MW01251280

"Magickal, beautiful, simply wonderful! Esmerelda Little Flame is like a breath of fresh air!"

> - Maggie Shayne, New York Times Best Selling Author

"This book radiates Light, Love, and Healing in a profound setting of a 'faery tale.' It's an easy read and it temporarily transport the reader to a different reality..."

> - Freya Aswynn, author of *Northern Mysteries & Magick*

"...prose is music to the mind...weaves a whimsical tapestry of warmth and delight..."
> - Silver Raven Wolf, Best Selling Author
> of *Teen Witch* and *Solitary Witch*

What Readers are Saying About
Temple of the Twelve

"This book is one of my favorites! It is filled with wonderful imagery and feeling that just lifts your spirits....I highly recommend this book to anyone who wishes to be inspired and who has an interest in the realm of fantasy/adventure."
> - G. House, New Hamshire

"I highly recommend this book to everyone who is seeking to grow in their spirituality. Reading it has been a great blessing to me."
> - C. O'Brien, Massachusetts

"Esmerelda Little Flame is a natural storyteller, & has created an absolutely charming mythology in Temple Of The Twelve."
> - T. Helene, Melbourne, Austrlia

"This book was wonderful - not only the story itself, but the journey on which it takes the reader....I absolutely love this book."
> - L, Miedzianowski, Lutherville, Maryland

Temple
of the
Twelve

Volume 1

Novice of Colors

Esmerelda Little Flame

New Gaia Press
An Imprint of Andborough Publishing, LLC

New Gaia Press
www.NewGaiaPress.com
3714 Bloomington Street #306
Colorado Springs, Colorado 80922
USA

Temple of the Twelve: Novice of Colors
Copyright© 2001 & 2008 Gemma Dubaldo
First New Gaia Press trade paperback printing January 2008
ISBN - 13 978-0-9774181-8-3

Cover design and book layout by Robert Yarborough

New Gaia Press is an imprint of Andborough Publishing, LLC
www.Andborough.com

Printed in the United States of America

Dedication

I dedicate this series to the Twelve.

Novice of Colors is dedicated to the color Black,
from whence all things come, and to whence they shall return.

Books by Esmerelda Little Flame

The Adventures of Charles the Well-Traveled Bear

Temple of the Twelve: Novice of Color

Look for More in the *Temple of the Twelve* Series
Beginning in the Summer of 2008

An Experiential Workbook
Vol 2 - Flight of Colors
Vol 3 - City of Colors
Vol 4 - Priestess of Colors
Vol 5 - Sisters of Colors
Vol 6 - Bridge of Colors
Vol 7 - Marriage of Colors
Vol 8 - Clan of Colors
Vol 9 - Vision of Colors

Temple
of the
Twelve

Volume 1

Novice of Colors

Chapter One

Caroline watched the heavy wooden door shut before her dazed eyes. This was really happening to her. This was really happening to her! She repeated that to herself a few thousand times, trying to absorb the words, the meaning. This was really happening to her. Right here. Right now.

Unable to think, much less do anything, she sat down on the unfamiliar little wooden chair beside the small window. She had no idea how long she sat there, motionless, lost in a trance. After a long, long while a bird flew by her and startled her mind back from wherever it had gone. A small, gentle smile touched her lips. She had always loved birds.

"Hello, little friend," she whispered. "Now I feel at home."

She eyed the setting sun in sudden dismay. She was supposed to be unpacking! The beautiful priestess who had led her to her new room had told her to unpack...and to await a visit from one of the Twelve. She, Caroline, was really here and soon to meet one of the Twelve!

And, if she didn't start moving, she'd meet her for the first time with her suitcase still unpacked and her bed unmade. Her. Now why had she thought it would be her? This place was changing her already.

Suddenly too excited to sit still even a second longer, she jumped up and began to put away the few things she had been told to bring.

There wasn't much...and now she could see why. The room was tiny and simple...an unmade wooden bed, a nightstand, a table and chair by the window, a second chair in the corner, a little washroom. Nothing more. The walls were of stone with many candle holders for light. These she filled first, with candles of different colors and scents she had brought from home and had helped to make.

Home. This was home now. It was certainly different from her room in the family house she had spent all her life in. Her parents did not have much, but they spoiled their children endlessly. Her old room had been full of pretty, feminine things...and colors. Colors upon colors.

Strange. She came to a place to worship color only to find the room plain and austere. She would have to ponder the meaning of that...*after* she finished unpacking. She had always been a daydreamer, but this place seemed to make her even more so.

Snapping out of it, she set to work. She hung up her few dresses, put a pile of clothes and her spare shoes on the closet shelf. There was a hook for a coat...she hung up her heavy black one, wondering if she would see the Winter snows through the little window. Would she be accepted? Would she pass all the tests, the requirements, the things she had no idea of yet?

She must. She would. Now she repeated that sentence over and over to herself as she laid out her brush and mirror, which had been lovingly crafted for her by her father. The image of his stern, proud face rose up in her mind. He was a woodcutter, and he loved her the way the forest loved tiny little birds. Harshly. Fiercely. Protectively. With honesty. That was what he called her...Little Bird. Always fluttering here, fluttering there.

Today, when he had left her, at the last minute he had turned around and said in his low voice, "I love you, Little Bird", and her heart had burst with feelings of all kinds. Then he turned, stone-faced, and simply left.

Her parents had not always understood her...had rarely understood her flights and dreams. But they had always loved her. And she had always known it. Impulsively she kissed the back of the mirror, where he had carved his initials. She missed them already, her parents, her three brothers, her little sister...yes, even her!

But it was right, her being here. This was where she was supposed to be. If she left this place her heart would break forever.

Try not to bring many personal mementos from home in the first year, the instructions had been. The goal is to create a new space, a new vibration, for the novice priestess. She should come to the Temple with only her selfhood, as much as possible. Caroline knew she could summon the priestess who had met her at the door and request to go home at any time. She also knew she wouldn't summon her.

The priestess (what had her name been? Sarah, yes)—she had seemed so happy. So strong. She was dedicated to Blue, and to Blue alone, for her robe was entirely of varying shades of Blue. She had radiated Blue, too—its clarity, its peace.

And I? thought Caroline. What will my robe be like? For I shall have one. I shall. This was where she was meant to be. The reality flooded her until the familiar ecstasy sang in her blood. Yes. Yes. This was *right*.

She sat in her little chair by the window, looked out over the meadow, and did as she had been told—she reflected upon the first moment when she had known she was called to serve the Twelve and could bear doing nothing else with her life. She had been a little girl of nine, running in a field of multicolored wildflowers not so very different than the one she was gazing at now—though this one was more sedate and obviously tended to by the priestesses. As she had thrown herself onto the grass and rolled and rolled in it, she had known that she wanted to understand colors. To serve colors. The longing pierced her then with such fierceness she gasped aloud.

It pierced her no less fiercely now, now that she was a young woman of sixteen, and beginning her first year at the Temple of the Twelve. She would grow into her womanhood here. She knew it; she felt it. Caroline had always known she'd find a special place in the world someday. Now she had.

Her hands were trembling, her lips were trembling with the ecstasy, when there was a knock at the thick, wooden door. Things happened so quickly. Though she felt sheer terror, it didn't have time to flood her before she opened the door. Her large, soft blue eyes were still brimming over with ecstasy and dreams. Which was exactly what her guest had wanted.

Yes, Caroline had been told that the Twelve took on a very "normal" human appearance, especially for the novices, so as not to frighten them before they were prepared for the full glory of the Twelve...or even part of the glory. Caroline's system was accustomed to ecstasy, more than most girls of her age, but still, the sight of the visitor to her room sent her to a level of ecstasy she had never felt before. It was almost...but not quite...too much. It pushed her to her limit, but no farther.

"May I enter?" a gentle voice asked, reminding Caroline that she was standing open-mouthed at the door, leaving her visitor in the hallway.

Hurriedly she opened the door fully and stood aside. Flowing black robes swirled into the room. Suddenly Caroline threw herself at the feet of the figure before her, kissing the hem of her robe and weeping.

"Lady," was all she could manage. It would have to be enough to convey everything, she thought wildly. It was.

"Come here, child." The voice was low, deep, soft. It calmed her.

Like a babe, Caroline threw herself into the arms of the Lady in black, still weeping and talking incoherently about how much she loved her, and how beautiful she was, and how Caroline would do anything, anything at all for her, anything; only tell her what to do and she would do it. The gentle hand stroked her hair, and the warm strong body absorbed Caroline's shaking until it stopped.

The newest novice priestess had no idea how long she stayed thus. When she became aware of herself again she was mortified and wanted to crawl into a hole and hide there forever and a day. With bright red cheeks she stood back from the Lady in black, wiping her tears and trying to redeem the situation. She bowed low and formal, the way she had been taught and had seen the priestesses do when in ecstasy before the Twelve.

"My Lady, I beg pardon. You...." Caroline, who had always been so good with words, had none.

The Lady smiled. "Do not apologize for loving me, Caroline. I love you, too."

"I *do* love you," Caroline cried, her whole body vibrating to that love. "I do. I do."

"I know, child. It is why you are here, is it not? For love of us."

Mute, weeping again, Caroline nodded helplessly. Never, *never* had she imagined it would be like *this*!

"Caroline. Who am I?" the Lady asked.

Without hesitation or fear, Caroline answered, "You are the color Black."

The Lady smiled. "Good. You know us already."

Caroline nodded. "I-I feel I have always known you, Lady."

The black eyes narrowed on Caroline's face, looking deeply into her. "Yes. Yes, I see that you have. But you have little control over your powers, Caroline."

"I want to." This was uttered desperately, in a choked voice. "I want to."

"Well." The serious moment seemed to crack like ice. "Do you like your room? There are others."

"This is fine. Thank you."

The woman smiled warmly at her. "You are homesick," she said gently. Caroline flushed. The woman put a hand on her shoulder and stared into her eyes. "We will take care of you," she promised.

Caroline became hypnotized by the black eyes. They seemed to spiral down into infinite worlds. They held all colors in them.

"Yes. Black holds all the colors in her. This is why I came to you first. You can only get to the others through me."

Caroline nodded, deeply lost in those eyes, those worlds within them. "I love you," she said simply.

"I love you, too. Let me remind you of what is to happen here, all right?"

Caroline nodded. "I would do anything you told me," she said.

The Lady sighed softly, filled with many emotions. "Child," she crooned, "you have been told, you have been called, you have been claimed by us."

"Yes. Yes."

"Do you understand that for your first year you will receive a task

7

from each of the Twelve; one of us will come to you on every New Moon and tell you our wish?"

Caroline nodded.

"At the thirteenth moon," the Lady continued, "we all meet with you to give you our decision as to whether you shall stay here for the next three years. We tell you of our feelings about your first year with us and how you can best serve us. I am always the first to come to a novice, the first to give a task to her. This is because all colors live in me. After that, it is different with each novice—the colors come as they will."

Here the Lady paused and then said dramatically, with a voice that seemed to hold infinity within it, "I will come to you tomorrow night, the night of the New Moon, and give to you your first task from me. On the night before the next New Moon, I will return to see how you have fared with the task, and to see if you are ready to go on to your next one. You may meet me here, in your room. For tomorrow, you shall be shown around the grounds by one of the priestesses or novices. That is all that shall be required of you. Do you have any questions?"

"One," Caroline said. "How do I become as beautiful as you?"

The woman laughed and touched Caroline's cheek. Her hand was smooth and soft and cool and womanly. Caroline closed her eyes, absorbing the feeling, touching ecstasy again. Then the woman was blessing her, kissing her forehead, and saying something about the first night at the Temple being spent alone in meditation; supper would be brought to her. Caroline had no idea what she answered. The Lady left silently.

Caroline flopped onto her unmade bed and lay staring at the ceiling, trying to absorb what had just happened. *I didn't even say farewell*, she thought. *I was a complete idiot in front of her.* Still, she couldn't feel too unhappy; it was impossible. Those black, black eyes were still singing in her veins.

That was it. That was what she had to do. Quickly she got the most precious things of all from her suitcase—her sketch pad and pencils. She began to draw the Lady. She drew the long, flowing black hair that seemed to melt into the black veil, the pale white skin and the liquid black eyes, thickly fringed and indescribably beautiful. She painted the delicate lips, so bright rose red, and the small, graceful bones beneath the black robes.

As usual, Caroline saw more than she had known she saw. She only knew what she felt about things when she drew them. She drew into the Lady's expression that strange combination of cold and heat which is a blanket of snow. As she drew, she talked to the Lady who was forming beneath her fingers.

"Yes, yes, you can be cruel—that is there in the eyebrows—but you are so gentle. No, no, that was not enough of blood flowing beneath your skin; I have drawn you like a corpse and yes, you are the Lady of Death, but you are so very, very alive. There, better...."

Then she began to draw herself, all dazed, stammering, gazing at the Lady in utter rapture. She laughed at herself. She cried with joy as the ecstasy flooded her again. When the drawing was done, the sky was dark, and her hands covered in colors, her hair mussed.

"I shall draw at this table with more power than I have ever drawn before," she said, and she shouted with sheer joy and began to twirl around the room, hugging her arms tightly around herself.

She bumped into the tray on her nightstand. Supper. Vaguely she remembered a priestess bringing her food in, but she had done no more than thank her and return to her drawing. Now she was famished, and she sat down to eat with fervor. They had told her that meals were usually in the common dining room, she mused. She hadn't really met any of the others yet. Now she heard laughter in the halls and talking as the novices returned to their rooms after dinner.

She was so happy. She was just so happy. It was good to be alone with her feelings, though. She was more in need of quiet this night than she had realized. She was grateful to be left alone to think.

When it was fully dark, she left the tray outside her door to be picked up, not knowing where else to bring it, and slipped into her nightgown. She made up her bed with fresh sheets and blankets from home, and lay down, not even lighting one candle. Tonight she wanted the black all around her.

Voices from the hall and from the field outside still chattered and laughed until the midnight hour. But Caroline heard them only as a distant background, like the hum of music you are not really listening to except unconsciously. They made her smile, those voices. They all sounded happy, and at peace.

In the dark, she summoned to her mind the vision of the Lady, until she almost felt as if the Lady was in the room with her.

"I am, Caroline," she heard the voice in her mind say.

"I love you so much," Caroline whispered back.

"I love you, too. I am the Lady of your dreams. You shall follow me into sleep," came the answer.

They were the last words Caroline heard before she fell into a deep sleep, far more intense and heavy than any she had known before. And as the Lady promised, Caroline met her there, far away in the land of the Sleepers.

***

The gentle knock woke her. Somehow her first thought was that she had everything to look forward to...the universe and all its stars were laid before her to play and dance in. Every knock was a chance, an exciting dream come true; every door was an adventure. She felt so *alive*...and she had not been aware how much of her lay dormant and untouched... until she had awakened.

As she walked to the door, she realized that she felt as if she had been healed of worry and stress in her sleep. She was definitely more *herself*. She knew that she understood herself better after only one day here. Excited, she belted her robe and opened the door, somehow knowing it was not one of the Twelve standing on the other side.

Her artist's eyes drank in the tall, thin woman before her, who bore a tray with fruit and bread and juice and tea. Golden brown skin, long brown hair, gentle brown eyes, an air of gentle strength, full lips, graceful, earthy, a novice since she wore no robe, but a simple dress of brown with little flowers embroidered on it in beautiful stitches.

"I am Lydia," the woman said, flushing a little at Caroline's intense gaze. "I have come to bring you breakfast and to show you the temple grounds."

"Come in!" Bubbling with excitement, Caroline welcomed her guest, anxious to hear about temple life from one who lived it. The priestesses were so private, no one knew much about the sacred mysteries practiced here unless you were in their midst. "I want to hear everything, I want to see everything, I want to do everything, I want to know everything." Caroline laughed.

Lydia's broad face lit up, causing Caroline to gasp inwardly. *Why, she is beautiful!*

"I have only been here seven moons," Lydia said shyly. "But I will try to help."

"What a darling," Caroline thought, and liked her instantly.

Sweet, unaffected, and sincere, Lydia managed to field the thousand questions shot at her like arrows over breakfast, and still remind them to eat something. The daughter of farmers and older than most novices at twenty years and two, she had come to the temple believing in her heart that she would be a priestess of Brown or Yellow. "I love them all...but it was Brown who called me here."

As Caroline stared at her in awe and amazement, she suddenly began to see the love of earth and trees and stone all over the girl's features. *She even looks like a forest nymph,* Caroline thought.

"I have no idea of what sort of priestess I will be...only that I *must* be one...and I am so excited!" Caroline said happily to her new friend.

Lydia said that she had been so nervous meeting Black on her first night in the temple that she had been sick to her stomach. They laughed together and dissolved...and crossed...barriers.

There is someone like me, Caroline thought. *I am not alone any-more. We are so different, she and I, and yet the same passions burn in us both. I am not alone any more.*

Lydia suddenly realized how long they had been sitting and talking and how much of the morning was gone and said, "Shall I wait for you outside?"

Caroline nodded.

At the door Lydia paused, then turned toward her again. "I do not know for certain, of course, but I think you will not be a priestess of Brown or Yellow alone. I usually can tell when a woman is born to be priestess of those."

Caroline smiled at her and laughed. "It's funny. Even knowing what I'm not makes me happy here!"

They laughed some more, and Lydia left.

Happily reminding herself of a little bird in a bird bath splashing itself, Caroline washed in the little washroom, singing a cheerful melody. She had a high, sweet voice, and loved to sing pretty melodies. She quickly slipped on a blue dress, almost unable to bear waiting even one more second. She put on her good, heavy walking shoes, and brushed her hair. She opened the door to her new life, her hair still wet and shiny in brown curls around her shoulders, her cheeks bright, her eyes sparkling.

Lydia led her out into the day. Together they walked hand in hand all around the huge fields full of Spring flowers, picking armfuls of them. They sat on the little stone walls watching the passers-by. They came upon a priestess of Yellow, whom Lydia knew by name, doing a ritual to honor the sun at noon but slipped away from her unnoticed.

"We must hurry or miss lunch," Lydia said, so they ran to the dining hall, Caroline keeping up quite well though she was much smaller, arriving there panting and laughing and hungry.

Luncheon with the other novices was an overwhelming affair. Caroline's mind swam with the names and faces and feelings all around her. Her heart swam in the loving acceptance, and sisterhood poured all over her from the others.

In the afternoon they examined those shrines and chapels open to novices. Lydia's favorite was one specifically dedicated to Brown, a beautiful cave of stones and earth in every shade of brown imaginable. Caroline could choose no favorite. She was beginning to feel a little lost, not sure if she would ever learn all there was to learn here...or even find her way around the complex grounds. It all seemed so massive...the grounds, and the magic....

By supper Caroline felt as though Lydia's calm voice, her practical good humor and her simplicity were a part of Caroline's soul now, that she would never again be able to do without. After the evening meal, the tall farmer's daughter embraced the tiny woodcutter's daughter. Caroline had told her she was called Little Bird, and now it seemed as if Lydia had told everyone, and she was to be Little Bird here as well as home.

With a kiss of blessing on her cheek, Lydia left her. All the novices were returning to their rooms, to await their New Moon messages and missions. Some had been told to wait elsewhere. But all waited with joy. Suddenly all was still and quiet in her little room.

As night fell, Caroline gazed at the New Moon, a soft crescent in the sky, whispering the incantations she had learned at her grandmother's knee...words of praise and adoration and power in the Light...and the Dark. Long before the moon had fully risen she was sitting in her chair, clutching her sketchbook in tight fists. Wondering what the Lady would think of the picture...desperately wanting to please...wanting so badly to know what the Lady would ask of her...simply hungering to see the face of Black again.

And when the Black came again...she didn't knock this time. The little room was filled with her presence and a dark silver mist she emerged out of. "Blessings, Caroline," she said softly.

Trying with all her strength to stay controlled this time, Caroline knelt. "My Lady," she said. This was all, but it was everything. *Mine,* she thought fiercely. *Mine to adore, to serve. To love. Mine.*

The Lady looked out at the crescent moon shining down on her, then turned back to Caroline and said, "It is the New Moon. In the name of the Twelve I ask, are you willing to accept your first task, given to you from the depths of blackness, from the depths of infinity?"

Caroline swallowed hard, then said in a choked voice, "I am willing."

As she knelt there awaiting her first task as a novice to be told to her, the Lady suddenly said, "What is in your hands?"

Caroline held forth the sketchbook, not able to meet the black eyes. When the slender white hands of the Lady clasped it, an electric current ran through Caroline and made her cry out. It wasn't pain...it was simply power.

The Lady smiled at her. "There is magic here," she said simply, "deep in these pages."

Caroline thought she would die or go mad from the sheer joy that consumed her at those words. "For you, Lady," she managed, out of lips gone suddenly dry.

The Lady gazed for a long while on the sketch. Her aristocratic face was expressionless and still. When Black desires to show nothing...she shows nothing. Wordlessly she lay the sketch pad on the little table, then said, "I am the color of selfhood. I am the deepest place within you. Enveloped in me, you become able to see more truly. I am often described as a place where you can hide the truth or hide from the truth. This is why people fear me...because they fear themselves.

"Caroline. In the darkness you see with all senses...you use touch and smell and taste to see. Your entire being sees, not just your eyes. Therefore, the first task for any novice who seeks to serve me is to be able to see in the dark. To be able to see with *all* of yourself, without lies.

"For you, Little Bird, that place of true seeing lies somewhere in the land between your heart and your hands, when you draw and paint. At those moments you are the most yourself. Therefore...Little Bird, I charge you in the name of the Artist of all life, whose servant I be, to draw with those hands and with that heart which is within you—*your own image.*

"But not just your body, Little Bird. You must draw your soul, as completely and fully as you are able. Put into each line and shading your essence and spirit. Draw the real you beneath all masks.

"And be aware, Caroline of the forest, that I can see in the dark. If you hide from yourself, if you hide from me, if in your work I see that you have not reached as far into yourself as you are able—then you shall try again in the next moon, and the next, and the next, and the next, until you either succeed or give up trying. For I tell you that no other of the Twelve shall appear to you unless I bid them entry.

"Be aware, you who seek to enter the Temple of the Twelve, that many do not pass out of the darkness of this first task. Child, there is a woman of seventy-one years who has been trying to do this since her girlhood. She does not give up. So I return to her. Again. She lives now among you, on the Temple grounds, though she has married, and so lives in a little cottage in the sacred woods with her husband, himself a priest of colors, although one who has not passed through the earliest levels after his novitiate years.

"Caroline of the forest, Little Bird, knowing that I shall see all lies, do you still desire to walk this path?"

"Yes, my Lady, I do."

"A third time I ask, for I always ask thrice, do you accept my challenge and my request of you?"

"With all my soul."

"So mote it be. I shall see you again, child, on the night before the next New Moon. Until then, I bless you in the name of the One." And the Lady raised up her hands, smoke and mist rose up all around her, and when it cleared, she was gone...leaving Caroline holding her sketchbook in her hands, not sure at all how it got there.

***

Images blurred as she fell into the rhythm of Temple life. She began to befriend the other novices, to learn her way around the grounds. Some days she assisted in the gardens—fruit, vegetable, and flower. This had been her assigned task for the Spring, and she loved it. She especially loved the plant lore and healing the priestesses taught her. She had learned a little from her own mother, but the knowledge given to her here was such a precious gift, she clung to it with all her might.

At night, under the stars, there were workshops and classes on different colors, their magical meanings, their special qualities. She attended as many as she could. Every moment was like a dream. She learned a few simple rituals and spells and began to speak of the Twelve as if they were actually familiar friends of hers. Every day she chanted, "This is really happening to me." Memories, so priceless, poured down on her like a shower of rain, and she could barely absorb it all, catch it all, keep it all. She wished each moment could be forever.

Because she was working with Black this moon, she always wore a black scarf in her hair or around her neck, which Lydia had given her. She prayed to Black, she meditated on it, and sometimes she felt the whisper of the Lady's presence. Mostly, though, she was so busy that she had little time to herself.

Small wonder, then, that the moon grew heavy and full and round without a bit of work being done on her self-portrait. Oh, she had been given a canvas and easel and paints from one of the priestesses. But it stood in her room untouched. She had sketched a few scenes in her sketch pad. But none of them were the inspiration she needed.

Who am I? I must draw the real me; I shall make Black proud, she thought to herself fiercely. But her mind only spun in circles and spirals. No idea seemed good enough.

On the night of the Full Moon she realized the time was half gone and became genuinely worried. That night she took a black candle and went off into the fields to do a ritual for help and guidance in her quest.

She was walking slowly, deep in thought, when a voice next to her said, "May I walk with you?"

A priestess was standing beside her. Caroline had not heard her approach. Startled, she bowed her head in greeting. "Of course, lady. I go to ask for help in my first assignment. My very first, and already I am failing!" Caroline wailed, feeling as if the world was coming to an end.

The priestess smiled. "As bad as all that?"

"Worse."

"You are Caroline, are you not? I have seen you among the other novices."

"Perhaps you won't be seeing me after the next moon," the newest novice said morosely, kicking a stone. "Black is never going to accept anything but the best."

"Ahhhh. Black. Yes. I see."

"Who do you serve, lady?"

In answer, the priestess stopped walking, and Caroline gazed at her robe. It was of orange, yellow, red, and brown, all equally present.

"My friend Lydia feels Brown has called her, and Yellow as well," Caroline said.

"And you, novice of the Twelve?"

"I do not know who calls to me. Only that I must stay here. I must." Her little fists and her jaw tightened in determination.

"Then you shall," the priestess said calmly, and with her simple words it was as if the universe went back into focus again, and Caroline breathed a deep sigh of relief and awe.

"How did you *do* that?"

The priestess smiled. "Oh, but perhaps *you* did it for yourself."

Caroline smiled back at her. "What is your name?"

"Elizabeth Anne. Why don't you stop here? This looks like a good spot for ritual work."

Indeed it did. There were some trees just ahead of her that seemed to make a little circle. Thrilled, Caroline raced to them as fast as she could.

She got so excited that she twirled around and around and around in the circle for sheer joy.

"I know I will find help here!" she cried. "I just <u>know</u> it!"

Elizabeth Anne laughed and came up to the circle. "May I enter?"

"Please!" When she did, Caroline impulsively grabbed her hands. "I think you were sent to me to help my magic work," she said earnestly, staring at Elizabeth Anne with her big blue eyes. "I do. I really do. How can I ever thank you enough?"

She studied the face of her new friend. She looked to be in her forties, with silver-white streaking the red-brown hair. The moon was so bright, even in the trees, that she got a good look at the gentle blue eyes with the round wire glasses and the kindly smile. *This woman is motherly...and special,* Caroline thought.

"I will stay for the ritual, if you like."

Caroline jumped up and down. "Please! It would mean so much to me!" She kissed the round pink cheeks, having to stretch up to reach them.

The ritual was simple, as Black was simple, but deep, as Black was deep. As Caroline and Elizabeth Anne called the powers of the four directions and elements to protect and assist the work Caroline was doing this night, a strange thing happened. Caroline felt a wave of energy such as she had never experienced before. This priestess was *powerful.* The circle began to glow with tiny blue sparks all around it, like faerie lights twinkling. When Caroline managed to get enough of her mind back to actually continue, her hands were trembling as she lit the black candle.

"Speak your heart," said Elizabeth Anne. "The truth."

Caroline knelt before the flame and began to pour out her fear, her longing. She cried about her lack of inspiration. She begged for help. She swore that she truly loved the Black, she did, and she wanted nothing more than to serve her. She swore that she would try, and try, and try some more to see her task done well. So intent was the novice on her prayer to the flame that she did not feel the energy shift in the circle. All of a sudden the blue lights went out, and the circle was cast into utter darkness. Caroline began to cry. Then she felt it. Black had come!

"Caroline," spoke a voice from the depths.

"I am here, Lady," she whispered. It had gotten so dark she could not even see her own hands in front of her, lifted in prayer.

"You have asked for help. Help I give willingly, abundantly, from my heart. Every novice is given a teacher, from among the sworn priestesses, on the first Full Moon of their arrival. This teacher shall be yours, for as long as you walk the path of the Twelve, unto death and beyond!"

The words "unto death and beyond" seemed to come from the bottom of a dark, dark well, or the depth of the night, or the bottom of the ocean. Caroline's whole body began to shake.

"Caroline, Novice Priestess of the Twelve, Little Bird—behold your teacher."

A silvery beam of moonlight broke through the heavy blackness. Caroline gasped. It lit up Elizabeth Anne's face in such a way that she was herself, and yet more than herself. She was all of herself. You could not see her body, only her face, half shadow, half light, deep in rapture and prayer to the Black. Caroline knew that she would never forget this moment, in which she saw for the first time the naked glory of a sworn Priestess of the Twelve. Her teacher.

She bent to kiss the ground, and tried to kiss Elizabeth Anne's feet or robe, but couldn't find it in the dark and bumped her head on Elizabeth Anne's leg. "Youch!!!"

Her teacher started laughing. The voice of the Black seemed to be laughing, too. What could Caroline do? She grabbed hold of Elizabeth Anne's legs to hug them, and laughed until she cried. Then the tears became real. She cried for all the longing in her heart for a real true teacher that had finally been answered. Gentle arms hugged and cradled her, and it felt as if both Elizabeth Anne and the Black were hugging her at the same time.

"Little Bird, Little Bird," Elizabeth Anne kept saying.

The hours passed. As the night approached its last hours, the two women rose and thanked the four directions and the elements and closed the circle. Wordlessly they walked back to their rooms, arms around each other. Caroline carried a black candle tightly in her hand. Though it had burned for hours...it had not burned down, even a little.

***

Elizabeth Anne began the very next day on helping to unblock her new charge. Old memories resurfaced, old feelings were dealt with. Misconceptions about Caroline's true nature were answered. Power was given to the novice that she needed. Once or twice she actually felt as if she had touched her immortal spirit. Then it flickered and danced away. But it had happened. Probing comments, hours of talk about seemingly nothing at all, a hint here or there about her artwork, a new way of tying up her hair—and Caroline felt reborn. Just being around Elizabeth Anne cleared up fog in her system she hadn't even realized was there.

The vision came, of all things, over blueberry muffins at breakfast. When it hit her, Caroline very calmly left her uneaten breakfast and went to her room, saying not a word of explanation to anyone. She began to paint. No one could see her work before Black did. She did not leave her room for the last eight days of the waning moon. She had to be bullied by Elizabeth Anne into eating from the tray brought to her. She did nothing but focus on her painting—and when she wasn't actually painting it, she was meditating on it. Every detail had to be perfect, she said.

On the day of the eve before the New Moon, she slept all day long. She was exhausted. Her dreams had been full of visions; she had been working even in her sleep. She woke to the light of the moon shining through her window. Oddly, she had no fear. She knew that the Black would understand that every tiny bit of self-knowledge she had, she had put into this painting. She stretched. Her body was sore. Her heart was at peace. She had given all she had.

When the Lady came, Caroline was staring out at the little sliver of moonlight. She did not even turn around to look at the Lady of Black. She said only, "I love you" to the figure who stood silently behind her.

"I love you, too, Little Bird," Black said softly. Caroline felt a gentle kiss on the top of her head. Then she heard the rustling as the protective cloth was removed from her painting by the delicate hand of Black. It was a thick, black cloth, Caroline thought as she stared at the moon. A veil of blackness....

There was a gentle gasp, then silence. Caroline's face went through a million expressions of feelings. After awhile, Caroline turned to look at the Lady. The dark eyes held no expression, yet so much was within them.

Caroline walked over to the Lady, and knelt before her and the painting. "For you," she said.

Black sighed, a tiny sigh. They stayed thus for quite some time, with Black's hand upon Caroline's shoulder, and her eyes upon the painting. Caroline had painted herself in a robe of feathers. Each feather seemed to tell a story. The patterns, the colors all meant something. The shapes and textures meant something. There were ancient symbols hidden in some of them, faces of animals and faeries hidden in places of the robe if you knew where to look. There were words, too, so subtle you could barely make them out. Each feather symbolized a person or event in her life, or a dream she had. The way they lay upon each other, their position and relation to each other, meant something. Some feathers looked like trees, or clouds, or flowers. Taken as a whole, it was magnificent. Taken in its parts, it was unbelievably magical. And the face under the feathered hood! It was Caroline, but it was more than Caroline, as it had been with Elizabeth Anne.

"What do you wish me to do with it now?" asked Caroline.

"Place it in my temple, the Temple of the Black. For now. Further instruction will come later."

Caroline nodded, and kissed the robe of Black. "I love you," she said again.

"Child, many are the hearts that shall open to themselves as they look upon this picture. You have served me well. Behold. As each task is completed, Little Bird, a novice is given a gift from the color she has served. When you have twelve gifts, you shall make of them an altar to summon us all, and there you shall hear our next instructions. Each gift will have great power for you, until that holy day of days when you receive your robe from us. Here then is my gift for you, Little Bird."

And the Lady handed Caroline a black feather. Caroline began to cry softly.

"Bless you," she whispered, and the Lady whispered back, "Blessed be, my daughter," and was gone.

The painting was hung in the Temple of Black the next day. Legend has it that many wonders and miracles have taken place beneath it. Legend has it that those who look at it learn something very special about themselves. Legend has it that it is still there, and you can find it if you enter the Temple of the Twelve, even unto this very day.

Chapter Two

Caroline forced herself to sit still though her nerves were quivering. Elizabeth Anne brushed and braided her hair with the good, strong brush Caroline's father had made. She was weaving some kind of spell into it, chanting softly under her breath as she did each twist and loop, so that Caroline could not hear her.

Tonight she was going to process with the other novices in the candlelight procession. Every New Moon the novices walked up the Hill of Novices, to the altar of stones at the top of it, where they left offerings and prayers to the colors who would be coming to them that night. Caroline's heart was racing so fast she was sure it was going to jump out of her chest. Many of the women who would be walking with her were no longer strangers, but friends. She had studied with them, laughed with them, created magic with them. They were like parts of herself now.

Lydia was coming. She had accomplished the task set to her by the color Orange last moon. This was her seventh completed task; she had only five more to go, and would receive one of them this holy night. She did not discuss much about her tasks, or what the colors said to her, Caroline mused. Lydia was quiet, steadfast, and determined. She did her work, she did it well and almost unnoticed, and yet the other novices depended on her constant good sense and kindness utterly. All she had told Caroline yesterday was that she had completed her task—she did not speak of what it was, or of the gift that Orange had given her—though she was wearing a cord around her waist of dark burnt orange which Caroline had never seen before.

Caroline sighed, a sigh of many emotions. The candles were flickering. Incense was flowing through the air, making her dreamy. The New Moon was shining in her window. Tiny wildflowers were being tied into her braid, in a spell she did not understand. Far off in the distance she heard the drums and tambourines and chants of the priestesses welcoming the New Moon. This was, truly, like a dream, yet she did not wake.

She missed her family. This was the longest she had ever been without them. She wanted to share all this with them. She knew she could not. She sighed again. Her eyes filled up with tears. She seemed to be doing a lot of that, these days....

Her mind wandered to the magic night ahead of her. She went over the words of the song they would sing as they climbed the Hill of Novices. She dreamed of which one of the Twelve would come to her this night...what they would say, what they would do. She imagined, she dreamed.

"You look beautiful. Your eyes are full of stars," Elizabeth Anne said softly. Caroline beamed, then turned around and kissed her on the cheek.

"You put them there," she said gently.

It was true. Ever since the fateful night of the Full Moon, Elizabeth Anne had changed Caroline utterly. She was so much more than what she had been. She could only dream of what she would become.

Impetuously, Caroline hugged her teacher. "Thank you. Thank you," she whispered to her. "Bless you." She could never get enough of saying it. She said it a hundred million times a day. She simply *had* to, or burst with it.

The two of them had gone over all her lessons, all her ritual work, had discussed her classes for hours on end, never tiring. Caroline liked to laugh that Elizabeth Anne was the only person she had ever met who could talk as much as *she* did! They were a pair, always chattering. The talks about everything else mattered, too. They talked of Caroline's old life, of her dreams, her fears. She said all the silly little things to Elizabeth Anne that she had never dared say to anyone else.

I am blessed, Caroline thought. *So blessed.*

A knock at the door had her scurrying to answer it, almost upending her chair and bumping into Elizabeth Anne in her haste. She grinned saucily at Elizabeth Anne's laughter, and opened the heavy door. Four novices stood there, ready for the holy night. A shiver ran up Caroline's spine. For a moment she just stood there and stared at them.

Lydia, in a brown peasant skirt and an embroidered white blouse with puffy sleeves. Flowers were in her hair, and the orange cord tied around her waist. She carried a plant in her hand. Lydia's room was a garden, so full of plants she could barely find space for anything else. "I would die without them," she had said simply. Caroline had helped her, often tending to those plants, learning the lore and uses of each. It had made her understand Lydia.

And there was Michella, who had spent two years as a novice, but had only two more tasks to complete. She was draped in a flowing green and blue dress, little castanets tied to her fingers. She was already dancing a little, there in the stone hallway.

Priscilla. Her sixth moon here, her fourth task. She had taught Caroline much about the stars. She wore a dress of stars of all shapes and colors and a crown of glittery stars in her hair. She intimidated Caroline. She was super-intelligent and seemed to know everything.

And Amanda—proud, quiet Amanda who was blind in one eye,—spoke five languages and always wore a black patch. She was certain she would have a special dedication to Black, for, she said, she lived so much within Her. Amanda was on her fourth moon, fourth task.

Caroline began to try to hug them right there in the hall. Lydia said gently, "May we come in?" So Caroline moved aside and let them in, and then hugged them. And cried some more.

"I shall leave you with my blessing," Elizabeth Anne said, and Caroline hugged her, cried some more...watched her leave....

Soon it was time. The girls walked solemnly to the Hill of Novices, each with lit candles. For Caroline it was the first time. She watched the others come, one by one or in little groups like hers, till they all met at the bottom of the hill. Twenty-one women in all and fourteen of the men from the novitiate priesthood. It was the first time she had even seen any of the men; they lived far on the other side of the grounds, and the women did not go there without reason. Caroline eyed them eagerly, wondering how their life was different from that of the women. They, too, carried candles or torches, and instruments and offerings. Like the women, they were of different ages, shapes and sizes, with differing expressions on their faces, from mischief to near trance.

Slowly, someone began the chant they had been taught, and everyone picked it up. "Come to me and show thy face, and I shall show thee mine...."

They began to walk, some singing, some just saying the sacred words that had been chanted on this hill from the earliest days of the temple, centuries upon centuries before. Caroline felt as if the spirits of every novice who ever walked these footsteps to the stone altar at the top were all walking beside her.

I am walking where all the great Priests and Priestesses of the Twelve have walked, she thought. I am one of them.

She loved to sing, and she did so heartily, holding Lydia's hand awhile, and Amanda's awhile. Her little basket of flowers was hung from her elbow, her candle burning bright in one hand. She wanted to look at the moon, the Hill, the procession, the candle, and everything else all at once. She couldn't concentrate. There was so much to see, to feel. Was she doing this wrong?

Once she stumbled. Twice. But did not fall. The top of the Hill shone bright and open in the moonlight. The circle of stones lay beneath the starry sky. One by one, each person lay their offering at that altar. The noise quieted, till there was nearly silence but for the sounds of the outdoors. Some knelt for awhile, then left. Some went a little ways away, but stayed atop the Hill. Some did magic at the altar.

Caroline knelt. She did not know what to do—stay or leave. So she did what she felt like doing—she stayed there, among the faces, amid the magic. She wanted to play the little wooden flute that was in her pocket, which her father had made for her. She wanted to sing. But she knew she was supposed to be silent, out of respect for the others. So she contented herself with the symphony going on in her brain. A few birds flew above, then flew off. She greeted them in her mind, thanked them for coming and blessing her. She waited for something to happen.

Awhile later, when only a handful still remained on the Hilltop, she saw a strange flicker of color in the grass. It was a quick flash, then nothing. Curious, she searched with her hands until she found it—a stone which shone pink, even in the dark of night. When she looked up, within the altar of stones stood Pink.

Pink was tiny, taller than Caroline but still tiny, and had delicate, faerie-like bones. She wore a dress of lace, of light and dark pink. Around this was a pink shawl on which were many pink hearts, and roses, both in bud and opened fully. On her slippers (ballet slippers) of pink were tiny roses. She wore a wreath of them on her head, too. Her hair fell in long blonde curls down to her waist. Her eyes were soft blue. Her china doll face had pink cheeks and pink lips. In her hand was a wand, embedded with pink stones like the one Caroline had found, with a bright pink crystal at the tip. All around her was an aura of pink light. Dazzled, Caroline stared.

Pink laughed softly. "Hello, Little Bird. I have heard so much about you."

Caroline's mouth fell open and stayed that way.

"You have my stone?" Pink asked. Her voice was silvery, like bells.

Caroline handed it to her. Pink's dimpled little hand touched her, and a wave of warmth passed through Caroline so intensely that she thought she might faint.

Pink laughed again. In some moments, she looked like a little girl. "Caroline. May I?" Pink picked up a handful of the flowers Caroline had brought as offering, pressed them to her face, inhaled deeply. "Mmmmm. I *love* flowers."

This is nothing like working with Black, Caroline thought.

Pink laughed again. "No, dear Little Bird. We are all very different."

Caroline touched the pink lace dress. She simply couldn't help it.

"Sweet child!" Pink put out her arms. Caroline hugged Pink. *That* was an experience. When Pink finally let her go—or rather pried her arms off her neck—she said, "Little Bird. Listen, child. No one but you can see me right now. They do not think you are standing there clutching at the air, either. They only see a novice, praying. I have so much to do. There is never enough time to say it all." Pink sighed.

Caroline tried to reassure her. "All will be well, my Lady."

The Lady's face brightened. "Yes. Of course. Now then. What do you feel from me, child?" The ballet slippers began to dance, a beautiful motion in the pink light.

"Love," breathed Caroline. "Friendship. Compassion. Kindness. Healing. When I look at you, I am happy to be alive."

Pink took Caroline's hands, an earnest expression on her face. "Yes! Yes! But my priestess must be loving to herself. A friend to herself. Compassionate to herself. Kind to herself. Healing to herself. Happy within herself."

Caroline stared into the gentle blue eyes.

Pink whispered, "Caroline. I can make any hurt transform into peace. I can bring gentleness. But my priestess must *want* this. Must reach for my hand." Pink had little diamond tears glistening on her cheeks. "I must be able to touch your heart."

Caroline felt the immensity of pain like jagged rocks cutting into her. Pink loved. Pink was too often shut out. Caroline must help Pink... or cease to exist entirely. She would not want life if she could not touch Pink's heart with love.

"How?" breathed Caroline, tears on her own face. "*How?* Tell me."

Pink smiled at her through her tears, and a wave of understanding and forgiveness washed over Caroline like holy water. "Caroline. Look into your heart. Find there the three greatest wounds your precious heart carries. You must face them with me. Name them with me. I will be there, Little Bird, right beside you."

At that moment Caroline felt as if she could do anything. That was the way Pink made her feel.

"It will not be so easy," Pink warned. "You will lose touch with how I make you feel...."

"Never!"

"Yes. You will. And you will find it again. And lose it again. And find it again. That is the way. But I am always there, Caroline. I am always there."

"I know. I know."

"When you have named those wounds, remember that I think your heart is beautiful. And I want to heal it. You must be able to tell me what you need to do to heal those wounds, Caroline. I do not expect you to do the work of a lifetime in a moon's time. Some things take a long time to heal. But you must know where to begin, how to begin. Do you understand?"

"Yes, my beautiful Lady. I understand."

"I am not like Black. Black is shadows and silence. When you work with me, you will find me there all the time. You will trip over me, bump into me. I will be everywhere you go. You will see me often this moon, Caroline. I seek to help you."

"I need that."

Pink smiled. "I need it, too. I am very open, very intimate with my followers. Very *present*."

"Like a hug."

Pink laughed. Caroline beamed at her. She loved Pink to the point that she thought she might go mindless from it.

Pink picked up a single flower and handed it to Caroline. "I am also one of the colors of love," she said gently. "Caroline. Did you know that the Twelve are mated?"

Caroline gaped at her. "What? W-what did you say?"

"We are mated," Pink said. "Six women, in love with six men. That is the Twelve."

"Lady!"

Pink laughed. "Child! What creative force did you imagine could be created without that love? All life is a dance between male and female." She began to dance again for a moment.

Caroline was speechless.

"Little Bird. One of the Twelve comes to you later, darling one, to teach you much, much more about that dance. That passion. But it touches me, too. It tints me; that passion tints me."

Caroline nodded mutely.

"My mate is the Purple King," Pink sighed, and she smiled wistfully and her eyes went all dreamy.

"I...see," was all Caroline could manage.

Pink giggled. "Little Bird. I shall tell you a great secret. Do you want to hear it?"

Caroline nodded.

Suddenly Pink changed, in that strange way she had, from innocent child to full-blooded woman. It was the woman Pink who said, gently, gently, but firmly, too, "The man *you* are mated to, Caroline, is the one my light is shining upon this very moment."

Caroline stared. Across the stone altar, on the other side, a young man stood in a pink light. Staring *straight at her.* Long brown curls. Gentle, wise blue eyes. A face full of shock and stunned amazement. A poet's mouth, beginning to curve in a smile, just a little.

"Right now, the color that has chosen him for this moon has shown him who you are, Caroline," Pink said, still gently. "Just as I have shown you who he is."

That did it. In utter panic, Caroline jumped up and began to run down the Hill as fast as she could. She did not say goodbye to Pink. She did not remember her candle. She ran so fast she stumbled on a rock and cut her knee. She did not think, through the pounding in her head, of where she was going. She heard nothing of the outcry that rose up when she bolted from the circle. She just ran. As far...and as fast...as her little feet could carry her.

***

"And then...I ran away. I just...ran. And now Pink won't want to have anything to do with me anymore. She'll have me sent home. I can't go home! I can't! I have to stay here! I love it here! I need to be here! I can't leave!"

Caroline sobbed onto Elizabeth Anne's shoulder. She was practically sitting on her lap like a child. She couldn't stop crying. She had cried nonstop since the terrible fiasco on the Hill of Novices. She began at dawn to pack her bags to leave. Elizabeth Anne had come to walk Caroline to breakfast, having a sense that something was wrong. She found Little Bird curled in a ball on her bed, next to a packed suitcase, sobbing.

"Now, Caroline. No one said you'll have to leave."

Caroline looked at her teacher with big, dazed eyes. "Of course I'll have to leave! I was rude beyond belief."

"Anything else?" Elizabeth Anne asked quietly.

Caroline's lower lip quivered, but she set it with determination. "I was a coward. The worst kind of coward. No coward is accepted into the priesshood!"

"Because you couldn't face him."

Caroline jumped off Elizabeth Anne's lap and began pacing around the room, throwing her hands up in the air. "Of course I couldn't face him. What do you expect?"

"A 'hello' might have been nice."

"I don't even know him," Caroline wailed.

"I think that's the point of 'hello'," Elizabeth Anne said. "Listen, child. We all run away sometimes. The point, really, is whether we stop ourselves before it's too late."

"What am I supposed to do now?"

"Stay," Elizabeth Anne said quietly. "Just stay."

Caroline threw herself onto her bed and buried her face in her pillow. A knock came at the door. "Oh, help," said Caroline.

Elizabeth Anne answered it.

"Is the lady Caroline, the artist, here?" a male voice asked.

Elizabeth Anne just waited for Caroline to do something. Hanging her head, Caroline got up off the bed and went to the door. She refused to look at the man standing there.

"Lady Caroline, I have a message for you from the novice priest, Gawen. The man you…met…at ritual last night."

Caroline forced herself to look up. Only the slight hesitation before the word "met" betrayed the fact that the messenger found the situation rather hilarious. That and the twinkle in his blue eyes. He was tall, and heavyset, with a long, brown beard. He had been dedicated to Blue alone, as his robe was all blue. And he had been called to be a Messenger. From among the Priests and Priestesses of Blue, some people were chosen to act as Messengers of the Temple to each other, and to the outside world when need be. They had more contact with the outside than others of the Temple had, except those who were called to actually live within the outer world again. This man was wearing the silver-winged medallion of the Messengers.

While Caroline stared at its beauty, and the sparkling blue crystal at the center of it, the man spoke again. "I am Robert, Priest of Blue, Messenger of the Temple, at your service, Lady Caroline." He bowed to her, and extended a note and a little wooden box.

At a loss, not sure of the correct protocol for dealing with a priest and a Messenger, Caroline simply took the things from him and said, "Thank you."

For a moment everyone stood there, silent and motionless, while Caroline waited for him to make a move to leave. Finally the man cleared his throat. Caroline jumped. It sounded suspiciously like he had stifled a chuckle. But his face was still sober, though his eyes danced merrily at her.

"I believe Gawen requested me to wait for an answer," he said gently.

Because Caroline looked to be about at her wits end, Elizabeth Anne gently led her to the bed, and had her sit down.

"I will wait in the hallway," Robert said respectfully, and shut the door.

Caroline opened the note and read:

"Caroline, I wanted to follow after you last night, to tell you everything was all right, not to be afraid—but Red (that's the color who showed you to me, Caroline) said to just let you go this time. I knew you'd be all right. Pink had surrounded you in her light, and I could see the pink bubble all around you as you left. This belonged to my grandfather. He was a Priest of Blue. He was also my best friend. He gave this to me before he died. Please take it. Caroline, you don't have to run from me. All I want is the chance to get to know you."

He had crossed out two lines at the bottom—Caroline couldn't read them—and had signed it simply, "Gawen".

She opened the box—and gasped. A gold chain lay inside, heavy and very well-made. Attached to it was a charm—a single streak of lightning. Caroline took it out of the box. As soon as she did, she dropped it back in as if it burned her. Touching it brought Gawen into the room as if he were standing right there.

Caroline shut the box, put it on the bed. "What do I do?!"

"What do you think you should do?"

"You're no help," Caroline snapped. Elizabeth Anne just stood there, and waited. Finally, in desperation, Caroline grabbed a piece of paper and wrote in a highly agitated hand:

"Gawen, thank you for the necklace; it is very powerful. I will draw for you a sketch in return for your gift. Send me a message to let me know what you would like me to sketch for you. Caroline."

Then she quickly went to the door, opened it, thrust the paper at Robert, said "Thank you" to him, and shut the door as fast as she could. With that, she collapsed on the bed.

Elizabeth Anne stroked her hair a moment. "Will you meet me at the dining hall?"

Caroline nodded into her pillow. Elizabeth Anne left, and shut the door gently behind her. After a little while Caroline felt another hand stroking her hair.

"Are you getting up?" Pink asked.

"Never," Caroline said into her pillow. "I am never leaving this room."

"But I thought you were packing," said Pink.

Caroline began to cry. At this, Pink pushed her head out of the pillow so she could look at her. For a tiny woman, Pink was very strong.

"Stand up, please," she said.

Caroline did, her head hanging.

"Look at me, please."

Caroline did.

Pink said, "I do not want you to leave here, Little Bird."

Caroline's eyes filled up with tears.

"But—" Pink held up a hand— "if you stay, you are going to have to allow yourself to get to know Gawen. Will you do this?"

Caroline felt her stomach lurch. Pink was dressed today in a long, pink silk dress, with some pink sequins on it, and a fluffy pink boa around her neck that hung to her hips. She also had on long gloves. At the wrist of one of them sparkled a diamond bracelet. She had a matching tiara of diamonds on her head.

"I like pretty things," Pink said.

"I'll stay," Caroline said.

"You have to put the necklace on," said Pink. "The spirit of his grandfather willed it so. He told Gawen last night to give it to you."

Caroline looked as if she was about to cry.

Pink hugged her. "Shh, Little Bird. We will talk about this as much as you need to. But for now, all you need to do is put on the necklace and go to breakfast. I promise, no one there will ask you a lot of questions or talk about all this."

Caroline look at her hopefully.

"I promise," said Pink. "Just a quiet breakfast. Go. Wash up. Go eat. I shall see you later."

"You really want me to stay?"

Pink kissed her on each cheek and forehead in answer, then left.

Caroline washed up and put on a dress, carefully leaving her ritual garb on her bed to be put away later. Then, with a big sigh, she took out the necklace and slipped it around her neck.

Immediately she heard Gawen in her mind. "Thank you," he said.

"For what?" asked Caroline.

Gawen sighed. "For wearing the necklace, Caroline," he said semi-patiently.

"You're welcome." Caroline paused. "Did your grandfather really ask you to give it to me?"

"Yes. I'd like to tell you about him sometime. Caroline?"

"Yes?"

"I wanted you to have the necklace, too."

Caroline was speechless.

Gawen's voice when he spoke again was gentle. "I will send you a message soon."

"All right," said Caroline. "What will you have me sketch?"

"I'm not sure yet," said Gawen.

"Oh," said Caroline. Then, "Why am I talking to you aloud when you're not in the room?"

Gawen laughed. "You're not talking aloud. You're talking to me in your mind."

"I am?"

Gawen laughed again. "I am a telepathist, Caroline."

"Oh," said Caroline.

He laughed again. "A very good telepathist, Caroline. When you wear the necklace I can hear everything you think."

Caroline said nothing. She didn't know what to say to that.

With one last laugh, Gawen said, "Have a nice breakfast, Little Bird." And he left her mind. Then there was only the silence of her room. And the lightning bolt that was sizzling hot against her breast.

***

From the onset, working with Pink was entirely different from working with Black. Pink appeared everywhere. While Caroline did breakfast dishes. When she was working in the gardens. When she was lying in bed, trying to fall asleep. In the middle of classes. Anywhere, anytime at all.

Pink always had bright, perceptive, witty comments about the people and things around her. She got Caroline in trouble during one class when she pointed out that the priestess had put on two different shoes, and Caroline burst out laughing in the middle of what was supposed to be a meditation.

Little gifts—flowers, crystals, shells, pretty beads, ribbons—all pink—were left for Caroline everywhere. On her pillow. Beside her vegetables at lunch. Next to her sketchbooks. Once there was a big pink balloon tied to her chair.

Lovenotes were left, too. "I'm thinking of you. Pink." "I love you, Little Bird. Pink." "I'll be watching! Pink."

Temple of the Twelve

Caroline kept fresh pink flowers in a vase Elizabeth Anne loaned her, and pink candles lit next to it. She heard nothing of Gawen. This was not surprising, since the men and women, especially novices, did not mix without reason, and Caroline was kept very busy. Still...sometimes Pink would get a certain little smirk and twinkle in her eyes. Sometimes the bolt of lightning she always wore would glow, and get warm, and she'd sense him there.

Caroline had a romantic heart, and letting her loose to work with Pink was a bit like letting a child loose in a candy store. All her friends were given cards and long, loving letters and gifts Caroline had made. She began to work on the sketch she promised Gawen. It was a drawing of her as a little baby, a little girl, a child of ten, and now as a novice at sixteen years.

She wrote poetry, pages and pages of it, and kept a diary in a pretty notebook. She wore flowers in her hair and on her dresses. She wore pink hats and scarves, loaned to her by the other women. She made a little box of gifts for her family, too, and planned to have a Messenger bring them to the forest house for her. It turned out she didn't need to. One afternoon, as she sat beneath a pretty, pink flowering tree, studying an ancient text that one of the priestesses of old had written about the color Pink, she felt a familiar hand on her shoulder.

"Mama!" She threw herself into her mother's arms, breathing in her scent, weeping softly. "Mama."

The work-roughened hand of the elder Caroline stroked her hair, hugged her close for awhile, then set her away from her so she could get a good look at her daughter's face. "You look well." The low, gruff voice Caroline remembered singing her to sleep as a baby was the same. Caroline began to jump up and down, trying to tell her everything at once, until her mother, laughing, said, "Always chattering. Sit down, then, and tell me all about it."

They sat on the old red and white blanket Caroline had spread out beneath the tree. Caroline held her mother's hand and stared at the dear, thin face. She had inherited her tiny, delicate bird bones from her mother, though her mother was thinner and her features sharper. Caroline told her all about Black, and her sketch, and her friends, and Elizabeth Anne; and her mother did what she always did. She listened. Her mother was very quiet, and spoke little. But she could listen like no one else

34

Caroline had ever met. And Caroline had a lot to say.

Her mother took it all in. She chuckled, she laughed aloud, she looked pensive by turns as Caroline told her stories. As usual, her mother said little. Her pride in her daughter was evident by the glow in her eyes. She often wondered how a plain brown bird like herself had birthed Caroline...but she never ceased to be grateful for the miracle.

When Caroline told her, stammering and tongue-tied, about what had happened on the Hill of Novices, the elder Caroline's eyes took on a strange expression. "I had a dream the other night," she said softly, then set her lips together. And young Caroline knew that, try as she might, she'd never get another word out of her mother about it.

They talked till suppertime. There was little news from home, though her brother, Dominic, had broken his foot in a fall from a tree while helping his father. Caroline was not worried. Her mother was a born nurse. She could heal anything that was able to be healed at all. Her younger sister Daria had inherited some of this, but had not nearly as much of the gift as her mother.

As they walked back to the little house where guests were lodged, Caroline thought of the strength of her mother. The small, delicate woman had ridden a hard three days on horseback to see her. She felt blessed.

She ate in the little dining room for guests this night. There were only two others there, in the small room with the pretty tables and lace tablecloths and curtains. And Caroline was full of peace.

Back in her room, she looked through the box of things her mother had brought her. A batch of cookies. Another sketch pad. A blouse Caroline had forgotten to bring before. A book of poems. A little box her father had made for her, with tiny birds carved onto it. She placed her black feather in the box, and looked for her father's initials underneath it, and kissed them. There was also a pretty cloth, embroidered by her mother. Caroline laid it on her little table.

She watched the stars come out, through her window, and thought of the conversation they'd had while walking back to Caroline's room. They'd gone halfway together, then she'd sent her mother back to the guest house, reluctant to make her walk so far, yet reluctant to have her leave.

"Daughter," her mother had said, her face hidden by night shadows. "You told me that Pink wants you to heal your three deepest wounds. Well, there's something I need to tell you, Little Bird. I know you don't remember this, but you were a twin, Caroline. I named your twin sister Serenity. She had that look to her face. Anyway, when you were both four, she died. At least we're sure she died. She wandered off into the forest. We …never found her. After we told you, you never spoke of her. It was like she hadn't existed at all. We decided you were in shock, and that we'd let you come to us about it when you were ready. When you told me about Pink—I had the feeling you were ready."

Caroline had stared at her mother, a flood of feelings pouring over her. "Mama?"

Her mother had hugged her. "Your mind was protecting you, child. If it lets you remember now, trust it. You're ready. And Caroline? I'll tell you all the stories I remember about her. When you need me to...just ask, honey."

Caroline held her, then walked back alone to her room, dazed. "Serenity," she whispered into the silence. No answer came.

The lightning bolt grew warm. "Caroline."

"I have a twin sister."

"I often talk to my grandfather. He comes to me. Would you like me to ask him about your sister?"

"Thank you."

"What was her name?"

"Serenity. Her name was Serenity."

"Caroline-"

"No. Don't say anything. I can't think about her anymore tonight."

Silence. Then… "I will need to see you again soon, Caroline."

"I-I know. Goodnight."

Silence. "Goodnight, Little Bird."

***

Caroline was up early to see her mother off. With four children and a husband at home, she could not stay away long. In fact, Caroline could not remember the last time her mother had left the forest, except to go as a family, and that was rare. *She loves me*, Caroline thought.

The beautiful brown horse had been cared for well in the guest stables. Caroline squealed with delight when she saw him. Next to birds, she loved horses. Their power. Their grace. Their freedom. Their flight.

"Star King!" She ran up to him, fed him a carrot from the bin nearby, stroked him. Large, wise, gentle eyes gazed knowingly at her. She pressed her face against him.

Her mother's lips curved, but she said nothing. Only watched. A big part of her daughter had died along with her twin. She'd never stopped praying that someday she'd get that part of herself back. She didn't repeat her promise, made by moonlight and shadows, to tell Caroline the stories she needed to hear about her sister. It was understood between them that her mother said it because she meant it. And Caroline would ask. When she was ready.

"I love you," were the last words spoken before the brown horse and the brown-haired woman rode off.

Caroline cried. Perhaps she cried because she knew that the next time she returned to the forest house, nothing would be the same inside her. Perhaps she cried for a twin, lost in the forest. Perhaps she cried without really knowing why.

One thing was certain. There in the stable, curled against the wall, full of memories and dreams, a part of Caroline emerged into being that had previously been wrapped in a cocoon inside.

***

There was a small pond on the grounds which Caroline loved for its peace and the huge white water lilies floating on it. That night she needed to be alone, and she needed the pond. Soft moonlight shone on the clear water. The priestesses often saw visions in this pond. Caroline wasn't expecting any vision. She had learned, though, to expect the unexpected.

She was crying over Serenity, her eyes swimming. As she looked into the pond, an image began to form. She saw a little girl who looked just like her—and yet was not her. The child, entranced by a bird (she loved birds, too!) ran after it, deeper and deeper into the woods. Suddenly a woman, tall and dark-skinned, and very strong and muscular, just appeared out of the bushes. She scooped up the little girl. One second she was there. One second she was not.

"No," Caroline whispered.

The vision changed to a forest she'd never seen before. It was thick and full of vines. There was the young child, a child no longer. She still looked like Caroline, only her hair was longer, wilder, carelessly tied back with a leather thong. Though her body was small, it was much sturdier than Caroline's. Her skin was darker and she had strange designs painted on her arms and face. This woman wore no shoes, nothing but a thin brown garment which looked coarse and rough. She had on an armband and a leg band around her thigh. Her ears were pierced. Feathers and beads hung from them. A black bird perched on her shoulder. A raven.

Caroline watched the little campsite as if her spirit had seen it before—with an odd sense of recognition. Men and women gathered around a campfire of sticks, preparing for sleep. Caroline recognized the woman—older now, with silver in her black hair—who had taken the little girl away years ago.

Why? Why did you take my sister? The question rang out across the stars, the miles, from heart to heart.

The dark woman looked up. Black eyes flashed in a stone sober face. She leaned toward Serenity, whispered something in her ear.

Serenity—*What do they call you, sister? I knew you as Serenity*—stood up. Wordlessly she walked to the front of Caroline's vision—and stared straight at her! Caroline drank in the proud, quiet features. *You are still Serenity*, she thought.

A thought whizzed into her mind like an arrow. "Flight." They called Serenity a word which in their language meant Flight.

"Little Bird," Caroline thought, as hard, as intensely, as she could.

The young woman smiled at her slightly. She had heard.

"Sister," came the thought into Caroline's eager mind.

"Yes, sister," Caroline answered. "My missing half."

The woman made some kind of gesture. Suddenly the vision was gone, and Caroline was staring dazedly at the little pond she loved. In place of this vision was a feeling so sharp, so clear that it was more real to Caroline than even her surroundings, which seemed like a dream. She had this feeling. She would see her sister again. She did not know where, or when, but she would see her sister again.

Suddenly it was all too much for her—the big move from her home, the self-portrait she'd done for Black, meeting Elizabeth Anne, Gawen, the work Pink had set her to doing, her mother's visit and Serenity—no, Flight. They called her Flight. Caroline couldn't take any more. She stretched out on the ground and sobbed. The ground became soft pink arms. She sobbed until it was all out of her. Then, nestled against Pink, she slept more deeply than she had ever slept before.

No one ever told her what had happened to her while she slept—where she had gone, what she had seen. All she knew was that the next morning, when she woke up, she felt healed. Calm. At peace. Supported by twelve pillars of Light and Love, who would carry her through everything. She belonged to Them. They belonged to her. Always.

***

When the next day dawned, the first thing Caroline did was to seek out a messenger. There was a special little building where the Priestesses of Blue who were messengers lived. Caroline had never been there before, and looked excitedly at the place as she waited for someone to answer the door.

It was painted in all shades of blue, with clouds painted on the sides, and the winged symbol she'd seen around Robert's neck hung in gold and silver over the doorway. A big glass house that seemed to hold fifty birds of many types within it was behind the main building. Caroline's heart beat fast. She must see those birds! Perhaps...perhaps she had a special connection to Blue....

The door opened. A priestess stood there, smiling a welcome. "I know you," she told Caroline softly. "They call you Little Bird. I have seen your painting in the Temple of Black. It is beautiful. Perhaps, after our business is finished, you would like to see our birds?"

Caroline almost swooned. She also nearly collapsed at the simply beauty of the little room she was taken to. Blue velvet. Blue lace. Accents of silver and white. A tiny white bird in a silver cage. Blue flowers in crystal vases. Blue stones in pottery dishes, which she held and played with to soothe herself. The whole atmosphere is soothing, she thought. Though the day was warm, a gentle breeze ruffled the curtains and cooled her cheeks. Soft music was playing. The sound of a small fountain of water splashing calmed her.

The priestess, whose name was Mariah, brought in a plate of light muffins and tea. She laughed when she saw Caroline's face. "So. You like the peace of Blue. Everyone does when they first touch the color. But Blue can be full of storms, and—lightning." She smiled at the necklace on Caroline's dress. "Your amulet is special."

Caroline nodded.

"We can discuss Blue later, Little Bird. I am always ready to speak about Blue." She laughed. The winged medallion around her neck glittered and flashed. "You have come in search of a messenger," she said gently. "Tell me."

Caroline poured out the story of Serenity, of her vision, with a few tears. "I must tell my family she is alive," she finished breathlessly.

The woman considered. "There are ten of us here now, and thirteen others. Let me see." From a little drawer she pulled out ten crystals, all of different shapes and sizes, but all blue, or blue with tints of another color, or clear. She lay them on a blue velvet cloth. "I am the crystal reader of the House of Messengers this moon," she explained. "We all take turns."

Caroline nodded, pretended to understand.

The woman gently moved her hands in a balletic gesture above the crystals. Soon one began to glow. It pulsated light so strong and bright that Caroline was a little afraid of it.

"Ahhh," said Mariah. "The priestess and the messenger Sasha. I will summon her." She rang a little bell. Caroline noted there were many little bells, in the window, on the door, hidden in many places. Blue must like bells, Caroline thought, and smiled. She liked Blue. She liked Blue very much.

A young novice entered, bowing to Mariah. Caroline was startled. She had not known a novice lived in the House of Messengers.

"Please bring the lady Sasha here," Mariah said. "She is in the kitchen." The novice bowed again and scurried off. Turning to Caroline, Mariah smiled as she read her thoughts. "Elena will be a messenger upon completing her novitiate," she said gently.

Caroline sighed enviously. To know what your destiny was in the Temple seemed an awesome thing to her. She felt ashamed that she had no idea about her own. And to serve Blue seemed like a very special thing. *Maybe...maybe I shall....*

Mariah laughed softly, then sighed. "No, dear. You do not belong exclusively to Blue—though those big blue eyes of yours are very beautiful. You have—other sides."

Caroline sighed and bit into a muffin. A priestess entered the room, and bowed to them.

"Sasha. This is Caroline, the novice known as Little Bird, who did that beautiful painting in the Temple of Black."

Sasha had a round, freckled face, red hair, and bright blue eyes that lit up upon hearing this. "Ahhh. You have been blessed by the Twelve indeed, novice, to use them with such power in your work."

Caroline blushed. She still was not used to such direct contact with the priestesses, and was in awe of them. She noted that their robes, though both blue, were very different. Sasha's was bright, electric, and flashing. Mariah's was darker, with traces of blue in it that were so dark they looked almost black.

"Tell her the story of your sister, Caroline."

As she again told the story, Caroline watched Sasha's face light up even more. *Adventure,* she thought. *Adventure, and a love of people, and an ability to forge links and chains. These things are Blue. I can see it in its priestesses.*

"But what good news!" Sasha clapped her hands. "Tell me more of your family, Little Bird. I would like to know more about how they will react, and who I should tell the news to, in what way. Who would prefer the direct facts?"

Caroline ended up spending two hours there, speaking of her family, and as she did her mind and heart seemed lighter. *I love Blue,* she thought. *And so. Blue is also words, stories, communication. Visions.* She told them, also, about the work Pink had set her to this moon, and how Serenity was the first of her great wounds.

Sasha's blue eyes grew thoughtful. "Ummm. Could it be that another wound lies with your family as well?"

Caroline looked at her questioningly.

"Well—from all I have heard, Little Bird—you lived your life as one of them—yet never one with them."

Caroline felt her heart shatter. Pain exploded into her in a million bursts of heat and ice. She had known. She had known, but to hear it so clearly, so cleanly.... *Oh, what am I to do now? How shall I live with this? Blue is also swords. Swords of truth with very, very sharp blades and edges.*

Mariah's soft sigh went through the room. "Breathe, Little Bird. Let it all in. Let it all out."

She did. After awhile the throbbing pain eased to something bearable.

"I think," Sasha said, "that your sister would have been like you in ways the others weren't."

Caroline looked at her in amazement. It was as if Sasha was already there, in the little forest house. How did she get there so fast?

"I also think," Sasha went on, "that you not only desire a messenger to your family, but also seek a messenger to your sister. Don't you?"

Caroline could only nod.

Sasha put a hand on her shoulder. "Blue flame is the hottest," she whispered, "but ice has tints of blue in the light. I will find a way, Little Bird. I will. But first, your family. They have suffered long and deeply. I go today."

The stables (evidently another totem animal of Blue was horses, as the messengers had their own stables) were clean and airy, like the house itself. Caroline had never seen stables that looked fresh and—sparkling! But these did. Sasha rode off on a beautiful, black horse, who also wore the wings on his head. Caroline watched her leave, feeling as if most of her heart had gone with her.

"Come." Mariah put an arm around her shoulder. "I shall show you our birds."

As they walked through the beautiful glass forest were the birds nested, Caroline was in ecstasy. She felt the birds' love so intensely she wanted to soar. Suddenly a little bird, of a type Caroline had never seen before, alighted on her shoulder. She was blue, black, white and brown. She chirped at Caroline, looking at her with bright eyes.

"Wait a moment."

Mariah held out a hand, sang a note. The bird flew to it white Caroline stood gaping.

"Sound waves—and translating the many languages of life—are a part of the magic of Blue as well," Mariah said to her, then stared at the bird, who stared right back. "Well," said Mariah. "Well, well, well."

"What?!" exclaimed Caroline impatiently. "What is it?"

"She wants to go home with you."

Caroline just stared at her. "Excuse me?"

"She wants to go home with you. And I should warn you, she is very determined. And very stubborn."

"But—but—"

Mariah laughed. "Blue is also the color of change," she said.

Caroline walked back to her room with a pretty white cage, a bag of food, so many instruction that her head was spinning, and the bird (whom Mariah had informed her was named Energy), still on her shoulder, because she staunchly refused to leave it and go into her cage. She seemed to think Caroline's shoulder was where she belonged. Caroline was beginning to agree.

Once in her room she allowed the bird to fly around it a bit. Energy soared, dipped and sang...and then returned to Caroline's shoulder. "Hmmm, I wonder...." She touched the lightning bolt, and wished to talk to Gawen.

"Hello," he said in her mind, so loudly she jumped and upset Energy.

"H-Hello. I wasn't sure if this worked, with me calling you," she said.

Gawen just laughed. "That's because you're silly."

Caroline sighed. "I wanted to tell you that I have a bird. And a sister."

"I know you have a sister—"

"She's alive. And someday I will see her."

Pause. "Tell me."

Caroline in great frustration tried to express the incredible vision.

"Whoooa. I got it," Gawen said. "You think very powerfully when you think in pictures, Caroline."

"Oh."

"Oh, indeed. Listen. That campfire scene struck a chord in me. Looks familiar. Do you want me to—"

"Please!"

"All right, I will. I'll find out all I can. Your bird seems happy."

"So am I. I didn't know I needed her. Then she was there."

Pause. "That's the way with a lot of things, Caroline."

"Gawen?"

"Yes?"

"Pink told me to begin to heal. But...healing from my sister involves change. Realizing things. Reaching for things. Making them different. But with my family— they're never going to change. They're what they are. I don't want them to be any different. Not really. How do I heal a wound when healing the wound would change things that aren't supposed to be changed in the first place?"

Silence. Then his voice, very gentle, very soft.

"I'll tell you what my grandfather told me."

"Yes?"

"There's no need to try to change the world. Because if you change yourself—you already did."

***

The moon was waning. Caroline decided to give a party in honor of Pink, who seemed to her to be a woman who loved parties and laughter and people. There was a pink flowering tree in the fields. Caroline went into the kitchens and got permission to bake little heart-shaped cakes, which she frosted in pink. She made pink lemonade, picked a handful of pink roses, and blew up pink balloons. The she asked six other novices to join her. They laughed. Caroline played her flute for them, the beloved flute her father had made for her. She told stories and sketched them all with flowers and ribbons of pink in their hair.

They left little gifts for Pink beneath the tree. Energy flew about, singing. Every once in awhile Caroline took her back to the bird sanctuary of the messengers to see her old friends. Energy loved it, but she was obviously not leaving Caroline. She barely let Caroline out of her sight.

It is like me, and my old home, Caroline thought. I need to visit. But I would die if I had to leave here.

Amongst the chatter and the laughter, a part of her heart had flown away with Sasha on the beautiful horse. *Mama...Papa...my sister if alive. She is alive, and someday I shall see her....*

***

The third great wound was harder to find. Nothing seemed to open it, to give her insight. As the moon sped downward in its cycle, Caroline grew so afraid. What if she could not do as Pink had asked? Would it always be this way, with all the Twelve—this desperate fear and longing as she traveled the moon-path?

She walked long hours. She couldn't sleep. And all of a sudden Pink, who had visited her often in the first half of the moon cycle, conveniently disappeared. In vain did Caroline call her, beg, plead, cajole her to show herself. Caroline was on her own.

She became morose. She lost weight. She wanted to try to see her sister again in vision, but she had no energy or will to focus. All she could think of was her family, and how they would react to Sasha's news. She waited impatiently for the messenger's return. Part of her wanted to quit and go home. But not truly. Never truly.

Energy was morose, too. She actually pouted. Caroline had not known that birds could pout. But Energy did most definitely pout. Then one day as she was visiting the bird sanctuary and sitting on a huge white stone, with five small birds perched on her and many more flying all around her, she watched Energy chatter with a pretty black bird.

"I wonder what they are talking about," she thought, and with that simple thought her mind cracked open viciously. Pain poured into her.

Oh, the animals. The beautiful, beautiful animals. And the plants, the flowers, the herbs, the trees. We cannot talk any more...we don't know how.

Images flashed in her mind, of lifetimes ages past, when she could look into the eyes of a tiger or a snake or a raven or a cat, or at a tree or a mountain, and *know* them. Lifetimes when she was taught by the tides. When she translated the sun. And it hit her so hard...*my sister does these things now.* Serenity could not bear not to do them, and so she left and went to a place where they remembered how a whale speaks to the ocean.

I wanted to go with her. All my life I wanted to go with her, and I could not go. I had to stay here, and be a good girl, and obey my parents, and cause them no heartache— but my heart broke a little each day. No one around me sang the song of the stars or the wind. No one danced with the wheat. No one's heart hopped from lily to lily with the frog. No one cared enough. No one opened enough. No one tried enough.

I love my parents, my family, the simple people of the forest where I grew up. I do. But I was without my friends. The starfish. The crane. The eagle. The beaver. They would pass by me and scurry away.

I lived in a cage of silence. Where was the music of life? I was satisfied with so little, so precious little. I made do. But it was never enough. It was never, never enough. Even now, now that I see the pain, now that I am living in it in my mind, I am still alone. The little flowers of these fields cannot call me sister and tell me of their sun kisses.

I can never go back again. I have to fly from this separation, this silence. I have to leave it. I have to find a way to breathe again. My spirit needs to fly again, to breathe again, to be again. They called my sister Flight. Flight. Now I understand.

Caroline wanted to run. There was nowhere to run. The separation was all around her, suffocating and choking her. She could not escape it by running. She had to find another way out. Somehow, some way out. She was trembling and crying. She stood up. It was so hard to stand up. It felt as if the world lay on her shoulders. It felt as if she was a billion years old.

How can I go back out there again, now that I know? How can I face it? It is as if a thousand tiny knives poke me with every move now. I shall

*go insane from it. I am so tired of fighting. No one knows what the smiles
I wore cost me. I did not even know myself....*

And Caroline lifted up both arms to the sky, and stood in the ancient position of woman, of the feminine energy of life. Open. Arms. Heart. Spirit. Eyes. Hands. Legs. Thoughts. All of me. Open.

And she said, "I swear to the Twelve, and to myself, that I will not take a breath without trying, even if only in my deep self, to find the links again. To find the ways of opening which I forgot. I will dedicate all I am to it; I will not stop until I can see the world again as I once saw it.

"I swear that no matter what it takes, or what obstacles I face, I will find a way out of this dark aloneness. I will find the way to my twin self. To the part of myself that never forgot."

***

Sasha did not return. She sent word that she was staying on at the forest cottage with Caroline's family for a moon, perhaps closer to two. A Messenger of the Twelve did not just deliver a message. The Messenger stayed to implement the message. The Messenger was the caretaker of the message...and that meant of its consequences as well. Caroline's family had need of the messenger to help them understand. Cope.

There was also a long, loving letter from the family to Caroline. This was delivered to her by Mariah. They talked for a long while. There were tears. There was guilt for not being with her family, and loneliness.

But that night, at last, Pink came. And wordlessly, until the dawn, just held her, wrapped in a blanket of pink light. So that at last she could sleep. And dream. In peace. Of peace.

***

Preparations were all aflutter in the House of Novices as the last few days of the moon passed. Everyone tried to finish up her their work, to ready themselves for the response of the Color.

Some faces were weary, some excited. A few were troubled, very afraid that they had not done quite enough to satisfy. Some women spoke of the task they were engaged in, others kept to a vow, or a preference, of silence.

For her part, Caroline had long talks before the little pink altar she had made in her room. She spoke of her three wounds, and of her plans to heal them. Sometimes she talked all night. And she knew that Pink heard.

***

The lightning flashed. "Caroline?"

"Hello, Gawen."

"Will you be walking the Hill of Novices this moon?"

"Yes."

"I will not be. I do not know where I am to go, but I have a very strong feeling I must go somewhere to meet my next color."

"Will you miss Red?"

Pause. A laugh. "Red isn't someone who lets you go."

"Oh. I *love* Pink. So much! But for such a gentle color, she is very draining. I am tired all the time."

"Little Bird?"

Yes?"

"When you walk the Hill of Novices, think of me."

"Yes. Yes, I will."

"Soon. I shall see you again very, very soon, Little Bird."

***

On the night before the New Moon, Caroline dressed all in pink. She had borrowed a pink dress and ballet slippers from one of the others. A pink scarf blew in the breeze behind her, tied around her hair. Pink roses had been pinned to her bodice. A necklace of pink stones glistened in moonlight and starlight around her neck. She carried a pink candle in a tightly clenched fist. Caroline giggled. Even her slip and underclothes were pink!

Elizabeth Anne had put pink eye shadow on her. One of the other girls had painted a pink heart on her cheek, and sprinkled her all over with pink glitter. Caroline rarely wore earrings; today she wore tiny pink crystals that sparkled.

The lightning bolt lay still and quiet against her skin. She wondered whether Gawen had succeeded in his work with Red. She wondered if

Pink would accept *her* work. She thought of Serenity...Flight. Energy chirped on her shoulder. Caroline's cheeks were flaming with excitement. Her pulse was racing, her hands trembling.

There was a beautiful bush of pink flowers, with a little bench beside it. Caroline went to the bush. She poured a little pink wine as offering to the bush, and set her candle beside it on the ground.

"Come to me, pink warmth of kindness. Come to me, pink light of happiness. Come to me, pink glow of healing. I have come to you, Queen of Dreams. Hear my call."

She sat down on the bench, and waited. She did not have long to wait.

Pink came. This time you could not see her body, for it was encased in pink mist and clouds, so that you could only make out her basic shape. The face above the pink mist wore no adornment at all, and was very serious.

"Novice of the Twelve, Little Bird, Caroline of the forest, painter of the Mysteries of Color, why do you call me?"

"My Lady, you gave me a task—to find my three greatest heart wounds and to begin to heal them. I have done so. I come to offer you my work."

"Tell me of your moon spent on my behalf, novice."

So Caroline did. She told the whole story, not leaving anything out. She talked till her throat was hurting. Pink stood sober and motionless, just listening.

I never saw the austere side of her till tonight, Caroline thought, but I will never forget it now!

Finally, exhausted, she finished her tale. "And so I have come here to give you these things, for I love you, my Lady."

A silence filled the little garden enclosure. Then, without a word, Pink's pretty little hand emerged from the mist, with a finger directly pointed at Caroline. A bright pink beam shot from the finger straight to the center of Caroline's forehead.

"Know this, Caroline, painter of the Twelve. I am not the only color you belong to. I am not the color you belong to the *most*. Your first loyalty is not to me, but to another of the Twelve. But I have claimed you as my own. Should you ever become Priestess, your robe shall bear Pink upon it. As a sign of my love, and a sign that you belong to me, for I demand much love from my priestesses, I brand you with my sign, and you shall bear it always on your forehead. Do you accept my mark upon you?"

Caroline nodded. A flash of warm heat exploded on her forehead, then stilled. Someone was shooting fireworks in the distance. They exploded in the sky, silhouetting Pink in many colors. *I wonder who the fireworks honor,* Caroline thought, then...*Lady! My Lady! I love you more than I ever understood....*

"Caroline. Little Bird. Listen to me closely, child. I will accept your offering, and give you a token of my favor. On one condition."

"Anything. Anything."

"You must continue your healing of these wounds for three more moons, and I shall come to you on the night before the fourth New Moon to speak of your work. Though you work with others, you must complete the work I set you to. If you fail to do this, then you must return my token to me, and you will go no further on this path until we resolve things between us. Do you agree to this, Caroline?"

"Yes. I will not fail you."

Pink's eyes grew softer. "See to it that you come to me in failure as well as glory, and I will be well pleased with you, for to do so is harder than it seems."

"I promise."

"Also, my novice, you must continue to learn of the man I led you to. Do you accept this as well?"

"Yes. Y-Yes."

"So be it. You have sworn allegiance to me, and I have accepted your oath. Receive then a sign of my love and blessing, and all my love go with you in the next moon as you begin your new work. And complete your old work. Blessed be, my novice."

A pink feather floated down to Caroline, who picked it up reverently. As she lifted up her face to Pink, Pink rose up her arms, let out a high, beautiful note—and disappeared into a puff of pink mist—then, nothing. Dazed, numb and overloaded, Caroline could not even begin to think. She sat quietly alone for many hours, just being.

When she at last rose up to return to her room, she thought for a moment how odd it was that she would not go to her mirror to see the mark branded on her forehead. She didn't need to. She knew what would be there, what she would see. She could see it clearly in her mind. So clearly.

A tiny pink heart...that looked like a birthmark. Which was fitting. Because a new Caroline had been born this night. And she served Pink.

Chapter Three

Caroline took the walk up the Hill of Novices feeling much older and more a part of the Temple than she had the last time. She was changed in so many ways she barely recognized herself as that same young, frightened woman who had run from Gawen and the messages of Pink.

Her bond to Pink was such that she felt a profound relief that her work with the Lady was not entirely over. She was not ready to let her go. In her spirit the words that Pink had spoken shimmered and danced. Pink had claimed her. Pink had chosen her. How to describe the depth of love Caroline felt? Her eyes swam with tears of joy and happiness. She belonged to Pink.

The little pink heart on her forehead did not hurt, but she knew it was there. She felt it. She wondered what it was for, other than to mark her as Pink's. It was for something, she knew, but wasn't sure what. It seemed to her, as she went through the chants and ritual motions with her friends, calling the new color to be with her this night, that part of her was not really there. The beloved friends' faces, the stone altar, the offerings, the words, did not stir her on some level. She was having trouble releasing Pink. She wanted to keep working with Pink. Other colors? Yes, but...she wanted Pink.

Chiding herself for not being reverent and for not being present emotionally in this incredible moment, she tried harder. She breathed the incense deep, felt the air blow around her, listened to the sounds of her friends. She tried to connect in. Then she heard it—the faint little stirring. She focused her mind as she had been taught, gave words and substance to the flicker of energy that had touched her.

"Go off alone now. Stay in the hills; you will know where to go."

So she walked. She walked a good half hour before she desired to stop. There was a spot, high in the forested hills that surrounded the Temple, which was open and clear. You could see for miles. Much of the Temple grounds were lain out before her eyes. She saw the rooms where the novices slept. She saw little fires lit here and there, and the beautiful main Temple. She saw, off in the distance, the edge of the building of the priests.

What was Gawen doing now? Who would his new color be? When would she see him again? The lightning bolt flashed in the moonlight, but was silent.

Her eyes sought the heavens for strength and wisdom. Tonight there seemed to be so very many stars! They seemed to be of all colors and sizes, some close enough to touch. They seemed to be talking. Caroline remembered her vow to Pink. She would heal her great aloneness by learning the language of life.

She whispered, "Stars so bright, what do you have to tell me?" Her candle was low. Still, she was unafraid. She was, after all, home.

After awhile, the voice of the stars formed clearly in her mind. "Touched by magic, touched by a dream." She began to chant it, over and over. Power grew in the little clearing. She could feel it. She chanted. She prayed. No question that she was fully present now! She was calling with all her strength...come...beloved one...come...a moonbeam slashed through the sky. She stared at it, hypnotized. Hundreds of tiny little stars began to dance in the moonbeam. Dance, play, sing, pray. Another chant. She said that one while trying to dance with the wind and the energy flow. Dance, play, sing, pray.

Come! Now! I need you!

The stars flowed together, came together. A man stood before her, bathed in moonlight. He had straight silver hair, to his shoulders, with a few streaks and strands of white in it. He was lean and thin. His bodysuit was of pure silver, but he wore white boots, and there was a clear crystal hung on his belt which pulsed in the moonlight. He was smiling at her.

She took one look at the silvery-blue eyes and almost fainted. Power. Leashed, magical power.

"Hello, Caroline," he said, in a voice that started her trembling with awe and love. "I'm Silver. Your candle seems to be nearly out." Suddenly in her hand was a long, thin, silver taper, aflame and beautiful. She gasped, and stared open-mouthed at him.

"Magic," he whispered softly.

And all of a sudden the clouds above her formed the pattern of the lightning bolt she wore.

"Magic."

And she looked at the tree next to her, and saw a face smiling at her from within it. She gasped, dropped her candle, but it floated back to her hand.

"Magic."

And all of a sudden the man turned into a large silver cat, rubbing around her legs, purring.

"Magic." He was standing before her as a man again, smiling, the silvery eyes twinkling. "Magic."

A belt of crystals hung around her waist, appearing out of thin air.

"Magic," he said solemnly, and pointed at her. Suddenly he had great, beautiful silver wings...and so did she.

"Magic," he said, as he came up to her and kissed her on the cheek. Then, "Sit down with me." A beautiful silver blanket appeared on the ground, fringed with white and with white stars. As he saw her noticing all the white, his smile grew wide and mischievous. "I am mated to White," he said, low and deep in his throat, with all the love he felt resonating in his voice.

Caroline swallowed hard. "Oh," she said, and then couldn't think of a word to say. Not that she could have spoken anyway. He was casting a spell on her. She was sure of it. Her stomach was doing flip-flops, her heart was pounding, and she couldn't take her eyes off him. "Tell me the story of Silver," she whispered.

And so, by moonlight and candlelight and starlight, he did. He held her hand, and the stars seemed to glow even brighter.

"Silver is the color of the metaphysical. Of other worlds, other dimensions. Of the future...and the past. Of the Universe, and the sky. Of dreams. Of visions. Of prayer. It is the color of the moon, of mysteries and wonder and enchantment. You travel, with Silver. You see your imagination come alive. Silver is starlight, and psychic energy, and worship.

"Silver has something in common with Gold and Black, and White. It sets off other colors. Enhances them. Worships them. Exalts them. It also reflects your face at you. Silver is mirrors, and water, and purity. But most of all, Little Bird, Silver is magic. You are magic."

Those hypnotic eyes were staring at her, peering through all the layers of her to the center. "Did you know that, Caroline? Did you know that you are magic?" Now the voice sounded sad. More than anything else, Caroline wanted, needed, to take that sadness away.

"Yes," she said. "I know."

He shook his head, and she felt suddenly cold. His mouth twisted a little, somewhere between a half-smile and a grimace. "Yes. I know. Silver can be cold," he said gently. "But Pink is not the only color."

Caroline's cheeks flushed. She hung her head. He took her face in his hands and made her look at him again. "No, no. I am not chastising you. I love you. But you must understand, Caroline, that I change everything I touch. Nothing stays the same after I have interacted with it. I bring the magic out of things." He stroked her cheek gently with a fingertip. "Don't you want the magic brought out of you, Caroline?" he asked, staring into her eyes. "I need you, you know. The colors need you as much as you need them."

Caroline began to cry, then to sob. She ended up in his arms, wishing desperately that she didn't cry so easily, unable to stop. "Yes. I want that," she managed to say. "Help me. Please. Help me."

For a long while they just sat there, until her tears had stopped. She pulled away from him, and finding handkerchiefs of silver in her hands, wiped her tears.

"Tears are silver, too," he said. "Let me." And he wiped her tears as they stared at each other, and the moon shone on them. He took the handkerchiefs and rolled them in his hands, into a little ball. Then he opened his hands. A pair of silver chain bracelets lay there.

"Yes, they are chains. Your fears and doubt and pain are chains. You have been afraid of your magic. You have not been strong enough to look at it, much less use it. Yes, I know you came here, and that is good. But the Temple outside must reflect the Temple inside. You have to feel like a priestess. You have to know your own power."

He put the silver chains around her wrists. They felt heavy and cold. "I made these of the tears you shed. Tears you shed because you wanted to be a daughter of magic and were sure you weren't good enough. Tears you shed because you wanted it more than anything but had let go of the dream because you thought it was beyond your reach.

"Little Bird. For me, go back to your world changed. Remember that you are the magic. Seek out your strongest magical gifts. Be able to tell me about them. Be able to look me straight in the eyes and tell me that these gifts are yours...even if you haven't developed them fully yet. Do this for me. If you have found them—if I can see it in your eyes—on the night before the next New Moon I will remove your chain of silver tears. From your wrists, and from your heart. If not—you shall continue to wear them."

Caroline was getting frightened. "Will you help me?"

He smiled at her, tenderly, a little sadly. "You see? You are afraid you cannot find the magic. The magic is in you. It is there. All you need to do is gaze into the mirror."

"I am scared. I do not want to let you go."

He hugged her. "Shh, Little Bird. If you need me, rub the bracelets. I will help you. And if you need special help, come back to this place. This hill. But, Caroline, you can do this. You *can!* You can. I have faith in you because I see the magic. It is there. It lives, it breathes. It's alive in you, Caroline. Just believe in yourself."

She found herself growing sleepy, and lay down on the blanket.

"Believe in yourself." She wanted to stay awake, but she closed her eyes. She felt the blanket being tucked around her.

"Believe in yourself." And he was gone.

But she dreamed that she flew among the stars with him. He told her stories about each star all night long. Or was it a dream? When she woke, she wasn't sure. When she woke, she did not have silver wings. The candle was gone. She found no trace of him, except the blanket wrapped around her. There was a bird, and a squirrel, peering at her from the tree above her. She felt stiff. Stretching and yawning, she stood up, keeping the blanket around her, looking around for signs of Silver.

When she woke, she found nothing but green grass, blue sky, and the temple grounds below her, as morning bells rang out, and people bustled and scurried like ants to begin the day's work. She wanted Silver. All she had were the chains around her wrists. She rubbed them gently.

"Thank you. I love you," she whispered.

Her eye was caught by a patch of blue and white wildflowers nearby. One was silver. She picked it, and carrying it in her hands, the blanket wrapped around her still, she began the long walk down the hill to the temple grounds.

***

Lydia was morose. Depressed beyond belief. She had not succeeded in completing her work this past moon. Now she would have to continue with Blue for another moon.

"I worked so hard!" she wailed, in a rare moment of sharing her private relationship with the Twelve. "I tried." She was in Caroline's room, crying into her hands while Caroline gently rubbed her back, and Energy chirped reassuringly into her ear. "I am so embarrassed. Blue said I had done *very* well, very well, but…. Oh, I am just dumb. Dumb and stupid. A dumb brown cow, that's what I am." She cried harder.

"No!" Caroline yelped loudly, startling poor Lydia, who stopped crying to stare at her. "You are not stupid! You are smart, and wonderful, and good, and…."

"Tell that to Blue! I was supposed to…to have gotten clear in my mind about some bad things that happened to me a long time ago…but…. So now what? Here I am. I *failed*. I want to serve Brown, Caroline. Will I ever get there? Will I ever, ever get there?"

"Now you listen to me." Caroline put her hands on Lydia's shoulders, shook her a little, and began to lecture her about her self-opinion. But somewhere along the way, the lecture changed. Caroline *saw* Lydia, robed in brown with a few small stripes of yellow, doing the Spring blessing of the earth with the other priestesses. "I saw you! I *saw* you!"

She pulled Lydia up, and began twirling her around the room. "I saw you, I saw you, I saw you! You were doing the Spring blessing of the earth, and you had on a robe of brown with a few yellow stripes, and you were so beautiful! You looked so beautiful! You're going to make it! You're going to be a priestess!" She was squealing and laughing and dancing a little jig. "We're going to have a party. We're going to celebrate."

"Celebrate?!" Lydia gasped. "But...."

"Oh," Caroline cried, "who cares if it takes an extra couple of months? It all works out the way its meant to in the end; the priestesses all say so, don't they? And you're going to be one of them. Lydia, you're going to be *one* of them!"

Lydia began to laugh. "Did you—did you really see—"

"Yes! Come here. Look." Caroline grabbed her sketch pad and began to draw a hastily scrawled image of her vision. She thrust it under Lydia's nose. "Look at you. Just *look* at you!"

For awhile Lydia just stared at her image on the paper. When she turned to Caroline her eyes were dry, but her face was pale, and her lip trembled. "Do you have any idea what this means to me?" she said in a strange, choked voice.

Caroline hugged her. "I'll make a real painting of it for you."

"You make people feel so special," Lydia whispered in her ear. "You have this way of making people feel so special."

The silver chains around Caroline's wrists grew hot, startling her. Then they stopped. It had been like tiny electric shocks. After Lydia left, Caroline sat on her bed, trying to figure out how making people feel good could lead her to knowing her magical gift. She thought and she thought and she thought, with her brow all furrowed up until she got a headache. But she couldn't figure it out.

***

Spring was full of life, and Caroline settled into a rhythm. She continued to tend the gardens with the others assigned this task. She made many friends this way, but it also grounded her. It made her less afraid. Yes, she was in a holy place, but the feel of earth in her hands reminded her that she was *home*. Perhaps, in their wisdom, the priestesses had assigned her this task with that reason in mind. She grew daily in respect for the wisdom of the women of the temple. They used each woman's strengths to create a harmonious whole that was awe-inspiring to witness. There was power here. Loving power.

To balance her physical work, she was always taking the classes and sharing in the discussion groups. There was an infinity of topics and of color lore to learn. Every day was an adventure, a joy.

Her work with Elizabeth Anne was also settling into a rhythm, as the two got to know each other. Almost every day Elizabeth Anne set her to doing something. Sometimes it was easy. Sometimes it was difficult. Always it was wonderful. Besides all this, she was trying to do as Pink had asked, and continue to heal herself.

Perhaps best of all, she was becoming known as an artist. Women were coming to her to ask for drawings for themselves or their families. And the artists of the Temple of the Twelve...a formal group consisting of 31 priestesses and 29 priests right now...had sent a delegate to her room one night. The woman had told Caroline that her self-portrait had drawn the attention of the artists, and she should consider applying herself as an apprentice to them. She could only be considered formally one of them when she became a priestess, but they wanted to train her. Work with her.

Caroline went the very next day to the artists' meeting. They met twice a week. She was accepted as an apprentice and given two jobs...to create a mural in the sitting room of the novices and to work with one of the priestesses on a design for a tapestry that would be made by the temple sewing group.

This woman's name was Katerina. She was a short, plump, jolly woman with bouncy brown curls and a loud, happy voice, who worked harder than Caroline had ever seen anyone work in her life. Katerina was opinionated and a perfectionist, and they got into many heated debates. But Caroline's art grew by leaps and bounds under her guidance, and she was already beginning to love the woman.

She was a priestess of primarily Blue, with Black and Brown as well. Every one of the artists had Blue as their only color or one of their colors. When Caroline mentioned this to Katerina, the woman laughed and said that Blue was the color of the artists. When she spoke to Mariah about it, the woman only sighed. *Impatient Little Bird. What will be, will be. In its own good time.* But Caroline noticed that every time they talked, Mariah began to discuss Blue Magic. Of course, Mariah was devoted to her color, Caroline thought to herself, but Caroline wanted to believe that it was more than that. That Mariah saw her as a possible Blue Priestess. So, Caroline being Caroline, that's exactly what she *did* believe. Because she wanted to.

Perhaps it was working with Silver, who seemed to her to be rather like Blue, or all the trips to the bird sanctuary with Energy for a visit. But Blue was always on her mind, it seemed.

So was Serenity. Caroline wanted to see her sister in vision again so badly she thought she'd explode of it. But she didn't. Caroline was not good at waiting. She did so, grouchily.

With all this going on, one would have thought that her life would have been full to overflowing. Something was missing. Thus it happened, that in a state of restlessness and seeking and questing for... something...Caroline sought out Gawen.

It all happened rather unexpectedly. It was a week before the Full Moon. She was painting in her room after the evening meal. As she did, she thought about how people were beginning to say that her self-portrait was magical. It seemed to her that if she did have any magical talent, it lay in the realm of her painting. But how? How? As with her ability to make others feel good, she simply couldn't make the connection into magic.

Abruptly she threw down her brush, spattering paint, and took her lightning bolt in her hands. "Gawen," she said in a voice that would be heard. A voice that would accept nothing less.

"Little Bird."

"I want to see you. Now. Tonight."'

There was a pause. Caroline could tell that he was mentally scanning her to see if anything was wrong. Finally, he said gently, "Meet me on the hill where you saw Silver."

She went, carrying another sketch she had made for him, of the view of the temple grounds from that very hill. It frightened her that they were so in tune with each other. It frightened her that she was actually going to see him face to face. She concentrated on the rhythm of her stride. It was a long walk. She felt winded and strangely lightheaded as she neared the clearing.

When she saw him, his back was turned to her. He was overlooking the magnificent Temple grounds, spread out before him. Sensing her, he turned slowly, and stared. Her breath caught in her throat. He had the gentlest expression on his face, as if she were something so delicate and precious and he was afraid she'd disappear if he closed his eyes. Looking into her eyes, he opened his arms.

She didn't walk; she ran to them. They sat for hours, wrapped together in the blanket Silver had given her, looking over the grounds. She felt warm. She felt safe. She felt as if she had come home. And wherever she went, from that night forward, she would never be truly home again without those arms.

Once in awhile they saw flickers of light as someone began a midnight ritual. Once they saw a shooting star. Mostly they saw each other. They just kept staring at each other's eyes. He stroked her hair. He touched the silver chains around her wrist. He played with the lightning bolt around her neck, fiddling with it between his fingers, and she played with his the same way. He told her of his days as a novice priest, and how it had been discovered that he had great telepathic ability (as if she hadn't already known that), and was very strong in the ability to receive visions, both literal and symbolic. He was a magician, and he made her laugh by pulling a flower from behind her ear out of thin air, and turning a pebble into a candy with a twist of his hand. He was working with Blue now, and he was so affected by Blue that Caroline knew he was desperate to have Blue claim him. (Was *that* why she kept thinking of Blue?)

Everything felt like a dream—his steady breathing, his voice, his laugh, his hands. It was surreal. She felt as if she were in another dimension. He, like Silver, loved stars, and spoke to her of the constellations and planets and movement of the heavens. She told him about Silver, and the request he had made of her. She told him of her struggle to understand her magic.

When she was done, he took her face in his hands, and looked into her eyes, and said, "Have you always drawn just what you see?"

She nodded. "Always. Except for the self-portrait Black asked me to do, because it was a—"

"Vision."

"And of Lydia as a priestess. That was a—"

"Vision."

She was too confused and overwhelmed to answer. She just stared at him, with her huge blue eyes even more huge than usual.

"Try something for me, from now until the Full Moon. Don't paint what you see with your eyes. Paint visions."

She was so engrossed in watching his mouth shape words that it took her awhile to realize he was waiting for an answer. "But—what if I don't—don't have any visions?"

He smiled at her, and her whole body turned to butter. "You will," he whispered. His brown hair lit by moonlight. Her heart was lost. Finally the first lightening of the sky appeared. "We should go back," he whispered in her ear. She nodded, but made no move to leave, only held him tighter.

After awhile, he gently pulled away from her. "When?" he asked softly, and she knew he was asking when he could see her again.

"Tonight," she laughed. He laughed, but shook his head. "What night are the artists' meetings?"

"The third night of the week."

He thought awhile. "Every seventh night of the week, then. We shall end each week together."

"Where?"

He smiled slowly, widely. "Everywhere."

She hugged him hard, and then he gently kissed the pink heart on her forehead. As he did, she felt again the power in that heart. But she could not get a sense of what it was *for*.

She walked slowly down the hill, turning around four times to see him. He stood and watched. When he was out of sight, she turned her face forward and began the long walk once more to her room...wrapped in a blanket of silver, lost in love.

***

Because Silver was the color between worlds, the color that bridged day and night, night and morning, Caroline focused most of her magic in those times when the veil of time and distance seemed thinnest, and easiest to pass through. Thus it was that she was back on the hill where she had met Silver one night, watching the last shades of day turn to black, and the moon rise. The blanket was wrapped around her. Dreamily, meditatively, she stroked the silver chain around her wrist. By and by she fell into a deep sleep, deeper than usual, and lay curled up beneath the stars, in her blanket of stars.

In her dream state she came upon Silver. He was standing beside her sleeping figure, a silver cape fluttering in a breeze, little sparks and bursts of light coming off him. Some were little flickers, some bright bolts. She realized that it was her spirit that was seeing him. Her spirit was standing outside her sleeping body. She could see a glowing silver cord connecting her to her body. She turned to Silver with wide, wondering eyes.

Caroline did not feel afraid. She had done this many times without remembering it when she woke. It felt natural. But watching Silver's face, she sensed that this time it would be her task to remember in her waking life, the journey she took during sleep.

Silver pointed again, this time to the stars. She felt herself lifting, lifting up into the night sky, and she had silver wings, and was flying. As she flew, the cord just kept lengthening and lengthening. She knew it would take her wherever she needed to go. Silver was no longer there, but she could feel his presence. She saw whirls of stars, spirals of color within the Black. They whizzed past her, sometimes she fell into them. She thought to herself, *I miss Black, and yet somehow she seems to be within and at the base of everything. She is always around me. Or within me. Or both. To serve Black must be so all-consuming.*

She thought of these things, and of Silver's strange, beautiful eyes, but mostly of the night sky she was traveling through. Falling, falling, falling, down, down, yet she was not afraid, just breathless with excitement and the sensations of being whirled through Space.

She landed in a forest, thick and heavy, mysterious. It was a part of the land which had not been worked and cultivated by humans. It felt prehistoric. It felt ancient, wild, dangerous, sacred. There were plants she had never seen before, and sounds of animals she was unfamiliar with. In the distance she heard a rushing waterfall and stream.

She floated instinctively toward the waterfall, flying through the air on her silver wings. There, in the waterfall, standing on the slippery rocks beneath the rushing water...Serenity. *Flight.*

Caroline flew through the spray, feeling the cool splash on her skin. Her mind seemed to focus. *I have been here with her often before, she thought. I have come to her in spirit, but never remembered. Not till now. Till Silver helped me.*

She stood beneath the rocks that sheltered her enough so that most of the water did not hit her. Her sister came into the same little clearing on the rocks, dripping, looking free and strong and alone. Wordlessly, they stared at each other. They did not have the difficulty of understanding each other's language that they had when Caroline saw her in vision. This was a spirit journey, and they were communicating spiritually, in a way that needed no words.

"So. You will remember this time."

Caroline nodded.

Flight eyed her solemnly. "Then I shall be careful what I say, for it will be important."

Caroline impulsively grasped the strong brown hands. "Will we be together again?" All her loneliness for the sister she had not known poured through her voice.

But Serenity shook her head. "We shall meet, Little Bird. But not to stay. Our paths are different."

"Yet the same," pleaded Caroline.

The wild eyes, so like Caroline's own, but glittering with strange sparks and fires in the blue, stared into Caroline's. "This much I will say to you, Little Bird. I am happy. I keep the old ways alive. I belong here. My spirit did not want to stay in the forest."

Caroline cried, "But I need you!"

Flight sighed softly. "We can help each other more, now that you remember. But you belong in the Temple. I am very proud of my sister."

Caroline's eyes filled with tears, and she wrapped her arms around her sister. "I love you. I am proud of you, too. You do much magic; you live within it. But I miss you."

Flight gently stroked Caroline's wet hair, and said, "Go, and I go with you. If you need me, you will know how to find me. If I need you, I will send a raven. If you see a raven, pay attention."

Caroline laughed into the shoulder that smelled of water and earth and sky. "You are bossy."

Flight chuckled. "Go. You have stayed long. Return home. Tell our mother and father I love them."

Waterfall droplets mixed with tears. Caroline felt herself spinning through Space again...the glowing silver cord pulled her back down, down, down...the part of her that wished to remain forever with her sister was not as strong as the part of her that knew she had to return to the Temple. Not as strong. Not as real.

She woke to the first rays of dawn. She knelt, arms spread open to greet the day, and thanked the earth and sky for letting her talk to Flight. Once more, wrapped in the blanket, she began to walk slowly down to the Temple, the silver chains on her wrists glowing in the sunrise.

***

Caroline was busy at the mural she had been assigned to work on, one afternoon when the sun was very warm, and she felt hot and irritable. Energy had not even stayed with her; feeling that Caroline was too cross to be around, she had flown off. The day's painting was not going well. The moon was waning. She once again had no answers for Silver. As she hadn't for Black. Or Pink. Was it going to be this hard every single time?

She missed her family. She threw down her brush in frustration and went to cool off her temper and her body in the shade. She found a tree, and sank down into the grass, spreading her arms and closing her eyes.

"Little Bird."

Caroline jumped up so fast that she hit her head on the tree. Rubbing her head, she muttered, "You scared me."

Pink's lips curved. "No greeting, Little Bird?"

Caroline sighed. "I am sorry, lady." She stood up, still rubbing her head, and knelt before the pink skirts blowing in the breeze. "How may I serve you, lady?"

Pink grinned and did a little dance movement in front of her. "No, no. It is I who can serve you," she said with a girlish laugh. "Come now, little one," she said, kissing Caroline on both cheeks. "Things cannot be so bad. You are studying with the Temple artists. You have found your lover. You have succeeded with two of the tasks given to you by the Twelve. You have found your long-lost sister. Has Temple life been so hard on you, then, dear one? You have even been chosen by—" here she danced around again— "*me!* Why so sad?"

Caroline's lower lip stuck out in a pout. "You know why."

"Ahhhh," Pink said. "Finding your magic. Yes. That can be difficult."

"Impossible," Caroline muttered.

"Then ask for help, silly," said Pink, laughing.

"Of whom?" demanded Caroline.

"You are pledged to serve me, are you not? Branded by me? Am I not even worth an attempt, a try on your part? Perhaps I can help you."

"Oh, lady, please...."

"Now shush yourself. I am not at all pleased with you. You show a lamentable lack of trust in me," Pink chided, a teasing, yet half-serious note in her voice. "Perhaps I should not help you after all."

Caroline grew frantic. "Lady, I...."

"Oh, for goodness sake, look at you taking me seriously," Pink snapped. "Come now. Wake up. I didn't choose you because I find you horrible. I love you." Her sweet voice took on that womanly power it sometimes had. "I *love* you. Now. Ask for help when you need it. And don't make me remind you again that I am here for you, Little Bird."

Caroline hung her head, flushing. "No, lady."

A soft pink, dimpled, graceful hand touched Caroline's cheek. "Look at me," Pink said softly.

Caroline did, all the love she felt for her Lady in her eyes. "I love you, my lady. I need your help."

"Then you shall have it," said Pink gently. "I have not one, not two, but three things to tell you that will help you find your magic."

"Yes?!" Caroline could barely contain her eagerness.

"First, young Gawen told you to think about painting your visions, did he not? And have you tried to take his advice?"

Caroline sulked. "What visions, I'd like to know? I can't seem to paint anything."

Pink sighed. "You did not answer me. Did you try to follow his suggestion?

Caroline sighed. "No."

"Then do so. The second things is, if you don't know what the heart I branded you with can do, perhaps you should…experiment…a little."

"I tried everything I could—"

"No, no," Pink cut in. "Not blindly trying anything. Ask the *heart!*"

"All right," Caroline said more quietly. "I promise."

"The last thing is, there is a young novice named Susannah. She is very unhappy right now."

"I have met her; she is darling. What is wrong?"

"Ask her. She, too, is pledged to me, though she knows it not yet. You two could use each other today. Seek her out."

"Yes, my lady. Thank you. I love you."

Pink smiled at her and tweaked her on the nose. "I love you, too, stubborn little one. Don't wait so long next time to come to me." And Pink was gone in a swirling mist.

And Caroline hurried off as fast as her feet could carry her to find Susannah.

***

In a distant corner of the Temple grounds, a young novice lay curled and weeping beneath an altar in a cave. It was the favorite altar of Lydia, the altar dedicated to Brown, which had every shade of brown imaginable in it.

Caroline approached softly, reverently, bowing to the statue of Brown, carved in wood and stone, buried within the cave walls. Brown blended in so well to the cave walls that she wondered briefly if she had really seen it. But there he was, the bearded, rugged face staring out at her with deep eyes. A shiver ran up her spine.

There was the sound of weeping, and there was silence. This cave was very, very quiet. Gently Caroline knelt before the figure in a plain brown dress and took her in her arms. Susannah went willingly, clinging to Caroline so hard that Caroline was almost breathless.

"Sister, what is wrong?" Caroline asked, stroking Susannah's brown-gold hair, her damp cheeks, her heaving shoulders until the sobbing quieted a little.

"I am afraid," Susannah finally managed. She had a deep, low, rich voice. It always startled the listener, because Susannah was small, but her voice was full and strong and boomed at times like thunder. It was also odd to see Susannah in the plain dress which was far too large for her. Susannah was elegant, refined; she had come from a wealthy family and had a flamboyant sense of style.

Seeing Caroline eye the dress, Susannah grimaced. "I borrowed it from Lydia. She is so beloved of Brown, I thought her dress could help me. Bring me luck. And I wanted to show respect. And I have no brown clothes," she finished, her words tumbling out defensively, in a rush like a waterfall.

"You cannot show respect to the Twelve by being someone you are not," Caroline whispered gently. Even the softest words here could be heard. The acoustics of the cave were incredible. Caroline reflected that Brown was deep and silent, yes, but seemed very much to have a strong talent for carrying or amplifying sound in a setting like this. It was two sides of the same gift, perhaps....

"I know," Susannah began to cry again, "but who I am is just not enough. Brown is not pleased with me. He gave me a task to complete, and I failed," she wailed dramatically.

"Tell me about it," Caroline said.

Susannah nestled her head against Caroline's shoulder and said, "It's not as if Brown is the easiest color for me. I know my hair has brown in it, but I always hated my hair."

Caroline burst out laughing. Susannah did look out of place in the simple, earthy setting—like a peacock trying to be a sparrow. "I can see why Brown is not easy for you," she said, still smiling, "but Brown *loves* you. Come, tell me what your struggle is."

Susannah threw up her hands. "Oh! I'm supposed to find a treasure, he says, only he can't tell me where, or what, or even give me any hints how to find it. It could be anywhere. I've searched all the altars of Brown the novices are allowed to worship at. I have searched the gardens and fields, but the Temple grounds are so *big*. I even tried looking in trees, but people began to think I was odd, poking my face into trees all the time. I just have to face it." She began to cry again. "I'll never find it."

"Shh," Caroline said. "Listen. Pink sent me to you. She said I could help you."

Susannah's face lit up. "Are you serious?"

Caroline smiled and nodded. "I'm having a hard time, too," she confessed. "Pink branded me with this heart. See it? But I don't know what it's *for*!"

"Oh!" Susannah impulsively reached out and touched the heart without asking. It was as if she was compelled.

And Caroline's mind split into a wide open place where she had never gone before. She saw Susannah growing up in her beautiful home, felt the stirrings of a young girl's heart as she began to love the colors. She felt those feelings as if they were her own, and the pictures were so vivid, they made Caroline cry. Then she saw Susannah as an older woman. She was one of the handful of priestesses sent out as preachers and teachers to the world. In each generation, only a handful were called to this work. And she heard the deep, rich voice of Susannah's. It sang. It told stories. It preached. It healed. It screamed. It created magical rituals. It once stopped a man from attacking her. Caroline heard the shout of Susannah's which caused the man to run; she heard it and she, too, screamed. It was a voice that welcomed babies into the world, ushered people into the next. A voice people wanted to be married by. A voice that was *listened* to and never forgotten.

Gasping for breath, now it was Caroline who clung to Susannah, who had become so frightened that she was nearly ready to run for help. "N-no. I am fine." Caroline breathed in and out, slower, slower, till her heart stopped throbbing.

"Caroline! The pink heart on your forehead—I have never seen anything like it—it began to *glow*, Caroline, and I saw Pink all around you, and—"

"Yes," Caroline whispered. "My gift is that the heart can show me the deepest dreams of others—what brings others to Ecstasy. That is what it is for. I know now. May I have some water, please?"

Quickly Susannah gave her the brown dish of water that was kept beneath the altar, but Caroline waved away the bowl of nuts and dried fruit. She splashed some water on her face, and drank a few sips. It grounded her a little. Her whole body was humming.

"Susannah," she said after a few moments, when the cave was again quiet, and Susannah's wide, frightened eyes had lost some of their panic. "Susannah, I have a story to tell you. It's about a beautiful young priestess, who becomes a wandering preacher and teacher. But first," she took Susannah's hands in hers, "the treasure Brown wanted you to find is not within the earth. It is within the sacred temple of your own body. Your voice, Susannah, has great magic in it.

"Let me tell you what I saw. What I heard. What I felt. Susannah, my sister, it was so very, very beautiful. I may not be able to express it fully. I may never be able to express the beautiful things I see and feel fully. But forevermore, I am going to try. I am going to try with all the strength I have."

***

As Susannah listened to Caroline tell her about her vision, about a life dedicated to using her voice to teach and heal and create dreams, she felt as if she were in a daze. She listened with a sort of detached wonder, knowing that this encounter would change her life forever, yet unable to react. She nodded. She heard the words. They seemed to fall like rain off in the distance.

In the distance, too, as she gazed off dreamily from her perch on some cloud, far off and distant...Susannah saw images. She saw pictures of her life as a wandering preacher for the Twelve. They were transferred, as if from Caroline's mind to hers, in startling, almost painful clarity. Susannah felt nothing, she just watched her destiny unfold. And when the stories were done, when Caroline had changed Susannah forever...Susannah stood up.

In the shadows of the cave, she watched Caroline's face for a few moments. "We will always be intertwined, you and I," Susannah said softly. "In many ways, our lives will touch."

Caroline recognized the pale, abstract expression on Susannah's face as shock, but was unsure what to say. *The Keeper of the visions can only speak them, she thought. There is no way to prevent the consequences. I am just the messenger...*

"Yes," Caroline whispered. "Our lives will mesh."

Susannah nodded. "You are not the only one who has the vision into tomorrow," she whispered. "I, too, have seen things about us. About you and I. I cannot share them with you. But I will. When the time is right."

With wide eyes, Caroline nodded.

Susannah started to leave the cave. Caroline watched her, motionless. Susannah stopped, but did not turn around. With her back to Caroline, she said, "Thank you, Little Bird." Then she left the cave.

Caroline did not know, could not yet know, what these visions would mean to Susannah. What they would cost her...in terms of family, love... life and death. If she had known, she would never have had the courage to speak. The ignorance of the visionary is his or her greatest blessing, as well as his or her greatest curse. No. She did not know. But she felt it. And it overwhelmed her.

So she curled up, at the altar of Brown, and there she slept for a long, long time...surrounded by colored lights she did not see. At least...not with her eyes.

***

The night before the New Moon came upon her so swiftly that she was unprepared for it. She spent the day frantically tying up loose ends as best she could. She took a ritual bath to calm herself in the sacred baths, and let the perfume of the bath oils transport her to a dream state. She cleaned her room, purified it with incense and fresh flowers. She spoke with Elizabeth Anne for last-minute instructions.

In the afternoon, she spent time alone. She walked and was silent. Her worried mind beat fast like the wings of her bird, Energy. She walked until she calmed it. Yes, she had perhaps not done as well with Silver's task as she would have liked. Still, she had tried.

The moon had overwhelmed her with its events. Gawen. Flight. Becoming an apprentice artist. She played with the silver chains around her wrists and thought to herself, *Well, I have survived this onslaught, and there were times when I thought for sure I wouldn't. So if that is all I can give Silver, so be it. I gave all I had.*

With these thoughts in mind and a stomach rumbling with hunger, she found herself on the mountaintop where she had met Silver. She picked some wild berries to eat, and drank from a stream. Then she sat, lost in prayer and her own thoughts, as the silvery stars came out, one by one. She fingered the lightning bolt, and felt Gawen's comforting presence. They did not speak. He sensed her need for quiet, and he, too, was preparing to meet with one of the Twelve this night. From her high perch she saw the lights of little prayer fires and candles being lit. All the novices were preparing to meet with their Color, and the priests and priestesses were busily preparing to usher in the New Moon. At last she fell asleep, but she remembered nothing of her dreams.

When she woke some hours later, a little stiff from the ground and dazed from her deep sleep, she focused her blurry eyes on the shining figures before her. Pink and Silver had come to her.

"My dear." Pink gave her an enthusiastic kiss on the cheek.

"Little Bird." Silver smiled at her.

Caroline lay down in reverence before them, then knelt, palms extended and upraised to them. "My Lord and Lady," she whispered.

Pink looked at her with loving eyes. "Little Bird. I have come to you because I instructed you to continue to work on healing your three great wounds for three more moons. I come to you now to ask you how you fared."

Caroline told her of her communications with her sister. She told her of the growing connection between them and of the first time she had remembered visiting Flight spiritually. Gratefully, she thanked Silver for his help in opening her to her spirit travels. She reminded Pink of Sasha's promise to work with her and her family, to strengthen the bond. She spoke of work she had done to reconnect to the life around her and of the times she had cried with Elizabeth Anne, letting out her pain and isolation. She spoke of how Flight was so connected to the plants and animals that she really had transformed Caroline already. She spoke for a long time, but Pink was not smiling when she was done.

"You have had a very difficult month," Pink said slowly. This night she wore a loose flowing dress with dark pink hearts on it.

Caroline nodded emphatically. "I am very tired."

"At times like this, you need to concentrate more on healing, not less," Pink said gently. Her pretty lips firmed with determination. "You threw yourself into the work with Silver wholeheartedly. Yet you did not remember that our lessons are like building blocks. They depend upon each other. How much of your magical ability can you use with a wounded heart?"

Caroline sighed. "You are right."

Pink shook her head. "You have done well, Caroline, but perhaps you need another moon with Silver and I. A lot has been thrown at you all at once, little girl. We love you. You must pace yourself." Pink looked at Silver, for his thoughts.

Silver wore a sleek silver tuxedo this night. He looked dashing, and he bowed to Caroline. "Little Bird. Will you dance with me?"

Taken aback, Caroline stuttered, "Uhhh..."

He held out his hand. She took it. She was whirled around, at first slowly, then faster, faster, until the sky began spinning and she felt the stars tilting. It seemed as if the solid Earth below her was not there; it seemed as if she were dancing on air and dreams. She became breathless, lightheaded, dizzy. Then she stared into the bright silvery blue eyes, and she felt her stomach fall back inside her. She focused.

"Good," said Silver, and danced harder, faster.

Time spun. Worlds spun. The past became a part of a circle she spun in. The future swallowed her, then spun her out again. All that was steady, all that held her, were Silver's arms. She forgot her name, her location, yet she could remember centuries before. She tore her shoe; she did not feel it.

Then it came. She felt a burst of energy explode out of her like fireworks. It was power and love and intense passion. It was life force. Around her, colors burst into the sky, as her aura sparked and then burst into flames of colors. Then she stopped dancing, and she watched as the energy her dance had risen up crashed and thundered in the sky around her. She felt detached from it.

Silver watched, too, his lean, handsome face lit by all the colors of her magic power. At last the colors died to a faint humming in the air.

Caroline was too drained to think, to speak.

Silver said, "Little Bird. What just happened?"

"I summoned up my power and sent it forth," she said.

He ran a finger down her cheek. "You say the words. But you do not understand that the lights were you. You know it is so. But you do not feel it. And you cannot control it."

"I could have died," she whispered. "If you had not been holding me I think I would have shattered in a million pieces."

Silver nodded, but said, "I *was* there."

Caroline sighed deeply. "It was untamed, that power. It was wild. I know that. I felt that. I could have burned something without meaning to. I didn't know what I was doing." Sadly, her big eyes even more huge than usual, she looked at Silver. "I suppose I must work with you again," she said. "I am not done with this work. I am not ready for another Color."

There was such weary sadness in her voice that Silver wrapped his arms around her tightly and hugged her. "You understand. You understand that you must work more with me. Because you understand, I know you will keep your word. Caroline, Pink and I were—*are*—very worried about you. But I wanted to see if you would understand your limits. If you would care enough. We have spoken with the color who is destined to work with you in the next moon. We asked for its choice, its preference. We asked if it wanted to wait.... Well?" He smiled at her, ruffled her hair. "Don't you want to know the answer?"

Caroline said, "It was no."

Silver chuckled. "No, Little Bird. The color in question felt that we three would make a nice triangle for you right now. You must continue to work with me, Little Bird. You must especially work on your visionary art. Gawen suggested you focus on it, and you did not have energy or time enough. You must this moon. So, we are not through yet, Little Bird. You and I are not through yet. But another of the Twelve...comes with the New Moon."

Caroline could only stare at him.

"Until you are done with my task, you shall wear the silver chains," he said gently. And he handed her a silver feather.

"Yes," Caroline agreed.

And then she was in the arms of Silver. He held her. They sat for awhile beneath the stars, until once again she slept, wrapped in a silver glow of love.

Chapter Four

It was rare for a novice priestess to wander into the grounds of the priests without reason, rarer still for Caroline to have a free afternoon to herself. But on the day of the New Moon, just days before the Summer Solstice, she found herself in a part of the Temple where she had never been before.

It was a quiet little garden. In a dreamlike state she walked, singing to herself, intoxicated by the fragrances and the promise of the color who would come to her that night. Oh, she still had much work to do with Silver and Pink, but today was a bright, glowing day. She felt she could do anything. She felt young and strong and invincible and free. Her voice lifted in song, she wandered where the whim called her, with Energy chirping along on her shoulder. *Sweet bird*, she thought. *Dear friend, dear little sister.* Energy allowed her to stroke her head lightly with a fingertip.

Drawn by a little hideaway behind a brick wall overflowing with ivy, she followed the wall to its end. There was a wooden door. Disregarding manners, she opened it, feeling somehow that she *had* to. It was a garden of early Summer flowers, surrounded by the brick wall, with a flowing fountain murmuring in the background. It was quiet, and Caroline felt odd, as if she had chanced inadvertently into the realm of Faerie. Energy flew off into a nearby tree. Puzzled at herself, at her bird, at this place,

Caroline looked around.

There was a man painting on a bench. He was young, with a sensitive, poetic face, and a gentle mouth. His long brown curls were tied back in a ponytail, and he was perhaps the sweetest-looking man Caroline had ever seen. Even her Gawen had a fierceness in his movements sometimes. This man seemed born of dreams.

He painted, not acknowledging her. She noticed that he sat with a circle of crystals all around him on the ground. She also noticed he had huge eyes. They were blue and so full of love that tears sprang to her eyes before she could stop them. This man's eyes were full of diamonds and stars.

She looked once. Twice. Three times. Then she knew. Those beautiful eyes couldn't see her. She cried out softly as the realization hit. "No!"

He didn't appear at all startled; he had known she was there. "Hello," he said, and Caroline's heart melted. The voice was like a kiss of wind.

"Hello," she said. "What are you painting?"

The poet's mouth curved a little. "I will show you later. Sit down. There is a pillow for you."

She sat on a little pillow she saw to his right. "You were waiting for me?" she asked.

He smiled at her. Caroline gasped. He had such a tender smile. But he said nothing, only painted. Energy returned to her shoulder. The man smiled. "Your bird is beautiful."

"Yes, she is—but you cannot see her," said Caroline, then was furious with herself at her runaway tongue. Would she never learn tactfulness? Ever?

The man turned his big blue sightless eyes straight on her. A shiver ran up her spine. "Since when have you only seen beauty with your eyes?" he asked. "You painted that little miracle of a portrait for Black. And you think I need to see your bird to know she is beautiful?"

Caroline protested, "Sir, I thank you, for I know you mean what you say about my painting. But you could not see it! How did you know what its quality is or isn't?" It occurred to her that this was a rather odd, bold conversation to be having with a stranger. Yet she couldn't stop her thoughts, even the stupid ones, from springing out of her mouth.

"There are no stupid thoughts," the man said, laughing gently.

Caroline sighed, irked. "Are you a telepathist too, then, sir? My... Gawen...is a telepathist and he is always reading my mind. It can be very provoking." Her lower lip pouted a little without her realizing it. Her eyes sparkled with irritation.

The man was still laughing softly. "Yes," he said simply.

"Yes *what?*" she asked.

"Yes, I am a telepathist. Yes, it is provoking. And yes, I do know that you're waving two fingers in the air right now. I am a telepathist, Little Bird. I don't lie," he said firmly.

Caroline flushed to the roots of her hair. "All right. I'm sorry. I'm being rude. I have interrupted your work." She got up to leave.

"You *are* my work, Little Bird."

With a huff, Caroline sat back down. "What do you mean?"

He sighed softly. "Caroline. Come before the easel."

She did. She stood in front of it, facing him. She could not see his painting.

"Close your eyes," he said.

She did.

"What have I drawn?"

Her eyes flew open. "How could I know that?! I don't like this. I'm getting very nervous. I'm going to go now."

"Little Bird."

She paused, unable to resist the voice.

"I said, what did I draw?"

She closed her eyes again. "Y-you drew me," she said in a choked voice after a minute.

"What do you feel, Caroline?"

She began to cry. "You drew me and Pink. And Silver. And you. All together. And you're forming a triangle around me." The tears were flowing fast and hard now.

"A triangle is a powerful shape," the man said gently.

Caroline nodded. "I know you."

The man stood up, walked to where she stood trembling before his easel, and wrapped her in his arms. "Shhh."

"You're too beautiful. I'm not going to be able to stand this. You're too beautiful. I'm not going to be able to take this much beauty." She wept.

"Little Bird," was all he said.

She stayed there a little while. As the planets turned, it was only moments. As the heart counted time, it was lifetimes. Finally, a changed woman, she pulled back from his arms. She knelt before him.

He put his hands on her shoulders. "Little Bird," he said again.

She spoke now in a voice numb and dazed with shock, as if she were sleepwalking. "You are the master artist. *Blue*. You are vision, vision of the mind and the hands. What do you want from me? What could I possibly have to give you that you cannot give yourself?"

"My sight back."

There was total silence. "Excuse me?" Caroline whimpered.

The man sighed. "Little Bird, I am one of the Twelve. I have power. But you have forgotten something vital. We come alive through you. Through the men and women who serve us. They are our hands, our feet, our voices." He paused. "Our eyes."

"I-I don't understand."

He sighed gently. He seemed to sigh a lot, sometimes like a breeze, sometimes stronger, as if breath was very sacred to him.

"Caroline. You are an artist. Yet you cannot see deeply enough. You see too much with your physical eyes. Your physical eyes are a *symbol* of your inner eyes. If your inner eyes can't see well enough, then your physical ones will lose sight, too."

"How?"

"If your heart can't see the beauty of a rabbit, will you be able to properly paint the shades of its fur?"

She shook her head.

"Caroline." His voice gentled, warmed. "You are my artist. You are my priestess. You are my brush, my paints, my instruments. Without you, I am a blind man. Because I see though your eyes. I live through your eyes."

Caroline only partially understood all this, but she understood one thing *very* well. "You feel I am shallow."

The man stared at her. "You hurt me," was all he said, and Caroline was at his feet, crying yet again.

"I'm sorry, I'm sorry, I..."

"Rise," he said.

She did.

"Little Bird. I chose you. I chose you as one of my own. You belong to me, now and always. I have a task for you. For this moon, you are to forsake your other art. Your studies with the other artists and your own personal work must be put away for awhile."

"What about Katerina?"

He chuckled. "I'll deal with Katerina."

She blushed. "Of course."

"I want you to be my apprentice for a moon's time." Caroline's world tilted, and began to spin crazily. She was dizzy.

"Y-you want *what*?"

"You must be my apprentice. Now, how hard a task can *that* be?" A smile spread across his face—a knowing, mischievous smile.

Caroline sputtered, "But...."

"And," he cut into her sputtering, "if you do the job properly, by the end of the moon I will see you with my physical eyes as well as my spirit."

This was *too much*! Caroline yelped, "You are telling me that I am responsible for the eyes of one of the Twelve?"

He pursed his lips thoughtfully, then nodded. "It looks that way, doesn't it? What's wrong? Are you that sure you'll do a bad job?"

Caroline just stared at him.

"Caroline," he said, his voice truly irritated for the first time, "I know your capabilities. I know your limits. I'd like it if you began to as well."

She hung her head. "I thought I did," she whispered.

He wrapped his arms around her. "You know them better than most people," he said, stroking her tears off her cheeks. "Little Bird. I need to create art with you. I need to paint with you. Paint with me. Please?"

Caroline fell headlong in that moment into unconditional, obsessive, and all-consuming love. "What time shall I be here tomorrow morning?" she asked, and that said it all.

***

The night was the seventh night of the week, the last night, when Caroline and Gawen were to meet on the hill. They had decided not to walk up the Hill of Novices this time, but to meet as usual. Caroline was glad. She was overwhelmed by what Blue had told her. She told no one about it, not even Elizabeth Anne. She wanted Gawen to be the first.

All afternoon she had wondered through her duties in a haze. Everyone was caught up in the New Moon celebrations and preparations for the Solstice and paid her no mind. They did not notice the odd look in her eyes. Only Lydia saw. She looked at Caroline oddly, then said quietly, "The aura of Blue is around you." She still looked awkward saying the name, and Caroline recalled how much trouble Blue had been for her in the last moons. Not everyone finds each color as easy or difficult as the next person. What was excruciatingly hard for one might be almost play to another. Caroline knew that Blue would always be hers. She knew she belonged to him, as Lydia did to Brown. Remembering the statue of Brown in the cave, Caroline felt a shiver. Perhaps, for her, Brown would always be intimidating.

She touched Lydia's cheek. "I am His," she said softly. Lydia watched her face for awhile, saying nothing. Then she nodded, touched Caroline's cheek in response, and left her.

She still had the blanket of silver and white that Silver had given to her. She took this, and a basket of food and some candles, and as dusk fell, began to walk to the hill. He was waiting for her. She had gotten used to the feel of his hands and was no longer frightened when he took her face in his hands and stared deeply into her eyes. Her heart raced, but she stood still and met his gaze. Their meetings had become as essential as breath to her. She could no longer imagine a week without him at the end of it.

As he loved to do, he kissed the pink heart on her forehead. "Little Bird," he whispered.

She looked at him, all the emotion of her encounter with Blue shining in her eyes.

"No," Gawen said. "Just because I can read your mind does not mean you can avoid telling me things out loud."

Caroline's lips twitched, then she laughed. It felt good. She needed to relax. As night fell (and the night was dark as it was a New Moon), she told him. She left nothing out. Sometimes he rubbed her shoulders; sometimes he stared at her. Once in awhile he'd ask her to clarify something, but he made no comments.

They ate as they talked, bread and cheese and fruit, and after awhile Caroline set up the candles she'd brought. When every word had been spoken from her heart and she had been wrung dry, she leaned back against Gawen, letting his arms and love enfold her, and she stared up into the sky. For perhaps half an hour they sat thus, in silence, as the candles burned and he stroked her hair.

At last Gawen spoke. "You know how much I love Blue. He belongs to me, too. This is something we share. He claimed me during the last moon, when I was working with him."

Caroline nodded. She had known this, had seen the blue crystal Gawen had been given for successfully completing his work with Blue.

"My grandfather was a priest of Blue," Gawen went on softly. "I loved him so much. I thought my heart would die when he did." Caroline kissed his cheek. "I will not serve only Blue, as grandfather did. I will have more than one color on my robe when I am a priest." Caroline smiled in the darkness. He did not say if, but when. She liked that.

"Little Bird, I miss him."

She turned around in his arms so that she faced him, and he buried his head in her shoulder. "Then talk to him," she said softly.

He shook his head. Caroline felt his tears against her dress. "I do. All the time. It is not the same as seeing him."

Caroline's love overcame her shyness. She tangled her fingers into the brown hair of the man who lay against her shoulder. "Perhaps," she said softly, "if we ask, we can get a special message from him this night. It is a magical night, is it not? And you have been chosen by Blue last moon; I in this one. If we ask, perhaps...."

Gawen leaned back, looked into her face, unashamed of the tears in his eyes. "Yes. Please," he said simply. Then he kissed her pink heart again. "We will do it together."

She nodded.

With instinctive understanding, they began without even asking what ideas the other had. Gawen spoke as he knelt before the candles. "Oh, you who are clarity and peace, you who have taught my mind how to be free, hear me. Blue of the sky, Blue of the water, hear me. I am your priest, and I call you to hear me. If there be any message from my grandfather, he who served you so long and so well and now rests with you, please open my spirit to hear it. I am here. I am willing. If it be your will, oh, Blue of my grandfather and now of me , hear my prayer!"

Caroline knelt beside him. Reverently she held the lightning bolt in her hands; she held it above the candles. Slowly she began to move it in a circle over the flames, round and round and round again. As it spun, each time it circled, she and Gawen said together, "Come to us" seven times. Then they just watched it spin. They blocked out everything else but the movement. The air around them changed. It seemed more clear, more sharp. It intoxicated them. It was as if they were getting drunk on breathing.

Abruptly, Caroline stopped. They looked up. Standing before them was a man in a blue robe. Gawen let out a choked cry. Caroline stared at the man with her artist's eye. Yes, Gawen was there in the face of this man. He had a long white beard past his chest and penetrating blue eyes. His robe was of dark midnight blue, and the hood was pulled over his head. Around his neck he wore a bright blue crystal that glowed on a thick cord. A staff was in his hand, studded with blue stones, with another blue crystal at the end of it.

Gawen got up to go to him. The man shook his head and in a voice bass and thunderous, said, "No, boy. You are too close to me. You will meld with me too much. Stay as you are."

Hands fisted at his sides, Gawen sank back to his knees, his eyes never leaving the beloved face.

The old man looked hungrily at Gawen. "You will be a fine priest, grandson," he said thickly, roughly.

Gawen, crying, said, "You are my example. You will always be."

"As the generations pass, fewer come to the Temple. And those that come do not have the gifts and power of even my generation. The world changes; it moves farther from the old ways, farther from the truth. Much magic is not even remembered anymore. My own grandfather taught me, as I taught you, Gawen. Ah, *that* was a priest in truth."

"You told me of him," said Gawen.

The old man nodded. "Remember it."

"I will," Gawen promised.

"He and I will guard you, grandson. You are our hope. You are our lineage. You shall carry our blood and our message on. Without you, it would die. We will guard you, Gawen. My grandfather, Arthur, Priest of Blue and of Black, will guard you. And so shall I."

Gawen nodded, crying too hard to speak.

The old man went on. "You will have four sons and finally a daughter. The third son will be a priest. Tell him that—that Arthur and I guard him as well. Tell him the stories."

At Caroline's gasp, the sharp blue eyes turned on her.

"Ha!" he said. "Are you afraid of bearing five children for Gawen, then? I can tell you each will be more work, more trouble than the last."

"Grandfather," Gawen managed, laughing helplessly through his tears.

"Well, what of it?" he snapped. "She is your woman, is she not? And fond of plain talk?"

"Yes, I am, sir," Caroline whispered. "How can I serve you, Grandfather Daniel?"

He stared at her a moment. "Love my boy," he said. "That's all."

Caroline nodded.

"I have a blessing. I would say a marriage blessing over you. Give you a marriage gift."

Caroline went pale.

"I know, child," the old man said. "Perhaps you are not ready. I am sorry. You have to be, whether you are or not. I cannot come again."

"Why?" Gawen pleaded.

"I will sometimes speak in your mind, grandson. That is all."

Gawen turned to Caroline. "Little Bird, if...."

She put a finger to his lips. "No. I am honored he wished to do this."

"I love you," Gawen said.

"Can we get on with it?" old Daniel interrupted. "I have not all night."

The young couple took each other's hands. The old man pointed his staff at them, then saying words Caroline could not understand, made a circle with it around them. A blue light glowed in the dark as he drew the circle. All Caroline knew was that she was being protected by something that would never leave her.

At last he said, "Love each other well," and Caroline saw tears in the old blue eyes.

"Sir," said Caroline, "the third son—we shall name him Daniel."

He looked at her soberly. "Thank you, mistress," he said quietly. "The child will have a hard life. The name will strengthen him."

Caroline smiled. It was a strange, sad, womanly, *knowing* smile.

"Sleep now," the old man said.

Caroline snuggled up next to Gawen, Silver's blanket around them. Gawen fought a few moments to keep his eyes open, but a heavy sleep overtook them both. They slept dreamlessly and deeply. Neither saw the old priest bend to kiss each of them on the cheek before he left. But both of them felt it, deep in their hearts. And would always remember.

***

It was Caroline who woke first, stiff from sleeping on the ground. She jumped up abruptly as memory of the night before and of what would happen this morning came to her. Oh! How could she have been so stupid? She was to meet Blue, and the sun had risen hours ago, and she hadn't washed up, hadn't eaten, wasn't ready at *all*. The thought of Blue *waiting* for her, while she was *late* to see him, had a pounding headache starting in her temples.

"Oh, help!" She literally threw up her hands. She gave sleepy, just rising Gawen a hug and took off running as fast as she could. *Blue, Blue, Blue* was all she could think. *I must get to him!*

It was a long walk to the rooms of the novices, and despite all her frantic efforts, she wasn't ready until nearly noon. Panting, frustrated, adrenaline pounding, she opened the door to the garden in the men's quarters where she had seen Blue yesterday. She had eaten no breakfast and was light-headed. She looked desperately around her. Blue was not there. She sat down on the ground, put her head in her hands, and began to cry. She was tired, she was hungry, and she was a fool. She could have painted with Blue as a teacher. The possibilities for growth, for learning! They were endless! Oh, what had she done?

There was no sign of him. No easel, nothing. She went over their conversation in her mind and realized he had never said a word about where they'd meet. She had *assumed* he would be here again. He hadn't *said* so. Stupid. Stupid. Stupid. She began to pace. All right. So there was a misunderstanding. All right. She could fix it. She could fix it. There'd been a mistake. He understand. She'd explain...

Oh, who was she kidding? Desolately, she began to walk out of the garden. She had every intention of packing her bags and returning to her family. She was a failure. And she could take no more. She was tired.

All of a sudden she saw a note. It was on the gate. Her eyes narrowed. It hadn't been there a few moments ago. Had it? She snatched it up in shaking hands. "Little Bird. Follow your instincts. You'll find me."

"Arrrgh!" she groaned in frustration. Then she neatly folded the note and put it in her pocket. She would find him, all right. Oh, yes. She would find him. Her huge blue eyes filled with determination. She began to walk. She had no idea where she was going, but sheer stubbornness kept her walking. She'd show him she couldn't be gotten rid of that easily!

It was a warm day. She had only one blue dress, which she had been determined to wear today, and it was a little too heavy for the weather today. She felt nothing but her single-minded goal. *Find* him. And when she did, she'd…she'd…well, she'd figure it out then. But she'd do something.

Wait a minute, Caroline thought. *Wait just a minute. I just felt a distinct impression that I should walk left. All right, I will walk left.*

It was a part of the Temple grounds she was unfamiliar with, still on the priests' side of the land. There was a grove of trees forming a perfect circle. Even before she entered it, she knew he'd be there. What she didn't know was that he'd be joined by a few dozen birds. And a few dozen faeries. Her mouth hanging open, she stood and tried to accept what her eyes were showing her. Faeries played tiny instruments, perched on branches of trees; faeries danced and swung on wildflowers; and one was even on Blue's shoulder. And the birds! Types she'd never even *seen* before—and she thought she knew most!

As for Blue, well, he was sitting at his easel again. He was barechested and had paint splattered all over him. He looked like a rainbow. His hair was in a ponytail again, and he looked like a wild animal himself. He had huge blue wings folded behind him. He also paid not the least bit of attention to her. His incredible blue eyes were focused on his painting.

With a sigh, Caroline acknowledged the truth: she would cheerfully rip out both her arms and legs from her body if he asked her to. And smile doing it. What could she do? She sat down at his feet and stared at him while he painted. Stared at him, and stared at him, and stared at him. They didn't talk. He didn't show her his painting. One of the faeries flew in front of Caroline's face, stared at her, then flew off, but otherwise the faeries ignored her, too.

It was an hour or more later when he put down his brush. The faeries all gathered around him as if hanging on every word. Caroline felt instant empathy with them. He said, "I am going to offer you three little visualizations to try before you paint, Little Bird."

She nodded, thinking about the way his eyes changed shades of blue.

"They're simple. But they *work*," he went on.

"Yes."

"First. Imagine you are in a hallway. Go down it. There's a door at the end. Open it. There's an easel in the room. Go up to it. It has a blank canvas on it. The canvas begins to form a picture. The picture may not be what you'll paint, but it will be what you need to see."

"All right."

"Second. Imagine a wave of blue. It can be water or wind, but it's clear. Pure. Imagine it washed through you. Let it carry off the negativity, the doubt, the fear, the lack of focus, whatever. Let it go through you until you feel *clean. Sparkly* clean. Crystal clean."

She nodded.

"The last one. Imagine the Twelve are around you. Imagine that, one by one, we flow into your brush. As each of us does, remember that we are in there now. We'll guide everything that comes off of your brush."

"I don't know all of the Twelve well yet...."

"Yes, you do," he said impatiently. "You just don't realize it."

"All right," she said. "May I hug you?"

He grinned a lopsided, clownish grin. "I'll get my paint all over you."

Caroline was laughing even as she jumped into his arms. "You can see how much I care," she said as she kissed him several times on his cheeks and forehead and nose. "I love you," she told him.

"I love you, too, Little Bird. Now, there's an easel for you set up over there."

Caroline looked to where he pointed. There had been nothing there before. Now there was indeed an easel, and she could tell it would be just right for her height. She beamed at him.

"Try one of the visualizations first," he said. "Then paint the faeries and me. But not just what you see with your eyes. Paint what you feel underneath it."

For a moment Caroline faced sheer terror. To paint for *the* Artist of the Twelve was like stepping into an endless sky and just...falling. She focused on the patient blue eyes that were steadily watching her. *What's the use?* she thought. *Why worry? He knows all about me already. If I don't paint for him, it's not like I hid anything from him anyway.*

He grinned at her. She grinned back and ran excitedly to her easel.

***

Caroline was high on Summertime. The day of the Solstice had been prepared for in every corner of the Temple. The kitchens were full to bursting with food that smelled so good, much of which had been magically prepared. Every available space had been made into an altar with flowers and fruits. Everyone wore special costumes, their finest ceremonial Summer garb. Every musician was outdoors, strolling the grounds and playing songs of love and joy and rebirth.

There were picnics by the stream, games of all kinds, dancing. All the animals were decorated with ribbons or flowers. Fortunetellers set up little nooks and altar tables and did readings for passers-by. Gifts were exchanged, strangers gave kisses of greeting and well wishes. Little plays were enacted. Many families visited. Clowns popped out from behind bushes. Jugglers and mimes performed. A young maiden might be startled by a young minstrel composing a song to honor her beauty. Magic was abounding. Spells were cast by young and old, novice and elder.

Caroline was in a daze of color and light. It was her first Temple celebration of the seasons...and one of passion. She was in love. On this day priest and priestess mingled as they would, so Caroline wandered with Gawen, holding hands. They ate snacks from the booths holding pastries and fruit drinks and special treats. They danced in the circles until they were breathless. They laughed themselves silly at puppet shows. He placed a wreath of flowers on her head, around her neck, around her waist. They had their palms read while Caroline blushed at the knowing look on the old priestess' face. They had friends to sing with.

In every little corner of the garden and woods, men and women were kissing and making love. Caroline's heart was racing. She was breathless with laughter and nerves. She just knew that he would kiss her—really kiss her—for the first time.

It so happened that the exact moment of the Solstice was mid-afternoon. There was a big ceremony for all the Temple in the main ground, but people were free to have their own. Caroline wanted to feel the power of the united Temple. The circle was large and wild. Someone painted a rose on her forehead. The images swam in her brain.

At the moment of the Solstice, when the power the group raised spun up into the universe in a whirl of colors Caroline could actually see, she was kissed into mindlessness for the first time in her life. For one instant her spirit split open, and she became one with the force of the spiraling colors of energy. She and Gawen were the renewal of life itself—he was God, and she was Goddess, and their kiss was creating the Universe anew.

When her eyes opened again to her surroundings, she blinked in a daze to see all her family—her father, mother, sisters and brothers—standing some yards away with Sasha! Sasha was laughing, her head thrown back, her eyes twinkling, joy-filled at the reunion and at being home. There were kisses and hugs. Caroline was tossed up into the air by someone. Everyone was talking at once. Caroline's mother was watching her with solemn, quiet eyes, seeing for herself how her daughter was coping with the news of her twin.

Sasha then said, "Tonight we must meet. There is a message from Serenity."

Tears of both joy and sorrow flowed at this.

After the Solstice the crowd went even wilder, crazier. There was feasting and drinking, and as night fell and the scents of Summer flowers and evening breezes were filling the air, the magic flew. It was a holy night. Fires were lit everywhere to honor the Sun. Candles and torches and bonfires and wands blazed.

In the special place where Caroline had first seen her sister, by the waters which had granted her the vision, the little group gathered at moonrise. Caroline's mother and father were holding each other for support. The children had wide eyes and were a little frightened. Gawen had been told to come ("You're part of the family, son," Caroline's father had said). Energy was perched on Caroline's shoulder, singing softly. The water lilies floated softly on the pond. Caroline remembered the night she had wept there in the arms of Pink until she fell asleep, so full of pain and longing for her twin.

Sasha was presiding priestess over the vision fire. Each family member, youngest to oldest, laid an offering in the flames. Caroline threw in a feather from Energy. Sasha's voice rang out clear and strong in the night. "Serenity. Flight. Sister. Daughter. Friend. We call you to this fire. Your family longs for you. Come to us."

And then it happened, on that sacred night, that one by one each person saw a vision of Serenity, each in their own way, according to their special relationship with her and their own strengths and weaknesses.

To Caroline came a vision of a very different Solstice celebration. One in the wilds of the planet where mankind had not taken over. One of ceremonies and spells even more ancient than those used at the Temple. One of a naked young woman, her sister, painted in the wild colors of the Sun, dancing around some firewood till flames burst from it. One of a wild, primal song, sung by her sister in the deepest forests. The call summoned the birds to her, and hundreds came. In trees, on rocks, flying wildly around, they all sang for the Summer.

There was much Caroline did not understand about the Solstice of her sister. But she knew this. She saw Serenity's spirit fly forth from her as a dark-winged bird. And the bird flew straight at Caroline's face, and the bird had Serenity's eyes. And Caroline became so frightened that she lost the vision, for the bird flew at her so that she was afraid it would claw into her face. She was ashamed of her fear—Serenity would never hurt her. She cried, for the fullness of Serenity's message had been lost due to her fear.

Sasha comforted her, telling her that Serenity understood and loved Caroline very much. But when Caroline pleaded with her to see if Sasha knew anything of the message Serenity had sent, Sasha could only shake her head. The message had been meant for Caroline alone.

It was not till dawn that Caroline returned to her room, drained and so weak that all she could do was lay her garlands in a basin of water, fall on top of her clean, fresh sheets, and sleep. And sleep. And sleep.

***

"Your family is gone." The sightless eyes of Blue gazed at her. So large, full, soft, and wise. So calm.

Caroline bit back an oath and a scream. Blue had given up his sight for her, to teach her where true Sight lay. And though he had taught her much, *much* already, she just *knew* that she wouldn't see truly enough to restore his eyes by the next moon.

Blue sighed. It was like a soft breeze. "You did not answer my question, Little Bird."

"It was not a question. You know they are gone."

Patient with her moods, he continued to stare quietly at her. "And you miss them."

Caroline closed her eyes. "Oh. Yes. So much."

"Paint it."

"What?"

"You heard."

"*How?!*" Caroline threw her brush down on the ground. "How do you paint longing? How do you paint need? I can draw their faces, but..."

"But not their souls."

"No."

"Yet you painted your own."

"I—"

"Try. You are my eyes, Caroline; you are my priestess. You are my artist. Look deeper."

"I love you!" Caroline screamed. "I *love* you, but I can't do this! I'm going home. I'm not worthy...."

A lightning bolt—out of a clear blue sky—zigzagged out of the sky towards a few dead branches near them. They were set on fire. Gasping, stunned, Caroline could only stare. "My Lord?"

"You wear a lightning bolt around your neck that belonged to a Priest of Blue. Yet you have forgotten my temper. You have forgotten blue fire. I am a calm and serene Lord. I represent peace. Yet it is the calmness of me which must have its balance, its opposite. I have one of the fiercest tempers of the Twelve when I am aroused."

Caroline stared at the sizzling branches. "Y-yes."

"You have been asking and asking and asking to see this painting I've been working on."

"Yes," she said softly.

Sparkling sightless eyes gazed at her. "All right. I think it is time." With a graceful gesture—for Blue is a dancer, as the wind is a dancer—he ripped away a blue velvet cloth that was covering the canvas he'd been working on. "*Look. See.*"

Caroline approached warily. When she did, she could no longer think or feel. Time stopped and reality shifted. He had painted *her*. Her true self. And she was absolutely beautiful. He had drawn her with such love that she could never again—*never again*—see herself in the same way. Nor could she gaze on herself. She was too bright. Too alive. Yet she could not turn her head away.

"I shall go mad," she whispered through dry lips. "I shall go mad."

The voice of Blue cut into her like a whip, each word lashing her. "So. You never expected to be painted by a God. Who, then, created you in the first place? You never expected a God to see you as beautiful. To love you. *Look! Look,* I said!" He had grabbed her, one hand on her shoulder, one holding her face still. "Look at yourself as the God sees you," he whispered into her ear. "I dare you."

Caroline shut her eyes, but the vision of her face swam before her. "Oh, my Lord, please…"

"Please what? Please don't love you? Please don't see you this way? Please don't expect you to see it, too? Please, *what?*"

"Please—I can't…"

"You *can*. You *must*. Or I will be blind forever. You are so beautiful. When you can look at your own beauty and not go mad, then you can paint the way you were born to paint. Not till then."

"My Lord…"

"My Little Bird…my priestess…I love you…."

Caroline ran. She knew not to where. She cared not. She only ran, as fast as she could, as far as she could. The branches that cut her she did not feel. The hot sun making her eyes blur she did not acknowledge. The lightning bolt burned a red mark on her chest and she knew it not. *I cannot live up to what he asks of me…to what he sees….*

And then Caroline ended up in a strange place. She was deep in a forest, so far away and hidden, with drums pounding a mad beat in her skull and the hands of her sister Flight weaving patterns in the air above her head. Caroline was on a bed of woven grasses. Strange scents were floating in the air. She was sheltered by long tree branches that made a sort of house out of the tree. She couldn't think anymore.

"Sleep, sister," Flight spoke into her mind. "You are safe here."

Grateful to escape the madness, Caroline ran deeply into the realm of dreamless sleep.   ***

Caroline awoke to see Flight's face above her as she gently wiped Caroline's face with a cool cloth. "I am dreaming," said Caroline.

"There are many names for it," said Flight.

"Do I have to go back?"

Flight's smile faded. "Yes. You are of the Temple of the colors."

"But—"

"You talk too much. You always talked too much," said Flight.

"I have so many questions...."

"No. Always you have too many questions, too. Ask me only one. The most important one to you."

"I don't know what to do."

"That is not a question. That is a statement." The tattoos on Flight's arms seemed alive. They were hypnotizing Caroline as Flight moved around the shelter.

"I cannot find one question."

Flight shrugged. "Then ask none."

"But—"

"What is this word, but? It is not a pretty word to be used so often. But. What is that sort of word?"

Caroline laughed. Flight's eyes laughed back. "I know my question," Caroline said suddenly.

Flight raised an eyebrow.

"What was the message of the dark bird you sent to me?"

"It was my spirit."

"What was your message?"

Flight nodded. "Good. Your easy life has not caused you to lose all your brains."

"Easy life!"

Flight shook her head. "Your world has taken the easy path...away from the One. Not you, Little Bird."

"Help me."

"This is why you are here."

"Why…why did the bird…fly at me?"

"Are you willing to find out?"

Caroline nodded. Flight began to shimmer black. Black hair, black wings. She became the bird. She flew around Caroline, who did not flinch. She flew at Caroline. Caroline stayed motionless as the bird's wings touched her face….Black. Black. Black. She fell into black. Within it, she fell so deep she no longer knew where she was. She was in the black.

There was a light. It was her own face. Caroline's face, as Blue had painted it. Caroline fell towards it. She looked upon all the parts of herself she had never let herself see. She absorbed the beauty of her being. She took it in.

"I will try," she whispered. "I will try…." Then, "I will try to be who I am."

In the blackness came Flight's voice, which sounded more like birdsong than a human voice. "Now go paint."

***

"I will try. I will try. I will try."

"She wakes!"

Caroline opened her eyes slowly. The healers of the Temple, those priests and priestesses skilled in healing, were around her in a protective circle. She recognized only one, vaguely. But she smiled. She was home. "I need to go to the gardens."

"You have been unconscious for hours. You will rest now."

"I need to see Blue!"

"Here, then, please don't cry."

"No! I need to see Blue! Now! My Lord! Blue!" she screamed. A blue light filled the room. All the healers stilled. "You may go," said Caroline. "I am safe. Blue has come. Thank you." They all nodded, and bowed, and left in silence.

Caroline gazed at the man standing over her bedside. "I have caused you much trouble," she whispered.

Blue's lips twitched. "No end of trouble."

"I'm sorry."

He brushed her hair off her face. "Shh."

"I am ready now."

"I know."

"I want to paint."

"Yes, Little Bird."

"Now."

"Sleep. Eat. Then come to our garden."

***

From that day forth, Caroline became more of a Master Artist every day of her life. The first painting she did was of her family...and she painted the longing. The next was of the bird in her face...and she painted the fear. And the courage. It wasn't just shape and texture anymore. Her art breathed.

***

He stood before her robed in blue sky. He stood in the center of a circle made by seven of her paintings. He turned, slowly. He felt the colors radiating from them. The hot red. The cool white. The feelings assaulted him on all sides. Need. Love. Lust. Pain. Joy. They hit at him. They hit so hard that he began to see the paintings with his eyes, because he could see them so well with his spirit. He saw them, clearer. Clearer. Clearer. Fully.

The god threw open his arms. He began to yell out a cry of joy from the center of his body that radiated out through all of him.

"I can see!" With a fierce, warlike howl he grabbed Caroline up into his arms and whirled her around and around till she was dizzy. Her tears blended with his on their cheeks.

"I can see. I can see. I can see," he kept repeating, and crying, holding her tightly. "Oh, you who are my eyes, never forsake me in the darkness again. If you do not see yourself, who then shall see yourself? And if no one can see yourself, who then can see the Universe? Who then can see anything, anything, anything at all?"

Novice of Colors

***

The New Moon drew close. Blue spoke to her in the last days of the old moon. "Little Bird. You need to understand something important."

"Yes, Lord?"

"It is destined that as a Priestess you shall serve four colors. So shall your mate."

"Why…why do you tell me this now?"

"Because, my dear, two of them shall be your primary Lord and Lady. The other two follow as helpers."

"I see."

"No. No, you do not. Not yet. Caroline, you believe that your love of Pink and I cannot be equaled. This is because there are two whom you have not yet met."

"I…."

"We—Pink and I—we are your Lord and Lady, Caroline. But there are two who could only come to you after you had learned how to love us. For your love of them will surpass anything you have ever felt till now."

Caroline whispered, "Why do you tell me now?"

"To prepare you, a little. Your spirit will be shocked too greatly when the time comes if I do not open you a little to the truth."

"Pink told me there would be another."

"Two others."

"Can—can you tell me anything else? Of who they are, of how I serve them?"

Blue gently kissed her on the forehead. "Simply know that they are coming, my Little Bird. They are coming."

***

"Blue is not my primary Lord," Caroline whispered to Gawen in wonder. "I do not understand."

Gawen stroked her hair, her cheeks. "I was told that there would be four for both of us—a primary Lord and Lady and a secondary Lord and Lady who will serve as helpers to the other two. But, for me, Blue will always be above any other Lord."

Caroline nodded, her love of Gawen in her eyes. "I see this truly," she said and kissed him. She had grown fond of kissing since the Solstice. "Do you know the other Lord you serve, Gawen?"

Gawen nodded. "Yes. I am of Silver."

Caroline kissed him again to let him know what she thought of that. "My Blue and Silver one," she smiled at him.

Beneath the nearly disappearing moon, on their hill on a hot Summer night, with the flowers scenting the air heavily and their young hearts wildly in love, he laid her down on the earth and kissed her with all the yearning of his heart and body.

*****

On the day before the New Moon, Caroline went to the mountain where she had met Silver. She went to the garden where she painted with Blue. No one came. It was not until she was nearly asleep in her bed that a pink and silver light flooded her room. Drowsy, she tried to focus.

"Relax, Little Bird," said Pink.

Caroline's eyes filled with love as she gazed at her Lady. "Hello," she said softly.

"Hello, Little Bird. I am proud of you. In the two moons you worked with Silver and Blue, you have kept your promise to work with me on your three great wounds. Will you enter this last moon with me ready to work harder than ever? The end is always the hardest."

Caroline nodded. "I am ready, Lady. I love you." Pink kissed her cheeks. "I will be more active this moon than I was with Blue. I have things to teach you," she whispered.

Caroline beamed at her.

"And as for your work with me," Silver put in, "I too am pleased and proud. You are doing well in finding your magical strengths. Your new paintings." He leaned forward and kissed the heart in the center of Caroline's forehead which was Pink's brand. Ecstasy exploded in Caroline, and she began to cry with joy. Silver hugged her tightly. "We all love you, Little Bird. We all love you so much." He stood back, and grew solemn. "What you did in being able to look at yourself as Blue sees you, that was very, very special. We of the Twelve want you to know how proud—how happy—you made us by looking at your true self."

Pink clapped her hands excitedly. "Little Bird. The Twelve are going to give you a special present." Her eyes were twinkling. "We have a gift—a blessing—for you. You will know it when you see it. It will come to you within the next moon."

Caroline stammered, "I—"

Pink stared deep into her eyes. "Shh. What you did was very, very hard for you. We are *proud*. We will show you how we feel." It was a simple, commanding statement.

Caroline bowed her head. "I thank you. I love you."

Pink laughed. "You're also consumed with curiosity and want your present now." Caroline grinned. With a joyful giggle, Pink disappeared in a pink mist.

Silver came over to her. As he did, Blue light filled the room, and Blue came in.

"Caroline," said Silver, "you are no longer chained. You have found yourself. But there is more to do to discover your magical strengths."

"Yes?"

"I will release your chains. But on one condition."

"Anything you ask, I will do."

"I will give you a sign, Caroline. Let it be a sign you discover for yourself. You will know it when you see it. It will tell you that you need to think about me, to think about your magical strengths. If I release you, will you swear to look for this sign, and when you see it, to return to our work together?"

Caroline nodded. "Yes, Lord Silver. I do swear."

Silver smiled at her. "As you wish, Little Bird." He looked at Blue. A silent signal passed between them.

Blue leaned over the bed and gazed into Caroline's eyes with his huge, gentle ones. It seemed they were a different shade of blue every time she saw them! She drowned happily there. "I love you," Blue said. It was all he needed to say.

Caroline touched his face gently. "I love you, too."

Blue handed her a blue feather, his eyes never leaving hers. "It is my turn to brand you," he whispered. Silver and Blue laid a hand on Caroline's wrist.

"Your chain is now the great circle of life," said Silver. They did and said the same with her other wrist.

"Caroline. You may remove them when you wish. Keep them and wear them as a memory of your triumph over fear and self-doubt. And of my love of you," said Silver.

Caroline found a clasp she could undo on each bracelet that had not been there before. Kissing them, she removed them. Where the bracelets had lain, on the insides of her wrists, were two brands, like her pink heart. They were blue lightning bolts.

Silver left quietly. Blue looked at Caroline with all his love of her in his eyes.

"You are mine now," he said. "You will be my eyes. Be my hands. Paint my visions." Caroline nodded, too full of tears to speak. "You are mine," he said again. Loudly. Firmly. Outside, she saw a lightning bolt race through the sky...again, a clear sky.

When she looked back, Blue had gone. But she heard his voice, clear and bright in her room. "I love you, Little Bird—and you are mine." It seemed to Caroline that the wind began to howl the words. "I love you—and you are mine. Mine. Mine. Mine."

Yes. The winds of blue had claimed their Little Bird and offered themselves for her to fly upon. She had sworn to surrender to their motion and pull and call, and they...they had sworn to take her wherever—anywhere—that she needed to go. In body, mind, or spirit. They would take her there.

Chapter Five

Caroline stared into the flames of the altar fires at the top of the Hill of Novices. She felt like an old hand at this by now and gazed wisely and knowingly at the new novices from the position of expertise after being an entire season at the Temple.

The Summer night was hot; even the breezes were hot and sultry. Her friends were all around her, and the words of the chants and prayers to summon the Twelve to this hill were like old friends as well.

Her beloved Gawen was standing with the priests on the other side of the altar, staring at her till her skin and lips tingled. She felt so strong and alive. Her future lay ahead of her, bright and beckoning with a thousand lights. Tomorrow seemed sweet. She was in love and a novice of the Twelve. Her dreams were all coming true. It made her tremble.

She was proud. She had passed the tests of four of the Twelve. Yes, she was still working with two of them. But somehow she just knew in her heart that she would become a priestess. For the first time, she had confidence in herself. She felt as though she were becoming a woman. She gazed steadily into the flames, feeling energized and awake. *Come to me, O Color of Beauty and Life, and let me serve thee and love thee with all my heart.*

Slowly the crowd around her seemed surreal and distant, the world within the flames much more real. The flames leapt and danced, crackled and hissed. Within them she saw two figures...dancing in the flames. Both were red-haired women with green eyes, but there the similarity ended. One was tall, strong, muscular, with curls of every shade of red imaginable. Her eyes were wild and cat-like. Her body was painted in black and orange tiger stripes. She moved with a sexuality that was open and natural as if she couldn't have moved any other way. Caroline felt a little afraid of her.

The other, Her hair was only to her waist, and she was not so tall, but she was round and curvy and voluptuous. She had eyes like Blue's eyes... only instead of many shades of blue, they were many shades of green. Like Blue, she loved bells, and wore them on her ankles. This was Blue's mate. Caroline knew it. This woman laughed as she danced and played and teased with her eyes. Her lips were full and bright red. She wore a green dress that clung to her curves and flowers all over her hair. Her cheeks were bright red, and she was barefoot.

Caroline watched them dance. She did not know what else to do. After awhile, they stepped out of the flames and stood before her, life-sized, real and breathing—no mere vision. But then, Caroline had known they were more.

Blue's mate spoke. "We greet you, Little Bird."

Caroline laid her body full on the ground in respect.

"Rise, Caroline, and share the magic!"

She did and asked, "What do you desire of me, my Ladies?"

"I am Green. Yes, I am the wife of Blue."

"And I am Red. Blessings, Little Bird."

Red stood behind Green as if she were a warrioress protecting Green's back from attack. She stared at Caroline steadily, never taking her eyes off Caroline's face, which made Caroline squirm. But Caroline refused to move or look away, and she tried to meet the wildcat eyes straight on.

"How may I serve?" asked Caroline again.

Green smiled. "Red and I came to you together because our tasks for you are closely intertwined—almost two sides of the same task. We will be working with you for two moons, and if you complete the task we set you to, you will receive feathers from us both."

102

Caroline beamed at them, having no words to express her excitement. She noticed that butterflies and small wild creatures seemed to flock around Green. A little chipmunk neared her now, unafraid. She also noticed that Green smelled of wildflowers. "What is my task?"

The Ladies exchanged glances, and private messages passed between their eyes which Caroline could not read. "We shall tell all, as things unfold and require it," Green said at last.

"And tonight?" asked Caroline. "What can I do for you tonight?"

Green laughed. "Enjoy the night! That is all. The moon and Summer are new. Your blood flows hotly. Savor it. That is all I would ask."

Several faeries, tiny and shimmery, appeared around Green then and danced around her. For Green was one of the Queens of Faerie. She danced, too, with the little bells jingling and her laugh ringing out. Red continued to stare at Caroline, never stopping or leaving her spot behind Green.

"My Lady Red," Caroline asked, for she was unused to such long staring and silences, "what may I do for you tonight? I will happily commit myself to any task you might put me to."

The woman became a tiger, fierce and wild. The beautiful creature did not leave its spot or move towards Caroline but continued to stare at her. Caroline did not ask any more questions.

"Dance, Little Bird! Dance for the love of the Summer! Dance for love of me. Dance with me!"

And so Caroline did, not caring that the other novices—and Gawen—were watching (indeed, she did not even remember it). Caroline danced with Lady Green on a Summer's night, and the faeries widened their circle to include her within it. And the eyes of a tiger watched it all.... Watching. Waiting.

***

Elizabeth Anne and Caroline were in the Temple gardens beneath the hot sun. Elizabeth Anne's robe of four colors was now mostly brown with dirt. Caroline had worn a brown dress she was not afraid to get dirty, one which her mother had brought when she visited on Solstice. It was a Summer working dress, light and cool. Still, Caroline was sweaty, hot, flushed, tired, irritable. Elizabeth Anne's round wire glasses kept sliding down her nose, and she kept pushing them back and smudging them with her dirty hands, no matter how she tried to be careful. Both women had pulled their hair back tightly in a bun.

Caroline was weary of her chores in the garden, now that it was so hot. She wanted to be discussing philosophy and magic with a group of sisters beneath a shady tree. The harder she tried not to complain, the more frustrated she got, for she was not good at holding back her feelings. So she gardened in silence, afraid she would snap at Elizabeth Anne unfairly when Elizabeth Anne was working twice as hard as a woman half her age.

Sighing, Caroline pulled up a weed. The Temple food was delicious, all fresh from the earth and prepared by cooks who put magic and love into each meal. Meals were made to be a pleasure, eaten slowly and savored, with your sisters around. Conversation was light, exciting, and pleasurable at meal tables. There were flowers and decorations. Caroline was beginning to understand how hard the priestesses had to work to achieve this atmosphere and quality.

As with the Temple artists and musicians and healers, there were the Temple cooks and head gardeners. Caroline noticed that many cooks were of Brown or Yellow, some were of Black or Green. As she put some berries in her basket, she thought about why these colors were good in the Kitchen. Orange was another popular color of cooks. It occurred to her that Elizabeth Anne wore three of these colors—orange, yellow, and brown. Yet she was not a cook. She was a housekeeper, one of those who tended to the grounds both inside and outside. She did, however, love to cook, and was always bringing Caroline tasty treats.

Caroline sighed again. "How is it that you are so patient when muscles ache, and you are hot and tired, and the little growing things take so very long to grow? How is it that you find comfort in doing the same dusting and washing each day, yet are never bored?"

Elizabeth Anne smiled and pushed her glasses back up yet again. The kindly round face was flushed pink. "It is fun. That's what artists like you forget sometimes. Housekeeping and gardening and cooking is fun. Yes, it is work, but so is painting. I honestly enjoy the work, the way you enjoy painting."

Caroline just raised an eyebrow.

Elizabeth Anne laughed. "Look," she said. A faerie was sitting on the basket of berries, watching them. Elizabeth Anne gave her a bright red berry, and she took it with both tiny hands. Then she bowed her head with thanks and a comical expression of delight that made the women laugh, and she flew off.

"I have seen many faeries recently," said Caroline. "Ever since Green came to me."

"There are sky faeries and tree faeries and water faeries and other kinds as well as Green faeries, you know," Elizabeth Anne reminded her. "And snow faeries and...."

Caroline nodded. "I know. But I have seen few, except with Green. What do you think they are trying to tell me? Why are they coming to me? It has been a week since the New Moon, but I have seen neither Green or Red. Only many faeries who never talk to me."

"Let us ask them."

"How best to do this?"

"Tonight we will do a faerie calling ritual, to ask for a sign as to their message for you."

Caroline grinned. Suddenly she was not hot or tired any more and returned to her gardening with a joyful energy that made Elizabeth Anne ruffle her hair, laughing.

"You see? It's all about having a happy, singing heart," Elizabeth Anne said with a laugh, and they began to sing as they worked.

***

They went to the gardens. They lit candles, laid down crystals, hung tiny silver bells in the trees. They called to the faeries with words the first men and women of the Temple had learned from the faeries themselves, centuries before. They sang and danced, for faeries love joy and laughter. As gifts, they left tiny silver ribbons hanging in the bushes, and cookies shaped like stars that Elizabeth Anne had helped Caroline bake that afternoon. In the trees they also placed tiny little lights and feathers from Energy. Energy had also come and was singing happily along with Caroline.

When the faeries came, there were hundreds! Some appeared only as little, many-colored lights. Some you could not see, but sensed. Some appeared misty and were hard to see, others you could see clearly.

One, a little bigger than the rest, approached Caroline, who was kneeling with Elizabeth Anne before the little altar table they had set up. In a beautiful voice Caroline heard only in her mind, the faerie said, "Little Bird, you have looked upon yourself as Blue sees you. The Twelve commends you. So does the faerie realm. We, too, wish to offer a gift to show you respect and friendship, to honor what you did when the dark bird flew at you."

Caroline sang softly, a song of friendship to the faeries she had learned recently. When she was done, the little faerie clapped her hands together. A dozen or more faeries flew towards Caroline. They carried a paintbrush, but one such as Caroline had never seen before. There were jewels and crystals in it, and it was made of silver. Little designs had been crafted into it. Caroline saw a heart, a lightning bolt, a feather, and began to weep.

The little faerie said, "This brush has very special powers. You will be discovering them your whole life long."

Caroline managed to say, "Is there anything I need to know, to use it as it was meant to be used?"

The faerie said, "The brush has a name. It is Beautiful Vision."

Caroline kissed the brush and made a holy sign over it that she had seen one of the priestesses do. "What gift may I offer in return that would please the faeries?"

The faerie had an answer ready. "There is a cave. We will lead you to it soon. You will know it when you find it. Paint it to honor us. Make it a place where people can go to speak to us." She nodded to Elizabeth Anne. "You who are her teacher; you help her to create a place of beauty. A faerie dwelling."

Elizabeth Anne began to sing a gratefulness song. At this, Caroline took out the flute she had brought and began to play. The faeries danced as she played; whether they were little lights or in more solid bodies, they danced and glowed and flickered. They also ate the food and drank from the chalices Caroline and Elizabeth Anne had brought. They got out some faerie instruments and began to play them. They took the silver ribbons off the trees and used them to dance with.

Many animals came when they heard the faeries laughing and singing and dancing...little mice and chipmunks and squirrels and birds and rabbits that wished to join the celebration and were friends of the faeries. Novice, priestess, and faerie celebrated. They celebrated the Summer, and the art of Caroline, and the arrival of Green in Caroline's life. They celebrated the vision of Caroline that Blue held. They celebrated each other. And Caroline began to understand that sometimes the simple joy of being alive holds within it powerful, powerful magic. Sometimes you need to do nothing but be, and exult in the being.

***

Caroline had just finished swimming in one of the ponds on the grounds to cool off. It was evening, and she had gardened and painted long hours. She was tired, but it was a happy tired. She lay on her back beneath a flowering tree, watching the clouds float by, seeing pictures in them, and daydreaming of Gawen kissing her.

Behind her she heard a tambourine tinkling in the air. She sat up quickly. A gypsy stood there. Her skirt was in patterns of red, orange, and yellow, and she had gold hoops in her ears and bangles around her wrists. She looked free and wild, her eyes painted in many colors. It took a second for Caroline to realize that it was Red standing there, for the body was a little different—smaller, rounder. The eyes were rounder, too.

"Yes," Red laughed. "Red is Shapechanger."

Caroline nodded, a little wary, but less afraid than she was of the tiger-striped warrioress.

"Are you afraid now?" Red changed into a small little elf with chubby red cheeks and a little green cap.

"Now?" She appeared as a graceful faerie, looking a lot like Pink, in red chiffon, with shimmery wings.

"Now?" She appeared as a sturdy little peasant with a basket of flowers and a kerchief on her head, tiny black boots and skin browned by the sun.

"Now?" She appeared as a belly dancer, all fringes and fire and passion.

"Now?" She appeared as a warrioress with a flaming spear, muscled and dangerous and very, very strong.

"Now?" She appeared as a sultry woman, glamorous and elegant, in red silk and sequins and rubies. She returned to her gypsy form.

"Which is the real you?" asked Caroline.

"A combination of all of them."

"Are other colors like this?"

"Some more than others. Sit down."

Caroline did, and Gypsy Red sat beside her. From her skirts she pulled forth a deck of well-loved cards, shuffled them, and handed them to Caroline.

"Pick seven," she said. Caroline did, and slowly turned them over. The pictures and images began to make her dizzy. Looking at them, she began to remember...

She saw lifetimes in which she served Red openly, long before the Temple even existed, amongst the people who had taken Serenity. She saw lifetimes in which she had totally forgotten who the colors were. Yet even in these, she could still see by her actions that she served Red unconsciously...and that Red was always, always there. In each life she was sworn to serve the color of passion, creativity, and the arts, love, and fire. Her life paths, each and every one, led in these directions, one way or another.

She began to cry, but was feeling so many feelings she did not know why she cried. All she knew was that every time she had fallen, Red had been there. Every time she had needed her, Red had been there. In defeat, in triumph, in the crowds, in aloneness, Red was beside her. Inspiring, prodding, lifting, exciting, freeing, maddening, serving, loving her...Caroline. Little Bird. No matter what face Caroline wore...or the shapechanging color she wore...it was always the same. A color and her priestess.

When it was over, Caroline found herself sobbing all over Red's shoulder, while Red stroked her hair. "You needed to remember," said Red softly, lovingly.

"Yes," Caroline whispered. "Yes. Very, very much."

"My novice, my Lady Caroline, Little Bird. My task for you in this moon is this: Find the way that you are meant to serve me in this *life*. Remember the others; see the pattern as you grow. But most of all, find how I wish you to serve me here. Now."

Caroline said, "To find *that* is all I desire to do. It seems nothing else matters."

Red smiled at her. Then she changed into a silly clown with red, orange, and yellow hair, a bright big red nose, a floppy hat, balloons, and a big floppy suit with polka dots of all colors, and huge floppy shoes. Caroline's tears turned to laughter until she was rolling on the grass with it. They did not need to speak more. They hugged and parted.

That night Caroline found she had a third brand on her. It was between her breasts. One red flame had two smaller ones on either side, looking like arms reaching up to the sky. Like a woman worshipping. Like a soul on fire.

***

High on the hill, where she had first met Silver, Caroline lay in Gawen's arms, looking up at the stars one Summer night. She gazed up at them, remembering Silver, how he had come to her as hundreds of tiny stars that flowed together to form him. How he had given her a silver blanket with stars on it to sleep in. How he had told her that she was magic. Then he had put silver chains on her that he said were formed of her tears and fear. He had begged her to find her magical gifts. Now Gawen was pledged to him, and Silver had told her the Twelve were going to give her a gift this moon. She meditated on how her visions created paintings that healed people, and how she could feel what people really needed to be happy. She thought of the power in her brands, and wished she knew more how to use them.

Gawen followed her thoughts with his mind. Though Caroline was not the telepathist he was, she had a little bit if it, especially with him, and he taught her, helped strengthen it. She remembered that long ago night when he had asked her, "Have you always drawn just what you see?" He was staring at her now, and she felt his pride in how far her art had come. Yes, she thought, *but not far enough.*

She took in his face. They met at the last night of every week and were slowly becoming more and more bonded. He was helping her again tonight, helping her thoughts to open up and flow to their true destination. She had told him all about Red, how she had remembered many lives of loving and serving Red, and how Red had asked her to find out how she was to serve her in this one.

Gawen mentally asked her, "Any ideas?"

"None. But something is in the air. "She looked at his blue eyes, twirled his hair into her fingers. "I want to go on a vision quest," she said, the thought coming out of nowhere. "I want to go on a vision quest to find out what Red wants of me. And you, you must help me. You must go with me. We must do it together." All this she said in her mind, to his.

Gawen smiled at her with love and excitement and a hint of magic. "Lady," he said out loud, shattering the silence, "I will take you anywhere you want to go. Anywhere."

***

The Hill of Novices was available to all novices who wished to do work with one of the Twelve. Many classes and lessons were taught there, and rituals were held often. On the night of the Full Moon, Caroline and Gawen set out to seek a vision. They kept the ritual very simple. Caroline sought a Red Vision, so she wore a red robe one of the priestesses had lent her and carried red roses and red candles. Gawen, too, had borrowed a red robe, and he carried a pouch of crystals and stones. For offerings they had some red fruit, apples and cherries.

On the Hill, they did not go to the main altar, which was used only on New Moons. There were a few other altars, made of stone or wood, around the top of the Hill. Most were plain so that the novices could use them for whatever purpose they wished. They had received permission from the Temple Elders to do this and were very excited. The night before they had gone up to prepare the site. They had wanted to be sure it was clear of any leftover energy and that they found the *right* place to do the ritual.

They *had* found the right place. It was a circle of stones and huge crystals of many colors and types, which was mainly a Summer altar, and taken away for protection in the Winter. As soon as Caroline stepped inside, she felt the energy of all the novices who had used it before, but subtly, like a background scent. Nothing unpleasant or distracting; it just added to the energy. She felt happy. That was her first, her central, her most primitive reaction. She was happy to be there on this night. It was where she was supposed to be.

Candles were lit. The couple joined hands and called to the elements to bless their quest. Then, because it was a Red Vision they sought, they chose to go into Flame. They had lit a blaze right in the center of the circle. Both stared calmly into it, feeling themselves grounded in the earth, but with spirits free to fly. Gawen, whose primary Lord was Blue and who was excellent with all things related to the mind, or vision, led the way. Caroline saw in her mind a path. It was lit by candles of red.

Gawen walked first. Caroline was awed at the ease with which he traveled into vision. He was so clear in her mind! She smiled at him. The surroundings were gone. She was no longer in a circle on the Hill of Novices, but following a path she knew not where, lit by candles. It led deeper and deeper into a forest. She knew that if the red candles were not there, placed in trees or on rocks, guiding her way, she would be lost in this forest, perhaps never finding her way out.

Gawen looked back at her, sending reassurance. *I will not let anything happen to you, Little Bird.*

I know, love.... I know.

After what seemed a long time, they finally noticed the trees getting thinner and less dense. They came to a clearing. It was a pretty spot. In the clearing it was bright daylight. A small cottage was there, and it was painted beautifully, with drawings and designs on the outer walls. Caroline gasped, for she recognized her work. There was a garden by the house, and she saw Gawen, much older, perhaps in his forties or early fifties, working there. There was a candle lit on the doorstep, so Caroline knew she was meant to go inside. The gardener did not pause in his work or notice them as they slipped into the house. A candle in one direction, a candle in another, and they found themselves in a room. There was Caroline, painting at an easel, in a robe splattered all over with many colors of paint.

I look so happy, Caroline thought.

Gawen grinned at her.

A young girl, a Priestess of Blue and White from the colors of her robe, was watching her intently. She looked to be about the sixteen years of age Caroline was now, and she was watching Caroline with great awe.

The older Caroline put down her brush. "I am just a woman, Jenni."

The young girl flushed.

"I am not the Goddess," continued the older Caroline. "I am Her priestess, a face of Her only. I have flaws, Jenni. Many."

"I am sorry, Lady. I will try."

"I know. I am sorry, too. Perhaps if we talk about it—get it in the open. *Why* are you so in awe of me?"

"Your power. You are one of the greatest artists the Temple has ever seen."

"So are you. Perhaps even more than I."

"No, never more!"

"At least my peer. You are young, but your gift equals mine. In your heart you know this. It is why you were sent to me to be trained. They told you this."

"Yes. But, Lady, your paintings and drawings are straight from spirit. You can *do anything* when you create! People ask you for a drawing of their spirit. When you draw it, you create miracles. You heal their diseases. You answer their deepest questions. You show them their hidden, most powerful dreams. I will *never* have that gift."

"No. You will have your *own* power. This is not the real reason, Jenni. Do I remind you too much of your own power? Are you really in awe of yourself? I have taken you to your future, Priestess. You know what your art will do, what you will become. Is it *yourself* that makes you tremble?"

Jenni lay her head on Caroline's chest, uncaring of the paint smears on her cheek from Caroline's robe. "Perhaps. Perhaps, Lady. Or perhaps it is not your talent I tremble before. Perhaps I tremble because I love you so much. I never had a family. You and Lord Gawen are my family. I am afraid to love you this much...and lose you."

Caroline stroked Jenni's hair, and they both had tears streaking the paint smudges on their faces. "Oh, Jenni. You are my spirit daughter, my spirit sister. We will always be bonded. In body or spirit, one way or another, we will always be together."

"Do you promise?" asked Jenni softly.

"Yes, Priestess. I promise."

Neither of the hugging figures had seen young Caroline and Gawen enter their private scene. Now it was getting to a sacred moment though—a moment that belonged to the Caroline of the future.

They left, hand-in-hand, and followed the path of candles, back, back, back through the forest…back, back, back…until they found themselves in the stone and crystal circle altar of the Hill of Novices, before the central flame, wrapped tightly in each other's arms as if they would never, never let go.

***

From that day forth, Caroline's art changed still more. Now she knew what she was seeking. Before each work, she looked for a vision. Perhaps it was a vision of the trouble that lay in people's hearts. Perhaps it was a vision of the joy they sought—and where it lay. Perhaps it was simply a way of seeing themselves that went deeper than the person had gone till that point.

Whatever she did, strange things happened. People's lives changed. She began to build a reputation; people began to seek her out. It began almost immediately, a day or so after the vision. Caroline sketched a priestess in a strange, unfamiliar place, high in the mountains. It seemed as if the woman was a snow queen in the drawing, for the high mountains were cold and still had some fierce storms even in early Summer. The priestess had paled when she saw Caroline's drawing. She said she had been sensing that her mother was ill, that she had been wanting to visit her mother, but her mother's letters claimed all was well.

The scene was nearby to her home , a place she had never told Caroline of, and the priestess knew as soon as she saw the drawing that her mother had been lying to protect her. Her mother *was* ill, just as her daughter had sensed. Something in the drawing *told* her this, and the very next morning she set out to visit her home, two moons' travel away. The picture had told her she would arrive before her mother died; she would arrive when her mother needed her most.

This sort of thing began to happen often, and as news of this kind will, it spread like wildfire throughout the Temple. Caroline's life began to change, even as the moon waned. She knew it would only continue to change. She knew because she had seen, in vision, in the eyes of the older Caroline, why she had gone into deep woods to live. She had hidden herself away because too many demands, too many hands pulled at her. And only those who could reach the cottage were truly meant to have her help. For the cottage was magically hidden by the Twelve, and only those whom the Twelve permitted could find it.

Many would seek it who were not meant to find it. They were a huge darkness to her, lurking just outside the light of the cabin clearing, lurking just outside the peace of her mind. It was a guilt that she did not deserve, but throughout all her life she would have to fight its claws. Yet the young Caroline continued to move towards that fame which she already knew would cause her one day to retreat to the woods. She could no more have said "no" to it than stop breathing. It was, simply, who she was. It was, simply, what Red called her to do.

And for Red she would have accepted fame, she would have thrown fame into the nearest trash pit, she would have spent her whole life walking around standing on her head. She would have lived a billion hells or a billion heavens and wouldn't have known the difference...for as long as she served Red, and loved Gawen, *all* was heaven.

Red called her to fall blindly and trustingly into a future she could sense, but not really understand until she lived it. Red called her to jump into the heart of the flame and create. Whatever the consequence. For its own sake...for the sake of the creating. And...loving her...Caroline did.

***

It was as the moon waned that Caroline found the two things Silver had promised her as he released her from her silver chains. She had been told that the Twelve were giving her a special gift, a special blessing to show her how proud they were of her for looking at her true self, as Blue painted it. She had been told that she would receive a sign, to focus her on her magical powers and Silver, when Silver wished it.

One Summer day she was wandering aimlessly, with Energy flying around her, just enjoying the grounds. She felt driven to go to the place where she had done so much painting with Blue as his apprentice. When she went back to the familiar spot, to her surprise the familiar, beloved easel Blue used was set up with a covered canvas on it. She felt she was being told to go look at it. Blue was nowhere around. Tentatively, she went up to it and pulled back the covering.

It was a painting. Black was there in it, and she was holding a miniature image of the self-portrait Caroline had done for her. Pink was there, holding out to Caroline a beautiful glowing pink heart in her hands. Silver was there, in his silver jumpsuit with the crystals corded around his waist and stars exploding all around him. Blue was there, with a blank canvas in his arms. Green was there, unfinished. Red was unfinished, too.

Blue was painting them all for her, the way they wanted her to remember them. Somehow Caroline knew what to do. She did not take the painting. She picked up a feather from Energy which was on the ground, laid it on the easel, and walked slowly away.

The next day she was sitting by the stream, throwing pebbles in. To her surprise the ripples formed not circles, but the shape of stars. She knew, without knowing how she knew, that if ever she saw a star-shape in something of nature not normally shaped like a star, this would be Silver calling her. Telling her to remember her magic, and him. And that this would be a sign from him that would return again and again, all her life long.

***

In the last days of the waning moon, Green at last came to her. Caroline had begun to wonder if Green was expecting her to do something on her own, something she was somehow missing, not seeing. But then, there Green was, as Caroline lay tossing and turning in her room in the night heat. Green was wearing only vines tied all over her, and flowers.

"Little Bird," Green said. "Hello." Caroline was thinking about how much like the blue eyes she loved Green's were. Green smiled. "A lot has happened to you this moon. You sought a vision. You found it. The faeries gave you a magic brush. Blue and the Twelve gave you a painting. You got your past memories."

Caroline smiled at her. "My Lady. All I want is to *do* something for you. Please. Tell me how. It hurts me not to be able to give to you."

"Then give to yourself." Caroline waited for an explanation. Green sighed. "What is Green?" the Lady asked.

"Growth. Abundance. Fertility. Life."

"All right. Go deeper."

"Green is…expression. Creation."

Green sat down on the bed. "Expressing what?" she asked.

"Selfhood?" Caroline offered.

"Define selfhood."

"Who you are."

Green nodded. "Who you are. Yes. Do you like who you are?"

"If you don't like you, then you're not being you," said Caroline.

Green beamed. "Yes! So it's not just about being you. It's about *loving* being you."

Caroline nodded.

Green said, "You can have self-knowledge, as Black showed you. But all your self-knowledge will come undone if you don't rejoice in being yourself." She reached over and stroked Caroline's cheek gently. "I want to take your lesson with Black farther. Build on it."

"How, my Lady?"

"You know yourself, but I want to help you know yourself better." She took Caroline's face in her hands. "Pink told you to find your three deepest wounds and how to heal them. I want you to find your three deepest pleasures."

"Oh, my Lady, that's easy! Painting and—"

"Why?"

"Why?"

"Yes, Little Bird. *Why* do you find pleasure in painting?"

"S-so *many* reasons."

"Not good enough. You must be able to explain to yourself as to *why*, exactly, the three greatest pleasures of your life please you so. The *central* reason. The *core* reason. There are surface reasons. You like painting because you can express yourself. But why is that a pleasure? What is it about yourself you love to express? The deepest reasons, Caroline. The task I give you is not as simple as it sounds. You will see, when you begin.

"Pleasure is a maze of sensation, and you can get lost in it. You can think you found the center. You can think you've reached the peak of joy, and more lies dormant you don't even see. I want to help you avoid getting lost in the maze. I want to stop you from ever settling for partial joy in life. I want you to have it all.

"If any parts of you are shut to pleasure, I want to open them. Go into the maze, Caroline. It will be full of sensation and wonder. You will be overwhelmed. It will put you in a daze. Little Bird, you will reach a point where you feel you can take no more pleasure, the same as there is a threshold for pain. In that moment, Caroline, I will be there. And I will break your threshold. I will take you past your barriers. I will make you strong enough to feel the pleasure you are afraid to feel.

"If you are lost in a dead end of the maze, drunk on pleasure and unable to move to the center, if you are too weak to reach for the deepest pleasure, I will pick you up. I will carry you. I will help you. I will not leave you abandoned in the maze. Remember that.

"My dear, people say they are frightened of pain. But they are frightened of pleasure as much. *More*, oftentimes. You do not feel afraid of this assignment? My Little Bird, you *are* afraid of pleasure. You are simply so afraid that you don't even realize it. I will help you be strong enough to hold pleasure. Do you accept my task, Little Bird?"

"Yes. Yes, I do, my Lady."

"I will stay with you."

"Yes, my Lady Green. Stay with me. I think I need you more than I understood."

"I am here, Little Bird. Open to me. I need to be let in. I am run from, rejected, ignored, denied, repressed. I want to love people, they *scream* for me, but they don't let me in. Give me a chance to love you, Little Bird. I am *always* here. Give me a chance to love you, Little Bird."

***

This time there was no feather on the eve before the New Moon to acknowledge that Caroline had completed her task, because both Green and Red had told her they needed two moons with her and would give her the feathers next moon if she was ready for them. Instead, Green and Red and Caroline had a picnic. They spread out a blanket and ate foods Elizabeth Anne made for them. They talked and laughed and sang. Caroline played her flute while Green and Red danced.

Caroline asked many questions, as was Caroline's tendency, about the colors Green and Red and how to use them magically. They did talk about this, but mostly there was giggling and laughter, teasing and frolic and dance. They teased her about Gawen. They tickled her feet. They told jokes. They threw her in the pond and got her wet. They played tag, chasing each other around trees. They made wishes on stars and wove garlands of flowers for each other. It was one of those times which, though seemingly simple and ordinary, have a profound impact, and Caroline remembered this picnic clearly and often, all her life long.

Pink had come earlier that night to tell Caroline that, once again, Caroline's month had been too busy to pay attention to the healing of her three great wounds. She was not angry—she understood—because Red and Green tend to carry people away in their intensity. But—she was firm—this next moon Caroline must attend more to her healing. Or Pink might take back the pink feather.

Caroline promised her earnestly that she would, and they talked a long while about why paying attention to one's healing is so often the last thing on a person's priority list. People made excuses. The work was too hard.

Caroline told Pink about how Green had said she was often neglected and ignored, because her pleasure and abundance and *giving* were too much for people. Pink held her awhile and told her how proud of her she was, and how much she loved her, and how beautiful she was. (Pink tended to do that sort of thing often). She showered Caroline with gentleness, praise, and tenderness, which Caroline badly needed. As always, Caroline found herself talking and talking and talking to Pink, unable to stop—just pouring her heart out about all that had been happening to her.

So Pink came for awhile to the picnic as well, in a mischievous mood, sprinkling everyone with pink glitter. But she only stayed awhile. Mostly it was Red and Green and Caroline, learning more about each other through play—one of the best ways of all to learn about someone.

Chapter Six

It was the last moon of Summer. The Temple was busy and bustling. The gardeners were harvesting and canning and preserving things for the cold months. The grounds-keepers were fixing any weakness in the buildings, anything broken. Everyone spent as much time outdoors as they could. All the rooms were decorated with flowers, all the altars draped in Summer colors. People were more playful, more relaxed, swimming or sitting in the shade with friends. Caroline thought she had never seen anything as beautiful as the Temple gardens in full bloom. She had never been happier.

Instead of meeting a new color on the New Moon, she did a private ritual outdoors to remind her of what she needed to focus on now. She needed to work with Pink on her healing. She needed to work with Red and Green so that they would be proud of her. The problem was, there was always so much to do. There were always outdoor picnics and parties and games going on. There were horses in the stables of Blue to exercise. There were paintings; so many ideas in her mind. There were her friends to talk to, and Gawen. There were interesting classes all the time, taught by the priestesses. Her work with the Temple artists and Katerina, her mentor. There was Flight to think about. It was all too much.

Within the first week of the moon, Caroline realized that she needed help or she'd never complete her work. So she spoke to Elizabeth Anne about it, who clucked sympathetically and said, "No, no, dear. Mustn't have that. Have you heard of the retreat cabins?"

Caroline nodded. "A little bit. You may go there to do special work alone."

"Or have some needed privacy. I'll speak to the elders, dear. Now don't you fret any longer, Little Bird. We'll set all this to rights."

Caroline was granted permission to use one of the cabins for two weeks. Already pining for the busy activity of the Temple in the last days of Summer, she said, "May I return sometimes?"

Elizabeth Anne said, "On the last day of the week, yes, if you wish."

Caroline told Gawen, amid many kisses and his constant reassurances that he'd check on her often. And when the day came, Elizabeth Anne took her to her retreat cabin. It was on a section of the grounds that had been marked clearly, "No Entrance Permitted Without Request." It was a forested area, with many evergreens and flowering trees. Caroline reflected as she walked that the Temple had more sides and facets than she'd ever see in a lifetime.

They came to a little cabin. It was very pretty, simple and quiet, made of logs and stones and covered with flowers. A little garden and a well were beside it. At the door they were greeted by a priest. He had a gentle, kindly face, but he wore a robe entirely of black, which made him seem austere. He smiled at Caroline, his serious, dark-brown eyes probing her face.

"Welcome, Little Bird. Do you know who I am?"

Caroline shook her head.

"I am David, a Priest of Black. Since the Temple was formed, this area has always been used for privacy, solitude, and retreat. And always a Priest or Priestess of Black was the keeper of this sacred space. We tend the grounds, we make all the visitors comfortable.

We are also advisors, here to listen should you need us. We know that those who seek the Inner Voice, the Deep Silence within the Self, are seeking Black. So we serve our Lady by being her messengers and intermediaries to those who come here seeking her.

120

"We live here, my wife and I. She serves Brown and Black. She assists me, but she is not the caretaker of this place. Only *my* caretaker." He laughed. "Only very rarely does she get involved with the visitors here. She serves them by helping me."

Caroline nodded.

"Elizabeth Anne, thank you. We will take good care of her." He put an arm around Caroline, who was watching with big eyes, suddenly a little frightened.

Elizabeth Anne kissed her on both cheeks. "All blessings to you, Caroline." She left to return to the priestess' quarters.

"Come, Little Bird. I will show you your cabin," said David.

He took her through a tangle of paths she couldn't ever have found her way out of, and she said so, fearfully. "I am afraid."

David patted her shoulder. "Dear child, if you needed to leave you would be able to," and that was all he said.

The cabin was small and rustic, made of logs and stone like David's, but even smaller than his. There were some vegetables and flowers growing.

"Come," he said happily, "see your new home. Here in back, some fruit trees. We have filled your shelves with food as well. I enjoy cooking and gardening. I find it... restful. Come inside! I think you'll be pleased."

Caroline was. There was very little furniture, only chairs and table, bed and so forth...the essentials. But it looked homey. It felt peaceful.

"Yes," David said. "That it is. It is a world within a world. It is of the Temple, a part of it, yet totally apart from it. Like a different place. You'll see what I mean. Here, now." He handed her a large crystal which sat on a small stand by her bed. "If you need me, hold this. I'll hear; I'll know what you need."

"All right. Thank you," said Caroline softly.

"You may not need to see me again at all until you leave." He smiled at her. "There is food and drink here enough for your first week, and fresh bedsheets and towels. I'll replenish your supply at the end of the week when you visit the Temple." His eyes twinkled. "Cannot stay away long, eh?"

121

Caroline flushed. "N-no."

He patted her shoulder. "Well and good. Well and good. He's a fortunate boy to have you." Caroline flushed deeper. David laughed. "I think you'll do well here, yes, well indeed," he said, and actually clapped his hands together like a little boy. "It is a grand adventure, this place. You are always learning here. Life is ever new here. You will find what you seek. Lady Black is good to us." He winked at her.

Caroline stared at him. "You really love this—the solitude, the quiet, the isolation. It makes you happy."

David smiled, but Caroline saw how deeply he was involved with Black, for suddenly it seemed as if he had drawn shadows around him and you could not see him so clearly. Was it a trick of the light? And why could she not interpret that smile? It was mysterious, like Black's. It could mean many things.

"Ah, yes, Little Bird, you will find, among those of us who serve Lady Black, that we are not the sober, serious, unhappy folk you might think. We are among the happiest people on the planet. Our hearts are joyful. There is great joy in deep silence. There is great peace in the dark. Good day to you, Novice Caroline, and may the Lady fill all the desires that lurk in the hidden places of your heart."

He bowed to her, hands folded before him, and slipped away, leaving Caroline alone in the cabin, clutching her two bags and staring at the door he shut quietly as he left.

***

There was not much to unpack. A few clothes. Some small things. She had brought her feathers from Black, Pink, Silver, and Blue. She had brought her paintbrush from the faeries, "Beautiful Vision." She had brought a sketch of Gawen that she hung on the wall.

She investigated. There were only two rooms in the cabin, and a washroom. There was a fireplace she wouldn't need, as it was Summer; and, as David had said, the shelves were stocked. Munching on an apple she picked from the tree in the back, she found many nice little spots. A few benches had been placed outside in spots where she knew it would be nice to sit and meditate and pray. There was a small indoor altar, too. She placed some black candles on it, and a piece of lace her mother had given her. The table was round and wooden. After serious thought, she lay the feathers there, and the brush.

She felt as if the area were *full* of faeries and elves watching her. She set up all her paints and canvas. She felt a bit afraid...but excited afraid. She felt as if she were on a great adventure. She picked wildflowers and put them around the cabin. It was strange. No passers-by. No knocks on the door. Nothing to do but think. It felt odd.

Caroline rather expected that Pink, Red, or Green would start working with her that very day. But it wasn't so. She just made her meals, took little walks, and settled in. The bed felt strange, but comfortable. She felt grown up meeting this wonderful new challenge. She was beaming in the darkness as she snuggled under her blankets and blew out her candle.

The sounds were different...the forest sounds, the outdoors. She had become used to her room at the Temple. But she liked this. She liked this very much. She hugged her pillow, imagining how much Gawen would like this place. Pretending he was holding her. Remembering their little cottage she'd seen in her vision. Giggling and laughing to herself in the dark. Feeling a warm glow of happiness rising up from her belly and spreading through her body. There were beautiful stars out. The waxing moon shone in. Energy was asleep in the little cage she slept in.

The lightning bolt around her neck began to glow, burn. "Gawen!"

"Goodnight, my love. Sleep well. Sweet dreams."

"This place is so beautiful..."

"Shh. I can see it. I can feel it. You are tired, more tired than you know. Sleep. I'll stay with you."

Caroline's eyes grew heavy. Was Gawen casting a sleep upon her? Or just helping her relax? "I love you."

"I love you, too, Little Bird. I'll stay with you."

"Stay with me."

Gawen's voice smiled. "I will."

"Gawen!"

"What?"

"Stay with me!"

"I will. Shh."

"Stay…stay…with me…." And she was asleep, holding the lightning bolt in her hands. It was then that she got another surprise. Pink, Red, and Green had left her alone all day when she expected to see them. One of them appeared in her sleep time, when she wasn't expecting it at all.

***

The dream was more feelings than pictures, more sensation than mere feeling. She understood things in ways she did not know she could, ways she did not know she possessed.

Pink was there, her pretty, ringed hands glittering with stones and jewels as she led Caroline through a story. She showed Caroline images of how the planet used to be, when all species were open to each other. She showed her a time of pagan glory when people could hear the voices of the wind, rocks, sea, and sun. It was an age that Flight and her people were struggling valiantly to keep alive. She saw this, her first sorrow, and then her second…being ripped away from her twin. Losing Serenity. Growing up without her. She had lost her best friend…her sister. Then again, unfolding like a movie, she saw scenes of her life with her family. So loved by them. So different from them. Never really seen.

Pink stood before her, holding her hands, staring into Caroline's eyes with her loving blue ones, her gold hair shining. Caroline could read the thoughts in Pink's heart. "Little Bird…what is at the center of this story?"

And Caroline saw that which she had been unable to see before. Her three pains were one. To lose Serenity meant losing her connection to Nature…for Serenity represented that. To lose Serenity meant to be alone in her own home, for Serenity was her home. The one who would have linked them all and connected them. To solve her pain, she needed to be taught what Serenity could teach her. She needed Serenity to show her the ancient ways, to reawaken her. She wished, in a part of her, that she had been stolen as well, taken as a baby to Flight's new world with her.

"Then you would not be of the Temple," said Pink, and Caroline released the jealousy she hadn't even been aware of before. To hear the voices of life again…

"How? It is futile," said Caroline. "Flight is not here. I can connect to her sometimes in vision, but so rarely. It is never enough. Flight has so much to say!" Caroline pleaded.

Pink sighed. "What is your magical talent?"

"Painting. Visions."

"What is your real self?"

"I am Blue's eyes. I see, I paint for him."

"What is your greatest pleasure?"

"To paint."

"Therefore, paint. Paint of the long ago days when a lioness could call to you and tell you of her thirst. Paint of a time when the land was kept holy. Paint of Flight's people—paint of their fight to keep the truth safe. Paint of these things. And in painting them, you shall remember them. They shall be yours again. They shall be always there in front of you on canvas to look at. They will teach you what Flight could not be here to say.

"My daughter, my sister, no one is taken away from a gift without being given one they need even more in its place. You can have that connection to Nature...you can have your sister back...if you paint it. For the artist always hears the voice of his deepest self through his creation. And when that voice is stilled, when he does *not* create, neither can he feel truly the life abounding all around him.

"If you do not paint, the monkey will not hear you, the roses will not understand you, the time you long for will be gone in truth! For now it exists only in you, Caroline, in your vision. If you bring it to life, it will live.

"Claim your sister, for she is yourself. Claim yourself, for she is all life. We are connected. We are one. You have looked in many places. You have searched everywhere. The power to heal yourself was always in your own heart and hands and mind and vision. It does not lie outside of you. Let Flight take you. Go home to yourself. You have been away too long, lost in the dark. Your home is within your own body.

"Create your dream. Create it of that magical, mysterious star-stuff inside you which makes you, *you*. That indefinable something which lets you be you. Do not seek to name it or understand it; it is a holy mystery. Live it. Live who you are. When you do, you set the universe free to live as well. For we love you, and we cannot live without you any more than you can live without air or water.

"Yes, Caroline. One pain, yet three. Three, yet one. Each of us has a Flight, has a voice of truth and life and love and joy that was stolen from us, is too far away from us, that we deem impossible to ever reach again. For earth, the voice is the sky, which it can never touch. But each of us has a way—a way to bring that voice back to stay. And that way is never distant, is never obscure. It is always right where you can touch it.

"For some, it could be baking a cake. For some, it could be building a house or dancing. For some, it could be healing the sick. For some, it could be swimming. There is always a way to hear once more the voice of the Gods. For earth to hear the sky, it opens to the rain and the sun. And then the earth flowers. Its seeds grow. Open to the help you have been given, and stop seeking the help you thought you needed. You already have all you need when you paint. Your paintings will heal others because first they healed you."

So spoke Pink, in the depths of a dream, and Caroline, upon waking, was not sure where she was. The cabin was unfamiliar. She felt like she had somehow been changed. Who was she? More, and less, than she had known she was. And Caroline, shaken to her core, remembered the dream and the message of Pink as she lay in the dark. She remembered it as she woke, ready for a new day, to the dawn.

***

Caroline awoke feeling sad. She understood the key to her three deepest wounds was her sister, Flight. But painting the visions she received of Flight did not seem to be enough at all. For one thing, she was still not expert at vision work, though she was improving. For another, even at her strongest power with vision work, this could not replace direct contact with Flight. Caroline wanted to be able to hear her sister's voice, to see her expressions, to have the chance to ask her questions and get direct answers.

The magic of the Temple was very powerful, but Caroline knew that even in the Temple, some—much—of the ancient ways and magic of the planet had been lost over time. Only Flight's people had remnants and the embers of it. And Flight's people did not share it easily or freely; it was too often misunderstood or misused. Caroline understood all these things. What she did not know or understand was how far into Flight's world—and the ancient knowledge—she was meant to go.

It was Flight, not Caroline, who had been claimed and taken by the ancient race. Though Caroline was still very angry at this, a part of her understood. Her parents would never have had the strength to give up Flight willingly, if asked...and Flight had to go. She *belonged* with those people. That Caroline understood most of all.

Perhaps it had been kinder to just sever the tie...but to let her parents—and herself —believe Flight was dead for so many years! What kind of people were these? Did they not understand family? Did they not understand compassion?

In the wild, dark eyes of the woman who had taken Flight, Caroline had seen love. This woman loved Flight. She had become her mother. Caroline could feel the deep regard with which the woman treasured Flight. She had given Flight everything she had to give...all her knowledge, magic, and love. They were family, and the bond was deep. It had existed for lifetimes.

But I love her, too! Caroline got angrier. I love my sister. Have I no rights at all?

She wanted to show the woman all the pain of life without Serenity. Caroline wanted the woman to understand her hurt. To answer her questions. How could this happen? She did not even speak the language of Flight's people, and she doubted Flight's foster mother would have anything to do with her.

It was a rainy day in the forest, so Caroline stayed inside the strange cabin, staring out the window at the unfamiliar trees and paths. The leaves and grass were wet with raindrops, and Caroline cried softly. She cried for all the years she had longed for Flight and Flight had not been there. Caroline sighed. She could not eat. She was lonely for the Temple, for Gawen, but she knew that these things would only give her a way to block her pain right now, because she would hide in all the noise and joy. She did not even have the energy to move around much. Just stared out at the rain. Despite the warmth of Summer, the cabin grew damp and could have used a small fire, but she did not start one.

She heard thunder in the distance. Through the trees she saw a flash of lightning. It was odd; when the lightning flashed, the amulet around her neck blazed, and the lightning brand Blue had given her grew warm. Caroline put one hand on the amulet.

"Little Bird."

Caroline grew totally still, then turned slowly. In her cabin was the woman who had taken Flight. Caroline just stared at the woman. She was beautiful, primitive. Taller than Caroline and her family, the woman's body radiated strength, the strength of one who had lived long with the planet and survived. She surveyed Caroline with no expression. Caroline took in her decorations of feathers, stones, beads, the offerings of the earth. Without knowing how, Caroline knew instinctively that this woman was much respected of her people and very wise. All of Caroline's rage and hurt rose up, but she tried to press it back down. This woman was not evil; she was profoundly loving, and she knew much that Caroline did not understand.

"No. Do not hold it back. You have held it back too long." The voice was deep and rich in Caroline's mind. The woman held out a stone. "Your anger is like fire. See it as a red, burning flame—and send the flame here, directly into this stone. Then we will decide what to do with it."

Caroline concentrated. She rolled up her fury as she stared at the calm face that had stolen her sister. She rolled it up into a red, glowing ball, and she could *see* it. With all her might she hurled it at the stone. The stone grew red, as if on fire, then brown again. Drained, Caroline sank down into the chair by the window where she had been sitting. She felt...empty.

"When there is an empty place, the Universe always fills it," the woman said in her mind.

Weakly, Caroline nodded.

The woman stepped closer. "Hello, Little Bird. My name in your language means Many Stars."

Caroline did not want her to have a name. She did not want her to be a real woman. A woman with feelings, just like her own. As long as she was just "someone" or "one of them," Caroline did not have to forgive her. Or understand her. She sighed softly. Already she was seeing much about the woman...about the things the woman herself had suffered. Caroline had suffered...but so had Many Stars.

"It is a beautiful name," she whispered.

Many Stars handed her the stone. "This is yours."

Caroline held it in her hands.

Many Stars said, "It is time to begin healing."

"What must I do?" Caroline realized that when they spoke mind to mind, there was no language barrier...or heart barrier.

"You must find a way to learn from Flight, to learn what she is meant to teach you. You cannot heal when you do not have what you need."

"What else?"

"You must let go of the dream...the dream of being with Serenity. In the past. Or the future. It will not happen. It was not meant to."

Caroline sighed again. "And who decides what is or is not meant? You? That is convenient."

Many Stars just stared at her with no expression and calmly said in her mind, "No. It is not I, or you. It is Flight who decides. Her spirit chose to come with us. Her spirit knew what would happen if she followed that bird as a child. She followed it. To me."

Caroline's eyes filled. "She chose you."

"And she chose rightly! You have seen her! You know she was meant to be with us."

Caroline hung her head.

"Your hurt is not cause for shame. My people honor pain. Pain is a great teacher. We honor your pain."

Caroline looked at the deep, dark eyes.

Many Stars continued. "It was written in the Book of Life. One twin would go deep into the past. One would carry the past into the future. You two are twins. That is sacred to my people. It means you have two sides of the same destiny. Flight needs you as much as you need her. Without your paintings, her message would stay hidden in the forest. The world would never know it. But you, you can present it to them in a way they understand. You do not understand, Caroline. My people did not choose only Flight. We chose you, too. We chose you to be our messenger to the world. You were the right one."

It was stated with such quiet simplicity. Caroline just stared at her. "Part of my pain was jealousy," she whispered.

"We know. And Flight was jealous, too...of the years you had with your family. To gain something, you let go of other paths. That is the way."

Caroline nodded. "How can I help myself heal?" she asked.

Many Stars smiled a little. "Healing will take a long time. But there is a way to talk to Flight."

"How?"

"Gawen. Gawen is a strong mind-reader. He can help you. He can tell you what Flight has to say to you."

Caroline blinked. "Oh," she said.

Many Stars laughed in her mind, though her face did not change expression. "What is a mate for, then, but to offer their strength to the other?"

Caroline smiled. "Do you have a mate?"

"No," came the quiet answer.

Caroline felt she should ask no more at this time. So she said, "Anything else, Many Stars?"

"You are twin of my spirit daughter. That makes you my daughter, too. We are family as well, Little Bird. I shall come to you this way, to help you heal. To help you understand that you, too, are one of us."

Caroline smiled, her whole heart in the smile. "*Yes.*"

"Your healing has begun, Little Bird. The heart of Many Stars is glad."

"I thank you, Many Stars."

"I will return," the woman said, and was gone.

And so it was that a day of gray sorrow and tears became filled with hope and wonder. Caroline's spirit was transformed by the possibility that perhaps her aching soul could be healed after all. She spent the day absorbing the visit from Many Stars and adjusting to the new lightness in her spirit.

That night she drew a sketch. It was of Many Stars, one hand on Flight's shoulder, one on Caroline's. She left it on the table. The next morning it was gone.

***

By the third day Caroline had become lonesome and sought company. As always, she wanted to talk! So she held the crystal in her hand, and said, "David, Priest of Black and Keeper of Her Sanctuary, I am lonely. When you are able, please visit me for a few hours." She sent the thought into the crystal, which glowed, then was still.

Early that afternoon David came, bearing a letter and a small gift. "Someone misses you," he smiled as she lit up with excitement. There was also a card drawn by Katerina and signed by all her friends with well-wishes. She put them away to look at later, after David was gone.

There was a spot beside a beautiful flowering tree, and she and the priest sat a long while. She found herself telling him her story...of the different tasks the colors had given to her, especially, and how she was faring. She also spoke about her vision of a secluded cabin none could find unless they were destined to...and of course, how very much she loved Gawen.

The people of Lady Black are very good, quiet, intense listeners who appear to be listening with their whole body. It was so easy to talk to David that she quite simply poured her heart out...all her hopes and fears and struggles. Black tends to cleanse you like a waterfall or rain shower as well. Caroline felt refreshed and reborn after their quiet hours. And she understood something about Black. Black is always there for you, constant and loyal and dependable. She had known this, but now she understood it much more deeply.

When they were done, she realized she had gotten much advice from David, without his saying a word. This, too, was part of her healing, for she had been almost six moons in the Temple, working with six colors, and she needed to take stock of how far she had come and how far she was still to go. She needed time to review her journey.

It had frightened her deeply to realize that Pink would take back her feather. It had seemed, in the three extra moons Pink had given her to work on her healing, that everything else came first. She had too much other work to do and healing took a back spot in her mind. Yet her need for healing, she could tell as she reflected on it, had adversely affected her work with Silver, Blue, Green, and Red. Pink had told her the lessons were meant to be building blocks. This was very true. She had found out the hard way.

Before he left, David gave her a present—nine beautiful black candles his wife had made. "Use them for a ritual to connect yourself to Lady Black," he said. "She is the first, the forerunner who holds all the other colors. When you lose her, all others tumble like children's building blocks, and you will have to set things aright with her before starting over."

Caroline nodded solemnly, surveying his calm, dark eyes. It was odd; she knew she was unlikely to see David again unless she returned to the Sanctuary. Yet somehow she felt he would always be with her. He winked, reading her thoughts on her face, made a sign of blessing, and took his leave.

Caroline sat for awhile, meditating by the pretty tree. A part of her wished this Summer would never end. She was filled with nostalgia, even in the midst of her novitiate. She knew that this time of adventure and innocence would never come again, and she tried hard to engrave it in her heart to keep forever.

Black's voice came in her mind. "Child, I am also the keeper of memory. All that has been, I hold to my heart, safe. It is never lost. Black is full of treasures, brilliant jewels of the moments you have lived. When you need to take them out, seek me and I will give them to you."

Caroline smiled to herself, and took out her sketchpad and began to draw a picture of Black, in whose belly and center she drew scenes of her own past. She titled it, "Keeper of the Memory".

"Very nice."

Caroline jumped, startled. There was Pink beside her, smiling at the picture. Caroline threw her arms around her. "My Lady!"

Pink hugged her tightly and sat beside her. They talked awhile, and finally Pink asked, "Tell me of the new ways you have discovered to heal your three greatest wounds."

Caroline said, "I must paint the visions I get of Serenity, to learn of the ancient ways of her people. I must work with Gawen, for he will telepathically reach her messages to me. I must get to know Many Stars, Flight's foster mother, to understand why it all happened. I must begin to understand what role I take with these people, how I too am one of them. I must release the false dreams of being with my sister in this life. And someday—just once—I need to hold her in my arms." Caroline wept softly on Pink's shoulder for awhile.

"What shall you do with the stone?" Pink asked.

Caroline said, "I am not sure yet. I do not want to let it go yet. I want to hold it. Is that wrong?"

Pink kissed her forehead on the heart brand she'd given her. "No. You are mistress of your pain. You will decide when you are ready to release it. No one else can. And you will decide the way. You will know what to do with the stone, my daughter."

Pink gently stroked her damp cheeks, and they sat and held each other awhile, wrapped in a rich pink glow Caroline felt but did not see. The flowering tree occasionally dropped blossoms onto Caroline's hair or dress or sketchpad. Pink gathered them, and with a little string made a small bracelet which Caroline wore around her wrist. They sat thus until the sun began to set. Already Caroline could feel tiny traces of Autumn in the air, see them on the trees and grasses. Perhaps it began to show sooner in the thicker forests of the grounds, which were cooler.

Then Pink looked at her deep in the eyes. She did not speak, but Caroline understood that Pink was pleased with her work. And though Caroline had what seemed like a lifetime of healing before her, Caroline knew her task with Pink was completed. For now, at least, she knew *how* to heal. She knew what to do. Pink would not be taking her feather back. It now belonged to Caroline fully in truth. Caroline understood this without being told.

When Pink left, she spent awhile just holding her pink feather and promising Pink solemnly that she would never forget, never neglect, never stop her healing, *ever*. Caroline meant this vow very, very deeply.

The gift Gawen had sent her was a small box with four compartments to it. He had made the box and said in his note to her, "For memories of your Sanctuary."

Caroline put the stone Many Stars had helped her pour her pain into inside the box. She decided to keep it in there until she knew more clearly what she wished to do with it. And she dried and pressed the blossoms from the flowering tree beneath which she had sat, and healed, with David and Pink.

***

The rest of the moon passed by very slowly...but uneventfully...at least on the surface! Much was changing within Caroline internally, and she had grown to love her little Sanctuary cabin very much. She ate the provisions left to her, but most often she ate directly from the forest trees, bushes and herbs. She saw many wild animals big and small. She went for long walks, and spent hours upon hours in quiet meditation.

She loved the nights in her little cabin, listening to the woods' sounds and the fire. She did a lot of thinking. She realized that once she completed her work with Red and Green, she would be half-way through her novitiate. This was amazing to her, and she spent much time reflecting on all that had befallen her in these six moons, and what lay ahead in the next six. Once or twice more she met with David to talk.

On the last day of the week she returned to the Temple, but the next week she only went back at night to meet Gawen on the Hill of Silver, as they had begun to call it. She had needed the quiet of the Sanctuary more than she'd realized and was fast becoming addicted to it. Upon her return to her cabin she would find it cleaned and stocked with fresh food, bedsheets and towels, and firewood. She asked for an extra week there. It was granted her.

By now she had accepted a sad fact. She had concentrated so much on healing and Pink that she had not even really dealt with Green. She knew that she would not get the two new feathers from Red and Green this moon. This saddened her, but she was at peace. Better to hold onto the Pink feather and not lose it, to finish what she had begun. She had needed the break badly, had needed to heal and renew herself. She promised herself earnestly that she would work hard with Red and Green next moon. She thought of how their lessons were connected but did not yet understand it. She thought of her three greatest pleasures, but got nowhere. So she let it go and accepted.

In her last week at the cabin, she did feel the presence of Flight. She was out walking when she saw a raven and remembered Flight telling her the bird was her messenger. But she did not sense more than that Flight was watching her closely.

Once she came upon Green. Green was sitting on a big rock, feeding a lamb from a bottle. Caroline played with her and the lamb awhile. Then Green took out her harp and began to play. Caroline ran back to the cabin and got her flute. She and Green played together a long while, and many faeries and elves watched. Caroline knew that she did not really know Green yet. But she would, she promised herself. She would. One thing she knew—Green celebrated abundance. There was a quiet acceptance between them. Both knew she would get no feather; both understood without saying a word. The last night of the old moon saw her alone in the Sanctuary cabin. No one came to her. She had expected no one. She prayed and meditated for a long while.

There were only two days left to her in the cabin, and she was thanking the Twelve and the Temple for her sacred time there. She lit the candles the Black Priest David had given her. She had them in a circle, with her stone from Many Stars, her box from Gawen, her flowers from Pink, arranged in the circle. Also a raven feather from the bird Flight had sent her. And many sketches she had drawn of the Sanctuary, which she wanted blessed by the candles' lights.

She watched the candles glow in the dark and smiled to herself. Black did not come to her with spectacular visions and wondrous miracles and theatrics. Nothing really happened externally. But Black came, nonetheless, when Caroline called her. She came as she often does, in the quiet places of our hearts, which we have to be very silent and still to hear. She brought forth from Caroline a new womanliness—a soft, yet strong, maturity. Caroline was growing into her womanhood. And Lady Black was gently leading her through the sometimes painful, scary darkness of growing up.

In the darkness, alone and at peace, Caroline, within herself, reached a major turning point she did not really understand. She just let it be.

Chapter Seven

It was the night of the New Moon, and stormy, windy, chilly, and rainy. Caroline sat near the comfortable and comforting fire, listening to the rain patter on the roof and walls. She gazed quietly around the now familiar room, saying goodbye to it.

She had spent the day preparing for her return to the Temple. She had walked around all the familiar spots by the cabin, saying goodbye to the trees and plants and animals she had grown to love there. In her memory box from Gawen, she had placed the remains of one of the black candles David had given her.

She felt ready to go back. She had a lot of work ahead of her and was eager to get on with it. She also missed her friends and the Temple life, for she was a very social person. She was rested, energized, peaceful, centered. She had grown up a great deal.

But the leaving was bittersweet. She had grown deeply attached to the cabin, and she already missed it. It was a strange place she was in emotionally...a place between yesterday and today, between endings and beginnings, between the worlds. The ritual she had done for Black lay heavy on her spirit. Black is a heavy, intense color to carry, and the effects of her ritual were still to be seen. Sometimes, with Black, things took a long time.

Caroline was meditating quietly on all that had happened to her in the Sanctuary. It was a good night to stay cozy and in one's rooms, a good night for listening to the rain and thinking. This moon, Autumn would come.

Lost in her thoughts, at first she did not hear the knock. But it came louder, more insistent, and finally she got up, startled. Who could it be? None were permitted to visit those in Sanctuary retreat cabins without prior permission. Was it David? Was anything wrong?

She opened the door. A man, not overly tall or heavily built, but not short and thin either, stood there, drenched. Caroline gasped and hurried him in out of the storm.

"Here, sit by the fire. We will talk when you are warmed." The man gave her a grateful smile and sat in a chair by the welcoming flames, warming his hands by them.

Caroline bustled around with Energy, getting a warm blanket and towels and hot tea for the stranger. He dried himself as best he could with the towels, and wrapped the blanket around himself. For awhile they sat, until he ceased shivering and was only damp, not soaked by rain.

Caroline watched him, full of questions, bubbling with curiosity. Who was he? He had long, orange-red hair in wet curls, a face full of freckles and mischief. His eyes were dark green and friendly.

He sighed, long and deep. "Thank you, mistress. I hope I have not troubled you."

"No, *no!* But where are you bound? None are allowed on the Sanctuary—"

"I know. I have had a cabin here for a few moons. It amazes me that I was so stupid, but I took a wrong turn and became lost in the forest."

Caroline patted his arm sympathetically. "These grounds are consecrated to Black, and the woods are deep, dark, and mysterious. There are many hidden trails. It is easy to get lost, especially in a storm, if you venture too far from your cabin."

The man gave her a wry smile. "So I see." He intently looked around her room. "Oh!" He saw several of her sketches and jumped up, going to see them without even asking her permission. He wandered around the little room, looking at the sketches she had lain out everywhere.

Wrapped in his blanket, lit by firelight, features that had at first appeared ordinary now appeared striking, fascinating, handsome.

Caroline watched his intense features as he studied her work. He focused completely on it. She sensed that he was utterly absorbed in her work, and the rest of the room had fallen away for him. That sort of attention and focus is what an artist craved. She found herself waiting with her breath held for his opinion, as if she really respected him, in her spirit. Perhaps she had met him in a past time and place, long forgotten. She wanted him to be pleased with her work very, very much.

He turned to her, his face lit up with deep inner lights. Caroline gasped. She had thought his features ordinary, common? There was nothing ordinary or common about this man, and he did not *need* the traditional ideal of handsomeness. He was, somehow, *more* than that ideal.

Now that he looked at her with that expression, she was *sure* she knew him and eyed him intensely. His expression suddenly calmed, as if he were making a strong effort to bank his inner fires. "I'm sorry. You are looking at me with such wide eyes. I didn't mean for my exuberance to startle you. It's just...these are excellent. Really, truly excellent."

Caroline beamed. It may have been dark and stormy out, but her heart was bright and joyful and sunny. It pleased her. Oh, it *pleased* her that he liked it!

"You are Little Bird."

She nodded, surprised. "You know of me?"

The man laughed, and it seemed as if the whole cabin was overflowing with the sound. "I am not of the Temple. I am one of those who sought Sanctuary here for awhile and was granted it by the Temple elders. I have heard *much* of your work. News of the newest Artist is *everywhere.*"

Caroline flushed. "Yes, thank you, my friend." But her happiness had been dimmed.

The man looked at her in concern. "This does not please you?" He sat beside her, peering intently in her eyes, and Caroline got the feeling that if he desired to know something, *nothing* would stand in his way.

She smiled faintly at him. "Last moon I was working with Red. She

138

asked me to find out how I was meant to serve her in this life. I found out that I was to create healing visionary paintings; they would greatly influence people. I am meant to become... famous."

The man grinned. "Obviously." His grin softened. "You are not pleased?"

"I am a little afraid."

All of a sudden Caroline realized that she was having a very intimate conversation with a man whose name she did not even know! "Who are you?" she asked. "You know me, but I know nothing of you."

He smiled at her. "You are trying to avoid my questions. I'll answer yours, but you must answer mine first. Afraid of what? Your talent is extraordinary, and you will help so many people."

"I am not sure. Perhaps I am afraid of them believing I am more than I am."

The man shook his head as if to say, "What matter about that?" He said, "Let them. You know who you are, do you not? Don't let the *others* frighten you, Little Bird! No matter how famous you become, in the end it is you and your talent alone who must deal with each other. Your talent is the only thing you need to answer to...the only thing you *will* answer to, in the end."

Caroline smiled. His orange-red curls appeared to hold many colors in them, the way the flames lit them. "You are, perhaps, famous yourself, that you understand so much about it," she teased gently. Yet a part of her was serious. He *did* seem to understand.

He grinned again, that quick, boyish grin that stole her breath. "We have all waited a long while for an Artist of your quality to walk through the Temple," he said, blatantly ignoring her question.

Caroline laughed. "Yes, all right. Your questions first. Sir, I have many feelings about what is ahead for me...many reasons I am afraid. They would take a long time to explain. I do not have this time. I am leaving here tomorrow to return to the Temple." Somehow she found it difficult to let her new friend go. She sighed as she absently played with the fire, which was dwindling.

"It is not easy to leave the world behind, is it?" he asked.

"Am I that obvious? I know I am. Yes, it is difficult sometimes. But there is nowhere else I would rather be."

"You are happy, then?"

"As a matter of fact, this is what I am to work on this moon. Green has asked me to find—and delve into—my three greatest pleasures."

"Ahhhh. Any ideas?"

"Painting. But that's hard to explain. Gawen, and that is even harder."

"Gawen?" He was smiling.

"My mate," she said softly, staring into the flames, blushing a little.

"My shirt is damp. Would you be offended if I took it off to warm it by the fire?"

"Of course not. Whatever possessed you to wander out on this stormy night?"

He smiled at her as he removed his shirt and laid it near the flames to dry. "Perhaps I was destined to meet you, Little Bird," he said.

She smiled at him and nodded. "Perhaps, in truth. I feel like I know you."

He smiled back. "I feel the same."

"Why is that?" she asked. She was staring at the shirt. It was sewn together of patches, as if the man were quite poor. Most of the colors were oranges, browns, and reds, but some patches looked strangely out of place—a yellow flowered print here, a bright purple checkered pattern there. It was truly the shirt of a gypsy.

"I could tell you a story of each of these patches," he said softly. "Each shows you a piece of my travels—of me."

Caroline fingered the shirt. "It is much drier."

The man only smiled. "You know," he said, "not everyone would be so welcoming. I know that the Temple is a place of hospitality and welcome, but I have interrupted your Sanctuary time."

"No. As I said, my time is over. I return to the Temple tomorrow."

"Is it not the New Moon?"

"Yes."

"You are a novice. Which color did you meet this New Moon?"

"None."

"I do not understand."

"Sir, I was unable to complete my tasks for Red and Green. They did not give me a token to signify my finished work, because I did not finish."

"And you can meet no Color?"

"No, not until I finish their tasks."

"The Temple requirements are harsh!"

"Not so. The tasks are building blocks. You need to have one completely understood within your heart before you can begin the next."

"There is no overlap?"

"No."

"But do not some colors blend well together? Do not they make a nice balance? Perhaps two lessons could work in harmony."

"So it was with Red and Green. They came together and gave me two moons to complete their tasks."

"You see?"

"Yes, but that did not involve the end of a task being left uncompleted!"

"I see. And you are neither angry nor disappointed." He sounded disbelieving.

She smiled a little sadly. "Of course I am. But they are *right*." She said it with utter sincerity. There was no doubt at all that she meant it.

"You are very special," he said.

Caroline smiled. "No. Just in love with the Colors. I want to do this *right*."

He nodded, staring at her. "I can see that."

Caroline tidied up the teacups. "You made me talk a long while, and you said nothing about yourself," she complained.

He laughed. "You are a very special person. And a very curious one." He walked over to her. "I like you," he said bluntly. "I need a friend. I need one very much. I have sought Sanctuary here because I needed a friend, and I thought I might find one. I was right. She is you. The friend I was needing is you. Listen. I will be here in my cabin another two moons. I have been granted Sanctuary here until then. I want to have you visit. A few times per week if you can manage it. I will talk to you. I will tell you my stories, all of them if you want to hear it." He knelt in front of her. "Caroline, will you do this for me?" He took her hands in his, staring at her, begging her with his eyes.

She took one look in his dark green eyes and said, "Of *course*. Yes. But you must tell me your name."

He still stared at her as if convinced that she would disappear or change her mind. "My name," he said quietly and slowly, "is Jonathan."

"Well, Jonathan. You cannot go out into this storm. As it is, you will be lucky not to catch a bad cold. You will sleep here by the fire." He made no protest, just kissed her hand in thanks.

She settled him, warm and snug, in blankets by the fire, and he fell asleep quickly. He was obviously exhausted. She looked at him awhile, wondering what had caused him such sorrow as to seek sanctuary here. Everyone knew that outsiders were only granted Temple sanctuary for very, very special reasons. Something horrible must have happened in his life.

She worried over him as she went into her bedroom. As she lay in the dark, preparing to sleep this last night in her cabin, all she could see was the strange beggar's shirt he wore. Had he no means of getting clothing and food? He was strong and healthy, strong enough to carve his way through life if need be. Or...he had said the shirt held memories. Was he a gypsy by choice; did he wear his multicolored patched shirt because he *liked* it?

***

When she awoke, he had already gone. There was a note. "Little Bird, Thank you for sheltering me from the storm outside and the storm inside. I cannot wait to see you again, come soon. May your last day in the cabin be blessed, Jonathan."

Caroline's day was a happy whirl. She packed up her things, making sure the cabin was as tidy as she had found it when she first came. She said a few final good-byes, shed a few tears.

Around noon, after a busy morning, David came and took her to his cabin. He had two black books. Pointing to one, he said, "This is private—only Lady Black and I see it. This other is for people to read if they wish to read the reflections of others who have come to Sanctuary. Do you wish to write in either?"

Eagerly, she nodded.

In the private book, she wrote a one-page letter to Black, thanking her for her healing and love. In the other book she wrote a blessing to all those who had come before her to Sanctuary, and all who would came after. They talked awhile, as David asked questions of Caroline to be certain she was ready to leave. When he was satisfied with her answers, he hugged her and wished her well.

When Caroline saw Elizabeth Anne—and Gawen!—approaching, she ran to them joyfully, flinging herself at Gawen so that she almost knocked him over. Arm in arm, the three walked back to the main Temple grounds. Caroline chattered all the way! She asked question after question about all her friends.

When she saw the little gathering of picnickers, at first she did not understand. When it became clear, she cried again. All her friends were there, and they were giving her a little party to welcome her back. There were balloons and a cake, and everyone was hugging her as she cried happy tears.

That afternoon there was celebration and joy, dance and music, for the novice had done well on her retreat. But at night, as she sat quietly with Gawen, she told him of the lonely beggar gypsy in the patched shirt who had come to her cabin and of how worried she was that all was not well with her new friend. She promised herself to visit him soon.

***

Jonathan's cabin was similar to Caroline's in style, though his was near a small apple orchard. The other difference, which she noticed right away, was that there were none of the tiny personal things that had filled her cabin. If he had family and friends, he never spoke of them and had brought no reminders of them to his retreat. He also had almost no clothes. He did have a warm jacket, worn but sturdy, but he had only a few shirts and pants; nothing more. Caroline decided to ask the seamstresses of the Temple to make him a few things.

One thing he was not was morose or self-pitying. He made her laugh and laugh and laugh. They played tag and raced each other around. They told jokes till they fell to the ground laughing. They tried to top each other with ridiculous, crazy stories, each sillier than the last. Caroline took to wearing silly outfits to make him smile. She'd wear silly hats or mismatched colors.

Gawen, who was improving daily as a magician, had taught her some tricks. She tried them out on Jonathan, who loved them all and told her she was wonderful. He had been all over the planet, it seemed, and he had many tales. She was never sure which were true and which were not, but it didn't matter.

They loved to make piles of Autumn leaves and jump in them. They loved to startle each other and make each other jump. Every time they visited, he had gifts from her—a red apple, a shiny stone, a bouquet of flowers, a handful of acorns, a pinecone, a feather.

When they were serious, it was to speak about Caroline. He was more full of questions than even she was. He wanted to know every-thing—all about her past, her childhood, her experiences with the colors thus far. She talked the way she loved to talk— for hours, in depth, and honestly. He was adept at turning all conversation away from personal questions about himself. He would only say, "What I need from you, Little Bird, is just to laugh and play. I need that more than any talk or words." So she accepted. He would be there another moon, anyway. Perhaps then he would tell her what was troubling him, and why he had sought Sanctuary.

The two grew closer and closer, and as the moon swelled, so did their trust and friendship, until it was a very bright, full, glowing source of power and light.

When she was not visiting Jonathan, she was working hard. Autumn neared, and there was much work to do at the Temple. Outdoor altars and benches were protected for Winter, the harvest was keeping all the gardeners busy, and the Temple was bustling. Caroline worked as well with the artists of the Temple, who were quick to notice her improve-ment after working with Blue and her retreat. Katerina pursed her lips and said only, "Hmmm," but Caroline knew her well enough to know she was impressed and proud. Her mural for the novices and the tapestry design were progressing.

She was happy. And right from the beginning of the moon to the end, she made herself focus on Green and Red and the tasks they had given her. She meditated on them daily. She wore green and red clothes, she decorated her room in green and red, and she sought out priestesses of these colors to talk to.

She tried to absorb the destiny Red had in mind for her. Red was there often. They walked and talked and spent time together, often doing nothing in particular. She told Red all about her fear and excitement as she looked ahead at her destiny. Red helped her to be courageous and confident; she helped Caroline to believe in herself and her talents. Slowly Caroline came to a greater peace about it. Red always made her too excited about the creativity, the art, to be afraid for long. The excitement and joy always took over.

She found Red to be a color of courage …inspiration…strength… motivation… energy. This she had known from past lives, but now re-remembered it. She found herself playing harder and working harder than ever before, for the Red fire was burning in her brightly. It was not a color of stillness, but of action and abundant external *life*. Between her talks with Gawen, Jonathan, Elizabeth Anne, her friends and Red herself, she was feeling as if the Red half of her assignment was under control.

The Green half was harder, somehow. She knew that one of her three greatest pleasures was painting and art, but she could not seem to understand *why* in a deep enough way to please Green. And though Gawen was her greatest pleasure also, somehow that didn't feel to be complete, either. And she had no idea what the third of her greatest pleasures even was!

By the time the moon was full, Caroline was whining to everyone who would listen about her failure and bemoaning herself as a stupid idiot. If a person does not even know what makes them *happy*, well, then, there must be something *wrong* with them. Wrong with *her*. Gawen and Jonathan and Elizabeth Anne all listened semi-patiently. Green, who came to visit often at Caroline's frantic pleas, only kept saying, "You are on the right path. Just travel deeper."

It was not until the second half of the moon, while it was waning, that she began to feel as if she might receive the green feather after all.

***

"I don't know what she wants!" Caroline was screaming at Jonathan, in near hysterics. "What does she *want*? How can I explain what happens to me when I paint? How can I explain how much I love Gawen? These things are beyond words. It's hopeless. I've failed."

Jonathan frowned over the chair he was fixing in his cabin. "Hmm," he said distractedly. "Seems to me like you've got the answer, and you don't even know it."

Caroline paced in agitation. "What? *What*? What, then?"

Jonathan banged in a nail. "It's beyond words, right?"

Caroline nodded, in tears.

"Don't use words," Jonathan said.

"Green told me that was not good enough...that I had to be able to explain in detail..."

"Caroline."

"What?. *What?*"

"Try not using words."

"But—"

"Shh." He stood up and came over to her, put his hands on her shoulders, and stared into her eyes. "Your paintings talk, Caroline. Maybe you need to go back to what you do best. Paint it. Maybe that will *give* you the words."

Caroline stared at him, then flew out of his cabin.

***

She worked as she had worked for Black...ceaselessly, night and day, in solitude, not eating or sleeping, driven, obsessed. She painted one of the works that would become known as one of her greatest masterpieces. She painted an image of herself. She *was* painting, in the painting. In her face was an expression of such ecstasy that Caroline was never able to express how she got it down on canvas. She simply *felt* it, so she *was* it, so she painted it.

The tiny, miniature painting she did, the one she was doing in the large painting, was of herself and Gawen kissing. You could see the love in the expression of the painter, you could see the love in the kiss. Then she painted, even larger, a beautiful hand, holding a huge paintbrush over the figure of the painter and her painting. From this brush came the twelve colors of the Twelve, shining down onto the little painter. To finish this painting, she made the kissing man and woman joined by a heart which also had all the colors of the Twelve. It shimmered between them as they kissed.

She titled it "Three Pleasures" and showed it to no one for a day after it was done. She meditated on it. And she understood herself. Her pleasure was to be open to the flow of the colors through her, because this gave her life. Her pleasure was to take those colors and pour them out of her again as a unique expression of herself. *That* gave her identity. Her pleasure was to make that unique expression one of love and joy and intimacy. *That* gave her purpose.

And Caroline understood, as she never had before, that the colors whirl into us, through us, and back out of us again, in an endless circle of life, and this is pleasure...to be open to receive and to release them. Pain comes when you are not open to one of these...the receiving or re-leasing of color.

Exhausted, having the words at last, she slept.

***

The last day of the moon came. Caroline was ready. She bathed in scented water. She put on her best dress and jewelry. She laid out the four feathers she had, and put candles of that color beside them. She decorated her room with red and green. She tied red and green ribbons in her hair. She made little gifts of tiny cakes for Red and Green, in their colors. She put a red ribbon around a green cloth to hide the painting. She was ready.

They came to her room, hand in hand. Green was all covered in vines, except for her face. Red was in a dancing skirt of many shades of red, with fiery sequins that caught the light, and red dancing shoes, and red roses in her hair. She had red jewels around her neck and wrists.

Caroline bowed to them. "My Ladies," she said. In her heart was peace. She knew she had done her best, and that was all she could do.

"Little Bird," said Red.

"Let us see," said Green.

"This is the first painting I have done with the magical brush your faeries gave me, my Lady," said Caroline.

Green watched as Red undid the red ribbon. Black had been quiet when she first saw the self-portrait Caroline had done. Green was not. Green threw back her long red hair and began to yell, a loud, primitive, animal scream of triumph and joy. It seemed to go on forever. Caroline was trembling and weeping before it was through.

Wordlessly, Green and Red knelt before Caroline. "Remember, you serve the colors. We serve you, too," said Red. "How does this pleasure connect to your destiny as my servant, Novice of Red?"

"I cannot achieve my highest destiny if I am not open to my highest pleasure."

They both smiled at her. Red kissed her, leaving a bright red lip print on her cheek. Red also painted her with some red designs on her forehead and cheeks and arms.

Green asked to hold the brush. As she did, she blessed it, and gently traced Caroline's face with the brush tip.

Caroline promised them solemnly that she would continue to study the magic of Red and Green, to grow in understanding of it her whole life long. It had become clear to her that one moon only scratched the surface of a color, that even a lifetime only scratched the surface of a color. One could always, always go deeper into it...eternally.

Red and Green told her to hold out her hands. She did, and in each they placed a feather: one of bright red, one of brilliant green.

As the self-portrait was hung in a chapel of Black, the "Three Pleasures" was hung in a chapel of Green. All year, even in Winter, the priestesses unto this day keep it surrounded by green vines. It is said, by the priestesses of today, that if you sit before this painting, within twenty-four hours your greatest pleasure will speak to you, give you a message in some way. Some laugh at this superstition.

Perhaps they need to sit before the painting before they make a judgement. Or perhaps the pleasure spoke...and they did not hear. In the end, one must decide for one's self, and the painting will have the power over you that you allow it to have. No more. No less.

It has also been said that one need not see the painting to receive this message. It has been said that the very first time you hear of the painting—even if you are nowhere near it—on that day your pleasure will speak to you. But that, too, really depends on whether or not you are open...whether you believe...whether you listen.

Chapter Eight

The New Moon came. It was getting colder. The trees were all turning. Energy did not enjoy going out as much; she liked the warmth of Caroline's room and often preferred to stay there. Caroline was very busy preparing for the walk up the Hill of Novices. She was excited to be meeting with her next color.

It had been two weeks almost since she had seen Jonathan. She had been so busy with her painting. It was he who had inspired her to try to paint her pleasure. She wanted to thank him...and to show him her new feathers. So, she put together a picnic lunch of fruit and sandwiches and tucked it in a basket with some late Autumn flowers. With a happy heart, she half ran, half skipped, to his cabin. As usual, he was playing outdoors. She found him sitting up in a tree when he shook the branches and made piles of leaves fall on her head as she walked past. He scampered down like a monkey while she shook the leaves off herself, chattering at him.

"I did it! I painted my three greatest pleasures, and it was wonderful. It was one of the best I ever did, and Green was happy. She couldn't stop smiling, and she gave me a feather, and I brought it to show you, and I hope you haven't had lunch yet because I brought a picnic! I am getting all ready for tonight, the walk up the Hill of Novices to meet my new color, and...."

"Little Bird."

"Hmm?" She stopped dancing around him in circles to look up at him, her head tilted, her cheeks flushed, her big eyes sparkling. She couldn't contain her joy for more than a few minutes, though, and impulsively kissed him. "How can I thank you? What can I do to repay you? I should have thought of this myself. I'll always remember you when I see the painting. You're wonderful, you...."

"Paint my portrait."

Caroline stopped, staring at him intently. "But, I don't understand. You have always told me you didn't want a drawing of you. I have pestered you and pestered you, and you always said 'no.' "

He tweaked her nose. "I changed my mind," was all he said.

"But, why?"

He smiled at her and kissed the nose he had tweaked. "No more questions, Little Chattering Bird, or I won't give you my surprise."

Caroline's eyes grew big. Jonathan's surprises were always fabulous and worth just about anything she had to do to win them. "All right. Okay. You know how much I wanted to paint you."

"I know," he said gently.

"Shall we eat first?"

He laughed. "I'm starving."

She watched as he sat beside her, savoring his food. "I have never seen anyone to take such pleasure in things—in sleeping or eating or breathing," she said to him. "You make me stop and think for a minute about how beautiful life is. You always do that."

He smiled at her, eyes closed in appreciation of the fine bread he was eating. "Mmmmm."

Caroline laughed. "I shall paint you just like this, eating *both* our lunches," she said, laughing harder. She began to sketch him with the pad and pencils she never went *anywhere* without. But things got very strange. She could not draw the man sitting beside her. She tried. But his hair she drew longer, even though she could clearly see its correct length. His face was the same boyish, freckled, laughing one, but it was different, somehow. Confused, Caroline looked at him.

151

"What's wrong?" he asked, eating a strawberry cookie.

"Nothing. Nothing." She shook her head and returned to work. But things only got worse. She found herself painting more shades of orange and red in his curls than he really had. She became frightened.

"Just paint," came the quiet voice.

So she did. And beneath her colored pencils emerged a glowing man...in a long orange cape which she had never seen before. Suddenly she found herself sketching Red. Her Red. And Red was putting her body against this man as if he belonged to her, staring out of the drawing with love-filled eyes. It was when she drew the matching tigers, orange, red, and black-striped, beside them, as if they *were* the tigers, that she accepted the truth.

She buried her face in her hands, unable to look at him. "I am a fool," she murmured. "A stupid fool." She felt a hand stroking her hair, but she could not look up.

"No," said a voice that was her Jonathan's, yet somehow *more*. "No. You always knew. You just hid the truth in your heart for awhile."

"Why? *Why?*"

"You had a lot to deal with all at once, Caroline. It is better this way. You needed time."

"I feel so ashamed. I talked to you as if...."

"As if I were a 'normal' man? I wanted you to. I did not want any secrets between us. I didn't want you to hide behind the old image of a color and his Priestess. It can separate us. I wanted you to know *me*."

"But you were not *you*. You were Jonathan. I acted like a child with you. I poured ice down your shirt. I hid your shoes," she moaned. "I talked about the most ridiculous...."

"And I loved every minute. My Little Bird, I am who I always was. I am the Trickster, the Jokester, the Changing One. I am never the same twice. I often come in hidden ways, surprising ways. I do this so that people have no time to put on false faces. Like Red, I am a clown. I understand what a mask can hide."

Caroline sighed into her hands. "You deserve *respect*. You are of the Twelve."

"Take your 'respect' and throw it in the nearest garbage heap. I don't want respect; I want love. Respect is already *within* love. Did you not think you were respecting me when...."

"I gave you charity. Shirts the Temple seamstresses made."

"We all survive on the love of each other. I am no exception. Look at me."

"I'm afraid. You'll be different. You won't be my Jonathan anymore. I liked my friend Jonathan. I am afraid he's gone. I am afraid you are a stranger."

"A stranger." He laughed gently. "Little Bird. Take my hand."

She did. Her hand was trembling and cold. As soon as she took his hand, he began to do what Red had done. He showed Caroline life after life in which she had served him with the same love she gave to Red. Weeping, Caroline threw herself in his arms, trying to run from the intensity of the visions, but he held her fast, pouring them into her mind. When it was over, she found herself clutching his shirt with both fists, and nothing, nothing inside her was the same any more.

"I am the bringer of change. I am the catalyst of change. I turn everything upside down. You know that. But I always set it aright, *better* than it was."

Caroline nodded.

Gently he put her away from him. "Look at me."

She did, and it took everything she had not to run. His beauty was terrifying. She was afraid she would lose her mind, that she could not absorb all of it.

"Focus on my eyes," he said.

She did. And in the dark, wild green, she found a quiet, calm place at the center of all the wildness and chaos.

"Breathe slowly. Focus."

She did, and she began to be able to see him with her physical eyes as well as her spirit eyes. His long, thick orange-red curls of fire. His deep, passionate eyes. His fringed cape of orange.

"Good," he said. "I thought for a minute that you would not come out of it. You have always loved me so much, Caroline. You easily lose yourself in loving me. It consumes you; you drown in fire. People can drown in fire, you know.

"Little Bird. What I want is to be your trusted friend and confidante again. I want you to be able to play games with me and put a whole new level to our closeness. In all your lifetimes of loving and serving Orange, you have never been able to give me your whole self. Part of you is afraid of me, in awe of me, distracted by my power. You do not feel 'good enough' for me. You think the little things—like whether you prefer almonds or raisins—are too insignificant for me. You want to hide your faults from me. You say you trust me, but you cannot be as free with me as you were with Jonathan.

"My task for you is, you must become as comfortable with Orange as you were when you did not know who I was. You need to be able to be as much yourself with me–no, *more* yourself with me—than you were with Jonathan. You need to feel as free with me as you did when you did not know my true name."

Caroline said firmly, "I do not think I can."

"You must." Like Red, he had a way of turning fierce and commanding and stern that no one dared argue with. He became that warrior now as he faced her fearful eyes and she faced his unreadable ones. "You must be more than my Priestess. You must also be my friend, my sister, my beloved. Or you will not receive my feather."

Caroline took a deep breath. "So be it," she whispered. "I will try."

***

Caroline lay in Gawen's arms, on the Hill of Silver, looking at all the Autumn leaves. They had buried themselves under a blanket of leaves of all colors. The sun was setting and it was chilly, but she had a warm sweater and Gawen's arms around her.

It had been an incredible evening. Gawen had at last completed all his work with the Twelve. He had spent the evening telling her how they had all gathered around him in a circle. Blue, his beloved Lord, had told him that all the Twelve felt he was ready to begin the three years of Priesthood training.

In this moon, they would prepare for his initiation into the Priesthood. There would be much, much to do. Gawen had many ideas of what he desired in the ceremony. He was so excited that he was sparkling with energy and life. Caroline had never loved him more. The love he had for the Twelve was so clear, it vibrated through his whole body and affected everything he touched. She was in awe of him, his strength and goodness and specialness. She could not believe how blessed she was to have found him. She was grateful.

A large part of her was also frightened. Yes, she had seen visions of herself as a priestess. She knew her destiny was to be a priestess. But the future can always be worked with, changed, recreated. She was *meant* to succeed, but she *could* fail, out of ignorance and blindness. The thought of never wearing the robe of her colors made her half insane. She needed to serve them as their Priestess. She also needed Gawen to be as proud of her as she was of him. Gently she twined her fingers in his hair, smiling at him. He sighed.

"Do not be afraid, Little Bird. You are full of love. That is all you need."

"I know." She stroked his face and said, "Tell me again of what task Orange set *you* to."

Gawen had told her the stories of all his work with the colors many, many times, but obliged her, telling her again how Orange had insisted on coming to him as a little boy of nine or ten—and having Gawen explain the colors to him as this child, with a child's mind and heart.

Caroline sighed as she listened. She was so afraid that she could not do what Orange asked of her. In some ways, this was the most difficult assignment for her of all. She had no idea where to start, and a moon seemed like too short a time.

Gawen said, "But you have worked with Orange not just for one moon, but *lifetimes*. You have come farther than you know already."

She tried to smile at him, but it did not reach her eyes. "All those lifetimes left me in still greater awe of him, each time. I cannot help how I feel! I feel as if he wants me to adore him less."

"No."

"I know it is not so, but that is how I feel."

"Then go into the feeling. Let yourself adore him, worship him, as fully as you can. Sometimes you must let a feeling run its course before you can grow. I think that if you fight the way you feel for Orange, you will never come out of it. Don't fight it by trying to repress it, or forcing yourself to change. Change happens naturally when it's real."

Caroline stared at him. "You have just saved my sanity. I *want* to worship Orange. I am not *ready* to stop."

"So do so. And in the worship, perhaps you will grow to simply love him as his own Little Bird."

Caroline enthusiastically kissed him all over his face. "I love you, I love you, I love you," she said with each kiss. "*Now* I know what to do. *Now* I have a chance."With one last wild and strong kiss, she began to run back to her room. "I love you," she kept shouting as she ran, and the wind carried it to Gawen, who watched her run while the stars came out, until he could see her no more.

*****

Caroline sought out Katerina. It was nearly midnight, but she didn't care. Katerina was her mentor, her teacher of Art. She respected her judgement very deeply. She knocked on the door, panting and wind-blown from running. She heard muffled noises as Katerina got out of bed.

"What is the...Caroline!" Suddenly wide awake, Katerina hurried Caroline into her room. She was in her nightrobes and looked disheveled and confused.

"When one wishes to express the complete beauty of something, I mean *all* of it, not just part of it, but *all* of the beauty one sees in it, what does one need to remember? What things make it open in you; what closes and blocks it?" Caroline had grabbed hold of Katerina's sleeves without realizing it and was clutching them tightly, staring beseechingly up into her face, looking slightly maddened by her feelings.

Katerina's wise eyes narrowed as she surveyed her apprentice. No, the child was not ill. The girl was in the throes of the beginning of a creative ecstasy. What Katerina said or did now would be very, very important. She had to help Caroline release those fires or they would eat her alive.

"All beauty is unique, and to each there is a unique way of express-ing it...or denying it. Come, Little Bird. Sleep here tonight. I will help you. I will help you do this. But you are in need of rest. We will begin in the morning."

"Do you promise?" asked Caroline, almost tearing at the sleeves of Katerina's robe. "Do you *promise?*"

"I do promise," said Katerina, and laid some blankets on the floor for her and got her settled warm within them. Then they both slept deeply.

***

Caroline dreamt of Blue. And Blue promised her that he, too, would help her express the beauty she saw in Orange, would help her unblock it all so that she could release it.

When Caroline awoke, a blue crystal was beside her pillow. She did not fully understand its use, but she understood one thing. It would help her see when she was opening the right doors to release her vision...and when she was walking in the wrong direction.

***

That morning Caroline, Elizabeth Anne, and Katerina went directly after breakfast to the offices of the Temple Elders, to ask permission for Caroline to create a special altar in one of the chapels of Orange. This was immediately agreed to, and Caroline left the offices holding both her teachers' hands and feeling a profound sense of relief. Perhaps, now, there was a chance that she could control this madness in her, release it in a positive way. Perhaps, as she expressed his beauty, she could learn to not distance herself from him.

"All I want is to be close to him," she whispered, and Elizabeth Anne smiled gently and nodded, "I know, my dear." Katerina just beamed at her proudly.

They went immediately to the chapel. It was located in a section of the gardens Caroline was unfamiliar with, but Elizabeth Anne knew well. She seemed to know the entire grounds as if they were part of her own body.

It was a stone chapel, made of red and orange and brown stones and crystals, and decorated with vines and many orange and red flowers. It was rather new, being created only a decade ago. And Caroline saw immediately that it had been waiting for her special touch. Inside there was room enough only for perhaps ten people. The chairs were plain wood and the altar as well. It was beautiful, well-made, but too barren, too empty for Orange despite the tapestries and altar cloths that hung there.

Caroline began to get idea after idea of what she could do with the chapel. They flooded her until she sank down weakly into one of the chairs. She was trembling, and the visions and inspirations just kept coming. "He is overloading me," she whispered. "He is always filling my heart past what it can hold."

"To expand it. To make it grow," said Elizabeth Anne gently.

Caroline stroked the sleeve of Elizabeth Anne's robe on the place where it was dyed orange. "You serve him well," she smiled, and hugged both her teachers. They all cried a little. Then Elizabeth Anne and Katerina left, and gave Caroline quiet and privacy. For a long while the novice sat in prayer and meditation, letting herself absorb the vision of all that she had to do here. She prayed for the strength to temper her worship of Orange with love and honesty. She prayed for the strength to not be swept away by him.

A large orange candle was burning on the altar. One of the Priestesses of Orange made certain it was always lit and replaced before it burned out. Caroline watched the flame for a long while, seeing his face in it, content just to gaze on him. Her prayers became a joyous thank-you for all she had been given, and for a Universe in which Orange glowed bright and alive.

When she left it was nearly sunset, and she left a bowl of fresh fruit as offering. She walked home, seeing the fiery colors of the sunset above her. *Yes!* The sky, when it is in that place between day and night, is touched with red and orange. And Caroline understood that this was the time of dying and rebirth. And that time belonged to her Lord and Lady.

***

Gawen was not the only one who had been accepted fully into the Temple. Lydia had completed all her tasks, and she was to be a Priestess of Brown and Yellow. Caroline had held her tightly, and they both cried. Caroline jumped up and down in circles around Lydia. It was told to Lydia that she was to spend the moon before her initiation in Sanctuary. Her teacher, a beautiful Brown and Yellow priestess named Estelle, would be given all instructions from the Twelve to prepare for the ceremony and would visit Lydia as need be.

Lydia came to say her farewell to Caroline and kissed her on the cheeks, and she was glowing with an inner happiness so that Caroline glowed as well. Caroline bid her to send greetings to David.

When Lydia left, Caroline spent a long time thinking about how fast life whirled. It danced past you so quickly that you could barely process the images. One had to make a real conscious attempt to be present in the moment, and it was easy to lose it in the fast flow of motion.

As she meditated on Lydia (she had promised to help tend to all the plants in Lydia's room while she was gone), it seemed to her that this was one of the purposes of Brown. To slow us, to make us heavy, to still us, to weight us with solidness. This, it seemed to her, was the attempt of the Universe to keep us from dancing into oblivion. To make us stop, look, listen, and be present.

Lydia herself had often taught her these things, balancing Caroline well. Caroline would bounce from thought to thought like her bird. Lydia would be so still, so quiet, you sometimes thought she was unresponsive, and then she would point out some little thing. It would be a thing Caroline had not seen or noticed, and it would deepen the appreciation of the moment a thousandfold.

Lydia would make her keep her goals realistic, she would not allow her to veer off on too many side tangents. This she would do gently and quietly, but firmly. Caroline shuddered to think what would have become of her if Lydia had not been there.

She remembered how Lydia had shown her the Temple grounds that first day, and realized what a perfect choice Lydia had been. On that special day Caroline had been overwhelmed with sensation to the point of really absorbing none of it. Lydia had steadied her, had been there for her to calm and focus her. This, then, appeared to be another quality of Brown. Constancy. Loyalty. Steadfastness. There was no more loyal friend than Lydia. She would be a beautiful Priestess of Brown.

As Caroline thought on these things, she began to dance, whirling around in circles until she was dizzy and fell onto the ground into some leaves. She got her balance back and watched the bright blue Autumn sky flowing above her. She was filled with joy, and her eyes stung. No matter how crazed life got—as long as there was Brown—and Lydia—all would be well in the end!

***

The moon settled into busy rhythm. She worked at a feverish pace on the chapel. She painted flames on the wooden altar. She made places for some paintings and hung up beautiful ones she had done of Orange. She gave the potters and sculptors of the Temple designs, and set them to work on offering bowls and statues.

She also had the seamstresses make a brilliant rug of orange and red, which looked as though you were walking on fire. She had the gardeners plant many more vines and orange and red flowers all around it, and then she *really* set to work.

She found a priestess who was willing to give some huge orange crystals to the chapel. She placed some orange robes in a closet so that people could wear them if they wished. Each had brilliant and startling designs embroidered on the back, and beads and fringes.

She had one of the instrument makers prepare a drum to be kept in the chapel, which also had orange flames on it. She had some other instruments stored in the closet as well. She had a shelf made, and placed copies of the books written over the centuries about Orange by his Priests and Priestesses.

Taking the idea from David, she got a book with blank pages and wrote, "Reflections on Orange" on the first page and left it on the altar.

She brought in vases. She brought in hand bells. She brought in orange feathers. She hung up wreaths. She brought in Autumn leaves of orange and red. She brought in orange pillows to sit upon. She brought in a wand made by a Priest of Orange and laid it on the altar and cried.

The woman mainly in charge of this chapel was named Alicia, and they became good friends. The bond of love they shared for "their" chapel was very strong.

In the benches she had woodcarvers carve sayings Jonathan loved or just words he had loved. *Inspiration. Laughter. Revelation. Appreciation. Glory. Uniqueness. Specialness. Hope. Passion.* These were placed in the walls as well, where people could meditate on them.

Caroline was demanding and bossy and had dozens of people involved in helping her. She knew exactly what she wanted and how she wanted it, and she would not take "no" for an answer. From *anyone*. She also had a statue to Red, Orange's mate, placed in the chapel, as she felt he wished it. In this statue Orange and Red stood together, kissing.

Caroline had made the design, and the resulting statue was so honest and real and full of passion that Caroline cried when she saw it, and she made Gawen come and see it with her. None of this seemed like work to her. It was sheer joy. That was a problem with Orange. You loved the work so much that you never realized when it was too much.

Elizabeth Anne and Gawen kept a watchful eye on Caroline, made her sleep and eat, bullied her to rest with them for an hour. Gawen was also busy at work with preparations for his initiation, and Caroline had things to do to help him and Lydia prepare. She was going to be actively involved in both initiations. Lydia's teacher, Estelle, and Gawen's teacher, a Priest of Blue, Silver, and Black named Simeon, were always calling upon Caroline for this or that.

Katerina, Caroline's Artistic Mentor, threw up her hands, said, "Forget the mural and the tapestry *this* moon; I can see that!", and joined in to help Caroline. Katerina was a very, very hard worker, and she accomplished *a lot.*

Then there was the *outside* of the chapel. There were outdoor statues, stone fountains, trees to plant, more meditation benches to make.

Elizabeth Anne was helping Caroline to sew special dresses for the initiations, and Caroline found herself frustrated, impatient, longing to get back to her chapel while Elizabeth Anne pinned her hemline or made adjustments. She'd cluck and scold at Caroline until Caroline stood still for her long enough to fix the dresses. Then Caroline would get all excited about the dresses when she looked at herself in the mirror, and she'd start jumping and squirming around till Elizabeth Anne was at her wit's end.

Word had spread all over the Temple, and daily people left offerings at the chapel, things to enhance it. Caroline was always careful to consult with Alicia so as not to hurt her feelings.

With all this going on, the moon sped fast upward, until one day Caroline realized that it was just beginning to wane, and let out a shriek. She felt no closer to meeting her task for Orange than she was when the moon started. She stared at the round orb in the sky, and sighed, and promised herself that *every day* she would visit Jonathan. Orange. *Him.*

***

"I am very proud," Caroline was telling him as they wandered by the familiar paths they had walked when he was just Jonathan to her. "The chapel is becoming so beautiful."

He smiled down at her, ruffled her hair. "I love you, Little Bird," he said.

She beamed at him. Then her smiled faltered. "But the more I do, the more I realize how much I adore you. And yes, that you are far above me."

He picked her up in his arms abruptly, startling her, and swung her around in the air till she faint with laughter. "Now you are above me," he said as she watched his face, staring at his eyes, trying not to get dizzy. Then he plopped her on the ground as abruptly as he had lifted her up. He lay on his back and stared up at her. "Now you are above me again."

Caroline lay down beside him. "Now I am *not*."

He turned his face towards her. "No. On the ground, we are neither of us higher than the other."

Caroline stared at him. He sat up, and she followed. "You see," he said, "I am the Lord of Opposites, the Lord of two sides of the same thing. You want me to be above you. But you also want to be above me."

"No!"

"Yes. You want to be more humble, to appear more holy, than me. You want to be insecure so that I build you up."

"This is unfair."

"Yes, it is. To *me!* Caroline, you do not think I will love you unless you are *better* than me." He took her face in his hands. "You also do not think you can win me any other way but through pity. If I look down on you, I will *have* to show you compassion. You know where you stand with me when you place yourself below me. If you are my equal, you are guaranteed of nothing. Not my pity and compassion. Not my worship and adoration of you.

"Loving me is a gamble. Worship of me is not. People distance themselves from the Twelve because it is *safe*. Love is always safe, Caroline. But only if you are prepared to trust with all your heart. I, the Lord of

Opposites, tell you this. The most frightening feeling in the world is also the only place you can go where you are totally safe."

And Caroline meditated on this and found it to be true. There is arrogance in insecurity, and insecurity in arrogance.

The final words of Orange rang in her mind. "As long as you are beneath me, you are in control. You know how to act, how I'll react; you feel safe. But you cannot control me, Caroline. Not even by throwing yourself at my feet. I do not give love out of pity or guilt or manipulation. No one does. That is not love. Love is given freely, and at its root is trust."

***

Things began to change, slowly at first, then rapidly. Once Red came along on one of their journeys together. She and Orange were holding hands and being silly. Caroline was basking in the glow of love surrounding them. Red had on a necklace of beads Orange had put around her neck.

"Caroline. Which is greater? The necklace or the bead?"

"The necklace."

Red looked at her, smiled, and said, "Here, then," and tore the necklace apart. The beads scattered. She handed Caroline a bead. "This is what the necklace is without the bead," she said. "So now, which is greater?"

"The necklace needs the beads. But the beads need to be a part of something. They are equal." Caroline was staring at Red with big, frightened eyes.

Red smiled at her. "You are a part of Orange, there are faint orange tints in your skin and hair. This leaf is part of Orange. This bead is, too. So am I. So is the sunset. We are all part of Orange. No, we are not the whole of him...and the whole is bigger than us alone. But without you... without its parts...Orange would fall apart like my necklace did. If even one part is missing, *he* is not him.

"The reason you cannot separate from him, Little Bird, and make yourself *less* than him, is that you are a part of him. You are really one with him. And one's heart and lungs do not say they are less valuable than one's whole body. How can you survive without them? Yet lungs do not see or hear or taste they way eye, ear, or tongue does. The lung is not the body, but if you were to ask it if it is more or less than the body, it would simply breathe. It would simply be. And allow the body to be.

"This is what you must do with Orange. Take your place as a part of Him that is irreplaceable. Rejoice in being within Him."

***

One day Orange gave in to Caroline's pleas to appear to her as a child, the way he had to Gawen.

He was a wild, energetic little boy, with orange hair in all directions and a mischievous grin. They played until Caroline was exhausted...and fell asleep, smiling.

***

Caroline had a nightmare one eve close to the New Moon. She dreamed that she was going normally through her day, working at her mural and the chapel, and being with her friends. But something was odd. Everyone was looking at her as if she were an idol. They made holy signs or bowed as she passed. They kissed the hem of her dress. They spoke to her only with quiet respect. If a group was playing or laughing, they quieted as she passed and nodded respectfully to her. If she tripped, ten people could see to it that she was helped, but everyone seemed afraid of her, as if her judgement on them would be fierce if they displeased her.

Even Elizabeth Anne behaved thus. In desperation she ran to Gawen, crying. But Gawen only said, "You are so beautiful," and kissed her hands and cheeks. He did not hear her pain at all.

A strange thing began to happen. Caroline began to be unable to see people or hear people. A mist was closing around her, and it kept thickening. She was becoming more and more alone with each second. No one really saw her, only their idol, and she was disappearing. Fading. With no one to see her, did she exist at all?

She awoke screaming. Orange was holding her and stroking her hair and wiping her tears. "Now you understand," he whispered.

"I'm sorry. I'm sorry."

"No. Do not be sorry. You are one of those who found me in the mist, who reached me through the fog. Who cared enough. I *love* you."

***

On the day before, the day of, and the day after the New Moon, there were celebrations to open the refinished Chapel of Orange. People from the Temple streamed in day and night. Alicia and Caroline were very busy. A sacred ritual was performed to honor the "new" chapel, and Caroline saw Orange there as the area was consecrated. He came as an orange mist that filled up the whole chapel and saturated it. At least that is what she saw. Everyone saw something different.

The response from the people was tremendous. Everyone *loved* the new changes, and Caroline was praised until she was spinning with it.

The Priests and Priestesses of Orange were especially joyful and kissed and hugged and danced with Caroline and gave her presents. Gawen was always at her side, his arm around her or his hand in hers. Elizabeth Anne and Katerina were standing together, beaming. Lydia returned from her retreat and came to the chapel, and she and Caroline hugged and cried. Dozens of orange balloons were freed into the sky as people cheered, and the candlemakers of the Temple had made hundreds of small orange candles. At night, people processed singing around the chapel, candles lit and held proudly.

What made her happy was that Orange was smiling. It was in this chapel, in a rare moment where she was alone there for a half hour, that Orange came to her. He was wearing a fringed vest, fringed pants, and had a gold crown with orange and red jewels in it, and was holding aloft his wand in a gesture of victory. Caroline later painted him thus, in his newly fixed chapel, his face glowing with light and pride of her. Lights of orange and red and gold were sparkling all around him like fireworks.

When he left, where he had stood was a brilliant, large, glowing orange feather.

Chapter Nine

The day of the New Moon, which began the last moon of Autumn, was unforgettable to Caroline. It seemed to be split into three distinct parts, all of which were like a lifetime, a world, unto themselves.

It began in the morning. Lydia had chosen to be initiated with the sunrise. She looked beautiful, draped for the first time in her robe of brown, with some yellow stripes. Lydia considered herself plain, even ugly, but Caroline could have told her that on her initiation day she was breathtaking. Her warm brown eyes glowed with peace and fulfillment, her brown hair and light brown skin blended perfectly with the shade of her robe.

It was to be a simple ceremony; Lydia preferred this. She had seven attendants; Caroline was one. Her beloved teacher, Estelle, was another. The women were all responsible for a different part of the ceremony. Lydia was led by the women, and all the assembly, to the cave of Brown she loved so well. She was taken from her room with the novices, and she and Estelle led the procession. Everyone was chanting an old chant to honor Brown, which had been written long ago by a priestess, and was especially loved by Lydia. Drums pounded, and some danced as they walked, and Caroline played her flute.

At the cave, Estelle led Lydia to the opening, kissed her on the forehead, and Lydia entered alone. Her initiation with Brown was to be private and for them alone. She never spoke of what befell her in the cave, but one thing was certain. She emerged changed. She was no longer a novice, but a priestess, and a woman grown. It showed; it radiated from her body. Caroline, the artist, was frustrated and intrigued. The subtle changes in Lydia would be hard to paint, and yet it was so striking and clear that Caroline ached to paint it. She watched her friend with bittersweet emotions. As Lydia journeyed into the cave, a part of Caroline had gone with her, had changed with her. She, too, felt different. Her childhood was ending; her friend was leaving. She would no longer room with the novices. Caroline was not exactly even sure what Lydia was to do now. She assumed that Lydia would stay at the Temple, but realized with a jolt that she'd never even asked Lydia if this was so.

For the half hour Lydia was in the cave, the singing and chanting and drumming continued outside it. Caroline's heart was pounding. She did not feel ready to come of age...but then, this was Lydia's day, not hers. After this, one of the attendants decorated Lydia in wreaths of yellow flowers. Lydia had another favorite prayer written to Yellow, and this was said aloud by her and echoed by the assembly. Lydia's usual quiet shyness was gone—she was calm, self-possessed, and strong of voice, never stammering or faltering. She spoke the words with great passion and joy.

Another attendant passed out gifts Lydia had made herself. There were many yellow and brown scented candles, and some stones she'd gathered, and some yellow flowers in tiny pots that she'd begun to grow. She had also written out many copies of the chant to Brown and the prayer to Yellow in her own hand. People took what they wished from the baskets the attendant carried around.

Caroline felt as if the world was moving very fast. She knew one thing–Brown and his Black wife made people grow up. *Matured* a soul. Even the feasting, as joyous as it was, was rather sedate. It was simple food which Lydia had prepared herself, when possible, with herbs or vegetables or fruits she had helped to grow. It was delicious and healthy, and all the plates were decorated with tiny yellow flowers. Among the best things to eat were Lydia's breads—she had made several, each better than the last. Nut breads and fruited breads, some spiced, some with different grains.

Lydia led the blessing, thanking Brown for the abundance of the earth which never ceased giving. She prayed that the planet might live close to and honor the earth and that her life as a priestess might be an example of the respect we owe the earth and all its creatures.

Caroline ate heartily and mingled with the crowd, helping the other six attendants to see that everyone's needs were met and all were happy. Lydia sat in a chair which was hewn out of rock. She sat there, and people came up to her one at a time with blessings and small tokens of affection. Amid the chaos of the bustling crowd, Lydia was a calm, quiet center, sitting still and watchful in her stone chair, talking quietly with those who came up to her. And, after it was all over, each person took their leave but were asked to say a small prayer at the cave of Brown for Lydia. So the crowd drifted slowly away, one by one, to the cave and back to their lives.

As for Caroline, she barely had time to hug Lydia goodbye when she was whisked away by Elizabeth Anne to prepare for a very different ceremony. Hurriedly, with her teacher's help, Caroline changed from the brown dress with yellow flowers she had worn for Lydia. This time she wore a gown. A gown of lace and silk. It was a beautiful, bright blue, over which she wore a silver shawl. She wore pink roses in her hair.

This ceremony began at sunset. It was held in an area of the priests' land she was not very familiar with. By contrast to the quiet cave, this ceremony was held in a large, open field, and a large altar had been erected in the center. This altar was magnificent. Many lights of blue and silver, pink and red shone over it, flickering and enchanted. Caroline had offered a large painting she had done of Gawen with his Lords and Ladies. This was on the altar, also.

Gawen was announced by several dozen musicians, by trumpets blaring and drums pounding and loud, glorious, rejoicing music. This began when the first star was seen, at which point Gawen appeared seemingly out of nowhere. Caroline was not sure where the priests had hidden him.

The crowd was large, much larger than Lydia's had been, and they parted to let Gawen and his teacher Simeon through, like a huge sea opening up. Caroline stood near the altar, and she began to cry as he passed her. She had never seen him in his robe before. It was of pale blue, but all over it were dark blue spirals and silver stars. There were also pink spirals that had a little bit of red at the very center. This robe was accented by crystals around his throat and shoulders, which caught the lights. Somehow the priests had managed to create a special lighting system, for a silvery blue light shone on Gawen as he walked up the altar.

And then everyone went wild, for this lighting show exploded. All over the field, from unseen mechanisms the priests had placed in the ground, brilliant beams of laser lights shot up to the sky. All over the field they rose up, as Gawen walked up the altar, which had steps to raise it above the earth and crowd.

No one—not Caroline—had any idea this would be happening. And the crowd was in a frenzy. To add to it, a potent incense had also been released (somehow, no one knew quite how) over the whole field. It, too, was rising up, and people were feeling the effects. This fragrance brought visions to some, strong emotions to others. Caroline recognized it as a scent Gawen often had on him, and it was making her feel very strange.

And then it was, as the crowd was still awestruck, that Gawen, the magician, disappeared. A puff of smoke rose on the altar and...he was gone.

Caroline knew he was creating an illusion. But she did not know where illusion stopped. For a minute she almost screamed, believing Gawen to be truly gone. Then she heard his voice in her head. "Did you think I would leave you, love? Watch." The smoke turned blue, silver, pink, red, back to blue. It did this three times, and then Gawen was back on the altar.

Oh, the symbolism was clear enough. The old Gawen had disappeared, had died, and a new one had been reborn from the colors. All Caroline could do was clutch the hand of Elizabeth Anne who stood beside her, until she nearly broke it.

And then there were fireworks. Brilliant explosions and colors flashing in the sky. The four colors appeared on the altar. All the onlookers agreed that they had come, though each saw them differently. All Caroline saw, as her eyes filled with tears, was that each blessed him. First Blue embraced him. Then Pink kissed him. Silver bowed to him. Red threw him a rose. This is what Caroline saw. What she felt was Gawen committing himself for Eternity to these Four. She felt it pouring through her. She stared at the altar, feeling at one with him as she never had before.

The celebration afterward was wild and unlike anything Caroline had ever seen before. There was music, the incense still heavy in the air, many people were half in trance or receiving visions. There was dancing; Caroline had never danced before with so many strangers. People had come in costume, as they had been invited to by Gawen, so there were elaborate masks of glitter and feathers and beautiful, strange designs. Caroline was whirled around from partner to partner, sometimes carried aloft in the air. The crowd was so full of energy Caroline was a little afraid.

It was near midnight when she found herself in a new pair of arms—and a new level of reality. He had violet blue eyes that turned a darker purple when he was emotional. He had on a flowing purple robe of fine fabric, and she knew right away who he was. Instantly.

His expression was sober, quiet. He had on a mask of purple feathers, and thick, straight black hair to his shoulder blades, which had a purple tint in the lights of the moon and stars. He smiled at her, a small, quiet, serious little smile, gazing at her with serious violet eyes with long, thick lashes. Caroline was out of breath from dancing and overloaded with emotion. She said nothing, just stared back.

"Caroline." His voice was low, soothing, and like dark velvet. Caroline's heart stopped, then began to race.

"Hello," she whispered.

He put a finger on the pink heart on her forehead, and Caroline felt her spirit melt.

"My woman has claimed you," he said.

"Y-yes."

He smiled, slowly and a little wickedly. "She will make your life interesting."

Caroline could not answer.

He whirled her to a bench; there were a handful scattered around the field. They sat down. A priest offered them a drink from a silver platter. He took it and offered it to Caroline. She was very thirsty and grateful to be sitting. Her head was spinning.

"There. You have had quite a day," he said gently. "Rest. Look at the stars. Listen to the music. Breathe the night air. Be at peace. Your man has come home."

Caroline's eyes filled with tears. "Did you *see* him? Did you *see* how he *looked* at the end?"

Purple smiled gently. "Yes, child. I saw."

Caroline flushed. "Of course, you did."

He was quiet awhile, content to absorb the evening. "This is good magic," he said. "Very good magic, this night."

Caroline nodded. "I feel it."

He smiled at her. "It is your man's magic. Of course, you feel it."

She was suddenly too tired to speak and just looked at him, knowing he would read her feelings in her eyes.

"My eager friend." His smile had softened. "How eager you are to please me—to please us all. Yes, little one. There is something you can do for me which would please me deeply. But it involves much study, much work, much discipline. Come to the chapel of Purple which is by the main library. Come tomorrow. You will get instructions then."

Caroline nodded. "I will be there."

He smiled gently at her again. "Enjoy the night, Little Bird. Your man is a good man. He has love and truth in his heart. He will make a fine priest. You deserve to be very proud of him. It is good to feel pride in one's mate—to respect them, to honor them. Hold this night deep in your heart. As you grow and change, never forget how he looks tonight. No matter how old he gets, deep inside he will always be as he is tonight. Young, alive, strong, with all of life ahead of him, full of hope and promise.

"If a woman can see a man that way, then no matter how many times he falls or fails in life, no matter how many dreams die or how weary he gets, he can be reborn in her eyes. Love provides the only immortality, Caroline. For love alone can die over and over again and come forth stronger. Love alone can always grow deeper.

"There is no death, Caroline, that does not involve growth. He has far to go in this life, child. He has much to do, many dreams to realize. Stand beside him. Help him. Keep him young and alive and burning with his plans.

"He will be a new man each day. Let go of the old one without fear. He will not leave you. Let him change before your eyes, even if it seems as if he turns to smoke, as he did tonight. He will always come back... deeper and stronger and more in love with you. Trust in his love. As he grows, he only grows closer to you. You are his home, child. Make it a warm, welcoming one."

Caroline stared at the violet blue eyes. She knew that she would never forget his words, in this life or any other.

"Carroliinne...." Gawen was calling her. He was wandering the crowd nearby, trying to find her. She stood up, waved to him. He came over.

Caroline turned to find Purple gone.

"Who was that?" Gawen asked as he hugged her close.

She smiled up at him. "Someone who admires you very much and is very proud of you," she said, and kissed him.

The celebration went on till the first ray of dawn. Caroline danced till her slippers had holes in them, and when all had gone home, she watched the sunrise with Gawen. The new day had dawned. And Gawen was a Priest of Blue, Pink, Silver, and Red. Her priest.

***

Her gown was hung neatly in her closet, her torn shoes put aside to see if they could be mended. As Caroline woke, the sun showed it to be past midday, and she wondered if she'd ever have a reason to wear the dress again. She stretched and yawned. She had felt like a princess... Gawen's princess. The pride in him Purple had spoken of had filled her heart until she could almost see her heart growing and expanding.

She washed up and put on a dress she had of purple and blue. She did not have many purple clothes. She brushed her brown hair till it shone. Elizabeth Anne had left her some fruit and pastry from breakfast on a tray by her bed, so she gladly ate it. Images of Gawen were singing in her blood—the way he looked in his robe, the way he disappeared.

What had Purple meant when he said it would require much study and discipline to complete his task? Brow furrowed, pondering this, Caroline headed towards the main library. This was quite a walk from her room. She began to think about Lydia, how Lydia loved to walk for hours, everywhere. Caroline would try to keep up with Lydia's long, strong legs, but her tiny ones had to take three steps to one of Lydia's. They'd walk, and Lydia would point out this or that flower or plant. She knew them all, their uses and properties. Though she was newly initiated only yesterday, people had been coming to her for many moons for herbal cures. Caroline vowed to go find her soon and talk about Lydia's plans.

Meanwhile, she had to try to put the stirring events of yesterday aside and think on her meeting with Purple. It was not easy; her mind was still dazed from the ceremonies and from the incense at Gawen's ceremony.

The library, a beautiful, sprawling white building, was a beloved place of Caroline's. She went there often; they had almost every book about the Twelve that the planet had ever seen. There were many little quiet nooks and crannies where Caroline could go to read and study. Nearby were a few small chapels. She had never been in the one dedicated to Purple, but she knew where it was. Like the library, it was shining white on the outside and classically beautiful. Elegant. Caroline felt a little clumsy and awkward just looking at it.

She slipped inside—and gasped. The carpet was wall to wall, thick, lush, royal purple. The benches were pristine white, with velvet purple cushions to sit on. There was dim purple lighting in the room so that everything was faintly tinted. On the walls were two small, quiet fountains, so you heard the sound of softly rushing water. Brilliant amethysts were embedded in the seats and walls—huge chunks. The altar itself was as simply elegant as the rest. A beautiful purple cloth lay over it, and amethysts and purple flowers decorated it. That was all. It was enough. It was powerful, magical, spiritual.

One could not help but relax, take a deep breath, and center one's self when one came in here. It was an instinctive reaction. Caroline prayed awhile before the altar and waited.

He came in so softly you could almost not hear him, and the carpet silenced footsteps even more. He sat beside her, and for awhile they said nothing, just looked at the altar together. He was dressed in a warm, soft pullover sweater and pants. He had glasses on, and every strand of his dark hair was in place. He carried with him three books. He looked like a scholar.

"I am a scholar," he said quietly. "I am above all else a spiritualist. A philosopher. A theologist. All these things I call myself, and my followers call me, yet I am more. I am a mystic, a healer, a ruler. I am law and I am reason. I am purpose. I am dignity and reverence. I am respect and understanding."

Caroline nodded.

"I love knowledge, the pursuit of it. I love to enhance the mind, but always and only for a spiritual purpose. Do you understand?" he asked her.

"Yes, sir. I do."

"Facts have a deeper truth. A fact can be surfacely valid and true, or seem so, but not be spiritually so. I define, clarify, and express spiritual truth, separating it from what is not spiritual truth."

"I see."

"I love the arts as well —music, writing, dance, your paintings, Caroline— when they are finely done. But again, to stir me they must have a deeper truth. They must be spiritual. They must *say* something."

"Yes."

His violet eyes smiled at her behind his glasses. "Really, all the colors have helped you to understand who they are, each in the way that best suits them. For Red, it involved action—a life spent in loving Red. For Orange, you had to open yourself to find the Orange within you. For Pink, you had to create a healthier reality. Each has their own style.

"I am a scholar. You will find me in study. It is not intellectualism that I seek—that is for Blue. It is Blue that is the genius of the Twelve, the one with the unrivaled mind."

"I *know*," whispered Caroline. "Yes."

Purple smiled that slow, devilish little smile of his. "But...I come close."

Caroline could only stare at him.

"I want you to study, child. Spend time with these texts on Purple. Study purple when you see it in Nature. Ask me questions. I love to answer them. At the end, I wish you to create a ritual. Create a ritual to

174

bring people closer to Purple. Have all your friends attend. I will know, by the quality of this ritual, whether you really understand me or not."

Caroline smiled at him.

"Like my wife," he continued, "I enjoy people. I am quieter than she at times, more bold than she in other ways. We both like to spend time with the people who are seeking us. But I will often ask of you—a solitary walk, so that we can talk in depth. A night spent in a debate, between us. I will ask of you alone time with me. Privacy. Quiet. The deeper a conversation, the more I like it. I hate shallow and superficial discussion. I want to dig into a topic, dig into the person I am with.

"I will ask you to be quieter than usual...more still. To focus on me and let other things go. I expect that if you seek me, you give me full attention. I will give it back.

"It is approaching the first moon of Winter. A good time to be contemplative, as the old year ends. Go for long walks. Visit this Temple often...and the library. Go off alone. You need some time to think. Pink and I are healers: she more of the heart, I more of the spirit. For you, Caroline—for most people—their three greatest spiritual wounds lie in what they do not know. Lie in ignorance. Look for knowledge, and you will find it. Look for understanding, and you will find it. Look for truth, and you will find it. *That* is what I stand for...and I am eager to begin work with you—you who love my wife so well."

Caroline's eyes glowed at him. Her whole face, her whole body glowed with excitement. "I shall start immediately," she said. "Now."

***

Caroline visited Lydia's new room. It was in a different section of the women's buildings, where the initiates resided. Once you were accepted by the Twelve, you had three years of training and teaching by the priestesses of your colors and the Temple Elders. This was supposed to give you a chance to clarify your life path and direction, and your role in Temple life. There were also Mysteries that were not taught to the novices.

Sometimes the initiates had specific work to do and places to go. If they did not, they roomed for the three years in the Initiate's Quarters. Lydia had chosen this option. It was the right of any initiate to live anywhere she chose, including the Priestess' Quarters. But those who were not certain where to go next went to the Initiate's section to find their way.

There was one thing Lydia did know. She wanted to work in the gardens and Temple grounds. There were many aspects to this work, however. You could be a gardener. If you were, you might concentrate on the flower gardens, herb gardens, vegetable gardens, or all three. There was also forestry, specifically working with trees and the wooded areas of the grounds. There was landscaping, which focused on creating beautiful areas outdoors for different purposes, groundskeepers like Elizabeth Anne, and there was earth healing. This involved protecting the crops against weather or animals, dealing with sickness in the vegetation, poor crops, or any imbalances in the environment.

There were still more distinctions. Within herb care, you could focus on herbs for food, medicine, or both. There were tour guides and naturalists who took guests—or novices—on tours around the grounds to explain all the nature there. There were those who simply kept the grounds clean, which was a lot of work. There were those who focused on the animals of the grounds, both wild and domestic. Some people were simply in charge of the general care of a certain area of the Temple grounds. There were people who organized nature hikes or retreats and gave classes and workshops. There were those who studied the weather. There were many, many paths to choose for the Priestess of Brown. Some were nurses and physicians, some cooks, and some focused on children or the elderly.

Caroline had not realized all of this until Lydia explained it to her. Lydia told her that there was much uncertainty inside her as to which path to take, so she was studying and praying on it. Lydia had set out on a three-year, intensive program of study. She wanted to learn everything she could about all these paths, to help her choose well. She was very excited. The priestesses had told her that once she made a decision, her studies would be geared towards that particular area. Excitedly, she told Caroline of still more areas—the study of rocks and crystals and their properties, the study of the environment of the planet—not just the Temple grounds, the study of crafts involving the earth, such as woodcarving or stone sculpture or carpentry or building, as well as poetry, music, painting, and dance. These could apply to all colors in various ways.

Then there were the mystics. In each color, there were the mystics.

Those were the spirits called to a life of constant prayer and meditation and communion with the color(s).

Lydia looked happier than she had ever been, and Caroline left her feeling warm and happy inside about where her friend had found herself in life, and promising to pray for Lydia and send her positive energy every day.

***

As Caroline had promised Purple, she kept her month focused and quiet as best she could, so that she could concentrate on Purple's studies with her. She told Katerina that she could not work long hours on the mural or tapestry this moon. She did not attend many classes and kept her visiting with friends to a minimum. She did have to do her part in the gardens, but she did not tarry there.

She put aside all things she could put aside, and she devoured the books Purple had given her. She read always in peaceful places—her room, an orchard, a solitary nook in the garden, the library or chapel of Purple. She read in places where it was quiet and she could think.

Then she formed thoughtful questions she could discuss with Purple, and she did so. They talked for hours, walking amid the late Autumn leaves, sitting quietly in the chapel before lit candles. They talked of the meaning of Purple and his lessons. Caroline found herself in a peaceful, introspective frame of mind as the moon grew full.

Purple, like Blue, did clarify the mind. But he went deeper and clarified the spirit. One of the things they discussed most often was the spiritual confusion which had led the planet to move away from the ancient ways of Flight's people. What was the planet afraid of and weak in? Caroline's great wound of being separated from the voices of Nature was addressed. Sometimes Pink joined them for their talks, if they involved issues of friendship and love and healing and kindness.

Pink revered Purple. She listened to him rapturously as he talked, savoring each word. She was in love with his deep wisdom, and would often sigh and grin at Caroline as if to say, "Isn't he *wonderful?*" Purple had black hair, and was a dark color in some moods, but she never let him forget his light violet shades and that he himself was not the color Black.

He loved spiritual ideas and growth and would become excited by them and animated and enthusiastic as he was about nothing else. He showed Caroline purple things in nature. Grapes. Flowers. Stones. Crystals. Feathers. A sunrise or sunset. Purple was in rainbows, and some fish, and so on. But Caroline began to realize that some colors...Black, Blue, Green, and Brown in particular...had spread all *over* nature. The sky, land, and waters were all covered with them. Other colors were rare and precious and not so often seen.

Purple explained that White, Orange, Red, and Yellow were in the middle of these two extremes. But Silver, Gold, Pink and he were on the rare side in nature. He explained that Silver and Gold were colors that *accented* other colors, enhanced them, brought them out. They also discussed that each color had a vibration. You could feel it. This vibration corresponded to the vibration of musical notes, and of numbers.

They talked a lot of Caroline's life purpose that she had discovered when working with Red, and of how she had to bring the knowledge of Flight's people to the rest of the planet in a way they would understand and accept.

Purple was soft-spoken and gentlemanly, but he could be very intoxicating. He was strong and potent, another reason for his rarity in nature...he could overwhelm you. His voice floated over her in waves and reached into deep places in her spirit. Like Black, he could touch the realm of the unconscious at times. He often taught her techniques of breathing. Posture. Meditation. Trance. Hypnosis. Altered states. Simple little techniques that made a great big difference.

He explained to her that the blending of harmonious colors creates a certain kind of energy, and clashing ones do, too—an energy that is very different but just as vital. He showed her simple techniques of color healing, as he was a great healer, and told her which colors to use for what results. They spoke of what emotions and vibrations are stirred by each color, and he helped her very much in the basics of handling these stirrings.

All this went on, and he told her often that he was pleased with her work. Theirs was a simple time, but deep. Sometimes he would wear a fine robe, or more exotic styles like Silver and Blue. But ordinarily he came to her as a Professor, in his warm sweaters or Autumn jacket, and glasses. Sometimes his long hair would be pulled back in a ponytail, or under a hat or cap. Yet despite his casual attire and mannerisms, there was to him an aspect of sheer royalty, of refinement. She could picture him sweating with laborers in vineyards or a construction site. She could see him as well dining with classical music in the background upon fine crystal, china and silver.

He was ever respectful and gentlemanly. He seemed holy and very wise to Caroline. As the days passed she grew to love him deeply. And she grew to understand why so often he was referred to as the Purple King. For he was showing her that true royalty was not about jewels or fine housing and clothes and a flamboyant aura...though he certainly had those things as well. He was showing her that true royalty involved inner dignity—pride in one's self, peace with one's conscience, self-understanding, and respect of all living creatures.

Purple taught her that morality was more than a set of rules. When she was around him, morality was a living, breathing entity. It pulsed, it had sensation and feeling. She could almost touch its face. He showed her that morality was not an abstraction, but a thing that was alive—very, very much alive. Alive in the rising sun, the turning leaves, the flowing streams. Morality lived and breathed in all Nature.

And insofar as she let it flow through her, she began to understand that morality lived in her, too.

***

Gawen, too, had moved to a new room, but unlike Lydia he felt certain of how he wished to serve the Twelve. There were two ways, and his only problem was in discovering how to combine them. This, he knew, would take some time. He wanted to be a magician of the highest caliber possible. He wanted to expand his art and become a Master of magic. This, to him, meant both stage magic for audiences and ritual ceremonial spiritual magic. The other side of his destiny lay in his telepathic and visionary talents. He had a great gift in these areas and wanted to develop this as well.

There was a small, remote building in the priests' quarters, big enough for perhaps ten to fifteen men. Those who wished to study magic and chose to live with other magicians, stayed there. Gawen had pledged himself to their service for at least the three years of his initiate. As the youngest and newest of an old brotherhood, he would be apprentice, and was expected to help and learn from the older men. He had been given a list of chores that were his responsibility as well, and in return the magicians would teach him.

He excitedly told Caroline about how, as his chores had been given to him, the priest had also told him a few ways to use those chores (simple cleaning and upkeep of the place) to increase his magical talent. The old man had said that the most seemingly mundane task had a world of magic lore in it if you knew how to unlock it. And that was the task of the magician to unlock the magic in things. Gawen never viewed things the same way again.

He proudly showed Caroline his new room. It was, as of now, much out of order, because he had not organized well yet. But he, like Lydia, was brimming over with excitement, and Caroline could not help but kiss both his cheeks and smile warmly at him. He was wearing an everyday robe, not his ceremonial one. Some people had almost all simple working robes that could get beat up and worn down with the hard work they did. Others had many fancy, elaborate robes. Gawen, as would befit a magician, liked robes with many different looks, and his small closet was overflowing.

His room overlooked a small building which was a theatre and ritual space for the magicians. He showed Caroline inside; it looked very barren. Gawen explained that they kept it so because each magic created needed a unique environment. Caroline helped him clean his room, and put a few more things of his in their proper places, and hung up a picture or two she'd done for him. She began to be almost as excited as he was, and clapped her hands like a little girl when he showed her a few new magic tricks he'd learned. She told him over and over how very proud of him she was; it seemed she couldn't stop saying it.

They talked, too, of her work with Purple, and Gawen listened to all her thoughts about the ritual she was planning, and gave her many ideas and suggestions which helped a great deal. They talked of all the things Purple was teaching her, and Gawen gave his impressions in great depth, thoughtfully and openly. She fell more deeply in love as each day passed.

***

One day Purple surprised her. They were sitting on a bench in the little garden by the library. After awhile, Caroline grew quiet and simply looked around, savoring the warmth of the late Autumn.

Purple smiled at her. "Would you like to go on a trip?" he asked.

She smiled back at him. "All right. To where?"

"Close your eyes," he said, "and visualize Purple."

She did, and soon the purple grew brighter, brighter, stronger, until she had fallen deeply into it. Purple was physically there with her, holding her hand, but spiritually they were bonding in a way they never had before.

In her mind she began to see images. She saw a beautiful purple and pink sky. Beneath it she began to see elegant, yet simple, buildings. Some were white or pink, most were purple. She got glimpses of fountains of crystal and amethyst, and some dark forests overrun with trees and wildflowers.

It was a place unlike any she had ever seen before. The lakes shimmered silvery blue, and the sky appeared full of odd lights. They sparkled and shone and glittered. She knew it to be a powerful place of magic, and she very much wanted to go down to see it and investigate. She could see a large castle in the distance that looked beautiful. What she noticed was that the place seemed both primitive and ancient and highly evolved and futuristic at the same time.

She felt as though much of the place was full of music, as if the waters and stars and stones sang there. But she could not hear or understand it all, only faint hints. It was very beautiful and made her cry.

Then she felt herself leaving, although she didn't want to, as if a powerful force was pulling her away. She had no choice but to go, and when she found herself back on the bench with Purple, she was disoriented and upset.

"It was so beautiful," she said. "Could I not have stayed?"

Purple gently shook his head. "You are not ready, my Little Bird. You would not have found your way home again. You would have gotten lost there."

"That would have been wonderful, to live there."

"No. It is not your home, child. This is your home. But someday, when you are a priestess, you will visit there."

"I will?"

"That was my kingdom, Caroline...the land of Purple. All the Twelve have a kingdom, and one day you will travel to them. But you cannot stay, for to stay you would have to become the color yourself."

"Yes. I felt as if I was Purple."

"Yes. I am happy you found my kingdom beautiful, Caroline. It will always be there, waiting for you when you need to visit it. So be at peace, Little Bird. It will always be there. I will always be there."

Caroline rested her head on his shoulder awhile. Her body felt strange, as if it were humming. Purple explained that her journey to his kingdom had brought out the vibration of the color Purple in her. That was what she felt. Her body was singing the music of Purple. There was also a very pale purple glow around her, which some others noticed. It did not go away for three days, but she only told people that it was because of her work with Purple.

She found she could not speak of the Purple Kingdom. It was too special, too sacred, and she told no one about it. With Gawen, she took his hand and remembered it all vividly, and he could see and feel what had happened.

In her heart she kept repeating, "I will go back. One day when I am Priestess, I will go back." She did this because leaving it had been very difficult for her. She felt as if she had left a part of herself behind in the Purple Kingdom and that she'd never be quite whole again until one day she returned there.

She began to meditate on Purple's promise that she would visit the kingdoms of the Twelve. She began to fantasize about what they would be like. And she painted a beautiful painting of the Purple Kingdom, which he instructed her to place in his chapel. In general, she tried not to think about it overmuch, because she found that thinking of it, even a little, brought her back there. And then she'd just have to leave again, unable to go down into it. She did not want to keep repeating the feeling of being pulled away when she wanted to go down into it. The next time she focused deeply on it, she wanted to be able to go into the kingdom and visit.

And so she held the promise of Purple deep and warm within her and vowed to grow strong and wise so that one day she could see and touch and feel that incredible beauty again.

***

She chose to do her created ritual for Purple on the last night of the moon. About a dozen people were present, gathered in the little garden beside the library. It was simple, really. Purple candles were lit. Caroline sat at a little table with an amethyst. One by one, the people came up to her and told her something they were having a confusion or difficulty with spiritually. They described to her what they hoped would happen.

Then Caroline sketched an image of their desire—it could be a very simple sketch or more complex. This was to give them something physical to touch and visualize with. The papers were all outlined on the edges in purple. Caroline blessed each, holding it over the amethyst and purple candle. With each sketch she tried hard to listen to the voice of Purple in her spirit, advising her about what each person needed. Yes, it was a simple ritual, but she felt she could best express her understanding of Purple through actual true life examples.

Afterwards people told her the pictures had been powerful. Each person meditated in the chapel of Purple with their picture for awhile. As the days, weeks, and months passed, Caroline got reports that her work had done much good. All who attended emerged changed and stronger and happier.

And Purple came to her after everyone had left and bowed to her and held out his hand and presented to her his feather of brilliant, royal purple.

Chapter Ten

Once again, Caroline took the long spiritual journey up the Hill of Novices beneath the New Moon sky. It was strange to go without Lydia at her side, strange to remember that Gawen would no longer climb this hill in search of one of the Twelve. Yes, life was changing. She wrapped her coat tightly around her. You could feel Winter in the air. The sky was so dark, so deep tonight, and mysterious. Caroline remembered the first day she had come to the Temple, and how she had gazed out the window wondering if she would be here in the Winter. She smiled to herself. Well, she was still here, but very, very different from the young woodcutter's daughter who had first come. She had the tokens of eight colors, all the feathers safe tonight in her room. She had fallen in love. She had found her sister, the one she never knew she had, but had always *felt*. She had learned that she was a Priestess of Orange, Red, Blue, and Pink in her heart, and that she was to one day be a very famous artist.

Her thoughts were turned inward as she placed the offering by the stone altar. She wanted to be a truly wonderful person, a noble spirit, very good and wise and truthful. Purple and she had spoken often of her strengths and weaknesses of character. He had instilled in her a firm desire to be good and righteous and loving. As she watched the bright flames of candles against the dark sky, she prayed that she would never lose her way but always hold to the truth and be a messenger for Flight's people, that they would be proud to call her one of their own.

At first, she was not sure if the shadow was her imagination or real. It seemed like a density in the dark night, like a thickness in the air—and she stared at it. Slowly, very slowly, a face and body emerged in the shadows. It was a long while before she saw him at all clearly, and even then he was shrouded in darkness.

Of the men of the Twelve she had seen thus far, this was the most muscular. Irreverently—or perhaps it was reverently—she considered that he looked to her exactly like a tree trunk. He was solid, immovable, and she knew instinctively that he was very, very strong. He had a rather wild, unkempt beard of brown, and deep brown eyes that seemed to see right through her. She could not tell if the expression in them was cold or warm, for it seemed to her to be both at once. He wore a heavy brown coat over pants, and walking boots, boots she could see were well-worn. He stared at her fixedly and intently and did not look away. She wanted to squirm but held firm.

"We are staring at each other rudely," he spoke in a bass growl from the shadows that made Caroline jump. When the flames lit his face she could see tiny color prisms in his beard. Black held all the colors in her, but she now saw that Brown had many colors in him as well. "We are still staring at each other rudely."

"I am sorry."

"No, you are not sorry. Your name is Caroline. They call you Little Bird."

"I, well, yes. I am Caroline. But I am sorry as well, for staring."

"No. You are not. You were interested in who I was. You would stare at me again. You are glad you did. Always say what you mean, Caroline Little Bird."

Caroline stammered, "I did not wish to offend you."

He said, "No, you did not. I know this. You trusted me not to be angry. You trusted me to understand. You were, in fact, *sure* I would understand. Had you *not* been sure, you would never have stared at me. You would have been afraid."

"Yes," Caroline nodded.

"Trust is good. Trust is a compliment to the character of another.

Trust is a statement of friendship. I believe that trust is good. But you must not misuse it. Do not use trust in another to excuse discourtesy or unkindness. Those you trust deserve more respect, not less, than those you don't."

"Y-yes. They do."

"I am glad you trust me. But the truth is, you were afraid or unwilling to ask me if you might stare at me. You *took* what you wanted. Which was it—were you afraid I'd say 'no, do not look at me'? Or did you think I would have no problem with it? Did you assume that?"

"I believed you would have no problem with it."

"Well, you were right. I don't. This time. But you are lucky. Next time I, or the next person, *might*."

Caroline stammered, "Sometimes, when you are close, you need no words."

"Then you communicate by touch or glance or movement. But still you ask for permission before entering the world of another."

"Is it never assumed, then? Between friends or lovers? Is it never *assumed* that you are wanted in their world?"

"If it is, then both people involved are lazy. One is too lazy to ask. The other is too lazy to let the person *know* they are wanted, over and over again. You have another assumption here—both that one person *knows* they are wanted and that the other person does not have to *show* them they are wanted."

"Where does trust fit into all this?"

"You find trust when you know that the other person will always ask you your wishes, directly or indirectly. You find trust in knowing that the other person will always let you know you are wanted and welcome. This is trust. Assumptions are a sign of uncaring."

"Do we then have to *ask* for love, over and over?"

"And so we have come to my task for you this moon."

"I am confused."

"I do not think you are confused. I think you are overwhelmed at my task and wish me to repeat it. All right. Your task this moon is to find out whether love is something you always have to ask for. Or is it given to you. Or perhaps you need me to clarify what I mean by 'ask'."

"Y-yes. Please."

"Do you always have to gain permission of another to enter their world, even in small ways such as staring at someone?"

"But, Lord Brown, if someone says they love me forever, doesn't that bring an assumption with it that I am *always* welcome in their world?"

"That is what I want you to find out. What assumptions come with love, if any? What does courtesy involve after you have been together a million lifetimes? Once you have been taken into someone else's world forever, what are the rules? How do you maintain trust and love?"

"I am afraid this will not be comfortable, this always asking. I stared at you because I was comfortable."

"If that is true, then I gave you a signal to make you know I accepted your staring and let you feel comfortable. What was that signal, Caroline Little Bird?"

"Well, you did not stop me or leave."

"I *let* you stare. Does that mean I *wanted* you to? Perhaps I was permitting you a discourtesy to myself."

"I see."

"No, you are hurt. You feel chastised, and are hurt and angry that I revealed to you your discourtesy. I can see on your face that you resent my honesty. You wish to appear in a favorable light in my eyes. However, if I did not think favorably of you I would not now be standing here on this hill on a New Moon night offering you a chance to earn my token of honor. Is that not so?"

"Yes."

"As you complete my task this moon, also consider the questions. How honest must one be with another? What is helpful, courteous criticism, and unkind criticism? Can you always tell the difference?"

"No. I cannot."

"This I know, which is why I am having you ask the question of yourself."

"But, Lord Brown, I have a question. I do not know much about you; I have not worked with you before. But I do know that you are a color of earth. This, to me, is about homes, building a home and family. Earth is our home and teaches us how to have a home. How does this task connect to those things?"

"Brown is also the color of truth and reality. It is the color of honesty and what really *is*. Without that there can be no home, no happiness or fulfillment."

"I understand."

"In that spirit, I will tell you something else. I am glad you stared at me. I think very highly of you, and I want your trust. You may stare at me again soon. I will be back to see you again tomorrow, Caroline Little Bird." And Brown disappeared into the shadows from whence he had come.

***

Caroline's mother visited once more. She said she wanted to spend time with her daughter before the Winter set in fully and travel became difficult. She came with Caroline's younger sister and brother this time and brought Winter clothes. They sat for a long while one afternoon, talking while the younger children ran and played. Caroline had her head on her mother's shoulder; she could not seem to get enough closeness. She missed her family so much, and yet she was so happy at the Temple.

Caroline told her mother all about the initiations of Gawen and Lydia and what they were doing now. She told her in depth all about her work in the Sanctuary of Black, when Many Stars had come to her to help release her anger and pain. That was a very emotional conversation. It was hard for the elder Caroline to accept someone else being mother to her child. There were tears shed, and Caroline showed her the stone in which she had placed all her anger when she hurled it at Many Stars. The elder Caroline wanted to take the stone home and take it to the place in the woods where Serenity had been taken. Then she would return it to Caroline. Caroline agreed. Forgiveness and understanding was not coming easily to either of them, but mother and daughter tried to help each other, and Caroline's insights about *why* it all happened were helpful to her mother. They also talked about the task Brown had given her.

"How do you feel, mama? Do you feel you need to keep asking for love from Papa? After all these years, what do you take for granted?"

The elder Caroline thought for a long while in silence. Caroline began to suspect she would never answer. Finally, in her low voice, her mother broke the silence and said quietly, "I think you're confused between trusting someone to always be there and taking them for granted. That is not the same thing at all, daughter."

"But how do you know the difference? Sometimes the difference is very clear, other times not."

"Well, I suspect that Brown is a practical-minded color. I don't think he'd be expecting you to be perfect."

"No."

"Seems to me he'd say if you make a mistake, learn from it."

"That's exactly what he'd say."

"All right, then. Just do your best. To me, it sounds like all Brown is saying is pay attention. Pay attention to the ones you love. Listen carefully when they talk. Watch them to learn about them."

Caroline smiled at her mother. "Do you watch Papa?"

The elder Caroline laughed. "I watch him even when I don't realize it. And not just with my eyes. I watch him with my ears and hands and heart."

This was an extraordinarily poetic speech for her mother, and Caroline stared at her. "How do you watch with your hands?"

"It's easy to know what he feels when I touch him."

Caroline nodded. She looked at her mother's face, which when speaking of her father took on the glow and radiance of a young girl in love. "I feel that way with Gawen," she whispered. "I could watch him forever."

Caroline's mother smiled at her and stroked her hair. "You'll do fine, then, child. You'll do just fine."

Thus it was that Caroline found the first rule of love which she could speak to Brown about. Pay attention.

Because both Caroline's mother and sister Daria had a love of nursing, they asked the Temple Elders if one of the Temple nurses and healers could be spared for a few moons to teach them. Not only was this agreed to, it was also agreed that if ever they visited the Temple, they might sit in on one of the classes held by the healers. Both mother and daughter were thrilled about this and excited to learn.

The priestess who was sent to live with them was an older woman named Shayne. She was a Priestess of Black, Brown, Purple, and Yellow—the strongest of these was Black. She was knowledgeable in many types of healing—herbal, crystal, and many more. She was studying to be a physician but found the Temple training very rigorous and was taking it slowly. She fit right in with the family, it seemed, as if she had always been a part of them.

When they rode off for home, Shayne went with them, promising to return in the Spring. Young Daria idolized her, followed her everywhere, and drank in every word she said. As they left, Caroline watched until she could no longer see them. And she reflected on giving. She reflected that if you give freely to another person of your love and time and attention, they do not need to keep asking for it.

And so Brown's question, "Do you have to keep asking for love?" became not so much of a problem when the love was freely given in the first place. She added another rule to the list. Number one was "Pay attention". Number two was *"Give"*. As she reflected on this, what seemed most clear to her was that the simplicity of Brown was deceptive. Everyone thought they understood these simple, basic rules of love already. Yet they always forgot them. They scoffed at these easy answers but consistently lost touch with them.

Brown was beginning to seem to her to be a color who shed off unnecessary complexities and got to the core of life. He refused to be distracted from what really mattered. She added, "Keep it simple," and "Remember what matters" to the list.

***

One night she was in her bed asleep, and she had a dream of Brown's kingdom. This land was much rougher than Purple's, though Purple had some wild areas in his kingdom. This land had forests so dense and thick and dark and primitive that Caroline felt afraid of them. The mountains were jagged and snow-topped and higher than any Caroline could have imagined. She saw canyons so deep that she was sure they went into the center of the earth.

As she saw all of this from afar, she also saw that Brown, far from being the "dull" color some call him, actually had many, many shades. Brown had more shades than most colors. Then, despite her fear, she wanted to descend into this land also, but she found herself awake in her bed. Her dream triggered another realization.

If you are happy, healthy, fulfilled within yourself, then you do not need to make unfair demands of another or drain their energies. Your needs do not go wild and chaotic. To avoid asking for too much, then, one should attend to one's self and be sure that one's needs are being met. One should be happy and peaceful deep within. Caroline added to the list, "Seek your true happiness."

***

Caroline asked everyone she could think of whose opinion she deeply valued for suggestions or help with her task for Brown. She asked Elizabeth Anne and Katerina. She asked Lydia. She asked the colors she had worked with already. She asked everyone. She gathered together all the information she could and reported it regularly to Brown. He seemed pleased with all her work, but she could not tell if he was satisfied. Like Black, he could be very unreadable, and you could get no information out of him unless he wished you to. But he always welcomed her ideas and thoughts. He listened carefully; he was a powerfully good listener, able to be very still and concentrate totally on you. Then he'd offer some comment that always took Caroline's thoughts to a deeper level. That was another thing he had in common with his mate, Black. He never seemed to have a bottom, but his spirit went on deeper and deeper, spiraling into an infinity of wisdom. He was bottomless and filled with layer after layer, the way a tree grows outward in circles, layer after layer.

He could be silent and brooding and thoughtful or talk at length with exquisite clarity and eloquence. His speech was plain and simple but beautiful to listen to, as he appeared to choose each word with great care. A sentence from him went a long way—you often remembered it and understood it more as time passed. His insights had layers, like he did, and seemed to grow with time. They began to seem more wise and pertinent and important as you thought about them, though at first perhaps they did not seem like much at all.

He was blunt to the point of crudeness, never hesitating to say what he thought, whether you liked it or not. Yet, in another one of those strange polarities of two sides of the same coin, he was exquisitely polite. You always felt honored in his presence, no matter what he was telling you about yourself.

When they were not deep in discussion, Brown would point out to her brown animals or things in nature. She noticed that animals of the air—birds—could be brown, and so could some animals of the sea. She spent time with brown horses and dogs and cats, and once Brown summoned some rabbits to her. She carefully studied all these.

He enjoyed animals; there were always animals near him. He would appear, and any animal in the area would come right to him. He often appeared with a wolf, fox, chipmunk or other animal at his side. He helped her understand the body language of animals, telling her what it meant when they stood this way or that.

They rarely met without him giving her some lesson about nature. If it was not animals, it was trees, plants, or weather. He sometimes appeared half-animal himself, sniffing the wind, or sensing nature around him in an instinctive way like animals do.

She became used to his penetrating gaze. She felt as though he was making her a better person. He had no patience with rationalizations, excuses, or lies. He was incapable of ignoring these. He also had little tolerance for the fear of nature that was in people's hearts.

Once he appeared to Caroline with a big black bear at his side and scared her to death. The bear was staring at her and growling. She tried and tried, but she could not relax with that big bear staring at her. Even though Brown assured her the bear would never harm her (*he* was there, after all, wasn't he?), she still feared. At last he sent the bear away, and he gave Caroline a long and stern lecture. He told her that people no longer listened to their instincts and never really understood when they were in danger or not. Nor did they know how to live in peace with the wild things.

This made Caroline cry bitterly, because her sister, Flight, lived there, unafraid of the wild things, *one* of them. Caroline felt inferior and weak. Brown made her understand how soft her life had been. He told her that he could help her a great deal with one of the wounds she had discovered with Pink—her disconnectedness from Nature. He offered himself as an ally and teacher in this, and gratefully she accepted. She was feeling closer to Flight. It seemed as if Flight was around more, or maybe she just sensed her more, with Brown's teachings so uppermost in her mind.

All this went on as Winter arrived. Once he lit a fire in his altar cave, and they sat before it as it stormed outdoors. He loved the outdoors, but he truly loved the coziness and warmth of home, too. He liked spending time in Caroline's room, especially at night. They would light candles and sit and talk for hours. The moon grew full, and Caroline remained a little afraid of him, yet she grew to respect and sincerely *like* him more and more as each day passed.

On the night of the Full Moon she had a vision. She was sitting quietly in her room, meditating. She had lit some candles and wrapped warm blankets around herself and was sitting before the flames. Suddenly she was in a tunnel that led deep into the earth. It was dark, but torches were lit on the rocks to light her way. She followed the tunnel deeper and deeper, knowing she was going far into the earth. She heard the sound of underground springs and water in the distance. There was a big opening. It was like a cave within a cave. She entered it. It had many shades of brown in it.

Brown was there, on a throne of stone, with Black beside him, veiled so you could not see any of her face except for her eyes. There was a small fire going in the center of this cave. Around it dwarves danced— little bearded men whom she understood were spirits of earth, dancing with their wives. Some played instruments.

The flames leaped, and the strange little men danced wildly around the fire. Hearing the music, Caroline began to clap her hands. With a motion of his hands, Brown encouraged her to join in. She found her flute in her hands. She began to dance and play her flute; it could have been for moments or hours. She lost a sense of time—time was just the beat of the drums. The laughter was wild and rowdy, the faces of the dwarves flushed by firelight and dancing, and Caroline danced harder and harder.

At last, weary, she went to the throne and bowed before Brown and Black. "My Lord and Lady, I thank you for allowing me to join in your celebration."

Brown nodded. Black said, "I have a gift for you, child. A help in understanding the task my husband has set for you." She clapped her hands together twice, and one of the female dwarves appeared, with a small potted plant in her hand. The little dwarf offered it to Caroline with a bow.

"This plant will teach you, child. It will teach you how to give and receive love. Take it with my blessings."

Caroline looked at the plant. It was in a simple piece of pottery and its red flowers looked as if they needed care. "It needs attention," Caroline said, "and I will gratefully give it. Thank you, my Lady."

She sensed that Black was smiling at her behind her veil. "We are all proud of you," Black said.

"Caroline Little Bird," said Brown, "the moon wanes. This is a time to pull within, to think deeply, to complete tasks, to look upon what you have gathered while the moon grew.

"You worked hard as the moon waxed full in the sky. Now put it all together, the seeds of wisdom you have gathered. Put all the puzzle pieces together and see what the picture tells you. Use the energy of the moon as it retreats into the darkness. This is also the start of Winter, the season of inward reflection and finding one's true face. Use that energy as well."

"I shall," said Caroline.

She found herself back in her room, blinking. Before her eyes she saw all the shades of the cave. Burnt orange. Light tan. Deep, dark red. Black. The colors of earth swam before her eyes, tinted by the flames of the dwarves' fire. She looked down to see that in her hands was a small potted plant. And it seemed to her, though she could not see them, that the dwarves had followed her back up the tunnel, to be sure she returned safely to her room. She could feel them watching her now.

She held the plant, staring at the red flower. How could something as simple as a plant help to teach her about asking for love? And the Full Moon shone down on her that cold Winter night, silent and watchful, bright white light. But it did not answer her question. Or, perhaps it did... but Caroline could not hear.

***

Caroline tended her plant with love and gentleness. She tried as hard as she could to learn from it. She worked to make it a little more healthy and basically succeeded. It did flourish under her loving care. She began to notice a few things. She noticed most of all that, though the plant was supremely vulnerable, she was also vulnerable to plants. Humans could destroy every plant species in existence...and they too would die if they did so! She thought a lot about interdependence...how all of life is connected and needs one another.

The Yuletide came, and she missed her family. She missed the tree they had decorated in the forest with food for the animals, the special dinner her mother made, the songs while she played her flute and her father played his guitar. She missed all this, though the other women and Gawen were very kind to her.

Her surprise came when Elizabeth Anne came in, loaded with a large bunch of gifts, and said, "Your mother left these with me when she came last. Yule presents from your family." She was grinning, cheeks red from cold, and laughing at Caroline's shock.

Suddenly it was the holiday time in truth, and Caroline joined in it all with a new heart. She gave little gifts to all her friends and to Gawen and joined the carolers singing Yuletide songs in the snow. She went to different parties and attended the big ritual circle to bring in the Winter. She no longer felt alone, and the gifts from her family had changed her whole attitude. They were all so perfect, so thoughtful, so right for her. As she looked out from her little window on the snow, she saw a black raven, dark against the white snow.

Flight was in her mind. She and her people had obviously retreated into caves for the Winter, for Caroline saw them all gathered in warmth together by fires, under many blankets, keeping each other warm. Flight was standing by this fire, staring into it, and the flames made her look so beautiful. Caroline's heart hurt to look at her beauty.

Like a wild animal, Flight sensed her and stared at Caroline with her dark blue eyes. "The wheel has turned again, sister," said Flight in Caroline's mind.

"May your new year bring you peace and joy and love," said Caroline.

"And to you, sister."

***

The next thing Caroline dwelled on was abundance. She thought for a long while on the principle that life is meant to be a place of abundance and plenty, a nurturing and warm place. None of our needs are meant to go unanswered, though we may not always like the way the Universe answers them. This means there is a certainty that we will receive blessings from life, in one form or another, if we are open to them. Why, therefore, ask? When you *know* you shall receive? If Gawen asked for her attention, did that not show a problem? Would he have to ask if there was no problem?

She decided two things. She decided that no two situations could be judged by one standard when it came to love. Every situation was unique. And she decided that the correct term was not so much ask for love, as be *open* to love. Yes, she liked that much better. You showed desire and willingness and need for love to come to you—but not distrust or lack of faith.

It seemed to Caroline that if you knew your own needs—really knew them—you ended up avoiding hurting other people very easily and naturally. One's needs were good and natural. They were never excessive or unreasonable, not if they were the true needs Nature had placed in you. Did her plant ask to be a rainbow? Did it claim a rainbow's needs as its own? A good lover, then, is a self-aware one. And the more you understood self, the better a lover you could be.

She began to feel that there was no one answer to Brown's question. Did a flower ask for rain? Yes, in its dry roots it begged for rain. Yet it trusted the sky.

***

Indoor games. Little gatherings in the rooms of novices to talk all night. Icicles. Stories and classes by firelight. Ancient texts read aloud by candlelight. Warm blankets. Ponds covered with ice as the people skated merrily around each other. Reflections. Long, long, cozy nights. Snowmen. Snow fights with her friends. Making angels in the snow. Indoor sewing projects that had been set aside for Winter. Mittens. Warm tea, many flavors. Nights of song and poetry. Gawen's and her footsteps in the snow. Writing "I love you" in the snow. These were the things that she would always remember of her first Winter in the Temple.

And she did as Brown had suggested. She reflected. She turned inward. She took stock. She looked clearly at herself—where she had been and where she was going. The snow seemed pure to her as if in the white the world was given a fresh chance at innocence.

***

She found something else out about Brown. Brown was a Craftsman. An expert Craftsman.

One time he showed her in vision things he had created, by sending her images one by one. She saw woodwork such as her father did—beautiful statues and birdhouses, lovely carved chairs and rocking chairs. She saw work done in metal and stone as well. Brown had the hands of a worker, rough and callused and strong from hard work.

He genuinely cared about each piece of work, the quality mattered to him. She began to understand Brown as the Patron Color of craftsmen, laborers, farmers, any who work with earth or stone. Brown had a special place in his heart for carpenters, builders, farmers...because he was one. He took pride in it. After Caroline grew more understanding of this side of Brown, he surprised her one day.

"This is for you, Caroline Little Bird." He handed her a box.

Wide-eyed, she opened it, and began to cry. He had carved a little figure of herself, with Energy on her shoulder, and he had made a tiny shelf for it to stand upon. Brown himself hung it on her wall in the place where he wanted it, while Caroline wept and hugged him.

One of Caroline's descendents is said to have it today.

***

The spirit of the flower came to her in another dream. It was a red faerie, a woman, and she glowed brightly. Caroline asked her why she had come to her, what she desired.

"I want to show you something," said the faerie. "Follow me." So Caroline did, into a red, circling, glowing spiral. She traveled down, down the spiral. They came to a bright flame.

"That is a flame of life," said the faerie. "Watch." Then Caroline saw dozens of faeries like this one. They fluttered around the flame, and Caroline knew they were other flower spirits.

Suddenly, one flew in the flame! And the flame blazed brighter for a split second, then was still.

Caroline cried, "But she was so beautiful!"

Another faerie flew into the blaze.

"Why?!" Caroline pleaded, as a third went in.

"Because the flowers understand that to keep the flame of life burning, you need to feed it."

"On what?"

"On the beautiful moments of yesterday, which, when they know their time is done, go gracefully into the flame. You do not understand, Little Bird. If the faeries stay outside the flame, they do not find immortality. In the blaze they will be immortal, for the fire of life never dies."

***

The difference between trusting in a person's continued support and taking them for granted still puzzled Caroline a little, and how to open yourself to love seemed confusing. On the one hand, if you had a need given to you by the Universe, you had a right to *demand* the need be met. On the other hand, you did not even need to ask. In despair, Caroline went to Brown one day with her worries. She told him she was afraid she would fail his task.

"All the things I have learned about love have been helpful, Lord Brown. I have learned so much this moon, and I am truly grateful. But it doesn't seem to answer the question fully. No matter what I do, I come to the conclusion that each situation is so unique, I cannot judge it by the standards of any other situation. Yet this seems to me too easy an answer, as if I were simply unable to work the question out to its true end. I feel I need help."

Brown listened in his careful, thoughtful, quiet way, and was silent a little while, pondering. After what seemed like a long, silent time, he said, "Caroline Little Bird, there is someone I think you need to meet. Will you come with me now?"

Caroline nodded. They were already outdoors, walking across a little hill. Brown made a motion with his hand and a beautiful horse appeared, coming up the hill towards them. Brown lifted her up and they settled onto the proud animal's back. Brown gently nudged the horse and they took off at a fast pace. Soon they were in an area of the grounds that Caroline was unfamiliar with. It was a pretty, wooded area full of pine trees. They came to a cottage. It was snow-covered, with smoke coming from the chimney.

"I cannot go in with you. Tell the woman you are a novice who was out riding, and went farther than you expected. You are stopping there for a rest before you return to the women's quarters. This will not be a lie."

And so Caroline knocked at the door. An old woman answered. She was tiny and frail, but her face was wreathed in smiles.

"Come in! Come in! We get so few visitors! Zachary, we have a guest!"

And Caroline was ushered in before the fireplace, given hot tea and her wet coat hung to dry, before she could even blink.

"What brings you here this cold day?" the man asked. He was sitting in a rocking chair, smoking a pipe, a blanket wrapped around him.

"I was out riding and went too far. I stopped here to rest before I return to the women's quarters."

The woman clapped her hands happily. "You must tell me all about it! It seems so long since I was there; it must have changed a great deal."

"What is your name, Lady?"

"I am Rhyanna, and you are?"

"Caroline. You are a priestess, then?" And Caroline thought, You wear no robe, but then a few priestesses prefer not to wear it all the time....

The woman smiled at her gently. "No, child. I'm afraid I never made it past my first task, with Black."

"I have heard of you," Caroline said before she realized it might sound rude.

The woman only laughed. "I daresay, child. I daresay. I must be legendary in the Temple. I don't think anyone else ever spent so many years with one color. I'm rather proud—I set a new record." And she laughed, but it was not insincere or sarcastic. Her laugh was heartfelt.

"Oh, no," Caroline said. "No, I didn't mean...."

"It's all right, child. It's all right, dear," the woman said kindly. "I have spent a life learning about Lady Black, and this is not a bad thing.

199

Not at *all*."

"Myself, I am a Priest of Brown," Zachary stated, "Brown alone." He puffed his pipe and rocked and looked content. "But I never really found out anything special I wanted to do with my priesthood. I have no great mind for study. All I wanted to do was live here quietly with Rhyanna. What could be better?" he asked.

Caroline smiled at him. "Nothing, I am sure."

He beamed at her. "This is so. This is so. It has been a fine life, and I would not change a moment of it. No, sir. I would certainly not." The chair rocked.

"Tell us about you, dear," Rhyanna said, and so for awhile Caroline told them her story.

"I am working with Lord Brown right now," she said to Zachary, who beamed at her.

"That's fine, girl, fine. I'm sure you'll do very, very well. I can tell. You have that look about you. You're a smart one. Yes, you are."

Caroline sighed. "I don't feel very smart right now. I am having a lot of trouble."

She explained what task Brown had set her to. When she was done, Rhyanna exclaimed, "Well, my goodness, perhaps staring at him *was* rude, but you needed to do it, I'd think, or else you wouldn't have done it. Maybe you needed to be rude right then more than you needed to be courteous. Maybe you needed to learn about rudeness and the only way was to be rude. Sometimes we can only learn from mistakes. Isn't that so, Zack?"

Zachary puffed his pipe and then said, "Yes sir. Seems to me it isn't about *asking* for love at all. Love is already there. Seems to me it's about looking around and seeing the love that's there already, instead of asking for what you've already got. Seems to me that no matter how bad things are, or how many mistakes you make with a loved one—and I made my share, eh, Rhyanna—you're getting just what you need at that exact moment, whether you know it or not. No sir. It isn't about asking for love at all, I wouldn't say. It's about seeing the love that is already around you, even if you don't *understand* the love.

"Now then. If you had been staring at Brown after he told you to please stop, just out of being ornery, I'd have said what you needed was a good swift kick on your backside. And you would have got it, too, one way or another. Yes sir. We get what we need, one way or another. It's just up to us as to whether we're smart enough to see that it's so. That's all. It's up to us, I'd think."

Inside Caroline everything fell into place, and she understood what Brown had wanted her to understand. She was filled with a deep, deep calm and happiness. She finished her tea and promised to visit the couple again, as they both longed for some visitors. She owed them a great deal, and she never forgot it.

Outside, the horse was waiting, and she and Brown rode back to the women's quarters in silence across the snowy hills. There was no need for any words, for between them lay a deep and rich and true understanding. They had forged a bond, a bond that would never be broken. For Brown, like Black, is about those rare things in life that never, never die, but stand firm and true through all ages.

***

She stood quietly beneath the dark sky. The next day would bring the New Moon. Snow fell softly all around her. She had gone to a forested area with many trees. She wore a thick, dark coat with a hood on it and was carrying a lantern in her mittened hands. The light cast patterns on the snow. In her hand she held the small figure that Brown had carved for her, of herself and Energy. She absentmindedly caressed it with her thumb. No one could know what the little statue meant to her. She wondered what power it held.

"Lord Brown, I, Caroline Little Bird, stand here in your forest, awaiting you. Come to me if you will, and speak to me."

From behind the trees, Brown emerged. He, too, had on a heavy, hooded coat, and boots. Snow clung to his thick beard. He had several animals around him—birds and small forest animals. There was also a beautiful deer, antlers lifted high and proudly as he gazed with soft brown eyes, much like Brown's own eyes, at Caroline. In his hands Brown carried a large wooden staff. It was glowing; there was a light around it. His deep brown eyes stared at her intensely.

"For what purpose do you summon me, Caroline Little Bird?"

"I have completed the task you have set me to this past moon. I wish to offer my work to you for your judgement."

"And how do you judge yourself, Caroline Little Bird? Do you deem yourself worthy of the feather of Brown?"

Caroline was startled to be asked. "Well, yes. I think I am." She felt uncertain now, a little afraid that Brown had not been fully satisfied with her work after all. Yet she had been so sure she had felt what she had felt. She had been sure she felt his pride and acceptance of her, especially after the visit to Zachary and Rhyanna. She gazed at Brown, wide-eyed.

"You must learn to trust yourself, Caroline Little Bird. For truly, you need to believe in your own feelings and insights more." Brown spoke quietly, but firmly.

Caroline bowed her head. "Yes. I will try."

"Tell me of your work this moon on my behalf," he said to her.

And she did. She told him everything, even the things they had already discussed at length. She listed for him all her insights about love, the need for love, the courtesy required in love. Here and there she paused, feeling that the silence of the snowy night needed some reverence and meditation. She noticed that Brown could speak with eloquence or be totally silent at great length. Most colors tended to be one way or the other, but Brown could be both ways. At last she came to the part about her visit with Zachary and Rhyanna. She spoke aloud all the things that had gone on in their cabin and how it had brought the pieces together for her.

"Though she never completed even one task for the Twelve, she is not bitter. She is a happy, contented soul, and she is very wise. She truly made me see. Whatever we need is within our grasp. We have to see it, grab it with both hands. It may not be what we think we want. But it will be right. Love is so giving that it is simply always there for us. Our mistakes, it transforms them into truth and wisdom. Our cruelty it heals. The question of love is not what do I need to ask for? It is, what have I been given? Am I seeing it?"

Energy sat on Brown's shoulder along with the other animals, gazing adoringly at him. Caroline spoke with all the eloquence and passion she could find within herself to explain what had happened to her. It seemed as if the little wooden clearing and the cluster of trees had become a chapel, and Brown its priest. The light from his wand glowed ever brighter and brighter.

At last he spoke, slowly. "This is a wand of truth. It connects earth to sky and myself to myself. It glows brighter in the face of truth. It glows dimmer and dimmer in the face of lies. It is fed by the energy of truth, and it has been fed by the truth in you. My staff has spoken. You have told me the truth, Caroline Little Bird. You have indeed learned all the things you spoke of. You have learned them well. You have indeed completed the task I set you to. You were diligent and you sought the true answer."

The wand glowed still more until its light encompassed Caroline also.

"Truth be within you, truth be all around you, truth become ever deeper in your heart. This is my blessing unto you, Little Bird. I wish for you all the beauty of Truth. Know that Brown is always there at your side to help you find it. Always. If your quest be true."

"I know." Caroline's eyes stung with tears. "I know."

"Come forth, then, and receive the token of Brown for a task well done." She did, and he handed her a brown feather. It had three shades of brown in it, and Caroline cried as she held it.

"Faithful Brown, warm, nurturing Brown, you who are always there, you who are so sweetly humble, you who are so rich with goodness like the soil itself! Let me serve you always!"

Brown smiled gently at her impassioned outcry. "I am always here, child. Always."

He stayed there awhile with her, in the quiet night. They simply gazed at each other. And then he left. He turned and disappeared into the trees. But the light from his staff stayed there around Caroline. And as she walked alone back to her room, the light stayed around her. And in her hand she did clutch tightly the beautiful figurine that Brown had carved for her with his own hands.

Chapter Eleven

The night of the New Moon was so wild and stormy that there was no walk up the Hill of Novices. It was too dangerous. Instead, there was a ceremony for the novices in one of the main chapels. It was very pretty, with stained glass windows portraying each of the Twelve. The novices processed around to each, meditating, staying at each as long as they wished. They lay offerings at the little altar beneath each window, if they wished.

It was a very beautiful ceremony, and Caroline was deeply moved. The smell of incense, the flicker of the candles, all took her to another world. It was a dreamlike night, as the novices uttered chants and prayers to summon their next colors to them. Everyone had dressed in finery, or at least dressed very nicely, out of respect for the Twelve. Soft music played in the background. Outside, the cold winds and ice and snow raged.

Caroline found herself staring a long while at the window which honored White. There were no words to describe its beauty. It showed a snow-covered field, with snow falling down, and White stood there staring out of the window. She wore a long white robe and hood, and had a beautiful, pale face, but Caroline found herself longing to see White more clearly.

White roses and candles were beneath the window and white stones.

Caroline lit one of the candles, staring at the window. And suddenly she was there in the snow-covered field with White. The sky was dark, but she saw White clearly, as the Lady had a brilliant glow of light all around her. Caroline stared at her face. It was classically beautiful. Her skin was pale and translucent, but glowed with health, and her bright red lips were shocking against the paleness. She stared at Caroline with pale, pale, light blue eyes fringed with white lashes. She had a hood over her, but you could see that her hair was white and straight, with little hints of silver. Snow covered her robe.

"My Lady," Caroline sighed. This woman was so exquisitely beautiful you never wanted to look away from her. It was an eerie, hypnotic, enchanting beauty.

Then there appeared next to the Lady a large white wolf, with the same pale blue eyes staring at Caroline, and snow in its white fur. In her hand Caroline held the white candle. She felt ashamed as she had no offering, but had come to White empty-handed.

"You may give me a gift later," White said.

Caroline smiled and bowed her head. "I shall. Thank you, Lady." She wondered a little why she was not cold, as she was outdoors in the snow with no coat, but then realized she was being kept warm by the Lady's white light. "Where am I?" she asked.

"You are at one of the entrances to my kingdom. It is a place in between your world and mine."

"You are very beautiful," Caroline whispered.

The Lady smiled. "As are you, Little Bird."

"Your husband, Silver, gave me a task of finding my magical strengths. He put silver chains on my wrists that would not come off until I could do this. Even when I was done, he wanted me to continue to learn more about my magic. He told me to pay special attention when I saw a star in nature that would not ordinarily be there. That would be his sign to me to pay attention to my magic. And to him."

White smiled, but did not speak.

"I have his silver feather," Caroline went on, "and a blanket with stars on it he gave me."

White remained silent.

"My beloved is named Gawen. He is a Priest of Blue, and of your husband, Silver, and of Pink and Red. He strives to be a Magician."

"And he shall be a great one some day," White said.

"Why am I telling you things you must know already?" Caroline asked.

White laughed. "You are nervous," she said softly.

"Tell me of white?" Caroline asked. "I am eager to learn everything."

"Tell me, instead, what *you* know of white, Little Bird."

"White is the color of purity and innocence. It is the color of cleanliness and renewal."

"This is so. What else?"

"I am sorry, Lady. I know little else."

"You have a very good beginning, child. You say white is the color of innocence. What is innocence?"

"Well, innocence is purity. Goodness. Loving, caring. A lack of hate and apathy. Holiness. Sacredness."

"Those are all great words, and they are all a part of innocence. Do you believe you are innocent, Caroline?"

"I am not totally innocent. I try to be good, but I have many faults."

"Innocence is complicated that way."

"I have never seen total innocence in a person. I see it in you, my Lady."

White smiled. "Yet a person becomes innocent, not so much through the absence of faults, but in *overcoming* them."

"Yes."

"Caroline, I think you need to expand your definition of innocence more. What *is* purity, goodness? How do you find it when your faults overcome you? You still too much see things as simply good or bad, when often they are both.

"Listen well, now. There is a woman coming to the Temple. She is meant to be a priestess, but she does not know this yet. She believes she is only coming here for healing and help. Caroline, she has done many things in her life that she cannot forgive herself for. She considers herself to be forever stained by these things and has no hope of ever feeling clean again. Her name is Tara.

"I shall tell the Temple Elders that you are meant to be the main companion of this woman while she heals. You will take care of her. Your task is to make her feel her own true innocence again.

"If you can do this, then I will know that you have a very good understanding of innocence and of me. On the last night of this moon, I shall ask you again the question, 'What is innocence?' And, according to your answer, I will decide whether you are ready to receive my token or not."

Caroline bowed her head. "As you will, Lady."

White smiled at her. "Blessed be your feet upon your path of truth, Caroline."

There was a whirl of snow around her, and when it cleared, White had gone. Then Caroline found herself back in the chapel, sitting before the stained glass window and little altar of White, a white candle burning in one hand...and a white rose that she had not had before in her other hand.

***

Tara entered the Temple two days later and was given housing in the Sanctuary of Black, where people might restore themselves and renew their strength. Elizabeth Anne summoned Caroline to her. She had been instructed by the Temple Elders that Caroline was to be the companion and guide of Tara. Being motherly and protective, Elizabeth Anne's heart was torn between not wanting to see Caroline get hurt in any way and a deep desire to help Tara. She gave Caroline many admonitions and suggestions and warnings before sending her off with a worried glance and a hug to find Tara.

As so once more Caroline met with David, the caretaker of the Sanctuary, and they greeted each other warmly as long-lost friends. He inquired about her emotional well-being, and she told him of the initiation of Gawen, and the task White had set her to.

David, too, looked worried as he listened. "Tara is a beautiful young woman," he said, "but very troubled. She has been through so much. Be gentle with her, Caroline, and gentle with yourself. Do not expect quick miracles."

"But miracles are exactly what I do expect," Caroline answered, smiling, and David sighed, smiled back, and led her to Tara's cabin.

"God and Goddess bless you, child," he said as he left her on the doorstep to the cabin. And Caroline could almost hear him thinking, "For you shall surely *need* blessing, child."

Caroline had become nervous about meeting this woman, and so she knocked quickly at the door, facing the inevitable.

"Come in."

Caroline went in, and was very, very surprised at her first sight of Tara. It was not at all what she had expected. Tara was petite, only five feet tall, and very, very small-boned and slender. She had a beautiful face that seemed to belong on a cameo, it was so lovely, with long blonde curls and big, soft blue eyes and delicate features. Everything about her screamed that she was a *lady*.

Then she spoke. "And just who are *you?* I was told I would be visited by someone from the Temple."

Caroline lifted her chin up proudly. "I am she. My name is Caroline."

Tara laughed. "Not even a priestess. I would have thought my situation called for some *real* help. No matter. All right. What do you plan to do with me?"

"Excuse me?"

"Are you hard of hearing? You are my...*helper*...while I am here. So *help*. What shall we do this afternoon?"

Caroline stared at her. "I-I have no idea. I guess we'll just...talk."

Tara stared at her. "Talk."

"Yes."

Tara began to laugh again, but it wasn't real laughter; it had pain in it.

"Fine. We'll *talk*. They haven't told you anything about my situation, have they?"

Caroline shook her had. "Only that you have done things which are hurting you very much," she answered.

Tara laughed again. "It figures. Well, I am certainly not going to be the one to tell you, *that's* for certain. So we'll talk. You tell me all about yourself, how's that? Tell me what it is like to be a Novice of Colors. You're supposed to be my helper, then I should know something about you. And you have to do whatever makes me comfortable. So, talk. Tell me about Caroline."

Caroline said, "Well, all right," deciding that she had absolutely nothing to lose at this point. If Tara already thought she was just a pampered Temple maiden who could not understand the problems of life, then Caroline might as well just be herself. Perhaps Tara would change her mind in time. And the snow fell hard outdoors while Caroline and Tara talked by the fire. Caroline told Tara her life story, while Tara asked questions now and then, but made no comment.

When Caroline as ready to leave, if the two were not friends, at least they were not encased in an atmosphere of icy tension. And when Tara said her farewell, she made no rude comment, but simply said, "I shall see you tomorrow."

Caroline had no idea if Tara's opinion of her had changed at all, but she felt proud that she had not pretended to be someone other than who she truly was. And she kept repeating to herself over and over in a mantra, "White knows what she is doing. White knows what she is doing. White knows what she is doing," as she went back to her room in the novices' quarters.

***

Caroline was shaking in her chair in her little room. The tension of meeting Tara had caught up to her. She had in no way expected to find the woman so closed and shut and angry. Even though White had warned her that Tara no longer believed in her own innocence, Caroline had not really comprehended what that meant. It was something that really had to be experienced to be understood.

Now she was softly crying as Red and White counseled her. One stood on either side of her chair, a hand on her shoulder, trying to offer her encouragement. White was dressed in a long white garment of flowing silk and lace, with little white slippers and a white veil of lace on her head. Red was in a flowing red peasant skirt and had on a white poet's blouse with fluffy sleeves. They both looked very concerned as Caroline spoke.

"I cannot do this. I am sure she will not in any way listen to me. I have nothing to offer her. I have not seen the horrors she has seen, and so she is firmly convinced that I will never understand. Even if she grows to trust and like me—which would take more time than a moon, she is wary as a wounded animal—even if she trusts me, she will never feel that I really can help her. She will always perceive us as different. In her mind, she is bad and I am good. And that is all there is to it, as far as she is concerned. She is one and I am the other. I truly do not know what to do. I am so afraid. She needs help; she needs *real* help. She came here to get it. If I cannot help her, someone must. Her eyes are so hurt. I do not want to leave her without assistance; it is dangerous. I fear for what she will do."

"What do you fear she will do?" asked White.

"I-I really don't know, but…but I sense that if she gets no help from the Temple, she will give up entirely."

"And how shall she do that?" asked White.

"Either she will just give in to her self-hate, and there will be no reaching her again —or her heart will break."

"And if her heart breaks?" White whispered.

"I-I don't know. But she could get very, very desperate. I can feel it. Please, please, I beg you, send someone else to her. Someone who knows what she is doing. Someone who can really help her. If I forfeit my white feather, well then, what else am I to do? We are talking about a human life here. My priestesshood would mean nothing to me if I failed this woman."

"First of all," Red snapped, "you are in the end responsible for no one else but Caroline. Your soul belongs to you, and Tara's belongs to Tara. You must understand that so long as you do your best, the failure would not be yours, but Tara's. And second of all, your priestesshood is your life. To throw that away would be to lose your life, really, and this is as terrible a thing as the loss of Tara would be. You are of equal value. You are both irreplaceable." Her green eyes stared angrily at Caroline, willing her to understand and to believe her words.

"This is so," agreed White, in a calmer voice meant to soothe. "Still,

Caroline is honestly afraid that she is the wrong woman for this task, and we must address that. Caroline, tell me, do you think I chose wrongly when I asked you to help Tara?"

"I...I do not mean to...sound...distrustful, my Lady," Caroline cried brokenly, "but I am so afraid."

"I can help with your fear. But you must trust me. I am White of the Twelve. I knew what I was doing when I asked your help. If you trust me, I can work with you. But if you do not, you effectively tie up my hands. I ask you to trust me just a little longer, Caroline. You *are* the right person to help Tara. I did not make a mistake."

"I-I know you made no mistake, Lady, but—"

"There is no 'but' in serving the Twelve, my dear child. Listen. Instead of putting your energy into all these tears and doubts, let us work together to help Tara. You have no idea why she is so hurt? She has told you nothing?"

"Nothing."

Red interrupted, "Little Bird. In your work here you have studied your magical gifts. You learned that one of them was a strong ability to visualize what would make people happiest. You can touch on their true, deepest dreams. You can inspire and encourage them to reach for those dreams. Yours is a spirit strong in optimism and hope. Use your gift now. Visualize Tara's dream. It will help you understand her."

"I need a few more days with her, my Lady Red. I am not yet close enough to her to do that."

"All right. But remember, perhaps addressing her pain directly is not the right way, if that door is shut. Perhaps you should address her joy instead." Red smiled at Caroline. "That has always been easier for you, my child. In all the ages you served me, you were always best able to work with, and through, joy."

"I think Caroline was afraid that Tara would not be receptive to joy or dreams or hopes. Caroline sees Tara as a woman unable to dream anymore. Is this not so?" White asked.

Caroline nodded quietly.

"Perhaps you were wrong," White said. "Perhaps Tara knows her pain all too well and does not need to know her pain any better. Perhaps she needs to know her joy. She may not trust you with her pain, not yet. But perhaps she will trust you to touch her dreams."

"Perhaps," said Caroline, sounding defeated and scared.

Red ruffled her curls playfully. "Now, Little Bird. I know Tara is afraid of dreams, too. But that's where you come in. Make her not afraid of them. Present her dreams to her so gently and warmly that she is not intimidated by them. Make her believe in herself. You are good at that."

"Yes," said White thoughtfully, "and there is perhaps another way we can help, child. It is simply this. If Tara feels you two are different, and she is bad, *you* must view it differently. If you run away from her and run away from her pain, you will only confirm her feelings of inferiority. You will give her the message that she is right to view you as different and unequal. I know you are scared, child. But try to feel confidence in yourself. If she has no confidence in your understanding of her, *you* must have confidence in it."

"I have none. I am very afraid she *is* right...that I cannot really understand or help her."

"Well, then, *be* afraid. But at least have enough confidence not to run. Stand still. You may be afraid, child, but you must not be afraid enough to let her push you away. Two people running in opposite directions will only create an empty space."

"I will not run," said Caroline. "I will not."

Red kissed her, leaving a bright lipstick kiss mark on her cheek. "I know you will not. I love you."

"I know, also," said White, "and I love you, too."

***

The moon continued its rise into glowing fullness, and it continued to be cold and stormy. Sometimes the snow interfered with her visits to Tara, but Caroline went there as often as she could. One warmer day, Caroline received permission to show Tara more of the grounds. They went for a long walk, and Tara saw many of the chapels and Caroline's little room.

They had become easier with each other, more relaxed, and Tara enjoyed playing with Energy. Caroline began to see that not only was

Tara beautiful, she was funny and smart as well. She often had Caroline laughing till she cried, and her observations of people were right on target. Her perception was keen and penetrating and cut past the masks people put on. Tara was very honest and demanded honesty back. Caroline began to feel great heart warmth and affection for her.

Yet all around the beautiful woman was a wall of ice, impenetrable and ever-present. No one was allowed to get really close to her. Tara was good at making people forget the wall was even there. Caroline never forgot. It was always forefront in her mind as she struggled for ways to break through the ice.

On the day Caroline showed Tara around, for some reason she felt more upset than usual about Tara's hidden inner world. She did not speak of it, but it was deeply bothering her. White seemed to sense this, for she accompanied them. Tara could not see her, but Caroline did. Caroline got much emotional support from her presence.

White looked like an angel that day. She had beautiful silver-white wings and a halo of light seemed to glow around her head. She had a silver harp in her hands and strummed it occasionally. It was very beautiful.

Caroline tried to remember what White and Red had advised her...to focus on Tara's dreams. One thing was certain: the situation could not go on like this for much longer. It was going to explode; Caroline could feel it. But it exploded a lot sooner than she expected, right there in her little room.

Tara sat on Caroline's bed, and Energy was on her shoulder. She suddenly reached out and touched the pink heart on Caroline's forehead, without warning.

"What is that for?" she asked.

Caroline was plunged into Tara's dream.

She could see, clearly, the beautiful Tara as a priestess. Her robe was mostly of white, with some silver and yellow in it. It took Caroline's breath away, she was so exquisite. But before she could begin to rejoice even for a moment in Tara's destiny, pain exploded in Caroline's heart.

She felt how strongly Tara was convinced that she could never be a priestess. She felt how painful it was for Tara to be visiting the Temple but unable to claim her right to stay there. It was so bad a situation within Tara that Tara was past the pain; she was feeling resignation instead. She was not even at all entertaining the idea of being a priestess. It was a dead dream inside her...or nearly dead. No, it still breathed...but barely. Caroline began to scream. She could not help it. The pain was like all the ice surrounding Tara had broken into tiny shards that were piercing Caroline. White held Caroline, but she just kept screaming.

Tara was frantic and about to run for help. She, too, was crying, for she believed she had done wrong in touching Caroline and had harmed her.

Then White intervened. First, she raised her hand, and Caroline stopped screaming. "I am mistress of pain and loneliness," she said to Caroline. "I know how to use them. And I know when enough is enough. The white light can be a blinding, searing pain."

Caroline sank weakly to the floor, gasping for breath, regaining control.

Meanwhile, White revealed herself to Tara, who was struck dumb at the sight of her. "I am White of the Twelve, Tara. The frozen world belongs to me. You do not own it. I am mistress of it. And as Lady of Ice, I tell you that there comes a time when the ice must melt or the land dies in eternal Winter."

Tara stood still.

"I can stop things, Tara. Freeze them into motionlessness. I do so to teach. I do so to force you to look at yourself when you are refusing to. When you move too fast to look around, I *make* you stand still. I do so now. But in the silence and stillness of the frozen world, I cannot make your decisions for you. I can only help you to look at yourself. What you do then is up to you. You have stopped running long enough to listen, because I froze you to stillness for a moment. Right now, Tara, if you tried to move or leave this room, you could not. Nor can you speak."

Tara just stared at White, feeling this to be true.

"You can listen, though. And you *shall.* Look at Caroline. Look at her. She barely held onto her sanity, Tara. She felt your dream. And she felt your refusal to accept it."

Tara became angry and tried to walk away but could not move.

"I have claimed you, Tara. You are meant to be one of my priestesses.

But you must accept *me*. You have a choice, Tara. Begin to accept your destiny, or your heart will wither up and die. There is no in-between. Talk to Caroline about this. You do not have to tell her what happened to you if you are not ready or willing. But you must speak of your desire. And your fear. I sent Caroline to you, to help you.

"If you turn from me, child, I will not stop loving you. But to turn from the face of the Twelve when they appear to you is very, very dangerous. You have lived long enough in this pain, child. I put a stop to it. I call you to end it, once and for all. Now what you do next is up to you."

White left. In Tara's hand was a white rose.

Caroline had curled up into a little ball and was softly crying. Tara knelt down next to her and put a hand on Caroline's shoulder. Caroline flinched.

"I know I caused you pain," Tara said softly. "I am sorry. I never wanted to hurt you. I should leave now."

Caroline turned and threw her arms around Tara and held her so tightly Tara could not breathe. Caroline could be surprisingly strong for one so small, and her grip now was like iron chains on Tara, because Caroline's pain added to her strength.

"Don't leave. Please. I don't know what happened to you, and I cannot pretend to fully understand your pain. But I know this much. Whatever it is could not be bad enough to cause White to stop loving you. Whatever it is is no excuse to leave White. White *loves* you. She knows what happened, and she loves you anyway. Don't turn your back on that kind of love. Whatever happened to you, White can heal it over time, but you have to *try*. You have to give her a chance."

"I am sorry," Tara whispered, "so sorry. I should not have come here. I was afraid something like this would happen. I should have known it would. This is not your fault, Caroline. Don't think that. It is me, not you. I wish you happiness in the Temple, Caroline. I wish you great happiness. I will go now."

She left the little room, shutting the door quietly behind her. Caroline grabbed her pillow from her bed and clung to it and cried into it. Tara had left behind her a great and terrible silence, a great and terrible emptiness. Before Caroline's eyes, unwavering, was the vision of Tara as Priestess. It did not falter or leave or fade. Caroline knew it never would. She had learned that a person can deny a destiny...but they cannot destroy it. It remains frozen...waiting.

***

Caroline was lost, beyond all comfort. She stayed in her room and refused to eat. She cried. She refused to see anyone, even Gawen. When one of the Twelve came to her, she just listened quietly, saying nothing, then turned her face to the wall.

Beautiful, beautiful Tara, you had so much ahead of you. Where are you now? When will the pain end?

Tara did not return. Days passed. If Tara was still in the Sanctuary, she was not willing to see Caroline, for she sent no word. More likely she had left the Temple entirely. It would explain the haunting, deep emptiness in Caroline's stomach.

At long last, the Twelve had had enough of this, as Caroline was slowly destroying herself. And they sent the one to whom she always listened, when she shut out everyone else. They sent Orange. He came to her room and sat quietly for awhile in her little wooden chair, saying nothing. Then she looked at him and burst out laughing. He had a shirt on, and on this shirt was imprinted the image of a huge, steaming plate of spaghetti.

"Orange of the Twelve is sitting in my chair in a shirt that has a picture of spaghetti on it," she giggled, as she went to him and threw her arms around him. As soon as the strong, loving arms were around her, she felt better.

He stroked her hair and shoulders. "What is all this I hear, Little Bird?"

She nestled closer to him, as if to bury herself in his warmth. "You know all that has happened."

"I know you're driving yourself crazy in this room. That's what I know. Come on. We're getting out of here."

"Where are we going?"

"I think it's time you saw a part of *my* kingdom."

The room around her disappeared. She was in a field outdoors. A beautiful white Pegasus was pawing the ground, her wings beating anxiously, eager to fly.

"Lady White," Caroline breathed, for she could see that the proud animal had the silver-blue eyes of Lady White.

"Of course. She is worried. She needed to come," said Orange.

They climbed up on the Pegasus' back and soon were flying into a sky of many-colored stars and lights. The sky looked like a wild kaleidoscope. Caroline clung to Orange and the horse, and they flew high and fast.

A beautiful orange planet shone in the distance, glowing like orange flames. Down, down, down they went. They landed—in a Ferris wheel! The Pegasus had changed into a tiny white faerie, who looked just like White did when larger but could fit on Caroline's shoulder and whisper in her ear. A tiny, white-winged, silvery little faerie.

The wheel spun. Caroline saw around her an amusement park such as the one she had seen once as a child...but so big and grand and colorful it made her crave to see it all. The wheel spun round. Sometimes far off in the distance, at the top, Caroline could see distant places of the kingdom...very unlike this part. A wild jungle. A magic castle. A museum. She felt, more than saw, it all. Other times, as the wheel spun, she could only see the park itself.

"Do you know what this really is?" Orange whispered in her ear. It was a warm, summery day here, and an ice cream cone appeared in her hands.

"N-no."

"Eat your cone. It's dripping."

Obediently, she began to lick her cone.

Orange went on in between bites of his own. "This is the wheel of fortune. It goes up, it goes down, and back up, and back down. It is a symbol of the cycles of life, Caroline. And—when you really are in a *magical* amusement park, like *this* one—it gives you visions. Glimpses. You never know what you'll see from the top."

They reached the top, and Caroline saw a forest below. The next time, a mountain village. The next time, her old childhood home. The visions only lasted as long as the wheel stayed on top. Caroline was about to question this, when Orange answered. "A moment of fortune, good or bad, is only *now*. You must live it *now*. That is the lesson of the wheel."

Caroline nodded. "Yes, my Lord."

White whispered in her other ear. "You release, my child. Release and accept, release and accept. Release and accept."

"I cannot release Tara."

"No, no. Release the moment. Release the moment when she left!" Orange said. "Here." He handed her a balloon. "Wait till we reach the top," he said, "then let it go. And with it, let go of that moment. It is gone. This is a *new* one."

Caroline did as he asked and watched the orange balloon fly off into the red-orange sky of this strange, wondrous land. She felt free, and she started laughing and hugged Orange and made their seat on the Ferris wheel rock. "I love you," she cried out, laughing and kissing his cheek, and crying a little. "I love you."

"You got ice cream on my shirt," he said.

She looked down and saw that indeed she had gotten his shirt dirty with her ice cream. But the picture of the appetizing-looking plate of spaghetti was gone. In its place was a picture of a grinning chimpanzee with a top hat on his head.

Caroline laughed and laughed and laughed. In between her laughter, she said to Orange, "I am going to do what you suggested I do with Green. I am going to paint the things I cannot say in words. I am going to paint the vision I had of Tara as a Priestess of White, and Silver, and Yellow. I am going to *paint* how beautiful she is. Then, wherever she is, I am going to *find* her. Even if I have to send every messenger of the Temple after her! I swear it, I will find her. And then I will *make* her look at herself, just as Blue made *me* look at myself. I am going to do this. And whatever she does next is up to her. She has the choice. But at least I will have done my best to show her."

White flew up and kissed Caroline's cheek lightly. Orange kissed it more exuberantly, letting out a little whoop. Even the small elf who was running the wheel made a victory motion with his arms, so they could see it from their lofty perch. Caroline made the sign back to him.

"Now is not a time for tears," Orange said almost in a hiss in her ear. "Now is a time for joy. Remember, joy is your power, Caroline." The wheel stopped a long while on top. "See?" he said. "At times the wheel gets stuck awhile. You never know when or for how long. That's part of the adventure."

"My frozen space in time," said White, fluttering to Caroline's ear so she could be heard.

The wheel began to turn again. "But see, it always goes forward again," said Orange. "Always, Caroline. Remember that."

"I promise," she said and kissed his cheek again.

A blur of colors spinning. A wild, kaleidoscope sky. Whirling back, back....Caroline was in her bed, sleeping the first good sleep she had known in days. When she woke...she had a large, healthy breakfast, for she found she was famished...and then...she began to paint!

***

The moon shone full and round and beautiful in the sky. That day, Caroline had finished her painting for Tara, and she was filled with an eerie calm. She knew, deep inside, that with this painting, she had done everything she could do for her friend. She knew Tara might or might not listen. She had accepted this. The next day she planned to seek Tara out. But now she felt tired and achy and sore, and a little restless. Snow had fallen softly that day, and the world was blanketed in soft white. She decided to go for a walk to enjoy the moon.

She walked a little longer than she'd planned and was very cold. As she looked around her, she saw a small cave and decided to enter it for awhile to get out of the wind before she began to walk back. It was a small cave, and when she entered it she found to her surprise an old woman already there. She had a little fire going in a torch she carried and was warming herself by it.

"Well. No one has come here in a long, long while," the woman laughed hoarsely. "Welcome, girl. Sit beside me. A little fire can go a long way on a night like this."

"Thank you," Caroline said and began to warm her hands and face by the torchlight which the woman had placed between some rocks.

"I'm curious, girl. How came you to be here tonight?"

Always one to love to talk, Caroline told the friendly stranger her story. When she was done, the woman laughed and patted her on the back. "Yes, you're a sweet one. You'll do just fine. Just fine."

Caroline began to feel a little odd. She was seeing strange shapes on the walls, in the shadows. "I should be getting back," she said.

The woman peered intently at her. "Something wrong?"

"No, no. I just feel...odd. For one thing, it just occurred to me to ask something I should have asked a long time ago. What are you doing here? You are no priestess. You are out alone on a very bad night. Why?"

Before her eyes, the woman's image wavered and became a young woman. She was not beautiful so much as captivating, her face full of grooves and planes and hollows and shadows that told little stories.

"Your face tells a thousand stories," Caroline explained.

The woman had dark black and brown hair and the same unique black-brown skin. She said, "I am the faerie of this cave; this is my home. I am the spirit of this cave. It is a place sacred to the faeries. A long time ago a spell was put upon this cave by the faeries, that none would find it without special reason and the blessing of the faerie folk. You would not be here without reason. But you must tell me that reason, or I cannot let you leave."

"But I know no reason why I came here other than shelter!" cried Caroline.

The woman's face set firmly in a stubborn expression. "Then you must try to remember." Caroline realized the woman looked very much like stone...and she had learned how immovable Brown could be.

"I don't know," she said helplessly.

"Talk to me, then. You'll remember," the faerie promised. She turned back into the old woman again. "Talk to me."

So Caroline did. And as she did, she remembered the day the faeries had told her that in return for her magical paintbrush, she was to create a special faerie chapel in a cave. She was to paint it and make it beautiful... a place for faeries and those who loved them, to honor the Faerie Way.

"This must be the place!" she said excitedly.

The old woman nodded. "We have waited for you a long time," she said in a strange, hollow, echo-y voice. "We always knew you would come when the time was right. Return here in the Spring. If it is a good day for you to work here, you will find the cave. If it is not, you will not find it. This is a very sacred place, Caroline of the forest. It belongs to a time when the people held the earth sacred. Now we protect it. And you shall be a part of the magic. Go now. Return home. It is late, and you must rest."

"I will return in the Spring," promised Caroline.

She left the cave, and the woman said, "Do not look back until you are outside again, or it will be hard for you to leave. This place calls you with a powerful magic, but it is not yet time."

"Thank you," said Caroline and bowed and left. Obediently, she did not look back until she was out in the woods again. When she did, the cave was gone, and only snow piled softly where it had been.

***

Caroline went in the morning to the Sanctuary and met with David.

"She's still here," he said worriedly, as he poured her tea. "But she has told me, Caroline, that she will see no one. I'm sorry—especially you. She was firm on this point, Caroline. She would only stay here if she were allowed total privacy. I told her forthrightly that she was making a big mistake. Lady Black is here to protect us but *not* to hide behind! There was no swaying her. I am sorry, Caroline. I am quite worried. I feel her retreating more every day. But this must be her decision. She and she alone can decide to reach for help, in the end." David looked sad, his brow furrowed with worry.

Caroline gently touched his arm in reassurance. "This is true, David. It is her choice. Do not be afraid. White will protect her. Here. I have made this portrait of her as I saw her in a vision. She is destined to be a Priestess of White, Silver, and Yellow—if she will! Will you see that she gets this, David? What she does after that will be up to her."

David looked at the painting a long time. "Yes. I promise, Caroline. Tara will receive this today." And for awhile they just sat together, looking at the painting, sharing the pain...and the hope.

***

Caroline had a dream that night. She had truly put away all the situation with Tara, allowing the Universe to work its will. She slept deeply and dreamed of a beautiful ballroom. The crystal chandeliers glowed, sending prisms of color. Soft music flooded in from the very walls, it seemed, but the only people she saw were Silver and White. They were dancing. Silver looked dashing in a silver-gray tuxedo, and White looked like a princess in a flowing white ballgown. She had on long white gloves and a little crystal tiara in her hair, which she had pulled up in an exotic, elegant style around her face. Diamonds danced on her ears and around her neck and on her wrists. They had eyes only for each other. They were staring at each other as they danced, and Caroline knew that, for them, the rest of the world had fallen away.

With her heart in her eyes, Caroline watched them. They were so beautiful. White had a white rose in one hand, and Silver had a white rose pinned on his tuxedo. The music flowed into her soul as Caroline listened and watched, enraptured and enchanted. It seemed as if spirals of silver and white danced around the couple in the air as they moved.

White had a faint blush to her pale cheeks, and her eyes were glowing. Those bright red lips were trembling with love as she looked up at Silver, her pale blue eyes lit with silver sparkles in them, as if she had taken silver into herself. They were full and expressive, and as Caroline watched, a single tear fell on her cheek. Then Caroline was alone, in darkness, but the single tear was floating in the air above her, glowing with white light.

White spoke clearly in the darkness, in a voice that surrounded Caroline. "Behold, that which gives us the greatest sorrow can also give us the greatest joy. Behold, tears can be shed of love and happiness as well as pain. Take this crystal teardrop."

The tear flowed into Caroline's hand, where it became a beautiful snowy-white crystal.

"Give this to my beloved Tara if she chooses to return to the Temple. I wait for her here. Tell her this is the tear White cried for love's sweet sake." And White was gone.

When Caroline awoke, she remembered the dream. A snowy-white crystal and a white rose lay on the pillow beside her. She carefully put the crystal on her table for Tara. It seemed to pulse with power and life. But Tara did not come that day, or the next, or the next.

White spent much time with Caroline, as they waited. One night she said, "We deserve a special treat!" and clapped her hands together.

Caroline found herself suddenly outdoors in a snowy field. A beautiful silver sleigh was there, with six white-winged horses prancing, waiting to fly! Silver held the reins.

"We are going for a ride," said White. "Get in."

Caroline didn't need to be asked twice. She jumped right in beside White.

They took to the sky, and Caroline was ecstatic. Little silver bells jangled as the horses flew. White had put her little mittened hand on top of Silver's as he drove the horses, and she was laughing. She had on a long, beautiful white coat, the hood of which framed her face in fluffy white fur.

Below them the sky changed. It was no longer black, but glowing white with silver clouds and tints and sparkles and spirals in it. Caroline gasped aloud at the beauty. Below them lay a beautiful world. White mountain peaks. Silvery forests and enchanted silver-blue springs and lakes. Fields of white flowers. Crystal caves. A beautiful faerie-tale white and silver castle. It was a land of enchantment, of faeries and magic and peaceful quietude. Caroline could not see much, for they did not get too close. But she could feel it so strongly she almost exploded with longing.

"My home," whispered White, "will always be open to you, Little Bird. Whenever you need it, come. And I will shelter you, until you need to leave."

The words were so beautiful and said so lovingly that Caroline began to cry. She lay her head on White's shoulder, and White put an arm around her. They rode the magical sleigh into the silvery white sky until, without a word, Silver turned them around and took Caroline back home.

***

More than a week had passed since Caroline had left her painting with David, and Tara had not responded. Caroline had begun to deal seriously with the possibility that Tara would *never* respond. Then something terrible happened, something that would give Caroline nightmares for the rest of her life. She returned to her room one night to find the painting there on her table. But it had been attacked. It had been chopped at with a sharp blade, cuts were all over it. Little chunks were missing or marred forever. In addition, a big red X had been painted over it.

First Caroline went totally still, then she began to scream as if she would never stop. Elizabeth Anne and Katerina came, hearing her heart screaming from their rooms. And a little later Gawen came, having run the whole way, looking frantic and terrified. He grabbed Caroline as if he would never let go.

Some of the Twelve came as well. White and Silver and Red and Orange. White gently placed a cloth over the painting. She went to Caroline and held her. "Little Bird," she said, her voice trembling, "I know you are hurt. But you must understand something. Tara is expressing her pain. The priestess in her was violated and attacked. She is getting some of that pain out of her. It is better that she is feeling, even if it is anguish and pain. Your painting has helped her, child, and I know this frightens you. But it is going to be all right, I promise. I want to fix the painting, Caroline, with a wave of my hand. I can make it be as it was. But I cannot do it. Not unless Tara lets me. I am sorry, Caroline."

Katerina said, "Lady White, what shall be done with the painting in the meanwhile? I surely isn't right to leave it in Little Bird's room!"

"No. I shall take it. The priestess belongs to me, whether or not she is cut and mutilated."

Silver spoke. "I love you, my wife."

White's face was still and calm, very expressionless. "When you need the painting, it will be here, Little Bird." And suddenly it seemed to Caroline that White looked very, very old. Her eyes held an ageless, eternal sadness. Caroline impulsively kissed White's pale cheeks, longing to take the sadness away. White made a sign of blessing over her head, and then the members of the Twelve left, taking the painting with them.

"Stay with her," Red said to Elizabeth Anne and Katerina, who were crying. They promised to.

That night, Elizabeth Anne and Katerina slept on Caroline's floor on blankets. Gawen stayed as well and held Caroline all night. She did not speak, or cry, or even move. She stayed still and motionless, wrapped in his arms, staring out into the darkness with wide, unblinking eyes. Until the morning came.

***

Caroline was awakened by a knock on her door, but she only buried her face in Gawen's shoulder. She was not ready to face the world. Elizabeth Anne answered the door instead. It was Tara.

When Caroline realized this, she sat upright, staring at the woman in the doorway. Elizabeth Anne was looking at Caroline to see what she wished to do next. "Come in," Caroline said softly.

Tara looked terrible. Her blonde hair was a mess, her eyes wild and red from crying. Her clothes were rumpled, and she looked ill. Caroline felt a wave of compassion move through her.

"I need to talk to Caroline," said Tara. "Alone."

Elizabeth Anne and Katerina exchanged worried glances, but Caroline nodded. Upon seeing this, Gawen sent Caroline a message in her mind to meet him later that morn. Wordlessly, they all slipped out of the room, leaving Caroline and Tara alone. The room was suddenly very, very silent.

Tara looked down at the floor, then into Caroline's eyes. "I am sorry I did that to your painting."

Caroline nodded quietly. "Thank you for saying that."

Tara flushed. "I had no right to touch your work." She began to pace. "But you— you had no right to do that to me! You threw my dreams in my face! Why? Why did you do that? Did you want to hurt me? Why would you want to hurt me?"

Caroline ran to Tara and embraced her and spoke in a gentle voice full of emotion. "No! No, my friend, I did not want to hurt you."

Tara was softly crying into Caroline's shoulder. "Well, you did."

"I am sorry, Tara. I am sorry. I never meant to hurt you," Caroline comforted her.

Tara pulled away and looked at Caroline. "All right. We both did not mean to hurt each other. Yet, we did. We have said we are sorry for it. It is why I came. Thank you, Caroline." She began to walk out.

"You were so beautiful," Caroline whispered.

Tara's hand stilled on the door, her back rigid. "Do not do this, Caroline. I am warning you. Do not do this."

Caroline laughed gently. "Oh, Tara. Do you think anything you do to me could hurt more than what happened last night? You have nothing left to hurt me with, Tara. You denied my friendship and cut at my painting of you. It hurt, but I am free now. You see, Tara, now I have nothing left to lose." She began to walk towards Tara, closer. "You do, though. You are afraid."

Tara did not move or speak.

Caroline put a hand on her shoulder. "I have something to say to you, Tara. And either I will say it to your face or I will say it in your sleep. I'll haunt you till you hear it. Make it easier on yourself. Listen now."

Tara turned towards her slowly. "You say I have more left to lose. But I have lost it all, too. I have lost my dream. Say what you wish. It does not matter now."

"You are wrong. You do have something left to lose. And it does matter. All right. I will speak. In this very moment, Tara, right now... as you stand here...are you doing anything wrong? Are you acting hatefully?"

"No."

"Then in this moment you are innocent. In this moment you are pure, and you can choose whether to be loving...or not."

"No. The past is a part of me now."

"A part which could be put to good use," Caroline snapped. "You should use your compassion for the pain of others because you have suffered yourself and you understand. There are other women like you who do not feel worthy of the Temple. Who have been attacked in many different ways. Physically. Emotionally. You can reach them, Tara. You can turn your horrible past into something priceless and valuable..."

"You do not understand," cried Tara. "You do not understand what happened. It is too late. I..."

"*Stop!*" cried Caroline. "I have decided that, for now, I do not want to know. Oh, someday, yes. But right now I want you most of all to understand that whatever you did does not matter. It is in the past. What matters is that you do not feel pure. Maybe a man stole your innocence. Maybe you stole from another. Maybe you were cruel and vicious. Maybe you were attacked physically. Maybe you hurt someone else. Don't you see? It just doesn't matter. Right here, right now, matters.

"You are given a moment, Tara. A pure, clean, white moment. And maybe, before, you made a bad choice. Maybe, before, someone hurt you. Now you're making *another* choice. Now you're letting that person hurt you *again*. Because you are giving yet another clean, white moment *up*. Throwing it away. And *you don't have to!*" Caroline yelled the last sentence, shaking Tara's shoulders. "You don't have to," she said more quietly. "You can choose to do something *good* instead."

Tara was crying. "I can't get the stain out. You say the moment is white. Maybe it is. But I-I am not."

"Yes, you are, as much as a newborn baby. In this moment you are neither bad or good. You are free to choose."

"A newborn baby! What happened to me, *happened!* It won't go away."

"No. It won't. But if you make the rest of your life into something special and good and beautiful, the past becomes different. It becomes part of a beautiful story."

"Caroline, I-"

"Shh," Caroline put a finger on Tara's lips. "What I think is, you have talked enough. Just do it. *Now.* No more talk."

Tara looked at her with tear-filled eyes. "I do not feel pure, Caroline."

"No novice does! We stay anyway." Remembering the crystal teardrop, Caroline hugged Tara. "Come on. We are going to see the people in the admissions offices. You are going to be a novice as of today."

Tara began to laugh. "You are bossy. It is as simple as that?"

Caroline laughed back. "I'll show you just how simple it is!"

By late afternoon Tara's things had been moved into her new room in the Novices' quarters. Caroline was helping her to unpack and settle in.

"I do not understand," Tara said, sitting dazed on the bed. "I came to you to apologize about the painting and leave the Temple. Now I am staying. How did this happen?"

Caroline laughed. "Come on. I am doing all the work here!"

Absently Tara began handing clothes to Caroline to hang up. "Caroline, is this a dream?"

Caroline grinned at her. "I'll introduce you to everyone at supper."

Tara began to laugh. "This is crazy. You are crazy."

Caroline hugged her. "*Life* is crazy. So enjoy it."

Tara squeezed her hard. "Little Bird. Thank you."

As Caroline held her, she saw something on the wall that hadn't been there before, and her eyes grew wide. Slowly, she pulled away from Tara, and pointed. "Look."

The painting of Tara as a Priestess of White, Silver, and Yellow was on her wall...unmarked, untouched, exactly as Caroline had first done it.

"I may have done the painting," Caroline whispered softly, "but the beauty was inside you."

***

It was the first night Tara was in her room as a novice. She looked around her, head spinning, unable to really understand that this was not a dream. She had dreamed of it so often that surely, *surely* that's what this was—one more dream from which she'd wake and cry in the hidden hours before dawn when she realized where she *truly* was.

But no. No. The little table, the little bed, the view of the grounds from her window—they were still there, not disappearing. She sat down in her chair, in her room, in her Temple. She laughed and said the words again. Her Temple. Her beloved Temple.

The faces came. She had known they would. Their black and shadowed forms filled her room. Many had come tonight. That she had expected as well. They stared at her. Some had hollow eyes; some had cold, yellow eyes; some had black pits for eyes. Some had no eyes. She did not scream. These were old and familiar faces to her. The horror of them did not panic her as it used to. She had learned long ago to look straight into what a human spirit could do to itself—and survive.

The leader spoke. "Well done. We have never had one of our own in the Temple before. You have opened up many doors for us. Doors we have wanted open a long time."

Tara laughed. "I stopped serving you a long time ago, remember?"

The voice ignored her, continuing on politely. "Of course, one of us is not enough. We will expect you to open the door to your sisters and brothers. But this was a fine start. A fine start."

"I have no sisters or brothers among you anymore. My sisters and brothers are of the Temple."

The voice ignored her again. "We wish to show you our appreciation; we always reward good and faithful service."

Tara grew afraid. She never liked their "gifts". "I want nothing from you. I did nothing for you."

"Your lack of greed is commendable. We have such power and wealth. Too many serve us just for what they can get from us. Not out of passion and devotion to our Creed, our Way. But you, you were always special. You never thought of yourself; you only cared about finding the best way to serve us. Well, your loyalty has paid off. You have entered one of the last places on the planet to which we have had no access. So. We will let you see him."

Tara went absolutely still. "There is no need for that. I left him with you. It was the price you demanded for my freedom. I do not wish to see what you have done to him."

"Now, now. I know you are upset. You miss the boy. We understand. But there was no choice. You had gotten into a bad crowd, gotten some bad ideas. We needed a way to control you. You were becoming a danger to yourself. As responsible guardians, we had to set boundaries. But now that you have shown yourself to be more mature and committed to the Way, there is hope. Perhaps you can be reunited with the boy someday. We will see. Continue to serve us well in your new position, and we will see."

"I do not want to see him! Leave this room!"

"Oh, Tara. You seek to punish yourself for any harm you did us as an adolescent. Punishment and discipline must be tempered with justice and fairness. Too much discipline, and you could grow to hate and resent us, instead of loving and serving us. And that's not the point at all. Discipline should bring one closer to one's guardian, or it was poorly thought out discipline."

"Leave!"

"Of course. You are tired. We will leave you to your sleep. But first, our gift."

"Nooooo!"

The faces left. The vision came. Tara could not stop it. A little boy, with her light curls and blue eyes. He was dressed for bed with a stuffed animal in his arms.

"Mommy!"

She got herself under control. She managed to smile. "Michael." Her voice was filled with missing him.

"I wish I could hug you and kiss you goodnight, mommy. I asked, but they said 'no, not yet'. Are you being good, mommy? Are you doing bad things to the Way anymore? I want to see you again."

She was crying softly as she saw the worried wrinkles on the little forehead and the sad eyes of her baby. "Yes, honey. Mommy is being good. Very, very good."

The face brightened. "That's what they told me. They said you did a good job for us today, a big job. I am proud of you, mommy. I know you're not a bad person, like they say. I know you're good. You love the Way."

Tara's nails dug into her palms. *Love the Way.* No matter what, the Way comes first.

"I love you, Michael. Go to bed, sweetheart."

He blew her a kiss with two chubby hands. "I love you too, mommy. Be good. I want to see you. Be good."

"You be good, too. Behave for Monika."

A woman emerged from the shadows of the dimly lit little boy's bedroom. "He's a perfect little gentleman, Tara. We hope to see you soon." She smiled at Tara, who almost got sick to her stomach.

"Take care of him."

"Oh, we will," the woman said brightly. "You know he's in good hands until you're ready to come back."

Tara laughed to herself, a little hysterically. *Come back. When you come back.* No. She forced a smile. "Goodnight, honey."

"Goodnight, mommy. I love you."

"Goodnight, Tara. Congratulations. We're all proud of you," smiled Monika.

"Th-thank you."

The vision left. Tara ran to her bathroom and vomited. When she was done, she crawled weakly into bed. There were no tears. She was past tears. There was no sleep, this first night as a Novice of the Temple of the Twelve. There were only lonely, quiet hours, like so many that had gone before.

Michael. My baby. When the moment comes that I must choose you... or the life of a true Priestess...may I have the strength. Help me have the strength.

In the end...I know what comes first.

***

On the last day of the moon, Caroline returned to the chapel where she had met White. She stood before White's little altar of white candles and flowers and stared into the stained glass window. Once again she was transported to the snowy field where she had first seen the Lady. Once again she awaited her sweet presence.

White came. She was dressed in a brilliant white robe. A white veil that hung to the ground covered her head. She was dressed very plainly, and though snow was on the ground, she wore no shoes. Though snow was all around, she had an armful of white roses.

"Caroline." Her voice was full of tenderness.

"My Lady."

"Tara has come home."

Caroline's smile was brilliant. "Yes, my Lady. She has."

"What of you, my child? What have you learned?"

"I have learned that we are all created innocent. And recreated innocent over and over again."

The Lady smiled gently. "Do you think that your ideas of Innocence have changed?"

Caroline thought about this. "They have formed more clearly. My Lady, I have imagined Tara in every possible scenario that I could think of. I imagined her stealing, or cruelly breaking the heart of someone. I imagined her lying, or witnessing a murder. I imagined as many things as I could being done to her, and her angry responses and actions to those brutalities. Nothing mattered. All I could see, in the end, was my vision of Tara as your Priestess, my Lady."

White nodded solemnly. "There will come a day when Tara will need to share her past. I want you to be there when that day comes, child. Will you give me your solemn promise that when Tara reaches out her hand to you—and she *will*, Caroline—that your hand will be reaching back?"

"Yes."

"Know, too, that innocence is not merely the absence of hate and evil and cruelty. Innocence is the presence of love. It is an active force. Help Tara to love, Caroline. Continue to teach her how to trust and how to give. She will have much work to do before she feels worthy of the white robe I wish to give her. Be her friend."

"I will. I am. Always."

"Little Bird. You were attacked this moon yourself. Your painting was ruined. Though I returned it to you whole again, you suffered much. I know the image still gives you nightmares. What have you learned about innocence as one whose creativity was attacked?"

"I learned that no one and nothing can really take away innocence. Though my painting was ruined, the vision that inspired it remained pure in my heart. Even when I thought Tara had left the Temple forever, the vision remained untouched."

"What if she *had* left?"

"My Lady, if she had left, if she had abandoned her own dream, I would have kept a place in my heart waiting for her. And I would have turned to you, my Lady, to keep me strong."

"And if she *never* returned?"

"Then I would have continued to thank you for the beautiful vision, and I would have let her go. But I would never stop loving her."

"I believe you," said White. "What you say is true. You would have done as you say. Tara will make a fine priestess, Caroline. She is a good, strong, loving woman who has much to give and deeply aches to be able to give it! What you have done, Caroline, affects not only Tara, but the Temple of the Twelve as well. She will give much to the Temple... because she was strong enough to dare to give even when she thought she had nothing to give.

"You, too, will be a fine priestess, my child. The Temple is a place of morality and integrity. Cruelty, lies, hate and evil are not the foundations of the Temple. Right action is. Yet you have understood that sometimes beauty grows in wild, harsh climates and is born of pain."

With a flourish she released the roses, throwing them up into the air, and they became a dozen white-winged doves, who flew off.

One flew over Caroline, and a beautiful, snowy-white feather fell to the ground. Caroline picked it up. As she did, she heard White say, "Love is the only law that truly matters, and love has many faces. This is my gift to you. We love you, Caroline."

When Caroline stood up, feather in hand, White was gone. She found herself back in the chapel, before the little altar and stained glass window. A white feather was in her hand. She lit a candle and prayed there. She prayed for a long time. She prayed for Tara to have the strength to become the Priestess she was born to be. She prayed the same for herself, and for true Innocence to dwell in her spirit. But perhaps most of all, she prayed for wisdom on that day when Tara reached out her hand and asked for Caroline to help heal her past.

Even if White had not told her this day was coming, Caroline would have sensed it. It was there in Tara's eyes, like an approaching, distant storm. And Caroline meant to be ready.

Chapter Twelve

The New Moon night came, and it was not stormy or too cold. So those novices that wished to bundled up in coats and scarves and hats and even blankets to make the walk once more up the Hill. And Caroline was one of them. She was three times her normal size, so many layers of clothes did she have on. But she was happily singing and chanting behind her scarf.

With a joyous heart, Caroline looked at the faces of the novices. Many of the women she had first walked the Hill with were priestesses now. Now *she* was the one whom the newer novices gazed at with big eyes, whispering, "She has completed ten tasks!" behind their hands and bowing to her as she passed. It had seemed to Caroline that she might well miss the rapture of being a brand new novice, but it was not so. In every day she spent at the Temple, she embarked on a new adventure of learning. The learning never stopped, and Caroline began to understand that it would always be thus.

She laid her offering at the stone altar. The candles and torches looked very pretty against the snow. The familiar prayers came to her lips. "Beloved and beautiful one, come, come show me your face, and I will show you mine...."

A ball of glowing light appeared before her. Caroline watched as it grew brighter, stronger, while her heart raced. When the light was very,

Novice of Colors

very big, she saw the shape of a man in the center. It came clearer, and clearer. Soon she could see his long, golden curls hanging to his shoulder blades, his flashing, fiery blue eyes. He had golden tanned skin, and the words that came to her mind to describe it were "sun-kissed". He was very strong and muscular, not as lean and narrow and trim as Silver, or Blue. No, this man was large, and very rock-solid, and very strong. He wore a gold robe that Caroline was beginning to be afraid would blind her, it was so bright. She tried not to shield her eyes or turn them away, but it was difficult, as looking on the brightness was painful. She tried to look into the blue eyes, but that was only a little better.

Remembering herself suddenly, she bowed low to him. He bowed back. When he stood up, she saw that he was smiling. It was like the sun, and made her gasp. He was incredibly, incredibly handsome.

"I am Gold," he said, and his voice was as powerful and booming as the rest of him and nearly knocked Caroline over.

"My Lord," she said. "I feel as if I do not know you well. And yet, I should, for the golden sun rises each day."

"You feel you do not know me because I am a color of enhancement. I decorate other colors and bring them out. I make them appear more startlingly brilliant. But a color who accents other colors can often be forgotten himself. You might notice a gold frame, but more you notice the painting within it; you might notice a gold necklace, but more the woman who is wearing it."

"That is not as it should be!"

"It is exactly as it should be. Myself alone, if you look upon me too deeply, directly, you are blinded. It is the same as looking into the sun. No one stares at me directly for too long. Without realizing it, Caroline, you have several times glanced away already."

"It is also because you are so handsome," Caroline said shyly. "Almost too much to look at."

Gold laughed, and it was a loud, full, rich, booming, rumbling laugh. "I like your honesty, girl," he said. "Very much."

"What else is Gold, my Lord?"

"Perhaps you should tell *me*, Caroline."

"Gold within the earth...this creates wealth and luxury and riches.

Are you a Lord of wealth, then?"

He laughed again. "Rather, of abundance, which does not always require wealth. Grains in the field can be golden. Think, Caroline. What else?"

"Wedding rings."

"Because gold is a color of permanence and also of purity. Yes, what else?"

"I cannot think."

"A king's crown. Gold is rulership and power. It is radiant health. It is also a color of victory and triumph."

"Yes, I see all these things. Yet—"

"What is it?"

"Green is abundant, white is pure, silver also enhances other colors, red is a color of power. I know all things are connected, but how are you *different?*"

"It is as I said. Gold enhances and can easily be forgotten."

"This seems odd. You are like a roaring lion. Who can forget you? Or the sun?"

"No, no, child. The sun is not pure gold. It is yellow, red, orange, white, as well. You see?"

"Yes."

"*Pure* gold is just that. Pure. The victory and abundance I offer, the health and power, come from purity of being. Perhaps that, too, is why gold is so rare. It is a color to strive for, to work for, more than a color to live moment to moment with. You understand?"

"Yes. I think I do."

"People spend lifetimes in search of gold, and often it does not bring them the joy they expected because they sought it for the wrong reason."

"Gold is treasure."

"Yes. Hidden treasure, sometimes. Other times not. It is a color of glory. It glorifies all it touches."

"How is 'glorify' different than 'enhance'?"

"To glorify is to bring out your own love of something. To enhance is to simply support another."

"And gold is glory?"

"Gold is glory."

Caroline thought on these things for awhile, then said, "I have much to learn. Will you help me? Give me a task to help me know you better?"

"Gold. Have you noticed how closely it resembles the words 'God' and 'Goodness'?"

Caroline had not.

"You see, child, I have given you much information about gold, yet you still do not really know what it is. That is often the way with me. Gold is elusive. It inspires the feeling of a quest. Would you like to go on a quest, Caroline?"

Caroline clapped her hands. "Oh, yes! Even the word makes me shiver!"

Gold laughed again. "Good! Do you recall how Brown asked Susannah to find a buried treasure, and she had such trouble because the treasure was within herself?"

"Yes. It was her voice...her incredible voice."

"Hidden treasure—that is a part of gold that lives in the earth. Part of gold is in the sky. Either way, the thrill is in the search, and the journey. I am sending you on a treasure hunt as well. I will leave you clues. You must first recognize the clues, then solve them."

"They are riddles?"

"Some."

"Is the treasure physical or spiritual?"

"Both, Little Bird. Both. As I am both."

Caroline frowned. "Will this be very difficult to solve?"

"Parts are easier than others."

"And this is my task?"

"Yes. To bring me the physical treasure I have hidden and understand what the spiritual power of the treasure is."

237

Caroline began to jump up and down. "When do I start?"

Gold laughed, and it echoed and resounded in her heart. She knew she would never forget it. "You already have, Caroline. You already have."

***

Caroline decided that she wanted to paint a large mural about her treasure hunt. She wanted it to tell the story of the search Gold put her on, from start to finish. She spoke to Katerina, and Katerina spoke to the Temple Elders. A place was chosen. In one of the chapels of Gold, there was a room (it was a larger chapel and had three rooms). One room in particular was not very decorated, and the Elders agreed to let Caroline paint her story on one wall, with Katerina's supervision. So they went to the chapel one day to see it.

When one became a priestess, if one were a priestess of only one color, it was possible to live in a building with only priestesses of that color, if you chose. These were not large buildings, but they enabled a priestess to focus very exclusively on her color if she wished. Such a building had a chapel of that color attached to it, of course, and it was there that Caroline went...to the building where the Priestesses of Gold lived. It was a beautiful building, round in structure and ornate, with carvings and gold designs on the outer walls and a heavy gold door, also elaborately carved. It housed thirty women, though right now there were only twenty-one.

Katerina and Caroline were ushered in by a beautiful priestess named Thomasina. She was tall and stately, formal and quiet, and her golden robe looked to be made of the finest silk. Caroline knew that not only the color, but the style and texture of a robe, showed the nature of the priestess. Thomasina's robe showed elegance, simplicity, and dignity.

She took them to the chapel where they would be working and spending so much time this moon. As the Elders had said, it was not very finished. The room was small, with a golden carpet and white walls. But other than the simple chairs placed there (which were plain wood and did not seem to fit the environment at all), and the altar table, the room was undecorated.

The altar table was also white, with gold inlaid in it in beautiful designs. The cloth was lovely and matched the gold designs of the table.

There was a small statue of Gold himself, made entirely of the precious metal that bore his name. And a few gold candles were in holders in the wall. That was all.

"We do most of our worship in the next room," Thomasina explained and showed them a much finer one. A gold and crystal chandelier hung from the ceiling. Beautiful gold velvet curtains hung at the windows. This room, too, was carpeted in gold, and there were fine mosaics on the wall. These chairs were white, inlaid with gold, with gold cushions. There were gold chalices encrusted with jewels, and gold and yellow candles in a candelabra. There was a small gold fountain and gold offering plates.

Caroline felt a little clumsy and awkward, afraid she would break something. Thomasina smiled at her expression. "Our Lord can be primitive and rough, like Brown, or celestial and sophisticated, like Blue," she said. "It all depends on what mood you catch him in." And she winked at Caroline.

From that moment on Caroline felt at home in the chapel, fine as it was. She noticed the gold, roaring lion statues and caressed and kissed them. Yes, Gold was a lion. A King. Graceful, yet strong. Proud. Roaring. Sleek and smooth, yet rough and wild, with a wild mane of hair.

Laying offerings at the altars, she set to work, painting her meeting with Gold on the Hill of Novices on a small portion of the wall, on its left side. The story would unfold left to right. Katerina watched and assisted. When she was done, seven Gold Priestesses who happened to be home at the time gathered to see the start of the mural. They were all excited and near tears to see their Lord painted with exquisite love. They hugged Caroline and blessed her and wished her success.

Caroline was a little overwhelmed. All the gold robes flashed and shone and stunned her a little. She kept blinking at the brightness and wasn't able to speak much. She felt dazzled. She looked at the blank spot on the wall, as the Gold Priestesses patted and praised and thanked her, and she wondered what she'd be painting on the rest. She did not dare to think of failure.

Before she left, she painted on the top of the wall the words, "Lord of Treasures". This was what she would call the mural.

***

Her mother and Daria came to visit, bringing back the healer who had gone to their forest home to teach them. They said they wished to visit now, before the busy time of Spring planting began. Winter had but another moon left, and Caroline was reminded of her childhood play. Rides on little wooden sleds through the woods, snowball fights, making snowmen, ice skating. At night there would be music (everyone in the family played something) and stories by the fire till the children fell asleep. These memories made Caroline miss her home, but she and her sister played in the snow as if they were little girls. So Caroline felt better.

She cried when her mother returned to her the stone in which she had placed her rage and pain over Serenity. Her mother had, as promised, taken the stone to where Serenity had wandered off and been taken away. Now the stone was even more full of emotion, and thus more powerful, but Caroline was still not sure what she wished to do with it.

She told her mother about the search for treasure Gold had set her on. Her mother got a strange look on her face. "Serenity had a little girl's ring," she said. "We got it from a traveling peddler. She loved it because it glittered and had a pretty stone in it. I kept it." The older Caroline went to her bags and took out a small box and handed it to her daughter. "Here, daughter. I think perhaps you should have it now. Maybe it will help you find the treasure Gold has hidden for you."

They hugged, and Caroline cried a little. Then she opened the box. The ring was not fine or expensive. But it was of gold. It was tiny enough for a little girl's finger and had a glittering blue stone in it.

Weeping, Caroline put the ring on a little ribbon around her neck. She was not sure how, or why, but she had been given the first gold clue. And though she had no idea what to do with it, or what came next, she was happy to have found it at all. And happy to have the little ring once worn by her twin.

As soon as she began to wear it, she felt more strongly than ever that Serenity was *with* her—and always had been and always would be. She had not lost her sister. Slowly, slowly, as the year unfolded, Caroline was beginning to understand this truth. She had never–really—lost her sister at all.

***

It seemed to her that she hardly ever saw Gawen these days...though that wasn't so, they really did see each other often. But Gawen was so busy with his magical studies, and it seemed as if she was always busy, too, and they ended up talking non-stop every time they saw each other. She was beginning to feel very tense, very afraid. There were only two more colors for her to finish working with before her Initiation. It was slowly becoming real to her that she might actually become a Priestess of the Twelve...and the emotion was so intense it left her breathless. So was the pressure! To be so close, so very close to success was terrifying and overwhelming. At times, images of her own Initiation played in her mind, bringing tears to her eyes. Sometimes she'd just stare at her ten feathers and try to absorb it. She had started out her year in a daze, and it felt as though she had stayed in one the whole time.

Many nights she took to sleeping in the Chapel of Gold, absorbing the spirit of the color. She'd lay on a blanket beneath her mural, praying that she would do a good job with it. She had added a picture of Serenity being taken by the fearless Many Stars and of herself getting the ring from her mother. (She had painted the ring on Serenity's little hand, clearly shining with a bright light; it was obviously the same ring). When she painted Serenity as a child, she also painted herself in the forest house with her mother. The story was very clear. But the purpose and meaning was not, to Caroline. And there was no more happening to her, either...the treasure hunt seemed at a standstill.

Until the night when Gawen came to see her...with a gift. He had gotten for her a little ring. It was of gold and had a red heart embedded in it. When he gave it to her and kissed her and put it on her, she grew dizzy. Very dizzy.

"This is no ordinary ring," she whispered.

He smiled at her. "No. I have put a spell on it. But I cannot speak of the spell, or it will be broken."

"Yes. I feel the magic. But that is not all! Gawen, this is another clue! I do not know why, but I feel it!"

He caressed her cheek. "Patience, Little Bird. It will all make sense in its own time."

She sighed. "I know. But I have two clues, I know I do...and I cannot at all understand them!"

He kissed her till she forgot to be upset and worried for awhile.

She painted Gawen giving her the ring, on the mural. She wore it as she slept, but she cried bitterly, for she could not understand what the clues meant.

That night she dreamed. She dreamed of Serenity, and her sister was standing very still, as some forest animal Caroline had never seen before was drinking from a stream. Flight paid no attention to Caroline; she did not seem to realize Caroline was there. But Caroline noticed something, all right! She noticed that Flight's armband was of gold. Strong, enduring, plain gold. It was beautiful. Flight was beautiful. And Caroline woke.

It was one in the morning, and Caroline was in the Gold chapel. She began feverishly painting the dream of Flight with her gold armband. She did not sleep that night. She tried to paint the beauty of her sister as best she could. Then she understood.

When the Seekers of old were sent on a Quest, they were given a magic talisman, by the Gods or by a friend. This talisman protected the Seeker from any harm and would provide magical aid when the Seeker was stuck or trapped at a phase of his Quest. The talisman was a key to the Quest, a way to open up the answers you sought. These three gold rings...the ring of her sister when young, the ring of her lover, and the armband of her sister, now grown, were her talismans. They would arm her on her Quest. She painted the words, "The Sacred Talismans," under this part of the mural.

***

Caroline was very sad. Days had passed, and still her Quest remained empty and futile. Finally, one night, she became very angry, and, determined to succeed, she began to meditate upon the rings, her talismans on this Quest. She lit candles and stared at her mural.

The one which drew her this time was the armband of Serenity. She stared at it on the wall, and it hypnotized her. Evening shadows fell. Darkness came. Caroline slipped into a whole other world. It began to feel as if she had an armband of gold on her arm. But her arm was darker, sturdier, and strange to her. One thing Caroline knew. She was a woman of the people of Flight. The armband was, in fact, a symbol of some honor among them. It was a symbol of strength and power to her people.

Then Caroline saw that her arm was burying something. A little box. She could not understand what was in the box, but the feeling—the feeling was *very* clear. She was burying the box for someone to discover, in future years. Someone, someday, would *need* the contents of that box. And Caroline found herself praying that the person would have the strength to find it, when the day came. She floated back into awareness of her room in the chapel.

She meditated on this all night, and by morning she understood what her vision meant. Once, long ago, she had been a woman of Flight's people, when the planet was young. She had been loved and revered among them. And in that life, she had buried a special box for someone to find in the future. In that life she had been spiritually prompted to understand that someday someone would *need* that box. Strong spells had been cast upon the box to help the person find it.

Caroline could not shake the eerie sense that the person who had to find the box was she herself—Caroline of today. This was the Quest Gold had sent her on—to find the treasure she had buried in a past life, a treasure she had buried so that someday she, as Caroline, would unearth it. Knowing this was a great relief to Caroline, because at least she at last understood what her Quest was about! She did not consider how difficult it would be.

There are times in life where a task is so daunting that we simply numb ourselves to apprehension and doubt. We just go forth and *do* the task, no matter what it is. Because we simply have no choice. Tara had experienced this when she entered the Temple as a novice. Now Caroline did. She instinctively shut off and put away the part of her which could not deal with the enormity of her task. And she prepared to try and just *do* it. There was, simply, no time to be afraid.

The moon was more than halfway to Full, and Caroline knew one thing above all else. In that life long ago, she had been correct. Caroline needed what was in that box. Needed it more than she consciously understood...but she felt it. Oh, she felt it. Oh, *how* she *felt* it....

***

Tara was alone the night of the Full Moon. As all novices, she had begun her work first with Black, the color from which all others emerge.

The timing couldn't have been more perfect. She needed Black, needed her desperately. Black was not only fully aware of the truth.... Black was the central force of the Creed, the Way. But the people had so twisted Black that Tara felt a deep, burning hatred for Black. She saw White as good and Black as evil, even though in her mind she knew this was not so.

So her task for Black had been to overcome her loathing of the Black, by correctly redefining it in her mind. She had to be able to explain what Black really was. Yet all she could see, all she could feel, was the pain as she remembered that she had once been one of those people. Now a part of her remained there. Her baby. Her sweet baby.

Perhaps they would hurt him, though she prayed not. He was an intelligent, bright boy, and they valued intelligence. They might hurt him, though, if they decided she was more valuable. If they wanted her cooperation badly enough. She had to do something. Something to guarantee that, if that moment came, she would stand by the Temple. Michael was lost. Whether she cooperated with them or not, he was theirs. All she would accomplish if she stayed on her old path would be to lose herself as well as her son. It was tempting to think that she could pretend to be one of them, live with them, while protecting Michael and showing him a better way. Until he was strong enough, old enough to leave. But it would never work.

Miserable and tired, she lit some black candles, trying not to cringe at the memory of other black candles for other purposes, in rituals of cruelty. The Lady Black stood before her, in her black robes. She gazed at Tara with compassionate black eyes.

"Yes, child. Black can be compassionate."

"It shields secrets. Bad secrets."

"If you choose. Or good ones. Black is a veil. What lies behind the veil is whatever the truth is—good, bad, or both."

"I understand."

Black sighed. "They worship the forces of chaos and destruction. They worship my power over death. You must understand, Tara, chaos and destruction are a part of life. They are not bad. Chaos is the swirling, creative spiral from which life and order is born. Destruction is a saving grace. What would the world be if those things whose time had passed could not die?"

"Lady, I am afraid."

Black frowned. "I will not lie. You have reason. These people worship ruthless selfishness. And they have a great power over you. Not only Michael, but they have power because they have stolen your self-respect. They will not easily allow you to take it back."

"Will you help me, Lady Black?"

Black looked very intently at Tara. "Yes. I will help you find the strength to cut your ties with them and to belong fully to the Temple. I will help you regain your self-respect. Yes. I will help you. And I will do what I can for Michael...but as to that, I can make no promises. Each soul makes their own choices. You cannot force the destiny of another."

"Michael is a *child*. He is helpless."

"*My* child, as *all* are my children, and children of the rest of the Twelve! You must give him to me, Tara. I cannot help you otherwise."

Tara hung her head.

"The necklace," Black said.

With a cry, Tara ripped a locket off her neck. It had a picture of Michael and a lock of his hair in it. She threw it at Black's feet, hard.

"Take it. *Take* it." She was trembling with anger. "They gave me no choices. They *said* they did. They said that to worship evil would liberate me. It did not. I served them like a slave. Are you, then, no better, Mistress of Black? Do you, too, demand and take and rule your subjects to achieve your own ends? Are we your pawns? I am sick unto death of being a pawn of men, of the hatred in us, and now—of you. Take my son." She was screaming now. "I no longer expect to get anything from any Deity—of the Dark or of the Light." And she began to cry tears of pain and rage.

Black stared deep into her eyes. "Tara, you were born to be a Priestess of White. You alone forsook that path to follow another. You alone reclaimed it and entered the Temple. If you wear the robe one day, it will be because you and you alone earned it. You asked for my help. I give it. But help is not easy and help is not gentle. Help is at times full of struggle. You will suffer, Tara. You will suffer deeply if you try to confront your demons. You may lose your child.

"You still, in the end, at least have your soul. Michael is mine, as all souls belong to the Twelve, to the Gods. Release him to my care. Tend to your own path. You are my child, too. I will protect you. I fight for your freedom, Tara. But you will have to be very strong. Very strong. And you will have to trust me."

Tara wearily nodded. "I worshipped evil, hate, and selfishness," she whispered. "It is not that I expect no consequences, no repercussions from my actions. I *will* suffer. I am *ready* to suffer...I am not afraid of it, for nothing could be worse than what I have seen already. But I beg you, Lady...if it is possible, spare my son. His only crime was being born of a mother who was twisted and sick inside. Let me suffer, let me suffer anything I must, but try to keep my son safe."

Black nodded gently. "I shall."

"My Lady," whispered Tara, "they will return soon. They will not let me rest long. They will demand that I *do* things for them...things within the Temple. I do not know what to do to end this."

"One task at a time, Tara; one moment at a time. All you need to do now is to learn to understand and trust and love Black for what Black really is. Concentrate on the work we assign you. Remember. You are no longer handling these people alone—you are handling them with the full force of the Twelve behind you. There is no power greater than the power of life and love, and it is in your possession now. Use it! Call on us! Seek our help and protection.

"You are no longer one of them, Tara. The Lords and Ladies you serve now can be depended upon to tell the truth and not lie to you. They can be counted on to be there when you need them. And they can be counted on to destroy all untruth, in the end, simply by being truth."

Tara nodded. "Yes, Lady."

"One final word. A peaceful heart gives no entrance to the ones who shatter peace. It is a troubled, vulnerable, fearful heart they prey on. You were an angry, hurt young woman when they found you, Tara. They saw your broken heart, and it was easy for them to crawl in. Fight to give them no such entrance now. Fill your heart with joy and peace and music. Then they will find no room in it for them. Enjoy your novitiate. Enjoy the Temple. This alone will be a powerful weapon, Tara."

Tara smiled a little. "All right. I will try."

Black smiled gently. "Good. I am here if you need me."

"Farewell, Lady."

"Farewell, Novice of the Twelve." Black left.

Tara touched her neck. She felt the naked throat there, with no locket around it. And she kept rubbing her neck until she began to cry and scratched at the bare skin. There were fingernail marks where once a chain was, and little trails of blood. At long last, near dawn, Black took pity upon her, and, as Mistress of Sleep, sent a heavy sleep upon Tara that she might rest.

***

Caroline was holding Gawen. In his arms she felt safe. All of the pressures of life changed perspective and became manageable. Once more, she faced the waning moon with a sense that she had not accomplished enough. Though she knew what she was looking for, at least, she had not the slightest idea of where to find it.

Gently and reassuringly, Gawen stroked her hair. He had a quiet confidence that she would succeed. It was a contagious confidence. When she was around him, she believed that she would succeed, would become a Priestess.

"My Little Bird," he said, and there was such love in his voice that Caroline's eyes filled with tears. She looked at the little ring on her hand, the gold band with a heart in it. She began to think about her memories of Gawen—their first meeting on the Hill of Novices. She remembered how Pink and Red had shown them to each other, and how Caroline had run in a terror down the Hill to her room. She thought of the round altar of stone atop that Hill. A circle. Another circle.

She began to jump up and down. "The treasure is buried somewhere on the Hill of Novices!" She began to dance Gawen around in circles. "I know it is! I can feel it!"

It took all of Gawen's persuasion to convince her that she could not go immediately, in the late Winter evening, to the Hill. He reminded her first of all that she did not yet know where it was buried on the Hill. And even when she found out, she had to get permission from the Temple Elders to dig there.

Reluctantly Caroline agreed, but her exuberance was still unbounded. She knew, she just *knew*, that the box was buried somewhere on that Hill! And she couldn't wait, she couldn't *wait*, to see what was *in* it!

***

They did not come to Tara directly any more that moon. They came in dreams. They invaded her sleep and sent her dreams of Michael. She dreamed of holding him as a baby, his sweet little hands waving in the air. She dreamed of playing with him. And there were dreams of her future, too—dreams of seeing him grow strong and proud, and her love of him nearly undid her.

Try as she might, she could not stop these dreams. She prayed for courage. "Lady Black, Mistress of Secrets, help me." And the Lady Black helped her to stay sane but could not stop the dreams. She comforted, she gave support—but could do no more.

The worst was when Tara dreamed of the day she left. She had thought to steal away quietly with Michael, go and hide quietly somewhere far away. When she entered his room late at night to take him and run, she found three of the High Priesthood there. They were dressed in full ritual garb, black-robed and hooded, and looked very serious. They told her that she was an adult and free to leave. But Michael had been taken to a house of one who was loyal to the Way...Tara would never find him!

"You may stay, of course," they said, "and try to get him back. But you have shown yourself to be untrustworthy. You would have to be carefully instructed, carefully monitored. If you do not agree to this, you may leave. But it is not good for the child to feel you searching for him. Michael is a sensitive boy; he shows great promise. You must not torment him further. His stability has already been disrupted by your unreliability. If you persist in seeking him, he will have to be sacrificed. You leave us no choice, Tara."

Tara was hysterical. In vain did they reassure her that Michael was safe and well cared for. In vain did they promise that they would not hurt him as long as she cooperated. She was inconsolable.

But it was too late. They had found out that she was leaving—she never did find out how—and they had taken her son. She grabbed the bags she had packed to run with. She told them that she would never, never follow their Way again. She left.

They never stopped in their efforts to get her to come back. Now they kept reopening the wound, not allowing it to heal. They sent her dreams to remind her of how torn and shattered she was when she left them. But Tara stood firm and did not falter in her resolve. She continued to work on her pain and bitterness toward the color Black. She never let the other novices see her pain; she was always bright and cheerful and friendly to them...if occasionally quiet. No one knew her nighttime terrors. Tara had become adept at hiding. An expert at it.

But she made no effort to hide from the eyes of Lady Black, which would have been useless and foolish and stupid. Tara was not stupid. What she began to understand was that there would be a long, hard struggle ahead of her to win her robe. She had known this, but now it was crystal clear to her. Tara did what she always did when faced with a seemingly insurmountable mountain to climb. She prepared to climb it one step at a time.

***

Slowly, gently, the Temple opened itself to the first hints of Spring in the air. It was coming, it was coming, and the promise seemed to whisper on the winds, from one heart to another. Soon now, soon. Caroline felt it especially keenly. It was a promise of hope, a promise of rebirth, and for her, it was also the promise of a new life.

As Caroline had promised Pink, she had been allowing Gawen to heal her wounds by connecting her mentally to Flight, and to all the wisdom of her sister's people...the people she was now thinking of as her own, in her secret heart.

The couple had long talks, and Gawen learned as he relayed the messages to Caroline. They both learned of the traditions and beliefs which the rest of the planet had lost. In Flight, Caroline found a true kindred spirit who was filled with passionate intensity and love for the Ancient Ways. Flight was honored by her people for her devotion, her courage, her self-sacrifice. As Caroline spent night after night listening to what Gawen was telling her, she grew to be conscious of how much she loved and respected her sister. Caroline would have done anything to help and aid and honor Flight, and the feeling was very mutual.

Little by little, step by step, she was losing her lonely disconnectedness from Nature. Sometimes she heard traces of the voices of the earth, hints of how rich and beautiful was the language of its creatures. But these were only hints. In the life in which she had been one of Flight's people, long ago, and had buried the treasure box (on what was now the Hill of Novices, but this had been long before the Temple was created)... in that life she had been so strong. So aware. So powerfully attuned to the Nature all around her. In that life, she too, like Serenity, had worn a gold armband to signify the esteem and love with which her people regarded her.

Wearily, Caroline rubbed her eyes. She had been working with Gawen for two long hours now, as he spoke Flight's words. No matter how hard Caroline tried, sometimes it seemed as if she only gained a miniscule portion of the knowledge and wisdom that she'd had in that long ago life. Sometimes it seemed to her as if her spirit had, instead of evolving, gone backwards.

"She says wisdom is never lost," said Gawen.

"No. But 'tis forgotten," whispered Caroline. "It is so much, so oft' forgotten...."

"Flight wishes to help you remember that day," Gawen said softly.

Caroline looked deep into Gawen's eyes, trusting him, trusting her sister. "All right."

"Lie still," he said, "and close your eyes."

So Caroline lay down and closed her eyes. Gawen, who loved to sing as Caroline did, began to sing a chant Flight was sending to his mind. It was in the language of the people, and neither he nor Caroline understood what the words meant. They understood the feeling, though. They understood the love.

The chant took Caroline back in time. She found herself sitting in a circle with her people around a sacred fire. The box that would be buried soon was being passed from person to person. They were chanting the same chant Gawen was. Caroline saw herself, dark-skinned and dark-haired and dark-eyed, wearing the gold armband. When she realized that her people were blessing the box, filling it with their love and energy, Caroline began to cry.

The woman from the past lifted up her head. "The Little Bird of the future weeps," she said. "I can see her. I can hear her tears." Caroline understood her words, and she knew the woman did see her. "She cries not only for love of us. She cries because one day she will be so far from us. One day she will almost forget."

There were murmurings of love and sympathy among the circle of people.

"Little Bird, I am Bird, too. I am called Free Bird."

At this Caroline cried even harder. It seemed Free Bird was everything she wanted to be, everything she dreamed of, but she was only a Little Bird. Weak. Helpless. Easily crushed.

"No, Little Bird. You are very strong. You went out into the world to bring them our message." The woman's dark eyes were compassionate and sad, and loving.

"Does it not hurt you, Free Bird, that in my life as Caroline I will no longer live with the people, live with the earth?"

"Wherever you go, the voices of Nature are there. You are not leaving us, Little Bird. You are a Messenger bird. A hope for our people. You became one with the world only for our sakes."

"And *why?!*" cried Caroline. "They do not listen! You who see the future, surely you have seen that they do not listen. They move farther from Nature. I gave up a life with my people, and no one listened anyway!"

"Oh, no." Free Bird shook her head. "Some heard, who would not have heard if you did not go into the world."

"What did you tell the people?" asked Caroline. "What did you tell them about the future life you would lead, as one of the world?"

"I told them that one day I would go into the world to bring the world our love, at a time when they needed it. I told them that to join the world, I would be born having forgotten much of the ways of Nature, and I would be unable to hear Nature's voices clearly."

"Your heart must be breaking!" said Caroline in agitation.

"No, Little Bird. I am happy to serve the people. And they have promised me— the earth and sky and the Great Waters—they have promised me that they would never truly leave me. This is my gift to you, Little Bird, a gift to my own spirit from a time long passed, to a time far distant in the mists. The voices of life live in you. Nothing and no one can take them away!"

The circle began shouting and cheering and whistling and stomping their feet in agreement. Caroline, crying still, looked at Free Bird deeply, to remember her always.

"We go to the place where your gift will be buried. It is a gift from all of us to you, Little Bird. You belong to us. We love you."

The image faded, and Caroline saw what she knew was the Hill of Novices, but there was no Temple there, only wild lands. Free Bird was burying the gift box, and she was softly crying. Caroline came up to her and put a hand on her shoulder.

"Little Bird," sighed Free Bird. "I can feel you but cannot see you."

Caroline spoke into her ear. "Be at peace. I shall never forget my people. I shall always love the planet, and I will always remember what you learned, Free Bird. It is forever a part of me."

Free Bird smiled a little sadly and nodded.

"Goodbye, Little Bird. I will not see you again, but I will never, never forget you."

"Nor I you."

Caroline hugged Free Bird, and Free Bird shivered, feeling the embrace. The vision faded.

Caroline found herself in Gawen's arms, her safe place of refuge, and held him for many hours. There was no need for words. But now she understood something she had been a little afraid to admit to herself. Now that she knew where the box was, there was also some fear in her heart. To find this treasure did not only bring joy. It brought back bittersweet memories. Bittersweet memories of dark, wild eyes in the forest—and a time when she had not been called Little Bird—but Free Bird.

***

Caroline spoke to Elizabeth Anne. She told her of her vision, and told her that she now knew where on the Hill of Novices the treasure was buried. Elizabeth Anne spoke to the Temple Elders, and it was decided that the box could be dug up with two Elders, a Priest and Priestess, overseeing.

And so one night Caroline and Gawen, with both of their teachers and the two Elders, went to the Hill. It was one of the most sacred nights of her life. Caroline was dry-eyed and calm, totally immersed in the power of what she was doing.

Because the ground was still Winter, cold and hard, the Priest cast a spell on it to soften it. But it was Caroline, and Caroline alone, who dug, as the chant of so long ago still echoed in her mind and on her lips. She gave thanks to the earth for protecting her treasure for so long. When she found the box, she discovered it to be in good condition. Though centuries had passed, the workmanship was such that the box was undamaged. Spells had also been woven into it to ensure its longevity. Her people took such *pride* in their craft! Gratefully and reverently, they closed the hole back up, as the Elders murmured blessings and closed the magic circle.

But the box was not opened then. Caroline opened it alone, later, in the Chapel of Gold, before the mural she was painting. She lit gold candles and she asked Gold to be present. He came, a silent presence, into the room, and she felt his love and approval, but he did not show himself. Still, she knew he saw, as she opened the box

A gold armband. It was so powerful that Caroline almost feared to touch it. In it were designs. She studied them, understanding some, not understanding others. Birds and lightning bolts and female figures were engraved into the armband. It told many stories and had many meanings. Jewels were embedded in it, also. Caroline knew that she would spend a lifetime interpreting it, for many of the symbols were ancient, strange, mysterious, and unfamiliar to her.

One thing was clear. Her people—and they *were her* people, centuries ago *and* today still—had made for her a symbol of esteem. A sign of the honor she was held in by them. And she understood that they did this to honor her difficult task now. Her task— of going far away from them and being one with the world. Her task—of trying to keep their world and the world of society from totally separating from each other. In herself there must always be a connection between the two worlds. And she was dedicating her life to connecting them for other people as well.

This was lonely and painful work, for she missed her people. As she held the band, she understood clearly perhaps for the first time how very much she missed them. But love does not consider itself a sacrifice, only a gift. She loved her people, and to serve them filled her with joy! Nothing else could have fulfilled her.

Temple of the Twelve

If she had rejected the task—if she had turned away from the inner voices that called her to the Temple of the Twelve—if she had found living with one foot in two realities to be too difficult and had chosen one over the other—then the box would have remained forever buried, lost in time, trapped underground—a hidden legacy, an unknown heritage. No one would have found it—and if they had, it would have been only of historical value.

Only she–Caroline—could bring out the magic! They loved her! Her people loved her!

Now, at last, she cried, as she put on the armband for the first time. She cried tears of sheer joy. They loved her. She was no longer simply Caroline. She was also Little Bird of the People. She who had worn the gold armband for them as Free Bird. She who now wore a new one for them. She whose sister was Flight. She was of the People, now and forever.

***

In the last week of the waning moon, Caroline finished her mural. She painted the scenes of her finding the box, and putting on the armband. This section of the mural she entitled, "Ancient Treasures."

When the night of the last day of her Gold Moon came, she met with him before this mural. He was wearing a golden, jeweled crown and had a heavy gold wand in his hand. His robe was rich in texture, embroidered finely, exquisitely. Even it had jewels in it. His long golden hair shone, and his blue eyes shone brightly, too. He looked like a King. This time he wore a golden beard.

Caroline bowed before him. "My Lord," she said, "this is the mural I did for love of you."

He smiled at her, and again it was bright as the sun. Almost too bright to look at. "What have I taught you, my daughter?"

Without hesitation, she answered, "Leadership. You have shown me how to claim my power."

"What else?"

"The purity of love. The endless stream of wisdom in the center of life. Who I really am. My place." She showed him her armband. "This means I am of the People. My sister's people are my people. No matter

254

how much the surface of life changes, that will never change."

Gold nodded. "You will have to work hard over your lifetime, understanding all the symbols and meanings."

She smiled joyously at him. "Yes. It will help me to learn more and more of my heritage."

"More of who you are."

She nodded, smiling. "So much pain has been eased," she said to him. "I had a great emptiness within. I was homesick for my people and the Ancient Ways."

"You have not lost them," Gold whispered, peering at her with his laser blue eyes.

"No. I have not. Oh, my Lord, what can I give you in return for all you have bestowed on me?"

He smiled warmly at her. "Your happiness is all I ever desired, Little Bird," he laughed.

She ran up to him and hugged him tightly. Then he blessed her armband, and he blessed the mural, and, with a great flourish and a ceremonial bow, he presented to her a gold feather. She took it. It glowed. Her gaze could not leave the beautiful, bright feather. It hypnotized her. She understood that gold had a very strong power to enchant and mesmerize you.

When she at last lifted her gaze up again, the Golden Lord was gone. But he remained with her, in the power she felt when she wore her armband. He had taken her powerlessness and replaced it with strength. He had taken her homelessness and replaced it with family. He had taken her disconnectedness and restored to her her past. He had shown her how strong and how loved she was.

The brilliant gold light of his love had forever changed her. She had deepened and grown into her womanhood. And she could never go back again. The treasure had worked its magic. She would never be the same again, having seen, having touched, having claimed the hidden treasure of Gold.

Chapter Thirteen

This was the one moon, the one time, when Caroline walked the Hill of Novices knowing which of the Twelve was to meet her there. There was only one of the Twelve left. And if she succeeded in this task, this would be the last time she walked the Hill as a novice. By the next New Moon she might be a priestess, accepted by the Twelve and preparing for her initiation. These thoughts were very surreal to her. Her life as a priestess might have been a breath away—but it also seemed an eternity away. There was still, there was always, the chance that she would not be ready—that she would not have the wisdom to complete her work for Yellow. None of her visions changed that reality. Whether she could achieve those visions in her life was up to her.

The chants, the familiar prayers. "Beloved, beloved, show me your face, and I will show you mine...."

Springtime. Just beginning, yes, but here nonetheless. You could feel it in the lengthening days, the softly warming earth, the beginning of life and grasses stirring in the soil. Sweet Spring. She had brought her yellow flowers.

The Lady came on wings of gold. At first, there was a golden light, and Caroline thought the Gold Lord was also appearing. But no. All that Gold did was bring his Lady to her. She heard the mighty, thunderous voice booming in her mind. "Behold, Little Bird, I bring you my wife, my lady, and my love." It made her shiver to hear that deep voice trembling and powerfully in love.

The Lady stood in a flowing, breezy-looking yellow dress. She had on little yellow slippers and yellow flowers in her hair and her yellow-gold hair hung in a riot of curls. Her lips were curved, as if she was ready to smile or laugh or sing at a second's impulse. Her blue eyes were gentle and kind, but playful and mischievous and sparkled merrily. Without a word, she held out her arms to Caroline. Caroline ran to them.

The love and warmth began as a tingle in her toes and rose up to her head. Yellow was giggling in her ear, and Caroline was laughing for no reason. She simply had to laugh. Caroline gently knelt before the Lady, who placed her hands on her head in blessing. There was such warmth, it was as if Yellow had hands of fire.

"Welcome, Little Bird," sang out Yellow in a bright, musical voice that seemed to dance. Caroline was beaming and glowing, just hearing that joyful voice. "Hello, hello, hello, hello!" sang out Yellow and took Caroline's hands and spun her around in circles. They laughed and spun.

At last Caroline caught her breath and, smiling at Yellow, she said, "Oh, Lady. You are so beautiful."

Yellow smiled happily at her. "Oh, darling, so are you!"

Caroline touched Yellow's cheek. "I want to do something very, very special for you," she whispered intensely.

Yellow touched her cheek back. "Oh, you will, sweetness. You and I are going to do something *very* special. Very special. Very, very special. I *promise*."

Caroline eyed the bright, smiling face of Yellow with a trace of suspicion. Yellow's eyes were laughing mischievously, and Caroline had the sense that you might never be able to predict what she'd do next.

"What do you have in mind, my Lady?" she asked, smiling in spite of herself. You couldn't help but smile at Yellow. She made you happy just by her presence. Her joy in life was infectious and contagious.

"Oh, no, no," Yellow said, wagging a finger in Caroline's face. "No, sir. It's going to be a *surprise*!"

Caroline stared at her. "But, my Lady, how can I get to work on a task if I don't even know what it is?"

Yellow shook her head and her curls bounced. "This task only works if you do it without realizing you're doing it!"

"Oh." Caroline was still befuddled. "So I am to do nothing?"

Yellow laughed. "Just go about your days, Little Bird, and trust me."

"Is there nothing I can do to help myself succeed, Lady Yellow? No hints? No preparations? Nothing?"

Yellow just smiled. "No, dear heart. You don't need any hints. Just stay close to me. Think about me. Learn of me. The rest will happen naturally, I promise! Trust me!" She kissed Caroline's cheek, and there was a delicate, flowery perfume around her. "Oh, don't look so worried," Yellow scolded, taking Caroline's face in her hands. "I love you, Little Bird. All will be well."

Caroline smiled. Yellow inspired her with confidence and optimism and faith in herself. It was hard to hold onto self-doubt and insecurity. "All right," she said with a laugh. "Gold led me on an adventure, and it looks as though you are, too."

Yellow picked one of the many yellow flowers from her hair and stuck it behind Caroline's ear. "You are a beautiful Little Bird," said Yellow. "A bright and beautiful Little Bird." Then Yellow began to sing. It was a sweet, wordless song, and very enchanting. Her voice lifted high and clear and strong and pure.

Caroline listened for a long while, her eyes closed, in silence. Yellow lifted her spirits with her song. When Caroline opened her eyes, Yellow was gone, and she stood on the Hill of Novices, looking at the altar. She stayed there for a long time, then slowly walked down the Hill to her room, knowing this might be the last time she stood on the Hill as Novice Caroline, Little Bird of the Forest.

It was a strange feeling, and so she put aside the feeling of uncertainty she had because Yellow was sending her on an unknown task and embraced freely this very special night. She let it absorb her. She let it fill her as completely as she could. For this night would happen only once.

**

2222

Tara had a very different experience on this night. Knowing that the sad and painful dreams of Michael were not swaying or influencing her, her old Clan decided on another way. They cast a spell on her to weaken her, and though Tara did fight valiantly, she could not fight it off entirely. She ended up with a very bad cold that left her weak and lightheaded and unable to appreciate or fully experience the New Moon.

Black had given her a token—a beautiful black onyx stone to wear on a chain around her neck. But Black had also told her that, due to her special circumstances and the violent repulsion Tara felt, she would need to continue to work with Black, probably the whole time she worked with every other color.

It was White who came next...with bright, white-feathered wings and *a lot* to say. Tara was resting in bed under her blankets, coughing and feverish. But she listened, and she heard. White made it very clear to Tara that she was to be her primary Deity and that her task would no doubt take the whole time she was working with the other colors. So all of Tara's remaining moons spent with colors would also be Black and White Moons.

White's task for her was to achieve a greater sense of her worthiness to belong to the Temple. But for Tara, this would be so difficult that White was going to attack the problem a step at a time. While all this was going on, Tara's teacher, whom she had met in the last moon, was tending her. Her teacher was a Priestess of Black, White, and Silver. Her name was Miriam. She was fretting over the cold Tara had. Miriam did not see or hear White in the room. Only Tara did.

As Miriam bathed Tara's face, she looked at her worriedly. "I know something of healing, Tara. And this is no natural illness. It is hate-filled. If someone has hurt you, I need you to tell me. I need you to be honest with me, or I cannot help you."

Weakly Tara shook her head. "No. Nothing like that."

White grew furious as Miriam pursed her lips and turned to get fresh towels. "Tell her."

"No," Tara protested. "I can't."

"You need tell no one else, Tara, until you're ready, but you need a friend, and I have chosen Miriam to be it. Tell her, or you will be unable to progress further in your work here!" White pleaded angrily.

And so Tara did. In a hoarse voice, raw with coughing, she told the basics of her story to her teacher. She did not elaborate on many details, but she did not leave anything out, either. When she was done, Miriam rocked her and gave her medicine to help her sleep. What Tara did not know, because no novice did until her initiation, was that Miriam was a Warrioress.

No matter which colors you served, there were twelve basic groups that every novice fell into. The knowledge of these groups was part of the preparation for Initiation. One group was the Mystics...those who dedicated their lives to contemplation, prayer, and the internal life of spirit. Another was the Artists, including every kind of creative expression. A third was Warriors and Warrioresses...those who fought, protected, and championed the Temple in different ways. Yes, all people had some of each group in them...but most novices overall fell into one.

Miriam was a Warrioress, well used to the tricks of Evil. Tara was meant to be a White Warrioress.

Now, each group had a Patron Color. The color of the Mystics was Black. The color of the Artists was Red. But you could be a Priestess of Red and be a Red Mystic, or a Priestess of Black and be a Black Artist. Each color had priests and priestesses in each of the twelve groups. Tara was a Warrioress to her very bones, and Miriam knew this. And she understood that a Warrioress must be very careful which battles she fought...and when, why, and how. They also had to know about their Patron color, and work intensely with it, whether or not they were actually a Priestess of that color. The color of the Warriors and Warrioresses was the Gold Lion of Justice, Truth, and Strength.

Miriam knew Tara had taken a big step in telling her the truth. She saw to it that Tara slept, and then she slipped away. She had business with Gold that night...about his daughter, Tara. And White watched it all. And so did Black.

***

Her moon with Yellow all began so quietly. It was a strange sort of ending to her novitiate year, because things were so calm and quiet. But it gave Caroline much time to reflect on all she had done. She spent a lot of time talking with Gawen and Elizabeth Anne, reliving her past year. It had been Spring when she first came to the Temple. Now it was Spring again, and she was so different...yet the same.

Though it was still chilly most days, she went for long walks with her teacher and beloved mate. She did a lot of talking. She did a lot of thinking. The only real work she did was to study Yellow, with the Priestesses of Yellow she knew. She tried to learn and understand what drew them to Yellow and what it meant to them to be Her Priestesses. Since Tara had a little yellow in the robe Caroline had envisioned, she studied Tara, too. She spent a lot of time with Lydia, talking about Yellow. And she spent a lot of time with Yellow herself. Learning. Growing. Sharing.

Sometimes Yellow appeared in farmer's overalls, her curls pulled into two long braids. Yellow loved animals and the outdoors, and she was always running around, climbing trees, getting dirty, riding horses, chasing kites. She loved to swim; she loved to dance. She loved to play ball. Spring was her beloved season, and she was often working with the newly awakened earth. She was physically healthy and strong, and as she spent time outdoors, her skin grew golden and so did Caroline's. Once she took Caroline on a rowboat ride on a lake.

Yes, all this was Yellow. But there were many other sides to her. She loved to nurse and was always tending sick or weak plants and animals and people. She could be very gentle and kind, although at times she was saucy and teasing. She loved food and often gave Caroline cookies or cakes. She loved to cook. She loved to decorate houses and had a good sense of style. Family and home mattered a great deal to her. She liked to help with carpentry and building, too.

She loved children. and any youngsters anywhere around were drawn to her energy. She often appeared with children and animals around her. She could at times be very romantic and pin her curls up and wear beautiful princess dresses. She liked romantic things...a cameo around her neck, a lacy blouse, flowers and perfume and poetry. There were hikes into forests and mountains, while Caroline tried hard to keep up. But there were also nights spent by candlelight, reading poetry.

She was open, warm, and emotional; she cried and laughed easily. She was very strong, inside and out. She liked to play with styles for Caroline's hair and to brush, braid, and curl it. At times she liked very much to be lazy and could curl up in a sunny spot like a kitten, once or twice even with a kitten, stretch out, get comfortable, and take a nap.

She worked hard, but she knew how to pamper herself. Special teas and baths, bright balloons, little presents. A ball of energy, she was a dynamo, always going, always doing.

She was intelligent and bright and quick, but not overly formal, intellectual, or prim. She was earthy and fun. Her body was lush, full, curvy. She took a sensual enjoyment in taste, touch, and scent, and really savored things. She looked equally well in a floppy hat or a tiara. She did not have White's delicate, ethereal grace and willowy body, or Red's constant shapechanging, but she was very aware of what she *did* have! She never tried to be someone else. She was happy to be her.

Simple and plainspoken at times, if you took her to be even a little slow or dumb or unintelligent, she'd knock you flat with a statement that showed you just how smart she was. She often said that she loved being a woman, and this really seemed true. She loved people, being surrounded by friends. She built up confidence in women who felt ugly, or believed they could not accomplish things, or felt they were unworthy. She hated to see women downtrodden or weakened. She loved being a beautician. She often said she wanted to see the planet full of strong women who knew they were women.

What she did to help Caroline understand her better was to have Caroline accompany her through her day. Caroline went where Yellow went, did what Yellow did. As Yellow often said, "I'd rather show you than just tell you. You'll understand more."

So Caroline witnessed Yellow energy in many settings—in sickrooms, in gardens, in forests, in houses tense with discord, in outdoor games, in the lives of animals, in the lives of lonely, scared, and friendless people. Caroline did not yet know what Yellow's group was (or even that there *were* twelve groups). But Yellow was Caretaker, as her husband was Warrior. And Caroline understood this, without the explanation or the right words.

Yellow gave hope. Yellow renewed you. Yellow excited you and energized you, at times softly, sometimes strongly. She brought light, laughter, strength, and new chances. She was a spirit of rebirth and new life.

All these things Caroline learned, and very deeply. It was Yellow who encouraged her to put perfume on parts of her body other than behind her ears. It was Yellow who left armfuls of flowers in her room and ushered in the Spring of the heart. With Yellow she danced, sang, talked for hours. Yellow loved to talk, and so did Caroline, so the two chattered all day like magpies. Caroline was happy. Very, very happy.

But as the moon grew towards it fullness, she became worried. No evidence of any task had happened yet. All her days were spent in learning, yes, but nothing *special* happened. And Yellow would not let her ask questions or speak about it. "Let it happen naturally," she'd say.

Caroline would protest, "But I don't know if anything is happening at all," but Yellow remained firm. The topic was off limits.

So, despite her increasing anxiety, Caroline tried to simply enjoy the bright, sunny warmth of their time together. She tried not to let worry get in the way of her beautiful friendship with Yellow, who managed to be mother, sister, and daughter to her all at once.

For Caroline, Black and White had been as mothers. Pink and Green were her sisters. But Red and Yellow managed to be mother, sister, and daughter to her in different moods. Caroline had certainly learned by now that all people reacted to the colors differently, uniquely. But this was how *she* did.

Yellow made Caroline want to protect her, as well as want to be protected by her. Yellow had sensitive feelings, a very giving nature. Caroline found herself very defensive if these things were trampled on. Yellow did not have Red's bite and Red's heat. She was softer. She brought out Caroline's red fire, by her very gentleness and softness and her big blue eyes.

The moon grew. Yellow loved the round, full, glowing moon, soft in the sky, bright and shimmering. Life at the Temple went on. Gawen continued to study with the Magicians and was supremely happy there. People were treating Caroline with respect and honor, knowing she was one step from Priestesshood. But Caroline herself looked up at the moon and worried despite her good intentions.

What was happening? Why, in this last task, did things suddenly get so quiet? So normal? The colors had swept into her life like a whirlwind. In the end...would Yellow really be any different?

***

What happened next was something Caroline was not to understand for many, many years. It happened on a plane that Caroline was not in touch with. She was not conscious of its existence, yet it existed, shimmering within her. It happened deep in the Within Land.

The place was dark and quiet, a woods that was sacred to the followers of the Dark Path. Caroline's spirit did not understand why she was there or where she was. Confused, she looked around. It seemed to her that figures emerged from shadows which had not been there only a moment before.

"Well," one of them was saying. "Tonight is the time."

The others nodded. Try as she might, Caroline could not make out their faces. They were shadowed.

"We have tried many different ways. It is time for something stronger."

The others nodded.

Slowly a black, whirling mass began to grow between the figures. Each wore a hooded, dark robe. The mass of black was so vile and ugly that Caroline was afraid. Very afraid. Without knowing *how* she knew this, she understood that this black energy was going to be hurled at Tara. There was no time to think, only to react. What was going to happen now would happen in seconds, very fast.

Caroline cried out, "No!"

The shadowed faces turned to her. Caroline knew her very life was at stake...but she was forced to act, not think of her fear. Instinctively she knew that black mass of energy was too much for Tara. Tara was still fragile, still weak.

She addressed the figures. "Send it to me."

There was no chance of the mass disappearing. It was fully formed and in existence—and it *would go somewhere*. They would never *allow* it to die, even if they could. She knew this. She was afraid of the black mass. It held horrors and nightmares and screams in it. But she was more afraid of Tara receiving its force.

"Send it to me," she said again.

"Ahhhhh," said the one who was the leader. "This could prove even more effective. Tara will not want to see her friend hurt." He spoke awhile to the others in a language Caroline did not understand. Then he spoke to her. "Why do you want to do this?"

"Tara is my friend."

"Do you do this of your own free will?

"Yes."

"We must, by Law, give you one chance to change your mind. Leave now if you wish to."

"No. I cannot."

"So be it." The man laughed. "Foolish child. You don't even know what you are doing. But fools deserve what they get." He lifted up his arms; in one was a wand, but again, Caroline couldn't see it clearly. He pointed at her.

Caroline trembled, then she cried with joy to feel a familiar pair of arms around her. "Stand quietly," Orange whispered in her ear.

The hooded figure paused. "You must not intervene, Lord Orange. She chose of her own will."

"As do I," said Orange. "I will not lessen your energy. I will simply add to her own. And you cannot stop me, any more than I can stop you."

The black mass hissed impatiently. It needed to move.

The hooded figure made a decision, though he was obviously less than pleased Orange was holding Caroline tightly against him.

"So be it." He spoke again in that strange language. The black mass began heading towards Caroline.

"Ohhh...," whispered Caroline, "ohhh...."

"I'm here," whispered Orange, "right here."

The black mass rose up and flew at Caroline. It entered her chest. It settled in her. At first Caroline did not feel it, she did not feel different at all. Then it began to seep in...slowly. A deep, dark sorrow. It invaded her very cells.

"Come, Little Bird," said Orange. "We must get you home." And Orange picked her up in his arms, and, placing kisses on her forehead and hair, he carried her away from the forest.

***

She was safe in her bed. She woke slowly. She looked around at her little room...her table and chair, her paintings, her little treasures, her special things. It took a moment to wake up. Then she realized she did not want to wake up. All she wanted to do was disappear.

With a little cry, she turned her face to the wall and began to weep. Sadness. Deep and profound sadness. It was just there, all of a sudden, when yesterday she had been fine.

All Caroline wanted was for it to go away. She would have given anything–anything—for it to just go away. But it didn't. It didn't. It sat there, inside her. She couldn't think of any reason why. She couldn't think at all. All she could do was feel pain. She was terrified. She had no idea of when—or even if—the pain would leave. Would it be there forever? She couldn't live with it. She couldn't. She could not last long this way...and she knew it, and she was terrified.

Around her bed appeared Orange...Red...Blue...and Pink. Also Ladies White and Black. Lord Silver came as well...and Lord Gold. So did Yellow. These nine encircled her, pouring love on her as she cried, her face to the wall. Red cried on Orange's shoulder. Pink sat on the bed and wrapped her arms around Caroline. Ladies White and Black held each other's hands. Lord Silver and Lord Blue were whispering together, planning how to help Caroline. Yellow and Gold were staring into each other's eyes, mentally conferring about the problem.

Caroline was so lost in her pain she was not even aware they were there. Vaguely she could sense their presences, but she could not see or hear them. After awhile they left, alone or in couples. There was much to be done if they were going to pull Caroline through this. It was agreed that someone would always stay with her, in case of emergency. From Orange's violent growl when they suggested he leave, it was obvious that he was not ready to do so. He stayed, arms wrapped around Caroline, staring at the wall with her, in a room silent except for her quiet weeping.

***

It was a very bad week. She did not leave her room. One of the colors was always with her, and Gawen refused to leave her. He was in tears all week himself, unable to sleep or eat. Because she was forced to by Gawen or Elizabeth Anne, she showered and dressed and perhaps ate a little. But it was obvious she was pining away. She'd stare out her window or at the wall for hours. She would talk to no one. She cried silently and sat in her chair. Often she'd wrap herself in a blanket.

Tara was devastated. As soon as she saw her friend, she knew what had happened. She could feel the hatred. And she raged but could do nothing. She was ready to leave the Temple if the sorrow would be removed from Caroline. But White and Black made her see that she had to stay.

Tara went to a high hill, and she shouted at the sky, "You have lost me forever. If you think I would ever be one of you after you did this... you never knew me!" She shouted this with all the passion in her heart.

Because Gawen was so inconsolable, and Elizabeth Anne, as her teacher, needed to know how to help her, Miriam insisted Tara tell them what was going on. It was one of the hardest things Tara had ever done, but she would have walked through seven fires to save Caroline. Gawen cried when she told him and hugged her. His understanding and forgiveness did something deep inside Tara's heart. When a person receives unconditional love...it changes them.

All this time, Caroline grew sicker. She was sick to her stomach. She was feverish and had nightmares. It was Yellow who made her walk around her room in circles, Yellow who brushed her hair when she would not, Yellow who shoved food into her, Yellow who sang to her, Yellow who comforted Gawen.

Lord Blue appeared to Gawen, his Priest. He told him that this would not last—a week, two at most. He said that Caroline would be weak afterwards, but fine otherwise. Gawen clutched his Lord and cried to hear this. The problem was...would she survive until then? She began to sometimes speak nonsense, for she saw horrid visions.

And Gawen knew what the others could not...her spirit had gone into hiding. When he reached for her with his mind, he could not find her. She was covered up by pain and sorrow, and the real Little Bird had flown. It was this that almost undid him. Mates are not meant to be mentally and spiritually disconnected.

A few times there was worry that Gawen would follow her deep into the insane despair, just to be with her. And the moon waned, unstopping in its flight.

***

A terrible battle was taking place on the Inner Planes. A life and death battle. The dark forest where Caroline had seen the hooded dark men was quiet. Caroline's spirit had indeed retreated, as Gawen had seen and felt. Her spirit had returned to the forest. In truth, though Orange had forced her and carried her back into her body, a part of her had remained in the forest. That part was growing stronger and stronger. Now her spirit was very fully there. She was sitting quietly, still in the spot where the black swirling energy had entered her. There was a vacant expression on her face. She was calm. Too calm.

Orange was screaming at her. "You cannot stay here! We love you!"

She did not answer him. She had stopped *feeling*.

"Let's go, Caroline." His tone brooked no argument.

She ignored him.

"Please," he begged. "Little Bird." He knelt before her then and forced her to look in his eyes. "Your life is awaiting you. You need all your energy. Come."

She ignored him.

"*Why?*" cried Orange. "*Why?*"

"Do not be upset," said Caroline quietly. "I just do not have the strength. I can't fight anymore."

"You must find the strength to leave." Orange shook her. "Caroline! You will die if you do not leave."

"I am very tired," she whispered and closed her eyes. "Please, just let me sleep."

"Nooooo!" Orange was crying hard.

Yellow appeared. She put a comforting hand on his shoulder. "Shh, brother of the Twelve. Peace."

He forced himself to be quiet and calm down.

Yellow looked at Caroline. "So. It's to end like this. All your dreams. In a hidden forest no one can find. Lost forever."

Caroline whispered, "I am thirsty."

Orange gave her some water. Still she did not open her eyes.

"Little Bird," said Yellow, "I have an important question to ask you."

Little Bird opened her big blue eyes. It took much effort, but she did it for Yellow, who had been such a friend to her. "Yes?" she whispered.

"Do you trust me?" asked Yellow. "Do you really and truly trust me?"

Caroline stared at her silently.

"I don't mean a little bit. I mean really, totally, trust me."

After a moment, Caroline nodded.

"Then if I tell you you *can* find the strength, you will trust me," said Yellow.

There was no argument to that. It was simply a true statement. Caroline nodded. "I don't—" she could barely speak, her voice was weak and tired—"I don't know what to do."

"I will tell you," Yellow said gently.

Caroline nodded.

"Trust me," whispered Yellow. "Sit up."

It seemed to take forever, but Caroline got her limp body to sit upright, with Yellow and Orange's help.

"Now. We will help you stand. Trust me. *Trust* me." They half lifted her to her feet, and though her legs were weak, she did at last stand up, with Orange and Yellow supporting her.

"All right, Little Bird. Now turn around. Slowly."

Caroline did. She was dizzy and almost fainted, but she did turn herself around. Now her back was to the forest.

"Now, child, you must say, 'I want to go home.' "

A little feeling stirred in Caroline—the first in days. "I miss Gawen," she said, and a tear rolled down her cheek. "I want to go home." She began to see a hazy outline of her room, of her body in her little chair. But it seemed so far away, so very far away, and Caroline despaired. The vision wavered, grew more distant.

"No, no, dear," said Yellow calmly. "Think about going home. Say it again."

Caroline did. "Please. I want…to go home." The vision grew clearer.

"One more time," said Yellow.

"I want to go home." Then she was in her body fully, in her chair, looking out through her own eyes. The pain was so bad that Caroline began to scream, but it was soundless. Her mouth opened, but no sound came out.

"What is happening?" cried Gawen.

Yellow was in the little room with them and said to him, "She will be all right now."

They all held her, and gradually, over that day, the pain got a little better. Then the next day, a little more. It did not seem like much at first. But within a few days she was eating and sleeping healthily and going for little walks outdoors with help. Gawen dared to begin to feel as if he might not lose her.

There was one small problem. Though all the Twelve agreed it was for the best. She did not remember. Not only did she not remember the forest and the black energy, she did not remember the days she spent half dead in her room, either. The last thing she remembered were the events of the night before she had gone to the dark forest. The Twelve told Gawen, Elizabeth Anne, Tara, and Caroline herself, that she would remember when she was ready, and not to worry. It was simply too much pain for her to absorb all at once.

Gradually Caroline began to regain her health and her vibrancy. Time would tell what changes the experience had wrought in her spirit. Gawen fell apart. He cried out his pain with Blue, until he had no more tears and slept like a child in Blue's arms. Tara did the same thing…with White. Only Caroline did not cry. She only wanted to get well again. That was all she wanted…to get well again. That was all.

***

The last days of the moon passed quietly. Caroline began to regain her health and peace, but she had lost the one thing she wanted most—the final feather of the Twelve. She knew, without asking, that she would get no feather this moon. She was a little wistful, but not deeply saddened. In the past days she had used all her tears...all she had left was a deep inner peace. Everything would happen as it was meant to—in its own time.

She really did not understand what had happened to her. She remembered nothing of the past days. She let herself walk and talk about light and happy topics with Yellow. She asked no questions. Something in her knew that she did not want the answers. She had been promised that one day she would understand...and she fully trusted in that promise, and was not worried or afraid.

Such a night it was when the last day of the moon fell...a quiet night of friendship. She walked the gardens with Yellow, laughing quietly at something Yellow had said. The air was mild and warm, the night peaceful. Caroline was happy.

Yellow turned to face her, and handed her a flower. "Tomorrow is the New Moon," she said to Little Bird casually.

Caroline nodded. "Yes. I am ready. I feel it's time to begin again. I look forward to the renewal."

Yellow smiled at her gently. "You have not asked about your task. Your work with me."

Caroline smiled back. "I am excited to work another moon with you," she said.

Yellow looked at her quietly. "Sit down, Little Bird." They sat down on a large stone. Caroline drew her sweater closer around her. It was not truly very warm yet. "Caroline, do you remember I told you that what you did for me, you would have to do without realizing it? I told you that if you knew what you were doing, the task I had for you wouldn't be properly completed. Do you remember?"

Caroline nodded, listening intently.

"Caroline, you have forgotten over a week of your own life! Could it not be, dear, that you *did* complete my task for you during this time—the forgotten time—and not remember?"

Caroline's eyes were wide. "Lady Yellow, what are you saying?"

Yellow gazed at her kindly. "Just answer my question, Little Bird."

"Yes. Yes. It is possible."

"Then," said Yellow gently, "perhaps you should ask me if it is so!"

Caroline began to laugh. "This is incredible. It would be something that would happen to me—to complete my novitiate and not even know what I did!" She laughed harder.

Yellow laughed gently and stroked Caroline's hair. "Yes, dear. It is."

"So," Caroline asked her, her eyes sparkling merrily, "is it so, Lady? Have I completed my task for you?"

Yellow stared into her eyes. "Little Bird. What does your heart tell you? Listen."

And so Caroline quietly sat, her hand in Yellow's, and listened. She listened to her heart. After a little while, she turned tear-filled eyes to Lady Yellow. They embraced tightly.

Caroline stood back and looked deep into the wise, gentle blue eyes of Lady Yellow. "With all my heart and all my soul, I will try to be the Priestess I was created to be," she whispered. Then she asked, "Lady. Is there *anything* I need to know about what happened to me?"

Yellow stroked her cheek. "Only this, child. There was a moment when I asked you to trust me—trust me unconditionally, with *everything. Everything!* And you did. And that was all I ever really needed from you.

'Without it, nothing else matters. Nothing else is even possible. *With* it—everything is possible. The Universe and all its wonders, my darling, belongs to those wonderful, brave, beautiful souls who can trust in the power of love."

It was with these words that Caroline passed through the barrier between Novice and Priestess. Beneath the Spring sky, Yellow handed Caroline a beautiful yellow feather.

***

'Twas the night of the New Moon. The last day of her novitiate passed in exactly the same way as her first day had. Caroline was in a daze. The things that were happening to her seemed surreal and dream-like. She went through the motions of eating and talking to others, but her spirit was far away, listening to the call of distant dreams.

And, as she had the very first day, she spent time alone. She walked by herself, and she sat in prayer in her room. She did not seek the company of others, though she at times felt the lightning bolt stir around her neck.

But today she wanted to be alone and quiet. No one disturbed her. She prayed and prayed and prayed with all her heart. She prayed with thankfulness and joy that she had been able to reach this point in her life. She prayed with hope and a sincere desire that she might be a worthy priestess. Sometimes she would cry, sometimes she would laugh, for no apparent reason.

She walked to her special places. She visited the Chapel of Orange she had decorated, and the Chapel of Gold where she had painted the mural. She visited the gardens where she had painted under Blue's guidance. She traveled to the Hill of Silver where she had been given the silver chains and where she met so often with Gawen. She went to the pond where she had visioned her sister, Flight. It was a day of memories and dreams.

Night fell. The hours seemed to pass so quickly. The little things of the day...what she wore, what she ate, who said what to her...were embedded in her mind. She knew she'd never forget any of this day, which seemed so ordinary and simple, and was so very special. She retreated to her room as the darkening sky deepened.

As Black had instructed her so long ago, she prepared for this night by creating an altar. On her little table she laid out her twelve feathers to form a circle. She lit candles. Energy, who liked to be present in her rituals, sat on her shoulder. She did not put anything else on her altar, but kept it simple.

With pounding heart, she began to say the beautiful words of the Temple prayer said only once in your life—on the night when you had completed your novitiate work and were calling the Twelve to you. It was a very long prayer, calling all the Twelve, but Elizabeth Anne had taught it to her well, and Caroline did not falter or forget anything. She was carried away and lost within the Spirit of the prayer. As she said the words that had been uttered by every priestess, once, since the Temple was formed, she truly, deeply meant every word. All other thoughts drifted away, and her only reality was her prayer.

As she called each of them to her, she could see their loving faces in her mind. The words ended with a cry of hope and trust, a statement that she knew that, now that she had called the Colors, they would come to her. In the quiet of the little room which had been her home for the last year, they answered that trusting, faith-filled cry.

They came, one by one, and formed a circle around her.

Black's dress was celebratory and elegant—black velvet and black lace, and her gorgeous long black hair had been pinned up with a black jeweled comb. Brown had his glowing wand of truth, and there were tears in Caroline's eyes as she saw its light growing steadily, stronger and stronger.

Green wore green silk and emeralds, and flowers in her hair. Her arms were around Blue, and she was smiling at Caroline with tears in her big green eyes. Blue was gazing at Caroline steadily, with a quiet, thoughtful expression, and in his arms was the painting of the Twelve which he had done for her. It was now completed, and so beautiful.

Purple and Pink were holding hands. Purple had on a royal purple cape with a hood, and Pink was in a dress of little pink roses. She was wearing a small tiara, and openly crying as she gazed at Caroline with a face full of love.

Silver wore his silver jumpsuit with his crystal belt, and a headband with a crystal embedded in it that Caroline had never seen before. White was in a simple, classical white dress. She held a white rose in her hand and wore diamonds.

Gold had worn his finest robes and jewels and had his gold crown and kingly wand. He was resplendent and glorious. Yellow was beaming with a bright yellow gown and yellow roses in her hair. Her whole face was lit up.

Orange, too, was openly crying. He was in his beautiful orange robe and had his arms tightly around Red. Red wore a brilliant, flashing, tight, sequined gown and a headband with rubies. She had a bundle in her arms. Orange and Red approached Caroline.

Red spoke in her emotion-filled, powerful, rich, theatrical voice. "I have been chosen as Spokeswoman of the Twelve unto you, Caroline. Why did you summon us?"

Caroline had been told to expect this question, and had her answer ready. "I have completed the twelve tasks given to me by the Twelve.

Behold my tokens of love as signs of my sincerity and willingness."

"And what do you desire?" Red asked.

"Full entrance to the Temple, as a Priestess of Orange, Red, Blue, and Pink."

Red smiled at her, a glowing smile of love. "The Twelve have heard your prayers," she said gently and held out the bundle to her. With trembling hands Caroline took it and unwrapped it.

The robe was made of brilliant splashes of color, as if on an artist's palette. Most were red and orange, and some were blue and pink. It was a kaleidoscope of color, and the strange, wild designs made by the colors could be used for divination. Symbols and shapes could easily be seen in the patterns. Caroline lay at the feet of Orange and Red and wept.

After awhile, Red spoke again. "Put on your robe, Priestess."

Caroline did as requested. She stood before the Twelve in her robe.

I am me, but not me-me, but a new me. I am who I was, and yet nothing, nothing is the same....

Orange spoke. "Pink branded you with a heart on your forehead. Blue has branded you with lightning bolts on your wrists. My Lady Red has branded you with flames between your breasts. I, your Lord, brand you now. If you accept."

Caroline could only nod. Orange knelt before her. Then he kissed her ankles. It felt as if a small electric current went into her as he did. When she looked, she saw on each ankle a design that looked like the wings of a bird in flight.

Tears ran down her cheeks. "I love you," she cried and embraced Orange.

"May your footsteps be guided by the flight of your spirit," he whispered in her ear. Red joined the hug. Then, after awhile, so did Pink and Blue.

Finally they all resumed their places, except for Red. Red stood before Caroline in a sudden, magnificent red light. "Your tokens shall make a circle, as we do," she pronounced.   She pointed a finger at the table. Where there were once just twelve feathers, now there was a headband of gold. Each of the feathers was attached to it by a crystal. They hung down, along with ribbons of the twelve colors. Gently Red took the headband and placed it on Caroline's head. The feathers hung in her brown curls. The ribbons and crystals were so bright they seemed to glow.

Caroline was overcome and clung to Red and cried. All she could say was "I love you," over and over again. Red said the same back.

At last, Red returned to her place in the circle beside Orange. Each of the Twelve raised their right arm over her in blessing.

Red began, "I, Red," and then all the Twelve stated their names, till it was back to Red, who continued, "We welcome you as Priestess of the Temple of the Twelve, Priestess Caroline, Priestess of Orange, Red, Blue, and Pink. We love you, honor you, and serve you into eternity."

"Into eternity," whispered Caroline back. "Forever and ever—into eternity."

An Invitation From The Twelve

Beloved Reader,

Does a part of you long to follow Caroline on her journey as she meets the Twelve? Does a part of you feel unable?

You are able. The love the colors have for you is very, very real. You can always access it.

Maybe you don't want to invest a year. Call upon one of them each week, instead of each moon. Let the tasks they give you be simpler.

Or perhaps you wish there to be no tasks at all...just a connection between yourself and the Twelve. Then have no tasks. But *meet* them. *Feel* them.

If there is worry because, to you, the Twelve are more easily felt as a leaf or rainbow, not a human form as in the Temple...simply connect to that green leaf. Maybe you perceive the Twelve quite differently than Caroline. We *all* perceive them differently! Each person's relationship to them is unique. That is what makes it special. So if, to you, Green is a mermaid, then Green is a mermaid. Every perception of them, if based in love, is *real*.

The important thing to do is be with them. Maybe you don't want to work with all the Twelve...just Silver. Then work hard and with joy, with Silver. But *do* it.

And *this*, Beloved Reader, means *YOU!* No one else can take your place in the eyes of the Twelve...or my eyes. Let Caroline's Quest become yours.

Seek the Color in Life! You will find it...if you truly seek it.

I wish you...

> The depth of Black
> The security of Brown
> The power of Gold
> The hope of Yellow
> The wisdom of Blue
> The life of Green
> The sacredness of Purple
> The caring of Pink
> The glory of Orange
> The passion of Red
> The magic of Silver
> The rebirth of White
>   and again...
> The depth of Black.

Blessed be the Circle of the Twelve.

Blessed be you who reside in its center.

      For Love,
      Esmerelda Little Flame

The Author

Esmerelda Little Flame lives in Connecticut, in the same old white house where her father was born and teaches piano at the music studio her parents built in the early fifties.

She is an avid tarot reader with a special talent for creating guided story journeys from the readings. Other passions include drumming, scrying, rune reading, creating ritual, working with the faeries, the study of theatre, and the study of empathy and human connection.

Esmerelda holds Baccalaureate degrees in English and Social Work with a Masters degree in Pastoral Counseling.

Her first book was *The Adventures of Charles the Well-Traveled Bear.*

Other Books Available from Andborough Publishing

Reiki is an Japanese system of energy healing through the "laying on of hands" that is simple enough for children of all ages to learn.

The Children's Reiki Handbook is a guide to energy healing that provides kids with the information they need to prepare for their First, Second and Master Reiki Attunement; and shows them how to use their new skills to heal themselves and others.

Only $17.95

ISBN : 978-0-9774181-5-2
72 pages paperback

Authors Robert and Pamela Yarborough are both Usui Reiki Ryoho, Karuna Reiki® and SSR Master/Teachers

"I found Children's Reiki Handbook to be a concise yet thorough introduction to the Usui healing system of Reiki. It's perfect for children and young adults"
- ML Rhodes, Amazon #1 Best Selling Author and Usui Reiki Ryoho Master/Teacher

"If you want to learn Reiki, this book will serve as in inspiration towards that goal... This Reiki handbook is a great resource to introduce the benefits of Reiki healing to children or grown ups who are just starting out."
-Erin Kelly-Allshouse, Review Editor Children of the New Earth

---

Let Us Praise Him in Poem is a wonderful collection of poems, written by Appalachian native Bessie Lee, that served as her personal testimony of her belief in God and the path of Jesus Christ.

This is a collection of twenty poems that will inspire, comfort, cheer, and help you in your efforts to get closer to God.

The poems are for all denominations.

ISBN : 0-9774181-1-1
58 page paperback $9.99

CPSIA information can be obtained at www.ICGtesting.com
Printed in the USA
LVOW010809040112

262330LV00003B/541/A